ALSO BY JEAN THOMPSON

NOVELS

*City Boy*

*Wide Blue Yonder*

*The Woman Driver*

*My Wisdom*

COLLECTIONS

*Do Not Deny Me*

*Throw Like a Girl*

*Who Do You Love*

*Little Face and Other Stories*

*The Gasoline Wars*

# THE
# YEAR
# WE
# LEFT HOME

## Jean Thompson

SIMON & SCHUSTER

NEW YORK   LONDON   TORONTO   SYDNEY

Simon & Schuster
1230 Avenue of the Americas
New York, NY 10020

First Simon & Schuster hardcover edition May 2011

SIMON & SCHUSTER and colophon are registered trademarks
of Simon & Schuster, Inc.

For information about special discounts for bulk purchases,
please contact Simon & Schuster Special Sales at
1-866-506-1949 or business@simonandschuster.com.

The Simon & Schuster Speakers Bureau can bring authors
to your live event. For more information or to book an event,
contact the Simon & Schuster Speakers Bureau at 1-866-248-3049 or
visit our website at www.simonspeakers.com.

*Designed by Kyoko Watanabe*

Manufactured in the United States of America

10   9   8   7   6   5   4   3   2

Library of Congress Cataloging-in-Publication Data

Thompson, Jean.
    The year we left home / Jean Thompson.
        p. cm.
    1. Families—United States—Fiction.  2. Brothers and sisters—Fiction.
    3. United States—Social life and customs—20th century—Fiction.
    4. United States—Social conditions—20th century—Fiction.
    5. National characteristics, American—Fiction.  I. Title.
    PS3570.H625Y43 2011
    813'.54—dc22
                2010047553

ISBN 978-1-4391-7588-0
ISBN 978-1-4391-7591-0 (ebook)

*To everybody who left home*

# THE
# YEAR
# WE
# LEFT HOME

# *Iowa*

### JANUARY 1973

The bride and groom had two wedding receptions: the first was in the basement of the Lutheran church right after the ceremony, with punch and cake and coffee and pastel mints. This was for those of the bride's relatives who were stern about alcohol. The basement was low-ceilinged and smelled of metallic furnace heat. Old ladies wearing corsages sat on folding chairs, while other guests stood and managed their cake plates and plastic forks as best they could. The pastor smiled with professional benevolence. The bride and groom posed for pictures, buoyed by adrenaline and relief. There had been so much promised and prepared, and now everything had finally come to pass.

By five o'clock the last of the crowd had retrieved their winter coats and boots from the cloakroom and headed out. It was January, with two weeks of hard-packed snow underfoot and more on the way, and most of them had long drives from Grenada, over country roads to get back home. The second reception was just beginning at the American Legion hall, where there would be a buffet supper, a bar, and a dance band.

The bride's younger brother had been sent to open the Legion building so that the food could be brought in ahead of time. He drove his pickup truck the mile from the church, playing the radio loud to shake off the strangeness of the day. He'd been an usher at the wed-

ding and he still wore his dark suit and blue-tinted carnation bouton-
niere, clothes that made him feel stiff and false. The whole import of
the wedding embarrassed him powerfully, though he could not have
said why. Many things had been disquieting: his sister in her overdone
bridal makeup, his mother's weeping, the particular oppressiveness of
anything that took place in church, the archness of the female relatives
who told him how tall and handsome he looked. "Pretty soon we'll get
to dance at your wedding, hey?" He'd shrugged and said, Well, they
could at least dance, which had made his girlfriend mad.

She was still back at the church and still mad, which was why he'd
managed to get away by himself, if only for a few minutes. As he was
leaving, she'd whispered that he should see what they had in the liquor
cabinet over there. He guessed that that was what it was going to take to
get her back in any kind of a good mood. A bottle they could show off
as a trophy, then drink some night while they were out driving around.

The radio was playing "Horse with No Name." He turned it up
and sang along:

*I've been through the desert on a horse with no name*
*It felt good to be out of the rain*

He wished he was out there right now, in some desert, instead of
smack in the middle of his family, who, because they knew his origins
and his history, thought they knew everything about him. He couldn't
account for this feeling when a wedding, after all, was supposed to be
this big happy thing. He guessed he must be some kind of freak.

The gray afternoon was already shutting down when he pulled into
the Legion parking lot, got out, and fumbled with the stiff lock. It gave
way and he stepped inside.

The hall was a big bare space with a much-buffed tile floor. Gloomy
light reflected from it in pools. To one side was a kitchen with a
large stainless steel double sink, two restaurant-style wall ovens, and
a pass-through to the main part of the room. Long tables covered
with white paper tablecloths were set up to receive food, and stools

and hightops were stacked in the foyer. He tried the bar closet but as expected it locked with a separate key. Then he heard another car pull up. He turned on the overhead lights and went back out into the cold.

His Uncle Norm and Aunt Martha were unloading their station wagon. "Ryan," his uncle said by way of a greeting, and handed him a foil-covered metal pan. "Careful, this one's heavy."

His aunt said it had been a beautiful wedding, hadn't it, and Ryan said it had. That was the extent of the small talk since there was all the food to manage, work to be done, and with Norm and Martha, work came before everything else. There were a dozen or more big pans to carry inside, and two coolers, and a cardboard box full of paper towels and pot holders and other useful items. "Just set everything out on the table," Martha directed, hanging up her coat and putting on the apron she'd brought from home. Ryan, peeking under the foil, found sliced ham with raisin sauce, a macaroni-and-tomato casserole, a green salad, potatoes topped with shredded orange cheese, beef in gravy, chicken and biscuits, corn pudding. There were sheet cakes too, and bags of dinner rolls.

He guessed that Norm and Martha had organized the supper, collecting the prepared food from different country relatives. It would have been a very Norm-and-Martha thing to do. They were not, technically, his aunt and uncle. They were his grandmother's cousins, his mother's mother's people. Tall, freckled, rawboned, they seemed not to have aged since his childhood. His mother had been a Tesman and her mother was a Peerson, and the Peersons were the scariest of the old Norwegian families. They lived out in the boondocks, what his dad called Jesus Lost His Shoes territory, and their church still held services in Norwegian the third Sunday of every month. Most of them farmed. They believed in backbreaking labor, followed by more labor, and in privation, thrift, cleanliness, and joyless charity. If you wanted a tree taken down or a truck winched out of a ditch or a quarter of a cow packaged for your meat locker, you called a Peerson. If you wanted lighthearted company, you called someone else.

The boy, Ryan, thought of them as part of some grim, old-country past that laid claim to him without his consent. Ever since he was a little kid he'd heard instructive things about Norwegian this and Norwegian that, like postcards from a place he'd never been and none of it any use to him, not flags nor fjords nor rotten jellied lutefisk, which nobody made anymore and nobody even pretended to like. Maybe if you poked around in the gene pool all the way back to the Vikings, you'd find some worthy ancestor. But all that had been beaten out of people long ago, or maybe it was just that the tamest and most boring Norwegians had settled here in Iowa, where they devoted themselves to lives of piety and sacrifice and usefulness.

But he wasn't going to spend any more time thinking about all that, since what really counted was the life you made for yourself, and the person you decided to be.

Once the food was brought in, he and Norm began setting up the hightops and stools around the room's edges. He guessed it about killed Norm and Martha to be in a place where drinking would go on, but they saw it as their duty to be helpful, and both the duty and the disapproval would be part of the occasion for them.

"So this fella," Norm began, and Ryan understood that Norm meant the groom, Ryan's new brother-in-law. "What's he like?"

"Jeff? He's OK." He was kind of an asshole.

"Ah." Norm nodded, as if this was convincing information. He reached for a rag and slapped it across a tabletop. Norm's hands were big and chapped and had been gouged and nicked and scarred and healed over so many times that the skin was as full of history as an elephant's hide. "Where's he from, out West someplace?"

"Yes, sir. Denver."

Norm received this in silence. Ryan wondered what was bugging Norm about Jeff, who was your basic bullshit artist, all fake smiles and manly handshakes. You figured somebody that straight and narrow would be a hit with the home folks. But guess again. Ryan knew better than to ask any kind of direct question, so he kept on with his work, carting the stools and tables out into the room so Norm could place them in groupings.

Martha was busy running pans in and out of the warming ovens. The smell of the food was making him hungry. Pretty soon the band, or what passed for a band, would arrive to set up. It was just four guys from Ames in leather vests and striped shirts and some pitiful attempt at psychedelic effects generated by a strobe light. And then the guests would come, a mix of his sister's friends and Jeff's, and any of the local invitees who wouldn't miss the chance for free food and drink. His girl-friend too, though he hadn't been thinking about her until now and he guessed that was one more thing he'd done wrong without even trying.

The tables were in place. Norm went to the front door and peered out. "No snow yet. I don't suppose we'll stay that lucky."

Ryan, looking out from behind Norm's angular shoulder, saw the gray gauze sky and a pink sunset behind it glowing like a lamp. House lights were beginning to come on along the street, small and bright, and Ryan registered that the scene was beautiful, without thinking the word itself. "Yeah, I guess it's supposed to start in later."

"June's best for weddings," Norm said, sounding unexpectedly de-cisive. "Then you can have your flowers and your pretty weather. They didn't want to wait for June, hah?"

"I think this was the only time Jeff could get off, you know, for the honeymoon."

"Oh, sure." Norm nodded and, turning away, gave Ryan a look he couldn't read, or maybe he was just imagining it in the light reflecting off Norm's eyeglasses. Embarrassment? Apology? It came to him that Norm thought his sister might be pregnant, and this was one of those hurry-up weddings. Oh, please. His sister Anita would probably still be a virgin three years after her wedding night because it would take that long for the industrial glue that held her legs together to wear off. But it was a weird thing to have to think about, or to imagine old Norm thinking about, or to witness him thinking about, and he was glad when Martha called to him, "Ryan? I need you a minute."

She was standing at the oven, poking at one of the pans inside. "Can you slide this out a little ways and hold it? Here, careful not to burn yourself."

He took the hot pads she gave him and supported the weight of the pan—beef, it was—while Martha lifted the foil and stirred and prodded the contents. She scooped some out into a crockery bowl. "All right, put it back now."

She fetched a knife and fork and a paper napkin, put two dinner rolls on a plate, and set it, with the beef, on the counter. "I expect you're hungry. Go ahead, it'll tide you over."

"Thanks, Aunt Martha." He didn't wait to be asked twice. He ate standing, filling his mouth with beef and bread. Martha took a Coke out of the refrigerator and he opened it and drank it down. "I bet you cooked this, didn't you."

"You like it?"

"S'great." He couldn't get enough of it.

"I'm glad you think so."

The room was quiet. Norm had gone out back to get something from the car. Martha ran water in the sink and looked around for something else to do, now that the food was ready and waiting for the guests. She was almost as tall as Norm. The two of them were like a pair of trees. And just like Norm, she wore plain, plastic-framed eyeglasses. Ryan couldn't have said if they'd grown to look alike, the way old married couples were said to, or if they'd started out as pretty much the same model, your standard Norwegian giant. She said, "I guess you're excited for your sister."

"Yes ma'am."

"She was just beautiful in that dress. Like an angel on a cloud."

"Sure." He'd thought she'd looked more like an explosion of tissue paper, but kept this smart-ass notion to himself.

"I'm so glad they got married in the church, even if that boy is what, Church of Christ?"

"I forget, exactly." He didn't think that Jeff was much of a church guy; Anita would probably make him baptize their kids Lutheran and send them to Lutheran Sunday school and everybody would be happy.

Martha said they made a nice-looking couple, and Ryan agreed with that too. He hoped she wasn't going to start talking about how pretty soon it was going to be his wedding, blah blah blah. People acted like weddings were contagious, like it was your duty to go out and get infected.

". . . because you never can tell, looking at it from the outside. How miserable people can be in a marriage."

Ryan, still occupied with the beef making its way into his stomach, looked up, uncertain of what he'd heard. He hadn't been paying attention, he'd missed something she'd said, some explanation. Who was she talking about? Who was miserable? Did she mean herself and Norm? Any of their grown children, all of whom had married and produced further legions of stoic, insensible, hangdog Peersons? He didn't want to believe that any of them had the capacity for misery. He wanted to keep them as they had always been, fixed and reliable components of his world. Or was she talking about Anita and Jeff, was there something she knew that he didn't? He tried to catch Martha's eye but she was looking away from him, embarrassed, maybe, at what she'd said. He was on the outside looking in. For a moment, he felt knocked off-center, no longer knowing what he had always known . . .

. . . and then the back door opened with a cold gust, and the band came in lugging their equipment and he went to help them. And not long after that the first guests arrived and one of the Legionnaires unlocked the bar and began putting ice in buckets and taking drink orders, and everyone waited for the next big moment in a series of big moments, the entrance of the bride and groom.

Ryan's mother came in first, taking short little steps in the shoes that hurt her feet. "Here they come, here they come!" She was in one of her wound-up states, where she might do anything: start crying again, or decide it was a good time for some uncomfortable, goopy talk. He moved to stay clear of her. His father and little brother and sister followed, and a few stray relatives. The guests lined themselves on either side of the room and a ragged clapping started up.

Called upon to register excitement one more time, Ryan set his face in a pleased, vacuous expression, just as his girlfriend crossed the room to stand next to him. She had another kind of look on her face.

She could have bit nails, people used to say, a way of speaking, and he understood what they meant by that now, he surely did.

"You were supposed to come back and pick me up," she hissed, and nothing he could say to that, not really, except *Sorry,* which he tried, sending it her way as a kind of mumble. But he hadn't known he was meant to go back for her, or hadn't paid attention, and then he realized he didn't care, although he had not known this until just now.

"I waited and waited and I was almost the last one there and I had to get a ride with Mrs. Holder, *God*!"

"I had stuff to do here."

"I could have come with you."

"You didn't want to," he reminded her, which was true, even though saying so wouldn't help him.

"Well you didn't exactly act like you wanted me here."

He shook his head fast, like a horse trying to get rid of flies. He couldn't win, arguing with her.

"What's the matter with you lately? You act like you don't care about anything. Not me or . . . anything." She flicked a hand to indicate the universe of anything. He guessed she meant the future she had mapped out for them, where they'd both head off to St. Olaf's for college in the fall, and she would continue to dole out limited portions of sexual gratification until such time as he could offer her a ring that would seal the deal.

He watched her tight little face as she went on and on about his despicable and inadequate behavior, keeping her voice low because there were people all around them. And because he must have sensed that she was about to disappear from his life in all the important ways, he was able to detach himself, consider her with cold curiosity. She'd done herself up for the occasion in a hard-edged, glamorous style, with a pouf of blond hair sprayed and clipped into place, and a shiny dress that left her arms bare and goose-bumped. Looking down, he was afforded a view of her small breasts in a brassiere of pink lace.

She caught him staring down the front of her dress. Her jaw began to shake with disbelief and rage.

"You are a filthy, perverted heap of crap," she said, just as the doors opened and a cheer went up, and Anita and Jeff, splendid and strange in their wedding clothes, swept in.

Ryan went to the bar and asked for two rum and Cokes and the barman served them up with a wink. He guessed there were some benefits to the wedding thing after all. He found a vantage point near the back door and watched as Anita and Jeff made the rounds, kissing and hugging and shaking hands. His girlfriend had taken herself off somewhere, but he didn't think he'd seen the last of her. The bridesmaids were carrying on and showing off, his sister's friends who were just as stuck-up as she was. The bridesmaids' dresses were sky blue velvet tricked out with floppy ruffles and bits of gauze and some other kind of fruit-salad trim, bad enough, but they'd really outdone themselves on the tuxedos. They were dark blue, with ruffled shirts and some shine to the jacket, and wide lapels faced with more velvet. Jeff and his groomsmen looked like they were about to emcee a wrestling match. When no one was watching, Ryan unpinned the carnation on his lapel, which by now resembled a piece of blue cabbage, and tossed it into the trash.

He drank one rum and Coke and then the other, and when people began to line up for supper, he felt a little blurred, and he sat down with some guys he knew from school and ate some more of Martha's beef to steady himself. He was working himself into a sad and rotten mood, which had something to do with his girlfriend, but was also about a loneliness that sometimes crept up on him without warning. Everybody else could have themselves a hilarious good time. He wasn't really part of it.

The band started up. Anita and Jeff danced and made moony eyes at each other. His dad and Anita danced. His mom and Jeff's dad. And so on. It was a regular festival of bad moves. The band had a keyboard player and a drummer and a guitarist and a scratchy-voiced lead singer who kept twirling and rocking the microphone and you had to feel sorry for them, trying to be cool when they had to play shit like "The Hokey Pokey" and "The Bunny Hop." At least now, with his girlfriend on the warpath, he wasn't going to have to dance. He wandered back to his spot at the rear of the room and stood there, arms folded, while in his mind he was in the desert on the horse with no name, silent, stern, keenly aware . . .

A hand landed on his shoulder from behind. "I don't know why it is," a voice intoned, "but I always cry at weddings."

Ryan turned to see his cousin Chip Tesman, grinning his crooked grin. "Hey man." They shook hands, a high-style fist lock. "How you been, I haven't seen you in the longest."

"Ah, I been my usual funky self. How's the happy couple?"

"Happy, I guess." They looked out over the room, the field of weaving, waving dancers struggling for space. They made Ryan think of a shipwreck, of bodies dumped into the ocean. In the pass-through he saw Norm and Martha moving around in the kitchen. "At least, Anita's happy. It's a big day for showing off."

"There you go," said Chip, by way of agreement. Chip hadn't been at the wedding, and showing up at the reception looked like it had been an afterthought. He wore jeans and a sweatshirt and his green army jacket with TESMAN printed above the chest pocket. His hair was growing out in scruffy patches. He was twenty-two, five years older than Ryan. The army had been meant to make a man out of him.

"Your mom and dad are here," Ryan told him, and Chip nodded, uninterested. Chip was really Ray Jr., after his father. Such boys were called Chip because they were chips off the old block.

Although Ray Jr. had never really lived up to that, had always been an oddball, a kid who'd collected comic books all through high school and never played sports of any kind and spent most of his time up in his room, reading science fiction and producing elaborate shaded drawings of robots, spacemen, and rocket ships. He'd managed to get himself graduated, barely, and then drafted into the infantry, and everyone had thought it was probably a good idea. There didn't seem to be any particular future for somebody like Chip, with his nervous, skeetering laugh, his habit of ducking his head instead of looking people in the eye, his lack of any practical aptitudes or skills. Somehow he'd managed to return from the war unshot, skinnier than ever but somehow bigger, alarming people by the way he looked and the way he acted and the knowledge that now he at least knew how to use a rifle.

Chip squinted at the bar station. "You think they'd serve me a drink?"

"Sure, why wouldn't they?" said Ryan, although he was aware that certain possibilities for friction and conflict attended Chip wherever he went. "You're family. Hell, it's the Legion, you're a veteran."

"Yeah, but I'm the wrong kind of veteran." He punched Ryan lightly in the arm and laughed his too high laugh and sidled through the crowd. When he returned, he was carrying two plastic glasses of Scotch and ice. "Hold these," he instructed, and Ryan watched him go back into the room, walking with his jerky, loose-footed slouch, like a puppet on busted strings, watched other people register his presence. Chip took a plate from the buffet line and loaded it up with whatever he could scrape out of the picked-over food pans.

"One of those is for you," he said when he got back, meaning the drinks, but Ryan took one sick-making sip and shook his head. "All yours," he said, setting them down on a window ledge.

"Get you something else, huh?" Chip asked with all the concern of a host, and Ryan said no thanks. He watched Chip hauling food into his mouth, gobbling away. Ryan was about to say Chip acted like he hadn't eaten all day, then thought better of it, since you never knew, Chip might just have woken up and this was breakfast. Chip had been out of the army for most of a year now, living in his parents' basement, and was having trouble getting his wheels underneath him, as Ryan's father said.

Chip finished off the food and set the empty plate on top of a trash container. He patted his pockets looking for cigarettes and found none. He took a drink from the first Scotch, put it down, picked it up again. Then he pointed out into the room. "Hey, Ry? Your hen's running around loose."

Ryan looked and saw his girlfriend, or at least that's who she'd been this morning, with one of Jeff's Denver friends, a guy with blow-dried hair and a lot of teeth. They were dancing together, dancing about as slow and dirty as you could get away with at the American Legion. Her face was pink, and he wondered if the guy had been feeding her alcohol or if she was just a slut and always had been for everybody but him. The Denver people had mostly been standing around all night as if they were watching a not very interesting television show, as if they were too good to be here in the first place, but now some of them were cheering their buddy on, and Ryan hated them and hated her and didn't care if they all fucked her upside down on the nearest table.

Chip tugged at his arm. "Hey, come on. Let's get out of here."

Ryan found his coat underneath a heap of others and followed Chip out the back door. It was cold, but that felt good after all the heat inside and the heat filling up his head, and he was glad to be walking out, even though there might be consequences to tagging along with Chip, the no-account, the fuckup, the guy everybody figured for a druggie and a criminal, though they couldn't have said exactly what sort of criminal.

"You got your truck here?" Chip asked, slapping his sides to try to keep warm. There was nothing to the army coat. Ryan opened the truck door and got in and Chip got in the other side and they breathed out clouds of frost and said "Whoo-ee" to holler back at the cold.

Ryan started the truck and the engine knocked a little bit before settling into a rhythm. "What is this, a 305?" Chip asked.

"No, a 325."

"Hah." Chip nodded appreciatively. It surprised Ryan that his dorky cousin might actually know something about engines now. Another part of the new Chip. He coughed his smoker's cough, again looked without success in his pockets for cigarettes, then continued, "I need to get, I don't know, a van, maybe. Something I could hit the road in, crash in if I needed to. What?"

"It's just funny, you saying *crash* like that."

"What? Oh yeah, I guess."

It was taking a long time for the engine to throw any heat. Ryan lifted himself one side at a time off the vinyl seat. His suit pants were useless when it came to keeping his ass warm. Being in the truck made him think of his girlfriend. A certain scent, a combination of wool, perfume, and cold air had accompanied their recent winter episodes, and in a wave of furious, hateful lust he saw again her white, white exposed skin. It staggered him for a moment, then he fought it down and made his voice casual. "So where did you want to go, Chipper?"

"Don't call me that, Lambchop."

"Ooh, that hurt."

"I was thinking we could sit right here for a while. You get high?"

"Sure," said Ryan. He did, he had, but not in any big-deal way. It had always been somebody else's stuff, he wouldn't have known how to get any himself or how much to pay for it or even how to roll a joint, a whole body of worldly knowledge he was still ignorant of. It hadn't done that much for him either, unless the lack of oxygen from the coughing fits was some kind of high. "Sure, you got some?"

"One great thing about the great Republic of Vietnam, they got the world's finest ganj. Jungle pot. Guys been bringing seeds back for years, starting their own little farm operations. Guys who know guys I know."

Chip rummaged around in his shirt pocket, came up with a plastic baggie. He shook and smoothed it with one hand and with the other switched on the radio. "Got to have tunes."

Yelps and whistles came out of the speakers. Ryan worked the dial and came up with the Cedar Rapids AM station, playing "Brandy (You're a Fine Girl)."

"Fuckety-fuck. There are like zero good stations around here, you know?" Chip complained. He was busy tapping leaves into a pipe bowl, and Ryan was beginning to get a little uneasy at the prospect of smoking up right here in the parking lot. The back door of the Legion opened and a man and woman he didn't recognize came out, walking carefully on the crusted snow. "Yeah, I'm gonna get out to see my buddy in San Francisco pretty soon. The summer of love is over, we missed that party, but they still make real music out there. The Dead still rule."

"Yeah?" Ryan echoed, not knowing what Chip was talking about,

not really listening as he went on and on, because after all it was only
Chip running his mouth, the way he always did, and anyway Ryan
sort of liked "Brandy" himself. The man and woman headed off down
the street without looking in their direction. He decided not to be a
chickenshit, to go along with the program. Otherwise Chip would give
him a hard time, and even if it was only gooneybird Chip, he wouldn't
let it drop.

Funny to think that his cousin, whom he'd known all his life
(though Chip had been too old and too uncool to be a playmate), had
been a soldier and been to a war and come back grown-up. Or at least,
as grown-up as he was likely to get. These days the war was going right
down the toilet, getting more and more lost every day. You knew it was
lost when they kept having peace negotiations. And though you still
had to worry about that shit, about registering and getting a lottery
number, odds were you weren't going to get called up or shipped off or
anything that was dangerous and important and *real*. It was another
party he'd missed out on, though that was a strange way to think about
a war.

Chip flicked a lighter over the pipe bowl, firing it up and inhaling.
He motioned for Ryan to take the pipe from him, then drew his breath
in and in until it exploded out of him, smoke filling the space between
them. They were both going to stink like chimneys.

When it was Ryan's turn, he fought to hold the scorching smoke inside him. The last thing you wanted to do was cough. He kept it going
as long as he could, then opened his lungs and took in air. "Anything
left? Gimme," Chip said, and Ryan checked himself for anything like
a high, found nothing. But after his third turn at the pipe he began to
feel it a little, and then without warning it snuck up behind him and
spun his head around.

"Whoa," he said.

Chip laughed, but his laugh had slowed way down. "Catch a buzz?"

"The top of my head is ten feet tall and filled with marshmallow."
Ryan laughed too because it was such a goofy thing to say, but it was
the absolute truth.

"Yeah, this ain't your local roadside hemp. You ever hear of Thai stick? Well, you have now."

"Not bad," he managed, pulling the words out of some box where all the words were kept.

"Who would have thought, a nice boy like you, smokin' out behind the barn."

"I'm not a nice boy, asshole," Ryan said, because nice boys were pussies.

But he guessed he might pass for one, if he was honest about it.

Chip reached to turn the radio down, then he seemed to forget about the conversation and absorbed himself with putting different parts of his body up against the truck's heater to warm them. There was a space of silence, except for the tiny radio noise. "Snow," Chip said.

Ryan, his brain by now operating underwater, took a slow moment to process this, then connect the idea of snow with the small, sleety stuff accumulating on the windshield.

They watched it coming down for a time. "Man, I hate winter," Chip complained.

"I don't mind it so much."

"That's the Norwegian in you. Me, it never took."

"I don't want to be a Norwegian." He guessed it was a stupid thing to say, but he knew what Chip meant. It was the same as being a nice boy.

Chip laughed another of his stupid laughs. Really, the guy should not go anywhere near a joke. "Little late for that, don't you think?"

"Shit."

"Maybe you could get yourself adopted by an Indian tribe. Your Indian name could be, ah, Hair of the Dog."

"Funny." The snow changed over to flakes, softer now but falling faster. Ryan thought about turning on the truck's windshield wipers, then remembered he wasn't driving.

A thin white layer began to veil the glass and fill the cab with reflected light. Chip loaded the pipe again and they smoked again but Ryan didn't feel any more stoned, just sleepy. Chip said, "Man, I need a cigarette. Why don't you have any cigarettes?"

"Bad for your wind."

"Oh yeah, I forgot. Track star."

"Eat me."

"Sorry. You know I'm just messing with you."

Ryan said Yeah, sure. Chip was an asshole, even if he was an asshole with good pot.

"It's just, you know I was never your all-American-boy type. Never climbed a tree or went fishin' with an old cane pole."

"Didn't go . . . fishing," Ryan managed. What was Chip complaining about now? He couldn't keep track of all the different gripes, which basically boiled down to all the ways Chip had been a total spaz. The snow was dragging his eyelids shut.

"Never had a girlfriend, hell, I don't think I even had a conversation with a girl, except I must have at least once or twice, right? Mathematically impossible not to. Lost my cherry in a whorehouse in Saigon."

"Yeah?" said Ryan, waking up. "What was that like?"

"The whorehouse? I don't know, stud. It's not like I got anything else to compare it to."

Ryan had meant something else, though now his meaning escaped him, *what was it like,* to travel across an ocean, to be in a war, to be afraid for your life, to kill someone or think about killing them, to buy a woman. They were quiet. The windshield was a solid white layer, though Ryan's window was still clear. The light above the back door of the Legion Hall threw a yellow cone downward, and in the light he could see the flakes falling steadily, then lifting when the wind swirled. It reminded him of a snow globe, one of those pretty scenes under glass, and then he had the sad, stoned thought that he was outside of the snow globe looking in. Just as something in him always stood apart, and he was not who people assumed he was.

". . . beautiful country," Chip said, as if he had been speaking all along and maybe he had, in his head. "Even after we bombed the shit out of it. It's hot, sure, but I don't mind that. Everything's green. Fruits I don't even know the name of. Mangoes. They got about ten different kinds of bananas, for Christ's sake. Mountains, there's all this fog or mist or something, turns the mountains this color, blue mostly but like, a rainy blue, if that makes any sense. I guess you'd have to be there and see it for yourself."

Ryan tried to make a picture of it in his head, blue mountains and green jungle, but it kept getting mixed up with desert, what he imagined the desert to be, red sand and yellow sand and bare rocks and the heat and feeling the horse's heat beneath him and when he looked out the truck's window he was surprised that the snow was still there. He guessed he was good and high.

"Beautiful country, fucked-up war. People here don't get that, they think all you do is show up in the middle of somebody else's deal and say, 'Hey, we're the Americans,' and everybody's happy to see you. You know what Martin Luther King said? 'America is the greatest purveyor of violence in the world.' You think the old boys at the Legion want to hear any of that?"

Ryan said he guessed they didn't. He was beginning to realize that there were all sorts of ways to be on the outside of things.

Chip fished around at the neck of his shirt and brought out a leather cord with a silver peace symbol hanging from it. "You know what the Legion boys call this? 'Footprint of the American Chicken.' I've seen the bumper stickers. They hate guys like me because we lost a war we were supposed to win and anyway we're a bunch of baby killers."

"Did you ever . . . ," Ryan began, but he stopped himself because you didn't want to say something stupid, like, you guys didn't really do shit like that, did you? Or find out just exactly what they had done.

And Chip must have heard the question Ryan didn't quite ask, because he started talking louder as if to drown him out. "Yeah, you want to learn a few things? I got all kinds of books I can loan you, like I. F. Stone's white papers that rips into what a big fat fraud the Gulf of Tonkin incident was, you know what I'm talking about? No? We need to educate you. Ever hear about Dien Bien Phu? You want to understand Vietnam, you start with the French. I thought everybody knew that. Shit, Ry, it's all out there, you just got to read up on it."

"Yeah, I could do that." But it was just something to say because it reminded him of Chip back when he was bragging about his comic books: "What do you *mean,* you don't know who Stan Lee is?" In other words, another load of bullshit, but this was different just as Chip had come back different, and it frightened him to think he might come to know all the things he didn't know and then there would be no place in the world where he would feel at ease, no place he would not judge or measure, no place that would be his true home, and just when he couldn't bear sitting there another moment, Chip muttered that he'd kill for a cigarette and got out of the truck and Ryan turned off the engine and followed him.

The snow had slackened though it was still falling at a steady, sifting pace. If it kept up all night they'd have to shovel out in the morning, and his dad would make sure Ryan did his share and more. It wasn't anything to look forward to. Chip was strolling along as if he didn't feel the cold anymore, sniffing the air as if falling snow was just another stoned treat. It was a pretty safe bet that Uncle Ray didn't wake him up early these days to tell him there was a shovel with his name on it.

They stopped at the door of the Legion. "You coming in?" Ryan asked, though he guessed he knew Chip wouldn't.

"Nah. I'll probably go on back home. I can only handle so much excitement." He laughed his unsteady laugh and slapped Ryan on the back. "Go on in, man. Join the party."

It's not my party, Ryan wanted to say, because it both was and it wasn't, and the people inside would welcome him and draw him in and he both would and would not want them to. "Hey, thanks for the . . . ," he began, but Chip was already walking away down the snowy street, raising his arm in a backward wave.

Ryan opened the door just wide enough to step inside. And because he was still high and he was afraid it showed, and also because his girl-friend might still be in play somewhere, he hung back.

The band was taking a break. People were sitting down and haw-hawing over their drinks, and his sister had taken off her veil and perched it on the table next to her like a doll or a pet, and her new husband was off somewhere Ryan couldn't see, probably being talked out of shooting himself in the head now that he'd gone and signed his life away.

Through the pass-through he saw the kitchen, wiped down clean, every pan washed and scrubbed and stacked. The band straggled back to the microphone, ready for one last set. They started in playing something fast and swingy Ryan didn't recognize, something with no words in it, nobody getting up because they didn't know how to dance to it.

Then an amazing thing: his Uncle Norm came out of the kitchen with a can of Dance Wax, sprinkling it over the scuffed floor. Little powdery flakes, like snow falling inside. Then Aunt Martha joined him, and the two of them clasped hands, Norm's arm around her waist. They stepped together, stepped and twirled and glided, up and down and round and round, some fast step they must have learned back when they were kids and had been practicing ever since in some unsuspected secret life that included fun, moving in perfect time with each other and the jazzy music.

Who would have thought it? People at the tables clapped for them. Norm was smiling. Martha, flushed with heat, almost pretty, smiled back. It was like the perfect heart of the snow globe, and Ryan guessed rightly that he would remember the moment forever.

# *Iowa*

## APRIL 1975

The drive from Iowa City was 150 miles and Janine said there were 150 redwing blackbirds, one on every milepost. She was from Chicago and she had these ideas about nature, which meant she got excited about ordinary things.

"You know what they're all singing? 'I'm the best bi-ird.'"

"Yeah, always a lot of blackbirds, this time of year."

"They look amazing. That one little red-and-yellow patch. You think they know how amazing they look?"

"Sure."

She made a fist and nudged it against his chin. "Don't get excited or anything."

"I promise I'm not."

"Hayseed."

"Snob."

"Boy, you're just trying to pick a fight, aren't you?" She wore a lot of silver bracelets. They made a busy noise when she moved.

"Hate to tell you, but blackbirds ruin crops, so farmers shoot em, or—"

She squealed and flailed at him, until Ryan caught both her hands in his free one, the silver bracelets jangling, and she twisted away and collapsed with her head in his lap, still laughing.

"Whoa." Ryan got both hands back on the wheel and steered around a slow truck. Janine arched her neck and smiled up at him. Did girls know what they were doing when they did shit like this to you? Sure they did.

They were on their way to Rocky Mountain National Park, where neither of them had ever been. They would camp in the snow, hike, swim in a cold stream. But on the way there they would spend a night at Ryan's parents', so they couldn't complain he didn't visit at all over spring break.

It would be the first time he'd ever brought a girl home from school, not to mention one they'd be pretty sure he was having sex with. They'd be able to tell. It would be all over them, a layer of happy guilt.

They were quiet for a time. Janine sat upright, though she still kept one hand in his lap. "It's just the one night."

"Yeah, I know."

"Parents. Mine would ask you every stupid question in the world."

"Oh, mine'll do that too, don't worry."

"What if they don't like me?"

"They'll like you just fine." His mom and dad would fall all over themselves with manners, while his brother and sister made google eyes behind his back. Janine wouldn't be expecting grace before supper, and she wouldn't offer to help with the dishes afterward, and she wasn't an education major and she didn't go around talking about how much she loved children. She had long, straight dark hair and a smutty sense of humor. She was the third girl he'd had sex with, and she was the crazy best. There wasn't much they hadn't tried these last few months. It had been just incredible.

And now all that weighed him down with dread. Janine wore a rawhide lace and some beads around one ankle, which would probably strike his parents as indecent, although they would not be able to say why, and she would be just one more way in which he had disappointed them.

They were almost to Ames. It wouldn't be long now.

This road was so familiar to him that he no longer saw it, only registered its landmarks—newly green overpasses and embankments, the Stuckey's off to one side, the billboard advertising a motel that had closed down before he was born. The car seemed to be pulling to the right. It was Janine's car, an obnoxious red Nova, and it irritated him to be driving it. But his truck couldn't handle the mountains, and the Nova was at least new and the carburetor wouldn't crap out when the air got thin. That didn't console him for the total embarrassment of it all.

"You ever get this car aligned?"

She was looking out the window again and she turned to give him one of her blissed-out, aren't-we-having-a-good-time looks. "What's that?"

"Alignment. It's so you don't wear the tires out faster on one side than the other."

"I don't know. I had some stuff done at Christmas. Oil change and whatever else the book said."

"You have to keep it aligned. It's stupid not to."

"Then I guess I'm stupid," she said lightly. "What?"

"Nothing."

"It's some kind of big deal, that I didn't get whatever done to the car? Chill. I want this to be a nice trip."

"It will be. We just have to get past this here family thing."

She swung her long hair around and studied him. "What's so hard about them?"

"I don't know. They worry about me."

"That's what parents are supposed to do," she pointed out.

"They don't know me anymore," he said, but Janine had found something new outside to look at and exclaim over, lifting her mood, and she didn't hear him. And he was glad for that, since the instant the words left his mouth he felt them to be babylike, or worse, girl-like, by which he meant whiny, injured, and self-pitying.

They were passing the Ames exits now, the Conoco station, the Case Implements store, everything familiar and drab, and which like everything about home, including his own sulking, made him feel impatient and shamed, as if he'd been discovered at something unworthy.

Back in his room in Iowa City was a letter from his cousin Chip. It had arrived just after Christmas. It was the only letter Chip had ever written to him. Nothing the whole time he'd been in the army, and nothing else before or since. The letter had been tossed aside and had occupied a shifting place in the room's architecture of crud all this time, then yesterday Ryan had come across it again. It was mashed and wadded and oddly faded, as if written in disappearing ink. Ryan lay back in bed to reread it. The windows were open and the noise of his roommates playing a stoned game of basketball reached him, along with the layered sounds of traffic. It was one of the first warm, lazy-making days. A green branch had unfurled itself just outside his window. He'd been living here since classes started last fall, and he hadn't even noticed there being a tree.

Chip was supposed to be in Minneapolis, studying electronics. At least, that was the word at Christmas. But he hadn't put in an appearance at any of the family gatherings, nor had anyone given an explanation for his absence. His letter was postmarked Seattle and didn't say anything about Minneapolis.

*Hey Lambchop,*

*How's the college boy? You any smarter now?*

*Strange days have found us. Yes indeed.*

*I won't lie to you, there have been some skanky goings on recently. I've seen amazing sights and had some rotten nights. Not everybody out there is a child of God. Plenty of people who take real pride in being lowlifes.*

*But enough of the sad songs. I'm doing pretty good here in Seattle. Was staying with an old Army pal for a time, but we had a parting of the ways, and now I'm living with this girl I met. Her name is Deb and if it ain't love, it'll have to do until the real thing comes along. She works at a home health care place*

*and she's trying to get me on as a driver, delivering oxygen tanks
and wheelchairs and crutches. Me, your friendly neighborhood
wheelchair guy. There's even a uniform.*

*So that's the news, but mostly I wanted to tell you about
this time a few months back when I wound up in the middle of
exactly nowhere, some big brown field in one of those big brown
states, either Montana or Idaho, anyway, one of those places that
sound more interesting than they really are, and I won't bore you
with how I got there or how I got out, but I can tell you there's
this moment of purity, that's absolutely the right word, when you
realize how alone you are in the universe.*

*Come out and visit sometime. There's things you ought to see.*

*Chip*

Ryan hadn't written him back. He figured Chip wouldn't expect
him to. It was the kind of letter you sent when you got tired of talking
to yourself.

Janine opened her purse and took out her makeup things. She
looked into a mirror, poked and smudged. Her face was too round
to be beautiful in any ordinary sense, just as her body was too
short-waisted and low-slung. But guys always noticed her. He certainly
had. She said, "Jesus Christ, I look like a hag."

"You look all right."

"Oh, thanks. You silver-tongued devil, you."

They were on the outskirts of Grenada now, though the town's borders were so ragged and undefined that occasional farm fields appeared
in places you didn't expect, like this one next to the elementary school.
A combine chugged along, making straight rows in the black dirt. He
said, "Listen, you can't say stuff like *Jesus Christ* or *God* around my parents. Don't take the Lord's name in vain. You know what that is, right?"
Janine had been raised without any religion at all, only books that
explained we celebrated Jesus' birthday because he was an important

person. In spite of himself he still thought of this as vaguely shocking. "Practice saying something else. *Gosh,* or *golly,* or *Jiminy Cricket.*"

"You're shittin' me," she said happily, intent on having as much fun as possible with him.

"Please. Pretend you're a nice, normal girl."

And now he'd gone too far, and the fun went out of her. "What's that supposed to mean, a nice girl?"

"I don't know. A Lutheran."

A lucky thing to say. So often with girls it felt like there was an entirely different language being spoken, words that inflamed or soothed, except you never knew which ones they were. Janine considered him for a long moment, then rolled her eyes. "It's not like I'm your affianced, or anything."

"My what?"

"Like we're getting married."

Even the thought of it was enough to unnerve him. "Yeah. I mean, no. Jiminy Cricket."

"God, relax. I don't ever want to get married."

"Sure." He didn't believe it when girls said things like that.

"Marriage subjugates women. It's another one of those paternalistic things."

"You might want to keep that opinion to yourself."

"What did you tell them about me? You better let me know."

"Nothing. Just that you were a friend."

"Oh, that's great." She shook her head. She wore Gypsy hoop earrings that went along with the bracelets. "*Friend,* that's only about the weakest shit you can say."

"I don't tell them stuff, OK?"

"Am I at least your girlfriend? Can you hang that name on it?"

"How about, 'If it ain't love, it'll have to do until the real thing comes along.'"

He thought it was kind of funny and was expecting her to make some joke, but she just looked at him, coldly now, then at the little town unspooling itself, the car slowing, the bland expanse of Main Street under the sparkling sky.

The Red and White Mart, the dry cleaners, the bank that never looked like it had any money inside. Row of false-front buildings, a painted ad for a fifty-year-old livery business sinking into a brick wall. Incongruous shiny new video-game parlor. The Grand Opera House block, a place everyone agreed was history. He waited for Janine to pronounce judgment, how small and fusty it was, or worse, how darling and quaint.

But she'd gone quiet. He'd said the wrong thing again, blundered into the trap he'd been trying so hard to avoid. It was only a few blocks to his parents' house and there was no time to make it right. They had fallen into a familiar trough of silence and distance. Something they couldn't help and couldn't predict, something false, unhappy, constrained, lost. Sometimes one of them fell in first and pulled the other one in after. Neither of them knew how to do anything except suffer through it. It wasn't exactly fighting, but a substitute for fighting.

And after such distance, how strange to make love, frightening, almost, as if everything between them, both good and bad, had been a kind of lie.

Here was the street, the block, the pinkish brick of his parents' ranch house—already he had ceased to think of it as his own house—and Janine stretching her legs beneath her too short dress and shaking her hair out, his smart-ass, hippie-slut girlfriend who really should have worn something else, because he wouldn't be the only one looking at the shadowy territory of her thighs. He hated that he was embarrassed, because hadn't he chosen her for just such reasons?

Ryan parked the Nova behind his mother's station wagon. It was two o'clock in the afternoon. The house was pretty and trim and sun-bright. His dad had been after the lawn already, he could tell, everything raked and clipped. The front door was closed, the sheer curtains in the living room drawn. It wasn't the kind of neighborhood where people hung out of windows or left shoes or bicycles strewn about, nor were his family that kind.

"Ready?" he said to Janine, and she said she was, not looking at him, still distant from him, and they got out and walked around back to the kitchen, where he knew they would be waiting for him.

His mother was first, pushing the door open and hugging and hugging him, and his sister right behind her, and back in the kitchen his lurking, beanpole brother. His father off somewhere, keeping out of the way. Janine was behind him and he turned to draw her in. She dodged his hand and stepped forward. "Mom, Torrie, this is Janine Pasqua. My brother Blake."

He watched them take each other in. It went about as well as he'd imagined, everybody keeping their smiling game faces on. Janine's alarming dress was a red-and-black print fabric with dramatic trailing sleeves. His family took in the silver jewelry and the ankle beads too. They were trying to figure out just who she was, and from just what dusky origin. His brother blushed dull red with embarrassed lust.

Janine said, "Wow, you all look exactly alike."

Hard to tell if she meant it as any kind of a compliment. But it was true enough; him, his brother and his sister, each some gradation of blond, long-boned Nordic-ness. There was a beat of silence, then his mother said, "Oh, wait till Anita gets here and you see all four of them together. It'll make you rub your eyes. Of course they get the height from their dad. I always say, they look like me, but stretched out."

"Anita's coming?" Ryan asked. His sister lived in Ames now, with her banker husband, and was often busy with the responsibilities and demands of her married state.

"She'll be here for dinner. Jeff too, if he can make it." Ryan's mother led them all back into the kitchen, ever the anxious hostess. "Would you like something to drink, Janine? Coke? Iced tea?"

"Iced tea would be great, thank you." Ryan's mother told them to go ahead and sit down and they did, Janine still not looking at him, and he guessed he was in for more of the same treatment until she got over it. His sister was out in the hall calling, "Dad? Dad? Ry's here," and then his father was standing at the kitchen door, looking down at everyone through his glasses like some big serious bird.

"Hey Dad." Ryan stood up and shook hands, watched his father register his shaggy hair and begin to say something, stop, and settle instead for a narrowing of his mouth. Then his eyes found Janine. "Dad, this is Janine Pasqua. Janine, my dad, Mr. Erickson."

Janine smiled and said Nice to meet you and his father said You too. Ryan saw little thought balloons appear over everyone's head, like a cartoon. His father's said, *Oh mercy mercy me.* His mother's said something like *Everybody settle down.* His sister's was *Now what?*, and his brother's was full of the kind of confused noise and word scraps used to ward away hard-ons.

And Janine's was blank. He couldn't read her and he didn't trust her. She was capable of saying anything, and if she'd decided to give him a hard time for whatever pissed-off reason, there wouldn't be much he could do except take it.

Ryan's father sat down at the kitchen table. His mother set out glasses of iced tea and a bowl of pretzel sticks, his sister was keeping herself busy looking into the refrigerator. He hadn't thought how weird it would be to have Janine sitting at the same table where he'd eaten cereal when he was a kid. The oak-veneer cupboards were marked with years of fingerprints, scrubbed down and reappearing again and again with the persistence of ghosts. Here were the same yellow-striped plates and cloudy-glass salt and pepper shakers, the same slant of afternoon light making the air in the room turn slow and brown. Everything here was familiar, a comfort to him, but at the same time he wondered how long he'd have to sit and endure it.

His mother asked them if they were hungry and Janine said no thank you, and his mother said are you sure, and Janine said she was positive, recrossing her legs in a careless way. His sister poured herself one of the Tabs she lived on. They seemed to be waiting for some other conversation to finish. "Camping," his father pronounced. "I never knew you to go in for that."

"I borrowed the tent and the rest of the stuff, so all we're paying for is food and gas." He could usually get off the hook with his father by claiming economy.

His sister leaned against the refrigerator. Thirteen years old and full of sass. "It is supercold up in the mountains. You guys are gonna freeze your heinies off."

"We'll manage," Ryan said, and because this seemed to conjure images of the two of them, him and Janine, burrowing into the same sleeping bag, everyone began talking at once.

"How high is—"

"I thought for supper—"

"Where are you going to—"

They all stopped themselves, then his mother said, "I thought for supper tonight we could grill burgers out back."

Janine said, "Oh, that sounds great." She gave Ryan a flicker of a sideways glance, as if to show him how *nice* and *normal* she was being. His stomach roiled.

His mother looked relieved. Ryan knew she'd already planned out the supper, written out lists, filled the refrigerator with her preparations. He knew that the hamburgers would be accompanied by potato rounds and three-bean salad and corn on the cob, with strawberry pie for dessert. Maybe they would get through everything with no real surprises. He began to relax a little.

His father said, "So where are you from, Janine? We didn't hear."

He stopped relaxing. They hadn't heard because he hadn't told them. And he knew that his father's question was designed to try and figure out Janine's parentage, which was an unlikely mix of Italian and Russian Jew. Janine said, "Chicago. The North Side. You know, where the Cubs are."

"You're a baseball fan?"

"Not really. It just gives people an image. A kind of cultural marker."

Another silence. Ryan's mother said, in her making-conversation voice, "So what made you come all the way to Iowa for school?"

"The Writers' Workshop. I'm a poet." It was about the same as saying you were an astronaut. Janine ought to know that by now. "University of Iowa has the best creative writing program in the country."

"Now I did not realize that," his mother said. "Iowa, famous for poetry." She seemed taken by the notion, as if those maps that illustrated the state's agricultural products—ears of corn, sheaves of wheat, and smiling pinky pigs—would add little pictographs of parchment scrolls. "What kinds of poems do you write?"

"Free verse, mostly. Just poems."

Janine didn't like such questions, Ryan knew. She thought they were uninformed. He hoped she would not provide his family with any of her poems, which tended to use words like *nipple.*

But it seemed they'd killed off poetry as a topic. His brother Blake, who had said nothing since they'd got here, spoke up. "I'm going to buy Ted's brother's '65 Impala and get it running."

His mother said, "Blake, we haven't said yes to that. It's going to depend on your grades."

"Hey, my grades are good enough to work on some car."

"Blake." His mother's warning tone.

Blake sat back in his chair with a hopeless expression. "This college thing is all your fault," he told Ryan.

"Yeah, right." He was aware of Janine watching. He didn't want to have to explain about his brother, how he'd never taken to school or books or anything that required sitting down and concentrating. Or that his sister Anita had spent a year at a community college, killing time until her wedding, and that college, in his family, wasn't anything taken for granted, since it cost good money. Then all of a sudden he was tired of his own caution. He said, "I changed majors. From business to poli sci."

"To what?"

"Political science. The study of government. Comparative politics, American and international political theory. Stuff like that."

"Heavy duty," his sister remarked, then left the room.

Blake got up from the table. "I gotta call Ted," he said, and he was gone also.

His father said, "Now let me get this straight. You're not in the business school anymore."

"That's right." With Janine sitting there, nobody was going to say anything too ugly.

"Political science, what's that, they teach you how to tear down the government? I bet they don't have that at St. Olaf's."

It was still a sore point that he hadn't gone to St. Olaf's.

"No, Dad. It's different ideas and theories about government." His father's face tightened at the word *theories,* which was likely to dredge up another whole speech about college not being an excuse to play around, but something you undertook to benefit yourself in tangible, vocational ways. "People get all kinds of jobs. You can work for state or local governments, or even at the national level. You can do research, develop policies."

His mother said, "You mean, you could end up working in Des Moines. That would be nice." His mother was also practical about higher education, but in a different way; she thought it would help her children "get ahead," by which was meant something that could be showcased in a Christmas newsletter.

Janine said, "It's a good major if you want to go to law school, or into politics. Or do community work, or labor organizing."

The thought balloons above his parents' heads now said *Outside Agitator* and *Communist.* Both of them were considering Janine warily. It was all right for a girl to be a poet, or any other fool thing she wanted. But boys had to make their way in the world, support families. The danger of sending your children to college was that they would be contaminated by subversive forces, bad influences, and bawdy women.

Ryan wasn't going to tell them that Janine's father was an orthopedic surgeon and that when she said they lived on the North Side of Chicago, she really meant one of the lakeside suburbs. It wouldn't change their minds and would be just another example of somebody's kid turning out wrong.

His father got up from the table. "What time's supper?"

"Anita's coming at five thirty."

His father said he'd check and see if there was enough charcoal. He went out the back door and they heard him out in the garage, something heavy being dragged around.

"He gets himself all worked up," his mother said. "I'm afraid it's going to take him a while to get used to your news. You could still switch back to business if you wanted, couldn't you?"

"I don't want to, Mom."

"You weren't getting bad grades, were you?"

"No, Mom."

"Of course you weren't. Ryan was always our little star student," his mother said to Janine. "Well, Torrie too, she gets awfully good grades. But Ryan was, what, an eighth of a point away from being valedictorian."

"Let's just drop it, Mom." He hated when she bragged about him, as if anything he'd done belonged to her.

"The government's kind of a sore subject around here," his mother went on, oblivious. "'Randy, that's Mr. Erickson, is still upset about President Nixon. He thinks everybody who didn't like Nixon in the first place ganged up on him."

"There's a sense in which that's probably true," Janine said.

*Stop*, Ryan ordered her telepathically, but of course she wasn't going to. She said, "I think everyone was just so hung up on getting even, that a lot of very ugly, unfortunate things happened."

"That's exactly what Randy says."

"She doesn't believe that," Ryan told his mother.

"Now how do you know what I believe or not?" Janine was hitting her stride now, charming and mean. "You have to tell me more about Ryan when he was a little kid. Did he get into trouble a lot?"

"Oh no, Ry was my sweetheart. My little young man." His mother leaned over to pat him on the arm. He felt himself becoming large and immobile, like a piece of furniture. "I mean, there were all the usual boy things. I'm not saying he was an angel. Now don't make that face. I'm your mother, I get to tell stories on you."

"I never did anything."

"I wouldn't say that, mister." His mother's heavy jokiness. She was the one person he knew who was never actually funny, either on purpose or by accident.

"I meant, I never did anything that interesting."

"Now why would you say that? All of you are interesting. And absolutely precious and special."

He pushed his chair back from the table. "I'm going to show Janine around, OK?"

"I'm driving you away." Her feelings were hurt, which she disguised by pretending to be hurt.

"No, Mom. I want to show her the house."

His mother rallied and produced a laugh. "Just don't be too critical. I always say, my interior decorators were four kids and three dogs."

Ryan led Janine through the dining room, with its sideboard and ceremonial fancy plates, into the unused territory of the living room, where vacuum tracks still showed in the rug. "Sorry," he said, once they were out of earshot.

"For what?"

"We should have driven straight through to Colorado."

Janine was looking through the layers of gauzy curtains at the street outside. He didn't know what else he was supposed to apologize for. She said, "Your mom's a little speedy, isn't she?"

"What do you mean?"

"You know. Uptight."

He hadn't thought about it. "I guess."

"You should be nicer to her."

He would have answered her, he wasn't sure how, but just then Torrie walked out of the back hallway. "She's gonna sleep in Anita's old room," she informed Ryan.

"Tor, it's rude to say *she* when somebody's standing right in front of you."

"Sor-ry." Torrie rolled her eyes. She seemed to have come into the room for the sole purpose of staring at them. "You screwed up about school."

"Yeah, thanks for your support."

"No prob. Why don't you take me along with you? On your trip."

"Let's see. How many reasons can I think of not to."

Janine said, "It'd be great if you came. We could make Ryan pitch the tents and chop all the firewood and cook for us."

"Drive into town and get us munchies."

"Catch fish and clean them."

"Shoot bears and skin them."

"You guys are tripping," Ryan announced.

"Ooh, druggie talk." Torrie tossed her hair and flounced off.

"She likes you," Ryan said.

"Why don't you show me the room, stud."

He was glad she seemed to be in a better mood. If abusing him helped, he didn't mind.

Anita's queen bed had been pushed up against one wall to make room for a sewing machine and a stack of plastic storage tubs. Luggage filled the closet. Anita's purple satin coverlet still presided over the bed, but without any of her other possessions—frothy curtains, posters, aggressively tended bulletin board—it looked frumpish and faded. Janine surveyed the room, found nothing to remark on, and asked, "So where are you?"

He led her down the hallway to what was still called the new part of the house, almost fifteen years after its construction, the L-wing with the den and the room where he and his brother had been segregated. "I don't suppose my mom made Blake clean it up," he said, without real hope.

The bed that was his had been cleared of its usual piles of books and papers, but the room still had its funky, inside-of-a-tennis-shoe smell, its wreckage of wadded clothes and *MAD* magazines and damp towels and empty Coke cans and tennis rackets and museum-like boyhood relics: sports trophies and a cabin made of Lincoln Logs and books thought suitable for boys because of their active, adventurous themes and lack of female characters.

"Looks sort of like your room at school."

"It does not."

"Missing only a hash pipe." She seemed to think this was funny.

The arching lines of her underpants were visible through the fabric of her dress when she leaned over to look at something. It was another hallucination-quality moment, having a real, fuckable girl here in this, the scene of so much beating off. He put a hand out, cupped one side of her ass.

"Don't." She stepped away, frowning.

"What?" he asked, genuinely surprised. She wasn't a girl who said "don't."

"This isn't the time or place."

Nothing he could say to that. He just hoped that whatever she was pissed off about, she'd get over the notion that it was his fault.

She asked for the bathroom and he waited outside until the toilet flushed and she ran water in the sink and came out. "Now what?" she asked.

"Take a drive?"

Janine shook her head. "I'm tired of the car. Let's sit outside or something."

"And do what?" He was still mad at her big touch-me-not act. What was that all about?

She punched him in the arm. She was allowed to do whatever she wanted. "It's just a beautiful day, dummy."

The picnic table was under a tree that threw a little shade. They sat on opposite sides of it. "What are those pink flowers?" Janine asked.

"I don't know, you'd have to ask my mom."

"Not a guy thing, huh?" He muttered and shook his head. "What? Didn't catch that. You know, your family's exactly like I imagined them. Exactly like you."

"What's that supposed to mean?"

"You're like the blackbirds. The blondbirds."

"Very funny."

"They're very nice. You always talk like they're Norwegian hillbillies or something."

"I do not." She didn't know anything about it.

"OK, you don't. Sure."

In the silence they heard a car rolling smoothly down the street beyond them, and, through an open window, a phone ringing. Janine was always the one who spoke first. She couldn't ever let anything go. "What's the matter with you anyway? You're being kind of a jerk."

"Me? You're the one with the bug up your ass."

"You've been acting like I'm some hitchhiker you just picked up."

"What's that supposed to mean?" He knew what she meant.

"Like you're embarrassed I'm here."

"Yeah, well you've been acting like you're at the zoo or something. Like everybody walks the earth just so you can write one of your big-deal poems about them."

He didn't mean it, or he did, but he didn't mean to say it, *poems,* who cared, and here was her face shoved too close to his, an angry mask, her eyes dark and staring, and if only they could lie down together, strip down to their naked selves without all the bullshit and even now he imagined himself putting his hands on her, drawing her in, making it *all right,* but that wasn't going to happen because whatever she was about to say she stopped. "Here comes your dad," she said, her voice flat.

Ryan looked over his shoulder and saw his father approaching from the garage, and whatever he'd been doing all this time he'd worked up a sweat that turned his face and forehead pink. "Need you to lend me a hand for a minute."

Ryan got up from the picnic table and Janine said, for his father's benefit, "Oh that's all right, I'll just wait for you," and he followed his father back to the garage.

His father had been trying to get to a stack of extra aluminum siding, but it was wedged in behind an old water heater, saved for unknown reasons, and now the two of them positioned themselves to grab hold of it. "Rock it forward," his father instructed, and Ryan struggled to get some purchase on it. It felt like an iron lung. He lost his grip and the thing dropped to the cement floor with a grating screech.

"This is no good, Dad."

"Little more and we got it."

"No, look, let's get a dolly and move it out to the curb and find somebody to haul it off."

"Count of three."

Ryan did his cursing silently. On "three" he put his back into it, budged the water heater maybe another foot, and straightened up, panting. "That better be enough."

His father took a minute to get his wind back. "Hoo boy. She's a pistol."

"Why you want to keep this? You can't even fit Mom's car in the garage anymore." His father's Buick presided over the space reserved for cars, its high-luster finish the brown of a beetle's shell. The car was eight years old and his father said it wasn't even broken in yet.

"It's a perfectly good water heater that somebody's going to be glad to have someday." His father bent to reach a length of siding and Ryan lifted the far end. "Like here I've got this extra siding and I can use it around the west side where the old stuff's starting to peel."

*Never mind.* "You want me to help you get started?"

"How about we just move it out to where I need it. Too late to get going anyway. With supper and all." By this he meant the occasion of company, and while he might not actually resent such company, it was understood that they got in the way of important home-repair projects.

Janine was gone when they came out with the siding, and Ryan was just as glad. She'd find something else to do with herself and have a chance to cool down. He'd say he was sorry, kiss her ass a little. By this time tomorrow they'd be in the mountains.

It took them a few trips with the siding, and then the infernal water heater had to get wedged back into its corner. His father reached for the overhead garage door, paused, and said, "Political what?"

It took Ryan a moment to shift gears. "Political science. It's the study of how people are governed and how they govern themselves." That sounded pretty limp-dick, so he said, "For instance, what do we mean when we say *freedom,* or *democracy,* or *justice*? Or, what makes the American system different than other systems?"

"What did they decide, on that last one?"

"We try to ensure that people who aren't privileged still have equal citizenship."

His father considered this. He seemed to be trying to decide if it was a good idea. "History. Like, the Declaration of Independence."

"No, Dad. It's how people live now too. Their place in the political system. Their, ah, equal participation."

"Their *rights,*" his father said with satisfaction, bringing the garage door down, a rolling rolling thud.

Ryan followed his father inside, wondering when *rights* had become a swear word. He guessed that to his father, it conjured up guilty-as-sin criminals hiding behind the skirts of the law, and sniveling, do-nothing intellectuals mouthing slogans.

Janine and his mother sat at the kitchen table. Janine had a bowl of strawberries and whipped cream in front of her and was busy working on it. "I got hungry," she said to Ryan, pausing with the spoon halfway to her mouth. "These are the best strawberries in the world, you should have some."

"No thanks. Spoil my dinner."

"Suit yourself." She picked up the Reddi-wip can and squirted another puffy layer over the fruit. The trailing ends of her hair got into the whipped cream; she used her fingers to wipe it away.

His mother got up to rinse lettuce at the sink. "How did you two get so filthy? Don't touch anything before you wash up." She looked happy, the way she always did when she was feeding people.

Ryan and his father obediently headed off. At the bathroom door his father said, "Well, if finicky eaters make poor lovers, I don't know what you got here."

He closed the door behind him. Ryan stood there a moment, then went out through the front door and used the garden hose to rinse himself off.

His sister Anita brought a casserole of chicken divan, the top covered with crimped aluminum foil. "This has to go in a 325-degree oven for twenty minutes," she announced, setting it down on the countertop, *thunk*, using the heels of her hands so as not to break her fingernails. "Hi, Ry." Then she pretended to be surprised to see Janine, even though she'd been told to expect her. It was a classic Anita move.

"Anita, this is Janine. Janine, my sister Anita."

"Nice to meet you," Anita said, and smiled. Ryan had seen that same smile on her before, that stretched and brilliant grimace. Keep Off The Grass, her smile said.

"Janine's from Chicago," their mother announced.

"Oh, really?" Anita was rummaging around in her purse. "Chicago," she repeated, as if it was a place whose existence she doubted.

*So my sister's this giant bitch,* Ryan tried to convey to Janine, but again, the telepathy channel wasn't working and Janine wasn't looking at him. He rested one hand on the back of her chair; she moved away from it. What the hell had he done, and was he ever going to be allowed to make up for it?

His mother asked Anita, "Is Jeff coming, honey?"

"He couldn't get away. Some dumb meeting."

His mother said that was too bad. Nobody ever actually missed Jeff when he didn't show up. He was still an undigested lump in the family group. When he was there he watched golf on television or volunteered to go out for ice, in order, Ryan suspected, to sneak a drink.

Anita didn't seem too broken up about his absence. She fussed with her casserole some more, then lifted her gaze to consider Ryan. "What's with the hair?"

"I was going to ask you the same thing. Let me guess. Disco Queen comes to Iowa."

"Very funny." She'd permed her hair to within an inch of its life. When she moved her head, the mass of hair followed along behind her a split second later. She wore one of her outfits, a matching shirt and slacks the color of cooked shrimp, and high, clunky sandals that made her wobble a little.

"So Janine, are you a student too?" Again, that billboard of a smile. This time it was saying, I Could Care Less.

"That's right."

"Oh, what are you studying?"

"Agricultural economics."

"That's a joke," Ryan said. "A funny."

Both women regarded him without amusement.

"Janine writes poetry," his mother put in helpfully.

"I didn't know you had to go to school for that."

"If you're serious about it you do. If you don't just want to be Rod McKuen."

There was no way Janine could have known that Anita and Jeff's wedding ceremony had featured a Rod McKuen poem.

"I was thinking we could put some brats on the grill," Ryan's mother said. "Anybody want brats instead of a burger?"

Torrie came in then, and his father also, and Blake returned from whatever he'd been doing with his friends, and the coals were pronounced almost ready to receive the hamburgers, and the business of the supper began. A card table was set up at one end of the picnic table. Paper plates and napkins were distributed. His mother made a little too much out of asking Janine if she liked eating this or that, and Janine answered politely that this or that was fine. It wasn't a good sign when she was this quiet, though it might pass for normal shyness around people you didn't know. Anita hadn't helped anything. But then, she never did.

After dinner they could go for a walk or something, cool out, talk about the next day's drive, the mountains waiting for them on the rim of the horizon. They could laugh about Anita (that hair! that outfit!), get back on the same side again. Or if he was lucky, she was now pissed off mostly about Anita, not him. He carried the extra folding chairs in from the den, brought his father the tongs and platter he needed to preside at the grill. Ryan guessed he shouldn't be surprised that the two of them, Anita and Janine, had sniffed each other over and hadn't much liked each other. Anita was what Janine called *bourgeois,* with her fussing about upholstery samples and appliance purchases and her waterskiing weekends at the bank president's lake house. Whatever *bourgeois* meant, he was pretty sure it was Anita, her constant brittle anxiety, as if she'd just missed out on some really important sale.

Janine's family had enough money that she could pretend it didn't matter, and people who were hung up on *consumerism,* another of her words, were small and pitiable.

But her new car was bought and paid for. Her out-of-state tuition covered.

Ketchup, mustard, pickles, buns. Salt and pepper, butter, mayonnaise. His mother loaded him down with jars and bottles, knives, serving spoons, plastic skewers for the corn on the cob. He moved automatically, while some distant, dreamy portion of his mind tried to formulate thought, something he'd been trying to explain to his father, the difference between people who had and did not have things, or not just things, but some other kind of ownership. There were people who felt themselves to belong to some common enterprise, and those who did not. People who took comfort in like-mindedness of all sorts, and those who had been set apart, or set themselves apart. . . .

His father put the platter of hamburgers on the table, each of them with its grid of black char lines, and announced that dinner was served.

Finally all of them were seated. Janine and Ryan were next to each other at the picnic table. Torrie and Blake complained about being at the card table, the kids' table. Everyone quieted. His father looked around. "Blake," he said.

"Dear Lord we thank you for the food we are about to eat and bless us this day we ask it in Jesus Christ's name Amen."

Ryan's mother said, "It's so nice to have the whole family together."

"Except for Jeff," Torrie piped up.

Ryan assembled his plate of food, started in on the potatoes. When his mother asked him when they were leaving tomorrow, he had to work through a mouthful of food before he could answer. "Early. It's nearly seven hundred miles to Estes Park." He looked to Janine, *Come on, help me out,* but she was taking particular care in buttering her ear of corn. Her silver bracelets clinked.

"I was hoping tomorrow we could all go up and see Norm and Martha. Martha's not doing so well."

"What's the matter with her?"

"Broken hip," Ryan's father said. "Didn't your mother tell you?"

His mother said, "It was last month. I did tell you, Ry, don't you ever pay attention? She fell right in their own driveway. The doctor said she'd heal up without an operation but the bone isn't setting the way it should and she still can't walk and sometimes this is how it goes, one problem leads to another, her circulation's bad, and then you get blood pressure and everything else. Of course Norm's right there for her, and Pat and the kids, but they're both getting up there now. Norm's what, seventy-nine? Martha, I forget."

"You're kidding." Ryan meant their age, or he mostly meant that. There was another kind of disbelief. Norm and Martha were like the carved faces on Mt. Rushmore. You expected them to weather but not really change.

His mother said to Janine, "They're practically like grandparents to the kids. Since their real grandparents passed away."

"I'm sorry," Janine said to him, but he didn't want her to be sorry. They weren't hers to feel sorry about.

"I'll come back the next weekend and see them."

"I know they'd like that."

Eating filled up the space that would have gone to talk. Everybody except Blake took some of Anita's casserole for politeness' sake: chicken and broccoli glued together with cheese sauce. Ryan said, "Great burgers, Dad." Everyone agreed, yes, they were great.

"May I be excused?" Torrie asked.

She hadn't eaten much, just dabs of salad and casserole, and half of a half of a burger.

"Don't you want any dessert?"

"Uh-uh."

"She's on another stupid diet," Blake said. "Except she gets up in the middle of the night and eats like a whole bag of vanilla wafers."

"Blake," his mother warned.

"Shut up, Blake."

"Both of you."

Torrie wore her persecuted expression and her mouth quivered. Anita said, "You should try Atkins, Tor. The weight just *falls* off."

His mother said, "She is not a bit fat. She's a beautiful, healthy girl and we love her exactly the way she is."

"Excuse me." Torrie grabbed her plate and headed for the back door. The screen door slammed behind her.

"Sensitive," Blake remarked.

"You didn't have to start anything," his mother said. Then she turned to Janine. "They always say, girls are easier to raise than boys, but I think that's only true up to a certain age. Do you have any brothers or sisters?"

"I have an older brother. A stepbrother, actually."

She couldn't have just said "brother."

His mother glided right past it. "Oh, and what does he do?"

"He's a psychotherapist."

"A what?" Blake asked.

"A headshrinker," Anita told him.

Ryan said, "Psychotherapist. It's a big word, but you can practice."

"All right," his father said. "Let's drop it."

"How many for strawberry pie?" his mother asked.

After supper his mother and Anita took over the kitchen and no one else was allowed to help even if they'd wanted to. Ryan and Janine walked around the block in the early twilight. Janine said she was cold and got her jacket out of the car.

"Better get used to it. It's a lot colder up in the mountains."

"Mhm."

"Don't get excited or anything," he said, trying to invoke the day's earlier mood.

"Sure."

"Come on."

"Come on what?"

"Can you lose the attitude?"

She was looking away, mostly to ignore him. So he guessed the answer was no.

"It looks like an old paddle wheeler."

"What does?"

"That house with all the fancy wood trim and the lights on. It looks like an old-style paddleboat steaming down a river."

"I guess." He was bored with her always pretending things were something else.

"It's pretty here. Green and all. Quiet."

He guessed it was. He didn't know what that had to do with anything. They walked on in silence. In the near dark Janine's neck and throat were white, her earrings thin silver glints. He imagined he could smell her hair, hear the faint friction of her legs rubbing together as she walked. Another spasm of irritation and lust came over him. He wondered, without any real hope, if they might wait until everyone else had gone to sleep, sneak down to the basement or out to the garage. They reached the end of the street and the alley of dark and whispering trees. As if by agreement, they turned around to go back.

He found her hand and squeezed it. "Things'll be better tomorrow. We just need to get out of here."

She kept her hand in his for a time, then it fell away as their paces changed. She said, "I don't see what difference that's going to make."

So she wanted him to crawl some more. "I'm sorry. My family always makes me a little nuts."

"Hate to tell you, but I don't see them doing anything that terrible to you."

"They make me restless."

He hadn't found that word before, but now it came out of his mouth like a snake disgorging a beautiful golden egg.

"Or making you act like a total asshole."

"How am I acting like an asshole?"

"Like you don't love them."

"Unfuckingbelievable," he managed.

Janine shrugged. They'd reached his parents' driveway. The darkness was nearly solid. Just outside the circle of front-porch light, he pulled her back and pressed her against the hood of the car, pulling her tight against him, and though he knew she wasn't happy with him and would withold herself to punish him, still he hoped that she would sense the *purity* of his need, another strange word squeezed out of him. He put his hands beneath Janine's jacket, found her breasts and tried to work them free. He pinched, hard, and her breath drew in as it always did and this was good, this was the two of them, who they'd always been, not the ugly, clumsy beings of the last few hours. She leaned against him for a moment, then said, "We can't stay out here."

"I know."

She patted his shoulder and he followed her to the back door. Tomorrow would be so much better.

Anita had gone home, and Torrie was still sulking in her room. His parents and Blake were watching television in the den. "Come on in, kids," his mother called, and there was nothing else to do except go in and watch whatever happy shit they were watching. His mother was in her place at the end of the couch, his father with his feet up in his lounger. His brother lay on his stomach on the floor, his head on a cushion, his shirt buttons twisted around to one side. He almost never wore T-shirts. He thought they made his arms and chest look too skinny.

Janine sat down on the opposite end of the couch but Ryan kept standing, pretending to be transfixed by *The Mary Tyler Moore Show*. No way was he going to squeeze in on that couch all cozy between the two of them or settle himself in the other chair. This was all too weird, too much like coming home from high school dates stirred up and mortified and hard, and so he did what he had always done, which was to announce that he was going to take a shower before bed.

He came back wearing sweatpants, his hair wet and combed. Janine gave him a smirky smile. Maybe she knew. He couldn't tell. His mother said, "You better have enjoyed your nice hot shower now, mister. They don't have those out in the woods."

"Yeah, I know." He settled into the free chair and turned his attention to the television. Out of the corner of his eye he studied them. His mother had her reading glasses on. They made her look like somebody else's grandmother. His father's mouth drooped. The chair always put him to sleep. You had to love your family. You didn't have any choice in it.

"Janine, honey, I put clean towels on your bed, and there are Dixie cups you can use in the bathroom for brushing your teeth. Is there anything else you need?"

"No, thanks very much. I'll be fine." Janine was sitting with her knees up on the couch and her jacket pulled over them. He imagined her sitting like that at a campfire.

His mother said she'd be turning in, then. Once she'd gone, nobody spoke, except for his father who asked what was on next. Blake said it was *Newhart.* The show started up with its noise and music. His father sat up in his chair and leaned in to watch. It was pretty clear that his father was going to stay put as long as he had to, rather than leave the two of them here together.

Janine straightened one of her legs and scratched the ankle with the beaded bracelet, a slow, thorough process.

After a while, she stood up and said she was going to bed.

"You get everything you need out of the car?"

"Yup. Good night." She stooped and kissed Ryan lightly on the mouth and walked out barefoot, carrying her shoes. They heard her running water in the bathroom, then doors opening and closing, then quiet.

Halfway through *Newhart,* his father got up and stretched and said it had been a long day. Ryan moved to the couch and lay down with his feet on the armrest, something you were not allowed to do in his mother's presence. Blake said, "I bet Mom and Dad have like, burglar alarms on that door."

"Shut up."

Ryan must have fallen asleep, because when he opened his eyes again, Blake was gone, and the television had been taken over by some cheap-looking kung fu movie, and the lights were too bright for his heavy eyes. He got up and shut everything off and stood for a moment in the darkness at the door of Anita's old room, listening, hearing nothing. His parents slept in the next room. There was no way he'd be able to keep quiet enough.

Blake was already asleep. He always laid himself down in one position and stayed that way until morning. Ryan drew back the covers and stretched out on the thin, clean sheets. It took him a while to fall back to sleep. The room, its shapes, its strips of light and of darkness, was both entirely familiar and entirely strange to him. Blake inhaled a snore, breathed out again, silent. He was on the gray deck of a ship and the air was gray or the air was really water and people came and went up and down staircases because they were no longer on the boat but at the sort of fancy party you saw in old black-and-white movies. He was supposed to get back to the boat because it was about to sail although it didn't have sails but some kind of loud engine.

He opened his eyes. He was still asleep because the air was gray, but no, it was early early morning and this was the first blurred sign of dawn.

He got up to use the bathroom, making sure he kept the door closed until the toilet was finished flushing so as not to wake anybody else up. He walked soft-footed out to the den, listened, heard nothing. In the kitchen the refrigerator rattled and hummed, then throttled back down. He ran the tap until the water ran cold, filled a glass with ice cubes, and drank it down. The backyard grass was wet with heavy dew. Birds were racketing and calling and he realized that he'd been hearing them all along.

He refilled the glass and carried it out to the living room. It was in a deeper shadow, and he pushed the smothering drapes aside to try and see the sun. A layer of cloud was just above the horizon, and a little light leaked around it from below. The light was dull, as if it emitted from some heavy metal, and he puzzled over it, just as the sun pushed the clouds away and shone forth and the last shreds of his dream dispersed and his eyes told his brain that Janine's red car was gone.

# Seattle

**Magic, magic!** Alive! Alive!

You could get so holy high. This air that turned into sky. Magic! Oh blue! Oh white clouds! The comical way they bumped and shoved each other. His own little giggly heaven. Nobody would ever guess. Him one smart guy. Sweet grass underneath his head, cool breeze in his hair. Who needed anything but this? He meant, the alive part. Something like that. It didn't matter. He knew what he knew. His mind unminded. Unwinded. A windup toy, a monkey in a jaunty little bellboy's cap, banging on a drum. Slower. Slow. er.

"Ray! Jesus, Ray, what're you doing out there?"

His eyes opened. Grass was in his mouth; he spat and rubbed it away with the back of his hand. Deb was standing at the back door with a look on her face.

"Fell asleep."

"In the dirt? There's chairs out there. Christ. I thought you were dead or something."

"Just relaxing." His mouth had gone dry. He didn't want her to know he'd been smoking up, or at least, he didn't want her to know it right away. Deb was home from work, meaning it was later than it should have been. The sky was still clear but the sun was low, and the

49

evening's chill was moving in. Dampness seeped in through his jeans and shirt, a clammy feeling. He stood up, trying to look spry and un-stoned. To distract and delay her from asking her questions, he got a cigarette going and said, "Why don't you grab a couple beers, sit out here with me."

She turned and went back into the kitchen, and he waited to see if that was the end of it. But a moment later she pushed the screen door open and stepped out, carrying two Coors in blue foam insulating jackets.

"So how was work?" he asked, once they were settled. The lawn chairs were made of woven plastic webbing that sagged in places, invit-ing you to burrow in and then get stuck.

"It was work."

She didn't offer anything more, which meant she was pissed off about something, him, probably. He finished his cigarette, stabbed it out in the abalone shell they used for an ashtray. He said, "I got some ham steaks for dinner. Tomatoes, green beans, and bakery rolls. Say the word, I'll get supper on the table in two shakes." Now that he was awake he was hollowed out with hunger. The beer sloshed inside him.

"Maybe in a little."

"Will Elton be here?" Elton was Deb's teenage son, who mostly lived with them.

"I don't know."

She wasn't going to give him the time of day, just freeze him out. "Hey," he said. "Big Chief Stone Face." He laughed, har-de-har. Deb was Indian, and sometimes he could kid her about that. Not now.

She lifted her beer as if it drink it, then put it down again. "You could have cleaned the place up a little."

"Those dishes? They'll take me thirty seconds. Watch me." Now he remembered that he'd put a load of clothes in the washer but had forgotten to transfer them to the dryer. With any luck he could sneak down to the basement and get the dryer going before she noticed.

"So why aren't they done already? What'd you do all day instead?

Are you listening, Ray? I get up at six in the morning, I spend eight solid hours—"

"All right," he said, but not fast enough.

"—getting phone calls from people who have real, actual things wrong with them, I mean they can't walk, or breathe, or crap, and them I feel sorry for, not somebody who's, what do you call it? 'Struggling with a sense of vocation'?"

"That was a joke."

"Yeah, like you're always so funny." She looked around her as if seeking the source for her disgust. "Your garden's not doing shit."

"Give it a little more time." They'd eaten lettuce and radishes early on, but the hot-weather vegetables, tomatoes and peppers and corn, were struggling. It was just too cool and gray here, nothing like summer should be. The corn was especially pitiful, a few scrawny stalks that were never going to produce ears. Anyone from back home would have laughed himself silly over it. Back home they grew hybrids so tough and sturdy, they'd stop a car.

"Tomorrow," he said. "Watch me. There's a couple things in the newspaper I'm going to check out."

"Good plan."

It wasn't like he never worked. He'd put in three weeks on a loading dock, he cleaned carpets for a realtor, he had a builder who called him whenever he had a demo job. But he wasn't the career type. Deb knew that by now. She just had to kick up a fuss every so often.

"How about I get busy with supper," he said coaxingly. "Kitchen patrol." He was starving and there was a taste in his mouth like old rags. "Need another beer?"

She shook her head. He extricated himself from the sagging chair and held out a hand to help her up. Deb was on the squatty side and sometimes she had trouble. "I'm gonna sit out here for a while," she said.

"Suit yourself." She'd get over it. She always did. He thought she sort of liked having that big pile of resentments and disappointments to rev herself up with.

He got the clothes in the dryer rolling and started in on the dishes. They were only dishes and not that big a deal. The front-door lock rattled. Elton was home.

Elton went into his bedroom and cranked up his music. Ray didn't like admitting it because it made him feel about sixty years old, but he hated a lot of the music these days. It was just volume, screaming, without any soul or melody or anything else that scratched you where you itched.

Elton was in the bathroom now. He stayed there a long time. When he came into the kitchen, Ray said, "What's up, Big Man?"

Elton didn't answer right away. It was a teenage thing, and Ray understood that. The music did most of the talking for him, crashing and shrieking from the bedroom, its moron refrain: "High-voltage rock 'n' roll, high-voltage ROCK 'N' ROLL!"

"Dinner in fifteen, twenty minutes." Ray had the kitchen all polished and wiped down and was getting his pans organized. Elton wasn't waiting. He made himself a salami-and-mustard sandwich, doubled up so he could get more of it into his mouth. He was a chunky kid, like his mom. Before Ray came out West, he never thought there was such a thing as a fat Indian.

Once he'd finished the sandwich, Elton said, "I earned twenty bucks helping Craig clear out the back of the shop."

"Twenty, that's good." He and Elton got along OK, mostly because they stayed out of each other's shit. He didn't need a kid, and Elton didn't need some fake dad telling him what to do all the time. "Couple more days like that, you'll be pretty close to a camera." Elton wanted a camera so he could take gritty black-and-white pictures of urban life.

"It was just the one day." Elton planted himself with his back against the door to the basement. "Where's Mom?"

"Sitting out back." Ray could see her from the window. She had her feet up on the extra chair and her head back, like she'd been dropped from some great height. It was Friday night and she had a week's worth of pissed off to get out of her system. "She's kind of tired."

Deb was always tired. He and Elton always heard about it. They

carried themselves with the jaunty indifference of men who are supported by women.

He got the green beans working and set the table, using plates that
matched, folding the cotton napkins around the silverware, placing
the salt and pepper, butter, salad dressing, everything they needed. He
wanted her to notice his making things nice for her.

Elton had gone back to his bedroom. There were times he left and
they didn't see him for days. Seventeen years old and it was summer,
what did you expect? He was a pretty good kid in spite of having what
most people would consider a fucked-up start in life. Deb being so
young and all when she had him. Sometimes if felt like she was both
of their mothers.

Ray sliced the tomatoes, put a little salt on them to juice them up,
arranged the bakery rolls on a plate, and set the ham steaks in the skil-
let. He cracked another beer and tested the green beans with a fork.
People always acted like cooking was this big hard thing.

The kitchen table was a lot smaller with all three of them there. You
had to keep your elbows pulled in. Elton got the mayonnaise out of the
fridge, split two of the rolls, and piled them with ham and tomato to
make a sandwich. There was nothing the kid wouldn't eat if he could
put bread around it. Deb was on a diet where you were supposed to eat
everything slow, so as to give yourself time to fill up. She put her knife
and fork down between each bite. He didn't think her weight was such
a big deal. He thought she got close to pretty when she smiled.

"Those beans turn out OK?" he asked her. "I pass the bean test?"

"They're good. It's all real good." She'd perked up some since getting
home, though not to the point you'd call jolly.

"Glad you like it, honeybun." Always in the back of his mind—
except sometimes it migrated to the front—was the need to make an
extra effort, keep her from thinking she was better off without him.
Then where would he be? Right smart nowhere, as his grandma used
to say.

Small, ripping, popping noises reached them from somewhere
outside. Firecrackers. Everybody warming up for the big, hairy Bi-

centennial Fourth. "Hey," he said. "Who wants to go to the parade tomorrow?" He chuckled, a joke.

"Big whoop," said Elton. The ham was gone; he was making a sandwich out of mayonnaise and tomato.

"What, you don't like parades?" This was just to give him shit. Elton was into Red Power. Elton made one of his faces, the one expressing loathing.

"We could build a float. Something historical, like Custer's Last Stand."

Deb said, "I keep telling you, you're not a naturally funny person."

"No, I've had to work really hard at it." Sometimes he could start her laughing, pry her loose from her mood.

Not tonight. She motioned that he should give her a cigarette. She lit it and turned her head to blow little puffs of smoke to one side. "Bunch of white people celebrating themselves. No thanks."

He didn't think he was celebrating anything. He couldn't remember ever having much patriotic feeling, even before the war beat it out of his backside. They wouldn't understand that. They thought anybody with blond hair and blue eyes had no reason for complaints. Not wanting to give up his argument entirely, he said, "Some of that stuff is kind of interesting. The whatsis. Tall ships. Fireworks."

"Well you head on down there if you want. It's a party I'm not invited to."

Deb was Yakama and Quinault and Umatilla and some other odds and ends of tribes that didn't exist anymore and probably a little whitey thrown in there too, though nobody liked to talk about that. She even had a white name, Potter, which was regarded as another injustice. She'd grown up on the rez. Ray had heard enough about it by now. The white devils. How they had—OK we had—grabbed their land, killed off all the salmon, elk, beaver, resettled the tribes on the most crapped-out acreage around, and then told them to be farmers. Ray didn't feel personally responsible for any of that, but he guessed this was where the notion of *tribe* came in. How they/we had turned their history into a bunch of stupid movies. Victor

Mature all oiled up, wearing a cheap, woolly-looking wig with braids and a feather.

It was one of Vietnam's bad jokes, one he didn't think Deb would appreciate, that hostile territory was called Indian country.

Sometimes he thought she liked his being white just so she could hold on to her grudges.

On the rez there was poverty, etc. Alcoholism, diabetes, hypertension, everything that came of eating the white man's food, following the white man's ways. The house Deb grew up in had neither running water nor electricity and sure, that was rough, but part of him wondered why it was so much worse than living in tipis or lodges or whatever they'd had a thousand years before there was an America. Of course the problem was more complicated. It was a soul-sickness having to do with shame, scorn, and the humiliation of having lost a war and yes, he knew something about all that.

When were you a tribe and when weren't you? Did Norwegian count? His Indian name: Ray White Rat, Junior.

"Hey," he said quickly, since the other two were stirring, ready to get up from the table. "I got a little surprise."

They looked at him without curiosity. He wasn't famous for his surprises. Elton said, "I'm going back over to Craig's."

"It won't take but a minute." Ray got up and went into the bedroom, his and Deb's room, navigating through the landscape of piled-up clothes and burdened chairs, finding his knapsack on the floor of the closet. "OK, outside."

They didn't want to go outside. What was the deal, anyway? They complained and dragged ass. It was barely dark by now. This far north was practically the land of the midnight sun. Not really dark enough but it was going to have to do, since they wouldn't let him wait and do anything right. Deb and Elton straggled out. "Now don't look," he instructed them. They weren't looking. Big whoop.

The yard was long and narrow, with unimpressive wire fencing separating them from the neighbors on three sides. Somebody who'd lived here before had constructed a porch on the back end of the house, a homemade thing roofed in corrugated white plastic and supported on a pair of three-by-five posts. Deb and Elton loitered here, bored and ready to go back inside.

"One second," he told them, hustling down to the far end of the yard, past the puny garden. Wishing he'd managed to smoke a little marahoochie. Half a joint still in his shirt pocket. Deb not approving of it in general, and especially not around Elton. Like the kid was some drug virgin. Please.

"One more . . . second," he called back to them, digging in the knapsack. He wanted to start with something big, wake them up, make them finally pay attention. He'd already carried out a bucket of sand he could use to anchor the loading tube. Now he broke open the cellophane pack, considered his choices. Giant Comet. Mad Dog. Sky Titan Triple Break. Dominator. They all sounded pretty good. The shells were packaged in fancy paper with tiny, gaudy patterns of lightning bolts and planets and whirligigs, funny, somebody going to all that trouble for something destined to be blown to smithereens. He picked the Giant Comet, loaded it so the fuse extended. "OK, watch this . . ."

It took three tries with his lighter to get it lit, from dampness probably. He had to squat down to get a good look and wouldn't it be bad form to lose an eye or a hand once he finally got it going but he stepped back in plenty of time. There was a sizzle and then WOOSH it was out of sight, spitting its way up into the sky so high he couldn't track it, a blue spurt, then a fountain of red above it and higher still a pop, and a green-gold starburst, and Jesus CHRIST it was big, like county fair big. He wasn't expecting that and his heart flopped inside him. What was left of the shell fell back harmlessly, floating cinders. Deb and Elton yelped and screeched, scared, sure, but then happy at the hugeness, the beautiful spectacle of it.

He took a little mock bow.

Elton came over to check it out. "What was that shit?"

"You liked it?"

"Let me do the next one."

Deb yelled at them to be careful, and they yelled back Sure, sure. It felt good to ignore her, the two of them in silent agreement because this was what women did, they were natural killjoys. Ray showed him how to load the shell. "Now back off, give it room and watch yourself when it comes down. Jeez, your mom'll scalp me if you get hurt."

"Yeah, yeah." Elton too excited, getting too close when he lit the thing and Ray had to yank him back, WOOSH.

This one was red and white and blue, a spray of glitter and sparks high overhead. *Oh say can you see.* Fourth of July just an excuse for some good old sky magic. Doors slammed. Neighbors came out to see what the hell was going on. A mild cheering. Everybody liking the show. The Triple Break, three separate BANGETY-BANG white waterfalls. They shot off some smaller bottle rockets and percussive pieces, a cluster of booming and popping white lights. The air had a gunpowder smell. Smoke drifted along the ground.

"What's this one?" Elton demanded, and Ray said he didn't exactly know, but there was a way to find out. It turned out to be a flare that shot up, whizzbang, and landed in the yard behind theirs, a little too close to the house for comfort. Nobody was home so it didn't matter. Then the loading tube fell over sideways when they lit the next shell and that might have turned out bad, then the fuse fizzled. Tricky shit but no harm done and that's what counted.

"Where'd you get this stuff?" Elton, impressed in spite of himself, forgetting his fat-boy coolness.

"Ah, downtown." Same guy he bought his pot from. There was no reason to advertise that. He felt for the joint in his shirt pocket. It was criminal not to be under the influence.

Dark enough now that Deb couldn't see him from the back porch. He fired the joint with his back turned to Elton, a feeble attempt at hiding, then he thought that was stupid, and because they were having such a good time being guys together, the way they almost never did, he passed it over to Elton, who sucked it down like a champ.

Ray dawdled a little, letting the pot do its thing. He was loose, expansive, peaceful, ready to appreciate the full potential and possibilities of this here beautiful light show. That magic holy high, the pure mindlessness of it. Him and Elton both with a case of the stoned giggles. Slaphappy, trying to get the launcher positioned exactly right.

"I got it," Ray told him, and he did, he could handle it, it was nothing new. Plenty of times back in the good old war, they'd light up all kinds of shit while lit up. Ordnance, tracer rounds, phosphorous grenades. Every day a twisted Fourth of July, or some big stoned carnival, with the other side getting prizes for knocking you over. Some guys, the most serious burnouts, were way way into speed, had eyes like fried eggs, skin that had stopped sweating, skin like chalk. Some guys smoked heroin packed into cigarettes. He tried that once but it just made him fall asleep. He never saw one goddamn Vietcong. It was just ready, aim, fire, miss everything. Big whomping rockets shook the ground. You couldn't tell who launched them, your side or theirs, but if one of them hit you, made you go up in the air and come down like snow, what the hell did it matter?

He didn't like to admit it, but aside from the getting-shot-at part, and the whole obscenity of the war itself, he'd actually kind of liked the army. It was the closest he'd come to a tribe.

They got the fuse going and the rocket fizzed and whizzed, climbed and broke open into the biggest brightest sizzling silver star he'd ever seen. A little murmer of ooh and aah came from the people watching, but then they were silent. The star broke apart into long tails of white shimmer, drifting down and down, bright, perfect, gone.

Then they started running out of luck. He didn't notice right away. Still lost in the admiration of it all.

"Sir? Sir?"

Elton? But he was gone. Sidling away all casual toward the house and then, total chickenshit that he was, probably right out the front door. Nope, this was the Man, strolling up the driveway like he was an invited guest.

"Sir? I need to talk to you."

Ray put on a smile, though it was too dark for the officer of the law to see it. But a smile rearranged your posture, made it less likely you'd get punched out or arrested or some other bad shit. You were just a harmless, well-meaning citizen, lacking any criminal intent. That was when he realized he was holding his lighter in one hand and a big ass rocket in the other.

The cop sounded pissed off. You could tell he was tired of chasing down a bunch of stupid fireworks. "All right. You want to give me the rest of your toys?"

"Ah . . ." Ray looked at the rocket in his hand, frowning, trying to suggest that the hand was an independent agent or third party, nothing he was responsible for. "Yeah, sure."

"All of them, smart guy."

"This is all that's left." Could he smell the pot on him? He could see the headlines now. Police hero busts drugs and explosives ring. Fuck it. Really.

The cop took the rocket, shone a flashlight around the yard, looking. Nothing but the peeled and charred paper scraps, leftover wrappings, and his stupid, slug-infested garden.

"You want to tell me where this came from?"

"Some guy, guy on a corner selling it."

"Let's take a hike, you and me."

He stopped to light a cigarette, hoping it would cover up the pot smell, and followed the cop down the driveway to the street. Deb was watching from the kitchen and he tried to make his walk slow and uncaring. Gave her a little wave, a tip of his imaginary hat. He heard the back door shut.

The cop had his squad car pulled up to the curb, idling, parking lights on. He opened the front passenger door. "Get in."

He dropped the cigarette to the curb. Front seat probably meant he was going to get a ticket or a fine, not a trip downtown. No big deal. He took in the leather seat, polished by a generation of cop butts, the ample legroom, the green dashboard light illuminating the blocky looking dash and gearshift and the cop radio making its static noises. Plymouth Gran Fury, he guessed, a 360 with a two-barrel carb.

The cop opened his door, got in, and switched the dome light on.

He had a heavy, gray face, an old dude who'd seen it all and didn't like any of it.

"ID."

He raised up off the seat to get to the wallet in his back pocket, extracted his driver's license and handed it over. "Iowa," the cop said. "You're a long way from home."

"That's a fact." Getting busted for kiddie shit. How stupid was that. So-and-so could screw up a wet dream, people used to say about somebody or other who never did anything right.

"What brings you all the way out here?" The cop was holding his license with one hand while he wrote with the other. It was just a question, but with judgment held in reserve, as if not staying in Iowa was some kind of suspicious circumstance.

"Ah, no good reason. Got out of the army, wanted to see the world. Nice town, Seattle. The three or four days a year it doesn't rain." This was pretty much the truth. He didn't have too many good reasons for anything.

The cop either had no opinion about this or couldn't be bothered to answer. "I got drafted," Ray offered. "'Greetings.' I always thought I had a heart murmur, but the army doctor didn't find it. So I was a lucky guy, huh?"

He wanted another cigarette. The street was quiet now that the fun was over. A steep slope climbed to the big intersection two blocks away, and the little houses gave the impression of struggling to keep from sliding downward. What was he doing here, anyway?

"Lucky," the cop said. Conversation over.

"Yeah, guess the army has to have you a hundred percent healthy before they kill you off."

The cop finished writing. He tore off a perforated card and handed it back with Ray's license. "This is your citation. You'll be notified of your court date in the mail."

"Seriously?"

"Call the clerk of court in ten days, see if it gets dismissed. The only reason I'm not taking you in is I don't feel like driving out of my way.

If you were old enough to be in the service, you're old enough not to shoot off illegal explosives. And don't give me any reason to come out here again. No more stupid stuff. You understand me?"

He guessed that meant the pot. "Yes, officer. Thank you." Prick. He'd almost rather get arrested than have to kiss up.

The cop radio came to life, a woman's garbled voice transmitting instructions to somebody answering back. Ray said quickly, "Hey, is it all right if I sit here a minute more, give the wife a chance to cool down?" He didn't know why he said *wife*, except it sounded more convincing.

He could see the cop trying to decide, irritated again, like this went on all the time, people wanting one thing or another: a break, a favor, let this one slide. "You can sit here while I finish my log."

"Thanks. Cigarette?" He shook one loose from his pack, held it out.

"You can sit but you can't smoke."

He put the pack away. He wondered if Deb was watching from the house. Probably not. Nothing he did, good or bad, made any difference to her anymore.

"Wish I'd never started. Two packs a day, that's a real ball and chain." He knew he should just keep quiet, he should always keep quiet, but he never did. "Didn't hardly smoke at all before the army got its hooks in me. They shouldn't make cigs so cheap at the PX. Bad policy. Healthwise."

He waited for the cop to say something about that, yes or no or who gives a rip. The cop just kept writing. Ray laughed just so the echo of his voice wouldn't be left hanging out there. "Yeah, then they ship your ass to the war and it's a very, very funky place, and the last thing you want to do is give up on your cig habit and get the shaky nerves."

In the house behind him, a light went on in the bathroom, then off again. It wasn't his house. He was just living there for a while.

"Saigon," he said, trying to make the word last in his mouth, taste it again. It tasted like a flower dipped in hot smoke. "Good old Saigon, now, that was like you died and went to sin heaven. Parties going on day and night. Pretty ladies. Card games, hootchy-kootchy, all the gin in the world." He'd only been there once and he'd got sick drunk. In his memory, rooms, faces, revolved around him like a kaleidoscope.

"Yes indeedy," he said, continuing his one-side conversation. It pissed him off that the cop was so good at ignoring people. A little interest, a little attention, was that so much to ask? Nobody wanted to hear about Vietnam anymore. It was as if it had happened to some different, humiliated country. Nobody wanted to believe it was guys like him who'd worn the uniform, carried weapons, stood posts, took fire.

"Saw a guy once, the jungle rot got into his tongue and burned a hole in it. He used to put chopsticks through it, wave 'em around. Another guy, this lieutenant, he ejected from his F-4 and broke all the bones in both feet, and by the time somebody found him, the bones had set wrong and his feet were all deformed. They looked like crabs. You'd see weird shit like that all the time."

You did and you didn't. Some things he had seen himself, others had been related to him by somebody who'd seen them, and other stories were regarded as a kind of community property. Nobody believed anything that really happened there because somebody else always came up with a better story.

"I was with a commando unit. Not Green Berets. Shadow Warriors. We ate Green Berets for breakfast. Very small, five-man teams. We were used for stealth missions. Times they needed somebody to go into Uncle Ho's backyard, do reconnaissance or retrieve personnel or 'handle with extreme prejudice.' That's what they called assassinations. Supposed to be top secret but hell, the war's over. Or it was the last time I looked."

He needed a smoke so bad, his brain itched. All he had to do was get out of the cop car. All he had to do was stop talking, keep from burning a hole in his tongue. "You had to do things. War things. We caught this spy. Double agent. He'd messed with my lieutenant. The man took it personal. Guys like him, it was always personal. His nickname was Skull. That tells you something."

The war was over. Everybody lost. "Things didn't work out so good for Mr. Spy. Skull set up a meeting with him. Little shack, middle of nowhere. He thought it was just him and Skull until the rest of us showed up. You could say, five on one, not much of a fair fight. But it wasn't a fight, it was punishment. A warning to every other scumbag spy out there. And it was a chain-of-command thing. 'Ours not to question why, ours but to do or die.'" He couldn't remember where that came from, where he'd heard it.

You'd like to think if it was you, you wouldn't beg for your life. You'd be some hero. *Hero.* What was the opposite of *hero, villain?* Words nobody used, except maybe in comic books.

"We had a roll of razor wire. Wrapped it around him. Head to toe and everything in between. Had some wood skewers about yay long. Long enough to go in through the nose and out the eye. I think that's what killed him. Least, I think he was dead. I didn't stick around to find out."

The cop had stopped writing. His pen made a blot of ink where he'd left off. "Get out," he said. "And get your nut-job self back to Iowa. Bunch of goddamn animals. They should keep you in cages."

Ray stepped out onto the curb and watched the cop car move away, slow at first, then fast enough so the big smooth engine displaced the air with a stinging sound.

The front door was unlocked and he let himself in and bolted it behind him. The bedroom was dark. Deb wasn't asleep but she was hoping he'd think she was. He knew that and he was just as glad. He got a cigarette going and walked through the kitchen, where the dinner dishes were just as they'd left them, food hardening on the plates, a mess in the sink.

The back door was stubborn about opening and closing, some complaint in the hinges that he should have got around to fixing by now but hadn't. He forced it open and stepped out into the yard. A scrim of low cloud was moving across the stars. It was always either raining here, or was about to rain, or had just finished raining. It was a stupid soggy miserable place to be.

He used the hoe to chop down every worthless cornstalk, laying them all flat, then he pulled the tomatoes and pepper plants up by the roots and hacked at them with the blade until there was nothing left but a heap of wilting trash.

*It had been either Idaho or Montana, one of those big brown states, in a field next to the highway. Skull wanted to prop the guy up against a fence so people driving past would see him. A lesson to any other smart operator. A cold night. The layer of sweat underneath his clothes turning cold. They were all tired. It was numbing, stupid, hard work, the effort required to reduce a human body to this state. Sound buzzed in his head, went away, roared back. Skull said Hurry the fuck up, did they want somebody coming by, stopping? It was understood that Skull had a particular effect in mind, a display, a tableau, and they were screwing it up with their lack of diligence and speed. But so much skin had been removed that nothing was easy to manage, and Skull got impatient and said to go get a goddamn rope*

*and then a piece was missing, blotted out or lost, because he was running, with an idiot's clumsiness, something coming out of his mouth, noise? blood?*

*and then he was on his back in the middle of a field with a twig working its way inside his shirt and something thick caked under his nose and a pale, dusty sky overhead and nobody else there, except a circling blackbird on lazy wings high, high up. He was alive. He was alone. Wherever you went, it was Indian country.*

# *Iowa*

OCTOBER 1979

"Big boy bed."

"That's right. Matthew has his very own big boy bed, and he stays in it all night long."

He wasn't convinced. He didn't trust her. His face bunched into a sorrowful knob.

"Do you need to go potty, sweetheart? You sure? Look, Pooh Bear's sleepy. Let's turn off the light so he can sleep."

"Car light!"

"You want the car light?" Anita reached up and switched it on. This was a night-light in the shape of a race car, glowing red and yellow, with oversize tires and fins. The room was decorated in a car motif. The sheets and coverlet were dark blue with a parade of antique cars. The curtains showed dogs driving sporty convertibles. The dogs' ears were outstretched, to indicate speed. Their mouths were open and their tongues extended, to signify enjoyment.

Matthew didn't want Pooh Bear. He said he wanted Daddy. Anita pointed out that he had already said good-night to Daddy. Matthew shoved his knuckles into his eyes. He wanted Daddy Daddy Daddy.

"All right. But then it's night-night time, mister. No more excuses."

Anita used both hands to lift herself up from the low mattress.

Sometimes she lay down with Matthew and they both fell asleep together. She was starved for sleep. It was as real as any other hunger.

Jeff was watching football in the den. He'd mixed himself a drink and it rested on a coaster within reach of his hand. The footrest of the La-Z-Boy was up and his legs were extended straight out. There was something stupid and self-satisfied about his comfort. She stood to one side of the television. "Matthew wants you."

"He's supposed to be in bed by now."

"He's in bed and he wants you to tuck him in."

"Huh."

She waited. The football game reached some point of great drama, and Jeff leaned forward to watch it. The television made its excited noise.

"Da-ddy!"

Jeff shifted his weight, tracking the play.

"Daddy!" Louder and more aggrieved.

"If you don't go in there, he'll get himself out of bed."

Jeff reached for his drink, took a big smacking gulp of it, got out of the chair and headed off down the hallway. Anita could hear his hearty, retreating voice: "Hey sport, why aren't you asleep?"

She sat down in the La-Z-Boy. The leather was still warm from him, a sensation she wasn't certain she liked. She wriggled her shoulder blades into the padded seat back, lifted first one, then the other leg onto the footrest.

Her eyes were closed when Jeff came back. She heard his footsteps approach, then stop. "Hmm. Who's been sitting in my chair?"

She kept her eyes closed. "Is he asleep?"

"Yeah." He seemed to be waiting for her to get up. When she didn't, he crossed behind her to pick up his drink. "What's the score now?"

"I don't know." She didn't even know who was playing. It was just football, and it was always on.

She must have slept. Matthew was calling her. She never dreamed anymore. Her dreams were Mommy Mommy Mommy. "What?" she said, buying time until she was really awake.

He was saying something she couldn't make out in his urgent peeping child's voice. "All right, honey, just a minute."

"Your turn," Jeff said. As if it wasn't always her turn, as if there were a joke in there somewhere.

Matthew had thrashed his way out of the blankets. His face was a furious pink and his hair looked like he'd used both hands to tie it in knots. Anita checked the nursery clock. She'd put him to bed fifteen minutes ago. "What's the matter, baby?" she said in her heavily patient voice.

"No sleepy."

"Sure you are. But you need to lie still and close your eyes and think about how tired you are." With the back of her hand she checked his forehead. Warm but not feverish.

"Go potty."

"All right, let's go." They were trying to make potty training as carefree and natural as possible, because otherwise you risked shaming and confusing your child. So people said. She couldn't remember its being such a big deal herself.

He wanted to be helped out of bed and then he wanted to be carried to the bathroom. He still wore a diaper at night and that had to be managed, but finally he was unwrapped and installed on the potty-chair.

She waited while he explored the different sound effects available to anyone persistent and inquisitive enough to drag one hand, then the other, around the circumference of the plastic seat.

After a time Anita said, "Did you go pee yet?"

"No."

"Do you have to go poop?"

He shook his head.

"I thought you had to go potty."

Again he shook his head. He was a chubby boy with a head of fine, snarled white curls. Aside from the hair, she could see nothing of herself in him. He had Jeff's square face and wide-set eyes. "Why don't you pee, since you're already here."

He squeezed his eyes shut, concentrating. A tiny spatter.

"Good boy, I knew you could do it."

"Pee!"

"That's right. Matthew peed in the potty like a big boy." You were supposed to praise them. He was pleased with himself now, one fond hand massaging the bud of his penis. Was she meant to encourage this as well?

She dumped the potty, flushed, got him back into his diaper and pajamas, washed his hands, filled a paper cup for a drink of water. She carried him back to bed, the warm weight of him, putting her face against his neck because his smell was still a baby's smell, not that of a boy already preparing for a lifetime of dick handling.

She was a bad, foul, unnatural mother.

There were further negotiations once he was back in bed, and a night-night story and a night-night song and a kiss on the tummy, and chin chucker chin chucker chin chin chin, and the bedroom door left open just so. She'd only gone a few steps when he called her back. "Mommy!"

"Matthew, you have to go to sleep now."

"What's his name?"

"The dog?" He was pointing to the curtains, to one particular dog, a beagle type with a comical black eye patch, just discernible in the red-yellow glow. "He doesn't have a name."

"Why not?"

"I don't know. Close your eyes."

"What's his name?" An Airedale who looked to be stomping on the brakes.

They don't have names, they are dogs driving cars on curtains. But you couldn't say that because after all, Big Bird had a name, Kermit had a name, Mickey Mouse had a name, and so on.

She sat on the edge of the bed, pointed to the Airedale. "His name is, ah, Arnold."

"Why?"

"That's just his name. This one"—she indicated the beagle—"is Bobby. Bobby Beagle."

He was entranced. Calvin Collie. Wally Wienerdog. Charlie Chihuahua. The dogs were all boys, the boys were all happy, driving cars. Matthew giggled. Some of the breeds she had to guess or just give up. Pete the Puppy. Mike the Mutt. Matthew yawned. Larry Labrador. Sammy Shepherd.

He was asleep. She smoothed his hair, felt the solid warmth rising from him. There were these moments. You came on them in the middle of something else, anger or fatigue or both.

In the den, Jeff had reclaimed the La-Z-Boy. "He asleep?"

"Yes. Turn that down some."

His hand hovered over the remote, the game distracting him.

"Jeff."

"These guys suck." He clicked the volume button and looked at her. "You shouldn't let him drag this bedtime thing out so long."

"It takes him a while to wind down, you know that."

"Once he's down he should stay down."

"Fine, you get up and change him when he's wet."

"He can learn to hold it." Jeff's drink was gone. He raised the glass, jiggled the remaining ice cubes and tried to get the last taste of it. "Treat him like a baby and he'll act like one."

"You're so full of it," she said, but his attention had turned back to the television.

She went into the kitchen to finish loading the dishwasher. Everywhere she put her hands, she felt something sticky. A yellow triangle of breakfast egg she'd missed before. The residues of milk, juice, Cheerios, the chicken and rice and peas left over from Matthew's largely unsuccessful dinner. Why did children need to be coaxed and threatened to eat, sleep, eliminate, anything that was supposed to come naturally? How stupid were human beings anyway?

It was a big, admirable kitchen, filled with all the things you were meant to admire. The appliances hummed and gleamed and clicked.

The house was only three years old and they'd chosen the floor plan themselves, as well as all the fixtures and finishes. She'd liked it best before they'd moved in, when it had been bare and clean and empty. It felt as if they'd soiled it with their living, with their shedding skins and hair and carelessness and anger.

When she was finished in the kitchen, she checked on Matthew, who was asleep on his back with both arms outflung, like a runner breaking the tape at the end of a race. On the curtains, the ecstatic dogs chased each other round and round.

In the den she said, "You need to switch the car seat so I can take your car tomorrow."

"Hm?" He'd opened a bag of Cheetos and his fingers were stained with fake orange cheese.

"You heard me."

"Yeah, but I forgot why you need my car."

"I'm taking my mom to see Aunt Martha and the station wagon makes her carsick." She waited. "Why don't you do it now?"

"Minute." He was eating the Cheetos in big handfuls, crunching them down to a deflated paste.

"You're getting fat."

He did look up then. "Hey," he said, injured.

Although she hadn't meant to sit down, she lowered herself to the couch. A beer commercial was playing, one of those with pals horsing around, pals throwing softballs, kidding each other, impressing cutie-pie girls. "That's what you all want. Life as a beer commerical."

"What who wants?"

"Matthew," she said, "is going to be different."

"Different from what?"

"From you."

"Nice attitude." He shifted around in the La-Z-Boy to look at her. The leather made a fleshy, squealing noise. "You spoil him, you know."

"When you spend any time taking care of him, then you'll be entitled to an opinion."

He gave her an unpleasant look, his nostrils seeming to enlarge.

"You aren't still having him sit down to pee, are you? Man, that is really going to screw him up. You don't want him thinking he's a girl, wanting to play with dolls, crap like that."

She reached down, grabbed the remote and shut the television off. "Hey!"

Remote still in hand, she started up the stairs. She heard Jeff peel himself loose from the La-Z-Boy, curse, fumble around on the television console until he found the ON button. "Bring that back here," he called. She knew he wouldn't come up after her until the game was over.

Now that she had the remote, there was the problem of what to do with it, what follow-up was possible. She would have liked to make a speech, something full of wit and scorn, but she was too tired to stay awake that long and keep the fight going. In the end she put the thing under her side of the bed, changed into her pajamas, and wrapped herself in sleep.

Jeff was trying to wake her up without looking like he was trying. He turned on the light in the closet, sat heavily on the end of the bed, took off his shoes and threw them, clunk, into a corner. She said, "Whatsa?"

"Nice stunt. That was really childish of you."

She couldn't tell how long she'd been asleep. Her pillow was damp where her open mouth had been. "Huh," she said. "Huh."

"You turning into one of those crazy women? Nothing makes you happy?"

She didn't answer. She heard him in the bathroom, then he got into bed next to her, tugging and rearranging the sheets. He turned off the lights and rolled from one side to the other. He spoke out of the darkness. "Just tell me what you did with the remote."

"Flushed it down the toilet."

"You did not." He was exasperated. Some other tone in his voice also, as if he was afraid it was true, she might be capable of such a thing. And maybe she was. By now she was fully awake. Maybe there were ways by which crazy women got revenge for all the things that drove them crazy.

She said, "First I peed on it. Standing up."

• • •

"Do you like Daddy's car?"

"Daddy car!"

"Yes, Daddy has a big fat important car. Because Daddy is that kind of guy."

Matthew, buckled into the car seat, was still able to reach the backseat window with one hand, leaving a trail of smears. She was going to have to clean that up or else listen to Jeff carry on about it.

She didn't drive his car that often and she was cautious about the way it handled. It was a Buick Electra as big as a boat, the interior all cream leather and burnished wood. The wheel glided beneath her hands, the brake and accelerator registered the slightest touch, like a kiss with the foot. The highway floated beneath you. She decided she could get used to driving this kind of car. You rode high, high up. You had all this taxable horsepower at your command. You could muscle your way through traffic, flatten pedestrians. "I am a big, big dog," she said. "Who's been driving my car?"

Matthew was asleep. Car rides always put him to sleep. He'd been drinking from his sippy cup—it had fallen onto the seat, she hoped it wouldn't spill—and a bubble of milk formed between his lips, blew in and out as he breathed, then thinned and burst. It made her slightly queasy. As so much about the necessary work of child care did, the diaper stink and spit-up and rashes and other excreted crud. You couldn't admit this to anyone, you couldn't even think the thought to yourself. You didn't read about it in any of the magazines. The magazines all had pictures of happy moms radiating baby bliss.

On the floor of the backseat was the loaf of pumpkin bread she'd made for Aunt Martha. It was from a box mix and wouldn't impress Martha or anybody else, but she couldn't show up empty-handed. Anyway, her mother would most likely be bringing a week's worth of casseroles. It was what you were supposed to do to people in any difficult circumstance. Clobber them with food. She guessed this was a good thing, a helpful thing, but Martha hardly ate anything these days.

The food would be consumed by Martha's daughter, Pat, and Pat's kids and anybody else who took a turn staying at the old farmhouse.

Norm had died last winter, a heart attack that the doctor said had probably meant about two seconds difference between being alive and dead. He'd gone out to the barn to break the ice on the cows' water trough—Norm, being a Peerson, saw no reason to spend good money on electric immersion heaters—and that's where the neighbor found him, collapsed in the sawdust and manure of the barn aisle, the rubber mallet he'd been using on the ice wedged beneath him, the untroubled cows stamping and shuffling around him.

Now Martha lived out the frail end of her life in the big bare farmhouse with the sloping floors and the bathrooms that smelled of Lysol and drains. For years she'd had breathing problems, balance problems, attacks of dizziness. Then she'd developed cancer in her female parts, had all the surgeries and treatments. So much inside her had already been burnt, cut, or poisoned, none of which had prevented the cancer from coming back, attaching itself to whatever was left. The doctors were vague about what came next, but no one expected anything good. A row of pill bottles was set out on her bedroom dresser like the row of spice bottles in the kitchen cabinet. Martha, who hadn't even liked taking aspirin for a headache.

If you had to die, and after all you did, Anita decided it would be better to go fast, like Norm. Then you wouldn't have to think about it. She didn't like thinking about Martha; it was horrible, really, how she suffered, how her body found new, complicated, queasy-making ways to fail her. Nor did Anita especially want to go see Martha, keep a cheery face on when everybody, including Martha, knew the only reason you were there was because things were really, really bad. That was a crummy, selfish way to feel and you weren't exactly proud of yourself. She couldn't help it. Some things bothered her more than they did other people.

Almost to Grenada. It was a gray day with a hurrying wind that reminded you winter wasn't that far away. She passed grain trucks and combines trundling along the road, and here and there corn had spilled like candy onto the shoulder. Their house in Ames was in a development on the edge of town, and sometimes ribbons of corn husks blew in across the yards. Everything around here was about farming: the weather forecasts, the TV commercials for hybrids and soybean cyst nematodes, or whatever it was that killed soybean cyst nematodes. She was just glad that she wasn't a farm kid, glad that she hadn't grown up ten miles out of town and spent her summers showing heifers at the county fair. She'd always felt sorry for the country girls. Even in a place as small as Grenada, there had been those distinctions. She hadn't missed it by much. Her mother had lived on a farm when she was a little girl, and the farm had been lost in the Depression. They'd moved into town and started over from nothing. It was all kind of lucky, in a way, a complicated sort of luck that had mostly benefited herself.

There weren't supposed to be Depressions anymore because they'd fixed all that. Still, everybody agreed that the economy was terrible right now. Not that she had any time to listen to the news! She just heard Jeff going on and on about the Arabs, Arabs causing all the trouble. Well what did he expect? That was what they always did.

Jeff's bank made a lot of farm loans, and now farmers had to pay more to dry grain and run equipment and everything else. The crop prices were too low and the farm debt was too high and Jeff spent a lot of time stewing and chewing about it. He referred to the president as "the peanut farmer," as if growing peanuts was laughable in some way, and inferior to growing corn, beans, and wheat. He'd got stingy about the money she spent on the house, on food. But he was the one who'd wanted to be the big shot in the first place. If business was that bad, he could go to work and do something important about it.

Her old street. The trees on her parents' street had begun to turn color. Dusty oaks and yellow sycamores and here and there a maple sending up a red flare. In spite of her father's and everyone else's best efforts, the neighborhood was showing its age, on its way to being just a little run-down, no place she'd want to live now. She pulled into the driveway next to her mother's car. Matthew was still asleep and she was able to carry him into the house without waking him.

Her mother had been watching from the front windows and she met them at the kitchen door. Anita made a hushing face so she wouldn't start in.

"Oh look at him," her mother breathed. "Little angel boy."

"I'll put him down." Anita carried him back to her old room. Her mother had taken to being a grandma in a big way. No one was surprised. She'd hauled out the old crib, stroller, and swing, and Anita, who'd wanted to buy her own things new, had to persuade her mother to keep them here for the times when Matthew visited.

Back in the kitchen her mother had coffee ready, and sour-cream coffee cake, and fried apples, and corn bread. Anita said she couldn't possibly eat all that, she'd already had breakfast, and her mother said just have a little bit. She shouldn't eat anything, it made her grouchy to think about eating. She still hadn't got rid of her baby weight and she hated the layer of padding over her hips and breasts and having clothes she couldn't fit into and probably never would again, and she was impatient with her mother and all her useless food. But in the end she ate two pieces of coffee cake and some apples and coffee with cream.

Just the three of them were living here now, her mother and father and Torrie. Blake worked construction and had a house outside of town with a buddy. Ryan was in Chicago doing his usual stupid Ryan thing. Her mother was finding it hard to adjust. "I should go down to Des Moines and cook for some orphanage," she said from time to time, one of her hopeless jokes. Even though it would be good for her to do something like that, anything to get herself out of the house once in a while.

They finished eating and cleared the plates and sat at the table waiting for what would come next. The furnace started up, rattling the vents in the floor. The kitchen smelled of cooking, but also of something else, a whiff of staleness, airlessness, the house less lived-in now. Her mother poured out more coffee. It was as if the two of them were always on the verge of having a conversation that would explain and reveal everything: *Is this what it means to be a wife, a mother, a woman? Is it what you expected? Should I have gone about it differently?*

But then they covered it over with other conversation, and the moment passed.

So that her mother wondered if they shouldn't go ahead and wake Matthew up, and Anita said to leave him be, since whenever he woke up, he was going to be cranky.

"I think I hear him," her mother announced, going out into the hallway. Anita knew that her mother was just anxious to see him, hold him, exclaim over him, and while she was glad to have some respite, someone else to help with him, there was an unwillingness also. He was her child, after all, not some especially desirable toy to be contested.

She heard his waking-up sounds, and her mother coaxing him, lifting him out of the crib he was really too big for, and then the two of them in the bathroom. She wondered if he'd woken up wet. She ought to go see, but she couldn't make herself get out of the chair just yet. All the food had made her drowsy.

Matthew was calling for her, Mommy, Mommy. "I'm right here, honey," she answered, still not getting up. Her mother's voice kept up its soothing stream of talk, and Matthew squalled a little—cranky—and then her mother came in carrying him. He squirmed to get to Anita. "All right, Matthew, I didn't go anywhere. I bet you're hungry, huh? Is Matthew hungry?"

"Would he like any ham and scalloped potatoes? I have some left over from last night."

"Mom, I brought SpaghettiOs." Anita balanced him on her hip and searched her carryall for the Tupperware container that held his lunch. With one hand she extracted the food, carried it to the microwave, and set it to warming. The microwave had been a Christmas present last year from her and Jeff. She suspected her parents never used it.

"Big bite," she told him, once he was strapped in the booster seat and a bib was in place. He opened, chewed, swallowed obediently. Her mother began hauling out the different baskets, boxes, and casseroles she'd prepared. There were stuffed pork chops and sweet potatoes and rice fancied up with sliced green olives. Baked beans and barbecued chicken. Corn pudding. Spaghetti sauce with meatballs packed in an old ice cream container. An apple pie and a tin of chocolate chip cookies and Matthew could have one if he finished his lunch like a good boy.

"This is more food than Martha could eat in a month."

"Somebody'll get to it. Besides, just the smell of food, good, plain, home-cooked food, cheers you up."

Anita gave Matthew half a chocolate chip cookie. He put it all in his mouth at once, so that she had to extract it and break it in half again. "All that missed me. Cooking. I never get anything to turn out right."

Her mother patted her shoulder. "You don't need to cook. You can just be beautiful."

She wasn't sure how she felt about that. Her mother made beautiful sound like a consolation prize. Besides, she didn't think of herself that way anymore. Beautiful was a long time ago, before she'd got pregnant with Matthew, back when she had more than two minutes to look in a mirror.

When they began carrying the food out to the car, her mother announced that maybe she wouldn't go along.

"Mom."

"Matthew could stay here with me so he doesn't have to spend all that time in the car."

"I'm not going by myself, Mom."

Her mother was searching the cupboards for some forgotten item, opening one door after another. "Oh, I don't know. I think it's probably better if . . ."

"No, we made a plan and we're going to stick to it. This was your idea! Don't you want to see Martha?" Of course Anita didn't really want to see Martha herself, but you didn't have to go into all that.

"I can't." Her mother shook her head.

"Mom! This is dumb! Do you even go to the grocery anymore? Do you go to church?"

"Of course I go to church."

"When's the last time you drove your car, huh?"

"Torrie drives it. Half the time it's not even here."

Matthew had been released from his booster chair and was careening around the kitchen. "Gmma!" he announced, hobbling her legs. "Gmma!"

"That's right, you are Grandma's very own precious boy."

"Maybe you should go talk to somebody," Anita said, although her mother was making a big fuss over Matthew as a way of ignoring her. And even as she spoke, she was aware it was a dumb thing to say. How did you get somebody who never wanted to leave the house in the first place to get out and talk to a counselor? She guessed that was what she'd meant, a counselor. She'd never been to one herself but she knew that people did such things. She tried to imagine her mother sitting in some depressing office and crying into a Kleenex and talking about her problems. What would she talk about, anyway? She never did anything anymore, that was her problem.

Anita said, "Come on, Mom. It's Jeff's car. You'll feel like you're sitting on the couch the whole way there and back."

"Matthew, do you want to stay here with Grandma and help me make more cookies?"

"He's not staying here. And I won't bring him anymore if you won't go with us."

She didn't mean it, or maybe she did just then, but anyway, it worked. Her mother sat, tense, rigid, expiring, in the car's front seat with her purse clamped in the center of her lap. Even Matthew's squalling away behind them didn't bring her around. Anita felt bad and guilty and exasperated. What were you supposed to do when people stopped making sense?

The big car rolled north, through the straggling edge of town: the old grain elevator, long disused; the barn fancied up to sell antiques; the drive-in, *Closed For The Season,* the *C* and *F* drooping off the marquee. All you ever saw from the road was the back of the screen, a giant bare space and scaffolding.

She hadn't been one of those girls who did things at drive-ins. She tried to remember why all of that had seemed so important back then. Making sure you were not a certain kind of girl, that you were not for an instant confused with certain kinds of girls. What difference had it all made? Matthew screamed and kicked his heels against the seat. "Matthew, stop that, Mommy can't drive when you do that!" Didn't they all wind up pretty much the same, trying to bargain with some furious child for five minutes of peace?

Her mother said, "You were never like that."

The muscles in Anita's arms jumped, and the car's steering overreacted. She had to pull back from the shoulder. "Like what?"

"The temper tantrums. The boys were the worst. Even Torrie had her moments. Not you. You were always happy with the way things were."

"That's probably because I was the only kid in the house." She was always cautious when her mother started telling stories she couldn't bear witness to or contradict, even if she was glad that her mother was perking up, coming out of her difficult state and back to her normal chatterbox self. The hard part was just getting her out the door in the first place. "Would you look in my bag, give him a toy? The frog that makes frog noises?"

"I think," her mother said, once the frog had been located and administered, "that you just always knew you were born to be the queen."

"Yeah, right, that's me. Queen." She laughed, an indelicate, snorting sound.

Matthew talked to his frog. Her mother remarked on the comfort and space of Jeff's car, and it wasn't a very cheerful day, was it, all those clouds. Anita thought her mother kept up her conversational noise to deflect the more difficult, embarrassing topics, as she'd always done. It depressed her to think that, aside from this peculiar remark about queens, she couldn't remember one important or necessary thing her mother had ever said.

Quickly, before she could change her mind, she said, "Have you ever thought about maybe getting some kind of a job?"

Her mother looked startled. "What would I do?"

"I don't know. Something you'd enjoy. Be a children's librarian.

Bake stuff, you could bake cakes and decorate them. People always want fancy cakes for birthdays and things."

"I wouldn't know where to start."

"Jeff could help you." Anita doubted this, but she wanted to sound encouraging. "You could be the boss."

"I don't think I'm the boss type, honey."

There was no way to argue with that, so Anita let it drop. She thought her mother was done talking about it too, but a couple miles down the road she said, "Why is it everybody thinks I ought to get some kind of job?"

"Who's everybody?"

"Torrie. She thinks I should take education courses and teach elementary school."

This was news to Anita, but it sounded like her sister. Torrie was always the one with the upsetting ideas, like deciding she was a vegetarian. "Well, you could do that. If you think you'd like it."

"Oh, I don't know. It used to be good enough if you kept a clean house and did right by your children and now you're supposed to go out and be some kind of world-beater."

"You're not supposed to do anything, Mom. Forget I mentioned it."

"It's the ones who have some kind of grudge against men. They'll never be happy no matter what they do."

"You're probably right, Mom."

The sky and rough wind gave the landscape an unfriendly look. Every so often they passed a stand of corn that hadn't yet been taken down. They were almost to Norm and Martha's place. That's what people still called it. How long after they were both gone would it still keep the name? Probably until everybody who'd known them was gone too, or maybe a while after that, until the next generation died off and the forgetting was complete.

"Look, Matthew, we're at the farm! Do you see any cows?"

"Cows!"

A small group of black-and-white Holsteins in a pasture, standing around in typical dumb-cow fashion. Norm and Martha had kept a herd of fifty, but most of those had been sold off or taken over by other farming kin. They'd grown hay and corn for silage and a couple of acres of sweet corn, kept chickens, canned vegetables from their garden plot, put up fruit from the apple and sour-cherry trees.

Her mother puckered her forehead. "It looks different somehow."

"I don't think so. Well, nobody did much with the garden this year." People like her parents decorated their houses with fanciful things that were supposed to remind you of farmhouses, like seasonal front-door wreaths, or a mailbox made out of a pump handle, or a miniature wishing well in the front yard. Maybe somewhere there were farms like that. But Norm and Martha's was all business. A rhubarb patch, an asparagus patch. A clothesline. For decoration, Norm had nailed his old license plates to the barn wall.

The lawn had been mowed, the white farmhouse sat as always in its square of windbreak trees. The cow barn, hay barn, silo, and all the other sheds and outbuildings were the same. A manure spreader was visible in a far field, one of Pat's grown kids, probably Art, keeping up with the chores. If things seemed different, diminished, it was only because you knew what had happened here and what was going to happen.

As soon as the car stopped, her mother got out and hurried inside with those food items that were in immediate danger of spoilage or bacteria growth and so might poison them all. Matthew wanted to climb the steps to the front porch himself, and Anita went behind him, ready to catch him or haul him up as needed. Finally they reached the long, dim hallway. It was as if she'd traveled a distance of lives since she'd left home this morning, from her own new and splendid house to her parents' smaller, fustier one, and now this plain old workhorse farm. She had the feeling that if she went any farther down the road, she might come across a sod hut.

The front-door transom had small squares of thick colored glass, red and blue and yellow, set around a central clear pane. A flight of stairs led up to the second floor. Like everything else in the house, they seemed undersize and narrow, the center of each wooden step shining with a crescent of wear. She guided Matthew past the front room and the dining room. The sofa of lumpy plush, the big gleaming dining-room table with a doily of stiffened, crocheted lace placed at its center. The piano, out of tune for as long as Anita could remember, with its framed family photographs on top.

She heard her mother and Pat in the kitchen. "Come on, Matthew, let's go see what Grandma's doing."

He wouldn't remember any of it, he was too young. Not the cows, or the whitewashed milking parlor, or the barn smell that inevitably seeped inside the house, or the grape arbor, or the old stereopticon with its 3-D pictures of the Leaning Tower of Pisa and the Grand Canyon, and certainly not Martha herself.

"Here he is!"

"Matthew!"

Her mother and Pat swooped down on him. He blinked, then his face crumpled and he began to wail. "It's OK, honey." Anita picked him up. He was getting so big. Her back always hurt these days. "He just didn't know where he was for a minute."

Pat said she didn't mean to scare him. He wasn't a scaredy-cat, was he? Everyone said that Pat looked like Martha, but she really resembled Norm. She had his reddish hair and lashless eyes and round chin, and of course she was freakishly tall, like all the Peersons. Pat was older than Anita's mother, past sixty, just as her children were older than Anita and her siblings. Everybody was about a half a generation off.

"How is—," Anita began, but Pat shook her head ever so slightly, meaning, Not now.

Her mother had already started back out to the car to bring in the rest of the food. Pat said she'd help. "Do you need anything for him?" she asked Anita, and Anita said no thanks, she'd brought juice and some graham crackers.

Pat nodded. She had the Peerson mannerism of seeming to be judgmental by withholding judgment. It was as if Anita had announced she'd brought a thermos of rum daiquiris for her child. "Coffee if you want it," Pat said on her way out.

She'd forgotten how bad their coffee was. For one thing the house had well water, another layer of smell in the rooms, whiffs of sewer or sulfur. She remembered visits as a child when she was told ahead of time, sternly, that she was not to complain about the taste of the water at Uncle Norm and Aunt Martha's. Maybe this was why they always made their coffee strong enough to float an egg. She took one sip, then poured the rest of her cup into the sink.

It was hard to find a place for all her mother's food in the old-fashioned refrigerator and freezer. It was like everything else in the kitchen, worn down long past the point where anyone else would have thrown it all out and started over. So there were bent spatulas, and pots and pans black and misshapen and scoured back into use, and these thin and shrunken dish towels, and the porcelain sink with the finish rubbed away, and the old soup can that collected grease drippings, for what purpose Anita would rather not know.

Pat said, "Why don't I go up and see if she's awake? Hey, Mr. Boy, here's something for you to play with." She put a basket of cookie cutters on the floor and Matthew set about scattering them. Anita recognized the shapes from different holidays: heart, star, diamond, angel, snowflake. Duck, rabbit, autumn leaves. Martha used to make sugar cookies with butter frosting, tinted and decorated with colored sugars and sprinkles.

They heard Pat on the stairs, then her footsteps above them. Anita's mother said, "There's a visiting nurse that comes by twice a week, but mostly it's just Pat. She cleans her and changes her and gives her the pain shots and all the rest."

"She gives her shots?" Anita asked, mostly so she wouldn't have to think about the cleaning and changing parts.

"Well, you give cows and everything else shots on a farm. It's not any different. I used to help my dad inoculate the hogs for scours."

"Ugh." Anita shook her head. Even the words, *hogs, scours,* sounded, as kids said, gross. It was hard to imagine her mother, with her clunky, plastic-framed glasses and strawberry-print blouse and arch-support shoes ever doing any such thing. What if she herself was called on to nurse her mother through some completely embarrassing illness? She just wouldn't be able to do it. But then, it wouldn't be expected of her. People went into hospitals nowadays and got themselves taken care of there. Only the Peersons took such things on. Laboring and suffering was what they did best.

Pat came back downstairs. "You can go on up. She had her pain shot about an hour ago, so she's good. When she first gets it, she's a little foggy."

"Should Matthew . . ."

"Oh sure. She'll get such a kick out of him."

Anita gathered him up. He wouldn't let go of the rabbit cookie cutter, so it came along with him. The stairs were steep and hard to manage. Her mother was behind her, puffing a little. They wouldn't be staying long, she was pretty sure.

Martha was propped up in bed on one of those backrests with padded sides. Her face was shrunken down in a way that made Anita think of a piece of fruit left out too long.

"Audrey," Martha said. "And Anita. And who's this young man?" She held out her long, bruised arms. Gauze pads were taped in place over each wrist. Her voice had sand in it, a rasp. She sounded like someone else.

"Matthew, say hello to Aunt Martha." Now that Anita had seen her, and the dread of it was over, she felt oddly calm, energized, ready to be one of those skilled and helpful women who managed things at times of crisis. She'd seen what dying looked like now. It wasn't as bad as she'd imagined.

"Now careful," she said, propelling Matthew closer. "I don't want him to kick you."

"He won't hurt me. And what would it matter if he did? Sit right here." Martha patted the edge of the bed.

Anita sat, keeping Matthew on her lap. Anita figured they had thirty seconds or less before he started in fussing. Martha stroked his face and fine white hair. "What's that you got there?"

"Bunny."

"That's right, it's a bunny. He's so big now."

"Yes, he's a handful," Anita's mother said. "How are you, Martha? You're looking well."

Martha didn't answer, either because she hadn't heard, or because it was a silly remark. Pat said, "Audrey and Anita brought us a week's worth of food. Are you hungry? You can have your choice of vittles. And apple pie for dessert."

"Maybe a little later." Martha held out one hand. The skin over the knuckles was loose and rubbed-looking. "Can I see the bunny?"

He considered this, then let it drop into Martha's hand. Martha said, "Here, you can have it back. Mommy can take it with you when you go."

"Oh, he doesn't need—"

"I'd like him to have it."

None of them spoke, then Pat said, "I have to get you some more of that warming cream, for your feet. Her feet get real cold."

Anita's mother said, "I should have asked you if there was anything you needed from the Rexall."

"No matter. Jane brings us whatever we need when she comes."

"We're a regular drugstore," Martha said. There was an odd-shaped plastic table by the far side of the bed, designed to swing into place over Martha if that was wanted. It must have come from a medical-supply place. The table held Kleenex and Chap Stick and baby wipes and a water glass with a plastic straw and a hairbrush and comb and a man's folded plaid handkerchief (Norm's?) and a jar of Vaseline petroleum jelly and an emery board and any number of other things, and though it all had doubtless been recently tidied, it gave an impression of disorder, of items assembled for unhappy purposes. The room had a medicine smell. Nothing worse. Pat must work hard to keep it that way.

Matthew wanted to explore the bedspread, pick at the chenille tufts (the kind that left soft indentations on your face when you fell asleep on them), and Anita's mother said she'd take him. He didn't like her holding him and tried to turn himself upside down, as if falling on his head was the shortest route to the floor. He was probably due for a bathroom trip. Anita said, "OK, Matthew, we'll get you fixed up."

Pat said, "Would he like to see the cows? I can take him out to the feed yard."

Anita's mother said to Martha, "We should let you get your rest."

"That's all I ever do is sleep."

"Best thing for you."

Martha shook her head. Her eyes closed. Probably because her face was so thin, her teeth looked overprominent, jutting out even behind her closed lips.

Pat made a sign. Anita started to rise from the bed, but Martha's hand touched hers. "Stay a minute. Your mother can handle Matthew."

"You're sure—"

"Stay a minute."

The others made their way downstairs. Anita wondered if Martha had fallen asleep. The skin of her eyelids was thin and discolored, like moth wings. Outside the window, the gray sky raced past. The room was smaller than you would have imagined for people of Martha's and Norm's size. The bed and dresser were bulky dark carved wood and took up even more of the space. The dresser was given over to Martha's medicines, and a cardboard dispenser of latex gloves. Over the bed hung a picture frame enclosing a cross and two linked wedding rings. Anita stared at it. It embarrassed her although she couldn't have said why.

Martha opened her eyes. "Here I am," she said, as if she'd been away somewhere. And maybe she had. She turned her head toward the table, searching something out. Guessing, Anita reached for the water glass with the flexible straw and held it for Martha to drink.

"Do you want me to get you anything? Should I go get Pat?"

Martha shook her head. "It comes and goes."

"I'm sorry."

"Such a nuisance." Martha's voice was fainter but more like her own. "You break down like an old car."

"Are you scared?" Anita was shy about asking. Maybe it was morbid, or rude.

"Was for a while. Then I got tired of it. You get tired of most things."

Anita felt the tears starting up behind her eyes. "I was afraid to come see you."

"Well who wouldn't be?"

That made Anita laugh, or try to, and then she put her whole heart into her crying and sobbed out loud.

Martha touched her hair. "So pretty."

"No I'm not. Not anymore. I'm an old sow."

"You are no such thing."

Anita took one of the Kleenex from the box and blew her nose. "Look at me carrying on. You're the one who's sick."

"He's a fine little boy."

"How did you ever raise six children? I can't imagine."

"We didn't know any better."

Martha eased herself lower on the cushion. She was wearing a blue nightgown trimmed with a lace placket and embroidery. Anita suspected it was for company visits. Do you believe in heaven? In angels with wings? Do you think you'll see Norm again, and the two of you will spend your time in some eternal version of Sunday church services? There were other questions Anita wanted to ask, but it was too late, and besides it might lead to a discussion of what she herself believed, which she preferred to keep vague. Anita would have said she believed in God, of course. Beyond that, she wasn't sure. God was rather like the president, except that he was God and in charge of more things.

Anita said, "Mom cooked all this food and all I brought was some pumpkin bread."

"I like pumpkin bread."

"I wish I was like you."

"Oh ho ho," said Martha, as if this was a joke, although Anita hadn't meant it as one. Was she fading out again? Anita hurried to get everything said.

"I wish I knew what I was supposed to do. What I want to do. I mean, except for Matthew, taking care of Matthew. I don't know. You always knew, didn't you? Or maybe you didn't have that much choice. Sometimes I feel like I ought to be more . . . happy," she finished, but she didn't mean happy, she meant something like "important," which wasn't quite right either.

"Well land's sakes." Martha said things like that, *Land's sakes* and *I swan*. They were a kind of substitute for swearing. She shook her head with some of her old energy. "You have to do something about that. You don't want to wait until you're some old lady laid out in bed and everything past deciding."


When Martha fell asleep again, Anita went downstairs. The others must still have been outside, amusing Matthew with the cows. She walked through the kitchen to the mudroom, where Norm's old boots and coveralls still resided, and looked out the back door. The path to the cow barn and the old chicken coop was edged with bricks turned with their long sides against each other to make a sawtooth pattern. She didn't see her mother or Pat and she was too tired and wrung out to walk out to the barn after them.

In the kitchen she found the tin of her mother's chocolate chip cookies and ate four of them standing up, one right after the other.

They were going to have to start back soon. She found her coat and carried the empty boxes and baskets out to the car. Although it was the middle of the afternoon, it had got colder, the clouds breaking up to let a bit of no-color, glaring sunlight through. A front pushing in from the northwest, a sign of an early winter. She got into the car and started the engine to warm it up. Air whistled through the vents and a steady current of heat blew across her knees. The station wagon took forever to get warm. Jeff needed a nice car for business, by which was meant, a banker couldn't be seen driving just any old heap. He'd probably explained ten different times today why he had the station wagon.

Say this really was her car, and she could go anywhere she wanted. She didn't get very far with the thought, because she would have to go without Matthew, and that would never happen, and say she didn't take Jeff. Where would that leave her? It was a stupid thing to think about in the first place.

Pat and her mother and Matthew came into view at the far end of the lane. They must have walked all the way to the pasture and then around. Anita started to honk the horn, but then she thought of Martha sleeping, and instead put the car in gear to go meet them. Matthew wanted to run toward her; Pat held him back, both women telling him careful, careful, the car is coming, he didn't want to get hit by the car, did he?

The driveway was bordered with a number of large, whitewashed rocks, another of Norm and Martha's peculiar notions of ornament. She got a little speed up. Here comes Mommy Mommy Mommy! She gave the wheel the slightest touch, and the car leaped forward to smash into one of the rocks, a crunch sound that stopped everything dead, an impact that she felt in her shoulders and teeth.

They all ran toward her. She shut the engine off and got out to see. "Oh my Lord, are you all right?" her mother cried.

"Of course I am, silly. I was wearing my seat belt." She walked around to the front of the car. There was a rock-shaped indentation in the wheel well, and the headlight drooped loose, connected only by its wires. "Boy," she said. "Jeff is really going to have a fit, isn't he."

# *Iowa*

NOVEMBER 1979

Mr. Milano was a guidance counselor, not a real counselor. But he liked having these little chats. He thought something was wrong with everybody, and he was the only one smart enough to trip them up and show them just how screwed they were. "Victoria," he said, "how's it going?"

"I'm great, Mr. Milano. How are you?"

"Fine, thanks. Busy time of year, college applications and all." Mr. Milano's nickname was Super Pants, owing to a time when he had showed up at a football game wearing a pair of white trousers with the outline of his underpants clearly visible beneath.

"I'm working on mine," Torrie said. "I'm almost done with the essay part."

"And you plan on applying to . . ." He shuffled through her file for his notes.

"Sarah Lawrence, Bryn Mawr, Vassar, University of Michigan, Northwestern, UCLA, and Berkeley."

"That's a pretty ambitious list."

She nodded. "Aim high."

Mr. Milano smiled, sort of. You could feel sorry for him because he was kind of a dork and this was his first job and he'd come all the way from St. Louis and here he was stuck in *Grenada*. Talk about aiming high. All the pencils in his pencil holder had chew marks. You could feel sorry for him until he started in on you. "Not that you don't have excellent grades. And all your athletics, and activities. But these are very selective schools. How about a backup, in case your first choices don't work out?"

"Like State? I don't think so."

"What do your parents say?"

Torrie shrugged. Her parents had no clue. "They just want me to be happy."

"Have you figured out the finances? Out of state tuition, private tuition, that's a big item."

"Scholarships. Loans. Work-study. If I have to, I'll stay home and get a job for a year and save money." She had no such intention. She'd go to New York or Los Angeles and wait tables.

Mr. Milano pondered this, looking for the hole in her arguments. Torrie occupied herself with examining his hair, which was another source of wonder and delight to everybody in the school. His hair was black and a little greasy, and even though he was probably only about twenty-three or -four, he wore a comb-over to hide his receding hair-line. This in spite of the hair that crawled out of his shirt collar and along the backs of his hands and no doubt other, even less appetizing places. Total dork.

Sometimes, without willing it, she imagined people naked, and the more she told herself not to do so, the more she couldn't help it.

He said, "I'm a little worried that you're making it too hard on yourself. Expecting too much."

"You mean, girls aren't supposed to be high achievers."

"That's not what I said. And it's certainly nothing I believe." He looked annoyed. It was something you could always say to guys like this, who thought they were so enlightened and down with the struggle and understood and sympathized with all the oppressed peoples of the earth. "What I meant was, you need to be flexible enough and mature enough to know that not everything works out as you plan."

Once they started talking about maturity, it was your cue to get your butt out of there. "I am. I will. I promise I'll think about some of the less selective schools. Could I be excused now? My great-aunt died and the wake's tonight and I have to get home."

He looked startled and a little guilty, as she had meant him to be. "Oh, I'm so sorry. I didn't know."

"It's OK. She was really old, and really sick. And now she's with Jesus."

He might have suspected her of putting him on, of mockery, but Torrie kept her face and voice absolutely serious, and even the new teachers knew better than to make fun of anything to do with Jesus around here. He told her she could go, and she gathered her books and turned toward the door.

"You sure you're not working too hard, studying too hard? You look like you're dropping some weight."

"Basketball season. Coach always runs us ragged. Have a great weekend, Mr. Milano."

Dorkydorkydorkydorky.

Michelle was waiting for her at her locker. "Where you been?"

"I had to go talk to Super Pants." Torrie banged her locker open, re-shuffled her books, and reached for her jacket. "Do you think he dates?"

"Oh yeah. Big dating action for the Pants."

"Maybe we could fix him up."

"With a nice hairy orangutan."

"Boy or girl orangutan?"

They laughed and the sound of it echoed through the long empty corridor, dark at the end of a rainy afternoon.

Outside they sprinted through the drilling rain to Torrie's car and flung themselves inside. Torrie found a towel in the backseat and they used it to mop their faces and their streaming hair.

"Sucky weather."

"Perfect for funerals."

"Oh hey, Tor? Is it OK if I just come to the wake? Joey's only going to be in town the one night."

"God, yes. The service is all the way up in Hardy. I don't think anybody's gonna come." Torrie meant, anyone from school. There would be about three busloads of family.

She dropped Michelle off at her house and went on home. Anita's car was in the drive. This day was just getting better and better.

"Hi Mom. Hi Nita. Hi Marmaduke."

"No-o!" Her nephew rushed at her, pounding at her knees.

"Percival? Barnaby? Chuck?"

He kept insisting that his name was Matthew, Matthew, and Torrie swept him up and said Well what do you know, it was Matthew, she just hadn't recognized him. Anita and her mother looked at her, unsmiling. "What?"

"We were talking about Martha," her mother said. She made it sound like everything was Torrie's fault.

"Oh. Sure."

Anita looked her over. "You're changing clothes, right?"

"Matthew! Can I wear your shirt?"

"No!"

"How about your pants?"

Howls of protest and giggles. "Guess I'll just have to wear my old jeans, then."

"Torrie," her mother said wearily.

*Lighten up.* Torrie looked in the refrigerator and selected a Diet Sprite. "When's Ryan coming?"

"Whenever he gets here. Are you hungry, sweetie? I'm making chili and everybody can serve themselves."

"I had an egg-salad sandwich a little while back, so I'm OK." Anita was really getting porky. Her slacks were so tight across her thighs that the zipper pulled and gapped. She'd skinned her hair back in a French-twisty arrangement that made her look about forty years old. Her boobs were huge. They bounced and flopped around in a totally gross fashion. Sometimes just thinking about bodies, other people's bodies, was enough to make her sick to her stomach.

Anita saw her staring. "What?"

"Just admiring your hair."

"Thank you." Still suspicious. Anita told Matthew that no, he couldn't play with Aunt Torrie, he had to get changed into his good clothes. Poor kid. He was always having to do something Anita thought was important.

In her room, Torrie unpacked her books and put each one in its spot on the desk on its own different-colored folder. She took off her wet clothes and put on sweats. *Blood on the Tracks* was already on the turntable and she switched it on, volume low so nobody in the kitchen would give her a hard time for being disrespectful. Not that Torrie saw it that way. She hoped they'd play Bob songs at her funeral.

She sang along just under her breath. Bob was so much better than the lame shit passing for music these days. The Bee Gees. Please. She'd missed out on so much, been too young for all the beautiful craziness and being a part of things that really mattered and anyway in Iowa it was as if none of it had ever happened.

She knew it was stupid, but she had a little fantasy about meeting Bob. Back in the old days, before he got all weird and Christian.

*She walked up to me so gracefully and took my crown of thorns / "Come in," she said, "I'll give you shelter from the storm."* Sometimes she pretended the songs were about her. It would be raining hard, just as now, and she'd have her own house, not here but somewhere else, the rooms full of velvet pillows and candles. She'd hear a knock at the door and there would be Bob. From here you couldn't force the fantasy to go any further, because it was never clear just what the girls in the songs did that made them so desirable. You weren't supposed to talk much, that seemed clear. You were just this soulful, totally cool being, instantly recognizable to other soulful and cool beings.

Another voice from the kitchen. Ryan had arrived.

He was standing with his back to her and she snuck up behind him and tickled him in the ribs. He must have heard her coming because he reached around and hauled her around by her arm. She wriggled loose and grinned at him. "Hey big shot."

"Hey small fry." The only time Torrie ever felt short was around her brothers.

"You look like a total hippie burnout," she said. His hair was in a ponytail and he wore a denim shirt under his corduroy sports jacket.

"Thank you."

Their mother said, "Please tell me you brought some other clothes."

He reached into a duffel bag and came up with a red paisley tie, which he looped around his neck and into a knot, then stood back to let them judge the effect.

His mother sighed. "How much can I stand."

"Relax. I brought a suit for the funeral."

Anita had a cloth napkin pinned around Matthew's neck and was feeding him chili. "I don't know what you're trying to prove with that hair."

"I could say the same thing about you."

Their mother said warningly, "Ryan, you haven't been in the house five minutes. Why don't you put your suitcase away and get some chili. Your father and Blake are going to meet us there."

"When's Jeff coming?" Torrie asked her sister.

"He can't make it tonight. He'll come to the service tomorrow."

"Oh, that's too bad."

Anita gave her an unfriendly look. It was almost unfair to make fun of her. She didn't have anything like a sense of humor she could use to fight back.

Their mother was putting out the bowls and spoons and crackers for chili. "Here," she said, handing Torrie a bowl. "You need to eat something. I made a vegetarian batch just for you."

Torrie filled the bowl halfway and ate a few spoonfuls. It tasted greasy, and the smell of it clogged her head. "I need to get dressed," she said, taking the bowl back to her room.

She found a white shirt and a pair of dark pants, added a gray sweater and low-heeled boots. She brushed her hair, scraped the chili into a plastic bag from the drugstore, twisted it shut, put it into the pocket of an old coat, and carried the empty bowl back into the kitchen. "OK, I'm ready."

She rode with Ryan to the funeral home, leaving her mother and Anita and Matthew to follow. Torrie and Ryan usually wound up together because everybody else in the family was so terminally uncool. "We're taking the long way there," Ryan announced, lighting a joint and getting busy with it.

"You are nuts," Torrie said. It was not yet dark and enough dinnertime traffic was on the road so that cars passed them on almost every block. "You want to get me thrown off the team? No, I don't want any. Besides, pot gives me the stoned munchies."

"Can't have that." He opened his window a crack and blew the smoke outside. The rain had diminished into drizzle and fog, the sky softening into a thick gray veil.

"You are something else," Torrie said, turning her face to the window to watch the uninspiring view of Grenada. Streetlights reflected on the wet pavement. The little houses looked lonesome in their big yards. It was impossible to imagine one interesting thing going on inside any of them. If they were the only shelter from the storm, Bob would stay out in the rain.

Ryan had put the joint out and was driving even slower now. She said, "Tell me you don't cruise around Chicago blowing dope."

"Not usually. Traffic's too heavy."

"It's messed up that you're a teacher." He was getting his master's degree and taught discussion sections of the big poli-sci lecture.

"If you're lucky, you'll have a teacher as cool as me in college."

"Yeah, can't wait." She only made it sound sarcastic. She felt a wave of longing for the life she hadn't started yet. School was the quickest way out of here.

"Sad about Aunt Martha."

"Uh-huh."

"Kind of the last of the old-timers."

Torrie didn't say anything. She guessed that somebody had to be the last.

"Look, Mom wanted me to talk to you. About this not-eating thing."

"She really, really does not have enough to do these days."

"Yeah. But she's worried about you. Me too. Your legs look like two sticks rubbed together."

"Gee, thanks."

He sighed. "Scratch that last part."

"I am not too thin. That's just her. God, could she just get off my case? Does her whole life have to be about stuffing people with food? What did she do, call you in Chicago? You guys were talking about me?" The minute Torrie said it, she knew she was right. They'd been having whole conversations behind her back.

"She worries, OK?"

"Just because I don't want to eat dead cows and pigs, it's some big deal."

"This isn't about being a vegetarian."

"Isn't it? You know what she's like. It's just too weird for her. If you don't eat three helpings of glop at every meal—"

"Not everything is glop."

"What am I supposed to do, whip out a milk shake and scarf it down? Would that make you happy? Huh?"

"Never mind. Forget I said anything. You should do whatever you want."

Without her realizing it, they'd reached the funeral home. The parking lot was in back and cars were already lined up, people hurrying inside through the early darkness. She was probably related to most of them. It wasn't a thought she liked having.

"Look," she said, talking fast because she didn't want him mad at her for some completely stupid reason her mother had come up with. "I'm sorry I'm being kind of a brat, but you don't know what it's like being stuck there with her picking on you constantly because nobody else is around. She never does anything anymore. Ask Dad. She watches TV and knits stuff nobody wants to wear and cooks stuff nobody wants to eat. She's the one everybody should be worried about."

"I do worry about her." He was occupied with finding a parking space. He seemed to be done with talking.

"Come on, Ry. Give me a break. I'm never going to do anything right, far as she's concerned. Dad too."

"Why's that?" He pulled into a space but let the engine idle. His arms were draped over the steering wheel. He didn't have to get stoned. It was stupid.

"Because I'm not Anita."

She was afraid he'd laugh, and he did. "Whoa! Good thing too. What?"

"Nothing."

"What? Come on. Why's it so tragic you're not Anita?"

"Because I'm not gonna hang around here my whole life and pop out grandkids and I don't think the world ends at the state borders and I don't live and breathe the gospel according to Martin Luther."

"Well I'm not that way either. But there's times I kind of wish I was. Come on, we need to get inside."

Half the town was there. The country relatives made up for the other half. They had to squeeze through a hallway packed with people shedding their damp coats, milling around, gabbing. Ryan saw some guy he'd gone to school with and stopped to talk to him. Torrie pushed ahead, looking for Michelle.

In the viewing room, flowers in clumps or sprays were arranged on pedestals. It was probably more florists' flowers than Aunt Martha had ever seen in her lifetime. The coffin was up front on a little stage. Torrie gave it a quick, horrified look. Martha, or what used to be Martha, was propped up with her hands folded across her chest. They'd left her eyeglasses on and dressed her in the same gray print dress she'd worn at Norm's funeral.

Almost the worst part of being dead was thinking about what people would do to your body. And there wouldn't be one thing you could do about it.

Michelle came up to her then. "Hey. Do you have to go view her?"

Torrie looked around and didn't see her parents. "I can just say I did." They sat down on one of the upholstered sofas in the back. A box of Kleenex sat on the table next to it, but she didn't see anybody in the room crying.

Michelle nudged her. "Oh. My. God. You brother is like, a hair queen."

Torrie watched him enter the room trying not to look stoned. He tucked his chin under and clasped his hands behind his back. Like he was really going to blend in. She hated being embarrassed about him. "He's a dick."

"Yeah, but he's cute."

Here were her parents, and her brother Blake and his skanky girlfriend. The girlfriend wanted to get married in the worst way, and as Torrie's father liked to say, that was probably the way it was going to happen.

Her mother waved Torrie over. Michelle said it was OK, she was going to go talk to Kurt and Denny. Torrie saw them leaning against a wall across the room. Two of the boring generic boys that everybody thought were so cool. Neither of them could carry on a conversation for more than three minutes. "Go for it," Torrie said.

"Hey Dad. What's up, Mom?" They were standing up front near the coffin. Torrie tried to keep her back to it. She thought she smelled the flowers, a cold, waxy perfume.

"Would you go watch Matthew so your sister can pay her respects? She didn't want to bring him in here."

"No prob." Torrie was glad for an excuse to leave. She wondered how old Matthew had to be before he got dragged in to see dead relatives.

"Thanks, sweetheart. Say hello to your Aunt Pat and Uncle Morgan."

Torrie did so, murmuring that she was sorry about Aunt Martha. Pat was Martha's oldest. Norm and Martha had been like the nursery rhyme about going to St. Ives, and the man with seven wives, and every wife had seven sacks and every sack had seven cats and so on, well, not the seven wives part, but they'd had a ton of children and all those children had a ton of children who were now busy making more big, round-headed, humorless Peersons. The world wasn't going to run short of Peersons anytime soon.

There was a gaggle of Peerson grandkids in the room, among them Bradley Goodell, who was her second cousin or second cousin once removed or something. He saw her and pretended he hadn't. She was relieved and pretended she didn't see him right back as she left the room.

Last winter she'd had sex with Bradley in the basement rec room of some kid's house, a party where the stereo kept playing "How Deep Is Your Love" over and over because it was stuck, and everybody else was passed out upstairs except for one guy who was passed out in a corner. Torrie lay beneath Bradley on the itchy tweed sofa, wondering how long it was supposed to take and if it was supposed to feel good or something. They hadn't said ten words to each other before, during, or after, and nothing since, and that was just fine with her.

God, a Bee Gees song! Could anything have been worse?

She found Anita and Matthew in the coatroom, where Matthew was running in and out among the coats, hiding and tangling himself in them. Anita looked frazzled. "Tag team," Torrie said. "I got him."

"He keeps knocking everything off the hangers, but it makes him happy."

"Don't worry, I'll put them back, go on."

"Thanks," Anita said, hurrying off to where the coffin action was.

Torrie told Matthew that she was going to wrap him in a coat and then sit on him, which made him shriek and flail harder. She followed in his wake, picking up coats and stray gloves and hats. She wasn't sure she got everything back where it belonged, but figured people could get it sorted out at the next funeral.

She looked up. Her Uncle Ray stood at the door, watching them. "Hey," he said. "That looks like fun, Matthew."

Matthew, of course, wasn't expected to answer, but she was. "Hi Uncle Ray. Yeah, he's a wild man."

Uncle Ray stood with his arms folded across his chest, smiling. He was the nice uncle. He was the one who dressed up as Santa Claus at

Christmas parties, the one who always had the best Halloween lights and spooky bats and skeletons. "Did you need your coat?" Torrie asked him.

"Naw, hon, I was just thinking, Audrey never lets us forget she had the first grandkid."

"Oh. Yeah." Torrie shrugged. It wasn't a topic she was anxious to discuss. "Yeah, Mom goes ape . . . she's nuts about him."

"All things come to he who waits," Ray said, which she guessed was supposed to mean that sooner or later one of his kids would get it together. The girls, you had to figure. It wasn't considered polite for people to ask about her cousin Chip anymore; he was assumed to be in murky, faraway circumstances, living a life of unspeakable and thrilling degradation.

The noise from the entryway welled up just then, more people arriving, and Torrie thought it was a good excuse to leave. She hauled Matthew up underneath his arms and walked him forward, his feet on hers. "Beep beep," she said to Ray, who was still in her way.

He patted her hair and then her shoulder, a clumsy pawing. "When you're older you'll understand how great it is, a time like this, to see a young one running around." He turned and walked away into the milling crowd.

She hated it when people said, When you're older, blah blah blah. It was like a present held up just out of your reach, one you probably didn't want anyway.


Ryan got his hair cut for the funeral service. He turned up the next day at lunchtime with the ponytail shorn three inches above his collar. It wasn't exactly short—was still some bushy stuff over his ears and in the front—but it was the shortest any of them had seen it in years.

"I bet they had a good time with you down at Hookstra's," Torrie's father said. Hookstra's was where elderly barbers in white smocks attended to men wearing seed-company windbreakers, and the radio was always tuned to the farm station.

"There were a lot of jokes about sending me down to the beauty college," Ryan said. He seemed pleased with himself, turning his head from side to side as if to catch the breeze on his newly exposed skin.

"Why now?" Torrie asked. "You could have gotten it cut in Chicago." It irritated her that he'd made himself into a spectacle twice. First when he'd shown up looking like a total dirtbag—like some out-of-it, granola-eating, clueless dirtbag—and now, when everybody would see the difference and talk about it.

"I dunno, I just felt like getting it cut. Sign of respect." He shrugged. "It's a funeral, you know?"

"It's not like Aunt Martha's going to notice."

Their mother came in then. She was wearing her church clothes and she smelled powerfully of perfume. "Victoria, I don't want to hear you say anything that ugly ever again. I think your brother looks very handsome."

"Thanks, Mom."

"Yeah, so does he." Torrie was still mad at him for getting on her case, for doing their mother's bidding. Like he cared in the first place. She'd eaten a whole bag of Doritos last night. She felt fat, soft, totally disgusting.

"What is the matter with you?" Her mother's made-up eyebrows gave her a menacing look. "Would you please try to remember that today is about honoring a woman who loved you very much and was never anything but kind to you and suffered terribly—"

"Maybe I should get all my hair cut off too."

Her mother sat down heavily on a kitchen chair. "I can't stand it. She was my sweetest, sweetest little baby girl. And now she hates me."

"Come on, Mom. Nobody hates you." Nobody ever knew what to do when her mother cried. It was the worst feeling, as if you'd killed somebody's dog with your car.

"All I ever did was love you. All of you."

"God, Mom."

"None of that talk," her father said. "You are way, way out of line, miss."

Torrie shook her head and tried to catch Ryan's eye: *See? This is what I was talking about.* But he wouldn't look at her. He was on their side now.

"Would you like to stay home by yourself?" her father asked. "Because that's exactly where you're heading."

Would she ever. If only they'd let her. If only she wouldn't have to sit in the backseat with Ryan, holding casseroles for the supper, while her father drove too slow and everybody in the car was mad at her. Instead she muttered No, she wouldn't, and waited until her father was in the bathroom and her mother and Ryan were busy with something in the den. She grabbed her coat and keys and yelled that she had to go pick up Michelle and she'd see them at the service.

She drove to the Casey's on the north edge of town, filled the car with gas, ordered a whole sausage pizza and ate it in the parking lot.

Once she was pretty sure enough time had passed, she set out for the funeral, still dawdling. Scouting the highway ahead and behind her, since she didn't want to encounter her parents' car on the road. It wasn't raining but the farm fields were soggy and soaked, the crops disked down for winter, and the sky looked as if it could go either way, clear off or dump more water. There had been a phone conversation she wasn't meant to overhear, her mother speculating with someone about whether they could get a grave dug in this kind of weather.

When she thought about being buried in mud, it made the pizza in her stomach turn into something hot and crawling.

She considered not going. Just driving around for a while and then heading back home, making some excuse later. Her mother would worry about her the whole time, which would serve her right for all her stupid guilt trips. They might even send somebody out to look for her. Torrie turned west instead of heading straight toward Hardy, trying out the idea. She wanted to make them worry, but it would be a seriously bratty thing to do at a funeral, which after all was about somebody dying, even if they had been really old.

She drove five miles or more into the country, deciding what to do. There was absolutely nowhere to go, and nothing to see except a treeline off in the distance. Hopeless. But when she tried to jog north again the road veered and curved, and a thick, ugly cloud cover was edging up on her left, and it scared her a little, because her mother's car sometimes stalled out or acted up, and when she finally got back to the main road she was glad and drove faster to make up time.

Hardy was one of those little towns built up around a grain elevator and a railroad siding. There was a crossroads, and an office and scales for the elevator, and always a few fertilizer trucks parked in a gravel lot, and a tavern that opened at 5:00 a.m. to serve coffee and sweet rolls, and a hardware and feed store containing a post office. Also a garage with a tractor-tire service, a hutch that sold hot dogs and ice cream cones in the summer, and three streets of houses, some of which doubled as beauty parlors or insurance agencies, places you could get knives sharpened, furniture reupholstered. The brick church was the biggest building in town.

She was really late now, the parking lot was full, and she thought that even from outside she could hear organ music. Her mother was going to kill her.

A side door led into the vestibule and she slipped in, hoping she'd be unnoticed. No such luck. One of the ushers, some dressed-up farmer, frowned at her and handed her a program. With his pointing finger, he indicated that there was room in the choir loft.

Torrie found a seat on the end, next to a row of little kids being minded by a couple of mothers. Looking down, she saw her family sitting in two rows in the middle of the sanctuary. Even Jeff was there. He was on one side of Matthew and Anita on the other, Torrie guessed to make sure he behaved, although it was also possible they just didn't like sitting next to each other. Her parents and Ryan were in front of them, with Blake and the skanky girlfriend on the end of the row. She didn't think they were going to look up, unless she launched a paper airplane at them.

The coffin was as big as a boat. Peerson coffins usually were. At least they'd closed the lid, and at least she'd missed the part where everybody took their last looks before the service. One more chance for people to stare at you. When you were dead, you had absolutely no privacy.

The organ reached the wheezy end of whatever dirge it had been playing and struck a new note. The pastor entered and signaled them to rise. Torrie grabbed a hymnal. She was glad for the little kids so she wouldn't have to share. "How Great Thou Art," the program said, and she pretended to look it up and sing along. Instead she let her gaze travel around the sanctuary, hoping to find anything that would let her eyes disengage from her brain. The stained-glass windows were the old-fashioned kind, everything done in bright colors and heavy leading. Here was an angel blowing a heavenly horn, Jesus the Good Shepherd, a dove descending, an open book representing The Word.

The hymn ended. They all sat down and composed themselves for the boring parts. "Let us pray," the pastor instructed them.

"Dear Lord, we gather here today to celebrate a new voice in thy heavenly choir, your faithful servant Martha Ann, who comes to you freed from her earthly labors and sorrows, glorified in thy presence. Even as we mourn her loss, let us not forget that in thy eternal kingdom there is no loss, only the peace that passeth all understanding. So that our tears will be dried and we shall be comforted by the promise of thy eternal mercy and goodness and love, we ask it in Jesus Christ's name, amen."

"Amen," the congregation responded. One of Martha's grandsons, a nervous-looking boy of twelve, got up to read the Scripture, from Matthew, the part about not knowing the day or the hour when the Son of Man would return, which was meant to remind you that you could keel over at any time and stand before the Throne. Kind of an odd choice for Aunt Martha, who everybody knew was headed that way sooner rather than later.

They stood again to sing "Just as I Am," and Torrie took this occasion to examine the program she'd been given. There was a picture of Martha and Norm on the front. They probably hadn't been able to find any picture of Martha all by herself. On the inside of the cover was an inspirational verse:

*God hath not promised skies always blue,*
*Flower-strewn pathways all our lives through.*

*God hath not promised sun without rain,*
*Joy without sorrow, peace without pain.*

*But God hath promised strength for the day,*
*Rest for the labor, light for the way,*

*Grace for the trials, help from above,*
*Unfailing sympathy, undying love.*

Now that really sucked. As far as Torrie was concerned, it was telling you to grin and bear it, put up with whatever miserable circumstances life threw at you, and you'd get your reward in heaven. No way.

It was time for the homily. The pastor waited for everybody to get settled. Torrie was pretty sure she heard Matthew pipe up in the middle of the silence. Looking down, she saw Anita drawing him onto her lap. Good luck with that. Once he got squirmy, he stayed that way.

"Dear friends," said the pastor, using his ordinary, sermon voice, not the exalted one he reserved for prayers. "I don't have to tell any of you what a good Christian Martha was. There's probably no one here today who wasn't touched by her faith, whether that shone forth in the love and care she gave to her family, her tireless work on behalf of the Ladies' Aid, or her fortitude during her last illness."

A sudden rattle against the windows and everybody looked up. A squall of rain hit hard, along with a high, dreary wind. It made you think of ghosts. *The wind howls like a hammer, the night blows cold and rainy / My love she's like some raven at my window with a broken wing.*

The pastor had to raise his voice to be heard. "She loved her family, she loved her dear husband, Norm. Can we even begin to imagine the joy of their heavenly reunion? Their two souls, no longer parted by death, reunited in glory. Oh, we do not mourn, we rejoice for them! She loved her church, and she loved her community. But today I'd like to talk about another community, that of our fellowship in Christ. A community of faith, a fellowship of believers."

Torrie hoped that Martha was in heaven. You didn't want to believe that people just *died*, and that was the stupid end of everything. Her stomach hurt. She was afraid she was going to have to get up and go to the bathroom, right in the middle of everything. Her mother was trying to look behind her, look around the sanctuary. For Torrie, most likely.

"How do we recognize our fellow citizens? Well, of course we come together in church. We know of each other's good works, the evidence of a godly life, like Martha's. Kindness, willingness to help, sacrifices on behalf of others. But good works by themselves do not lead us to salvation. It is faith and faith alone that makes us truly one with Christ."

If she was little, like Matthew, she could just start hollering, Hey! I'm up here! It was a little creepy, her whole family down below her wondering where she was, and her right there all along.

The rain drove against the windows and the old church creaked. People shifted in their seats. There would be a tent erected over the gravesite, but still . . .

She thought she'd missed part of the homily, some thread of argument. She shifted around in her seat, trying to ease the pressure on her stomach. The preacher never ran out of things to say, because there was always something people were doing wrong. "How can we ever see into the heart of another, or those others into our own hearts? Even those nearest and dearest to us. We struggle with the pressures of everyday life, and too often we are frustrated, hurried, angry, confused. We are not the people we set out to be. We are not true to our best selves. Jesus is the only one who sees that best self and loves us as we are meant to be loved. Every day he stands at the entrance of our hearts, waiting patiently for us to invite him in."

Her abdomen was cramping. She felt flushed and sweaty from the pain of it. She wondered how bad Martha's cancer had hurt. The wind howled like a hammer. That sounded great until you really thought about it, like a lot of Bob's lyrics. Jesus wanted shelter from the storm. He was a raven with a broken wing, a dove spiraling down. The dove was the Holy Spirit descending to men on earth. Jesus was mad at her for being a total brat and making her mother unhappy and eating all that pizza.

"It is our choice and ours alone. Open our hearts to the Savior and be a part of his church, his loving and faithful community. Or hold ourselves apart, excluded, alone, unhappy, lost."

Torrie had to get to the bathroom and the bathroom was all the way in the basement. She got up and made her way down the spiral staircase, to the empty vestibule, then the flight of cement steps to the basement, half-running, then finally reaching the little washroom beneath the stairs, latching the wood door and rippng her pants down just in time. She flushed, waited for the tank to fill, then flushed again. She felt weak and hollowed out and ashamed of the filth that came out of her.

Above her head, the floorboards thrummed with the deep sound of the organ. Smaller sounds reached her too, a stack of plates chinking together, footsteps. The supper was being made ready, and in a minute or two everybody would be down here, hungry.

Right there on the toilet she asked Jesus to forgive her for her snotty behavior and her smart mouth and everything wrong and stupid and unkind she'd ever done.

She ran water and washed her hands and unlatched the door. Some of the women had put on aprons and were busy taking the tops off casseroles and putting serving spoons in them. Coffee was brewing in an urn. They smiled at her and she wondered if she should offer to help. Probably not. They were the kind of women who had to do everything themselves.

Now there were voices and feet overhead, and just as Torrie was trying to decide if she should go upstairs and find her family, her mother came down the steps. When she saw Torrie, her mouth popped open. "Where have you been all this time?"

"I got here late and I had to sit upstairs."

"I don't know where to start. I truly don't."

"Mom, I'm really, really sorry about Aunt Martha. I mean I'm . . ."

Then she was crying and her mother hugged her and her mother's hair was tickling her nose and that was weird but she guessed it was all right. Her mother released her and produced Kleenex. "Here, blow your nose."

Torrie blew. "Are you all right?" her mother asked. "You look so pale. Did you get a chill? Does your head hurt?"

As usual, her mother would have to go through a whole catalog of ailments to see which of them applied to you. "I'm OK. Just kind of tired."

"You come sit over here. I am going to fix you a plate and you are going to eat something and I don't want to hear any arguments."

Torrie sat. People were making their way into the basement and lining up at the supper table. This church was smaller than the one in Grenada. It was going to be wall-to-wall eating. Her seat was in a corner and she was glad she was out of the way. Her mother came back with a plate and a plastic cup. "This is 7UP, you'll drink that, won't you? None of this has meat so it should be perfectly all right."

Her mother hadn't done badly. The plate held green-bean casserole, carrot slaw, a roll with butter, macaroni and cheese, and a brownie. Torrie actually felt a little hungry, hollowed out, and anyway it was kind of nice to have her mother wait on her.

"It looks good, Mom. Thanks. Oh. What did they do . . ."

Her mother lowered her head to whisper. "It's still raining, so they left her coffin in the sanctuary and they'll inter her tomorrow with just the kids there."

Not that it made any real difference, but it seemed less awful that way, as if Martha wasn't quite gone yet. Torrie ate a little macaroni and cheese, then some green beans. Her father came over and stood looking down at her. "How's that mac and cheese?"

"It's good, Dad. You should get some."

"Your mother made turkey and gravy. Oh, I forgot, meat."

"That's OK, Dad." She thought of the sausage pizza. She was never going to eat pizza again. Her father patted the top of her head and moved off toward the supper line.

Her brother Blake was next. He was wearing a corduroy sports coat he'd outgrown. He had monster arms and shoulders from working construction. She said, "That jacket just screams, 'I haven't dressed up since high school.'"

"Hey Tor. Where were you?"

"Up in the choir with the rest of the peanut gallery."

"Mom thought you'd been kidnapped."

"For real?" She was interested in this thought, wondering who, in Grenada, you could get to kidnap you. "No such luck."

"Yeah, she keeps thinking Patty Hearst."

Torrie made a sound of pained disgust. Blake just laughed. He didn't get worked up about things, at least not about complicated things. Now that he was getting laid on a regular basis, he probably didn't have a worry in the world. His eyes strayed over the crowd, no doubt looking for the skank, who for the first time in recent memory was more than three feet away from him. "OK, I gotta go. Catch you later."

"Later." She ate a little of the slaw, since carrots were a healthy food, at least until you soaked them in mayonnaise. She moved her chair farther toward the wall so she could lean back. It was warm in the room and she felt sleepy, and glad she could sit and watch everybody moving, eating, talking, and nothing about them ever changed, and that was fine.

"You awake?"

She'd closed her eyes, and here was her brother Ryan standing over her. She had to remember all over again that he'd cut his hair. "Is everybody in the family going to come over and pay their respects?"

"Not Anita. They went home already." He sat down next to her.

"Look," Torrie said, indicating her plate. "Me. Food."

"It's a start."

She poked him in the shoulder and ate a piece of buttered roll. She said, "Aren't there wakes, funerals, where they have bars?"

"I think you have to be Irish. Maybe Italian. This is OK, though. It's so, I don't know, normal."

"Yeah, I was just thinking sort of the same thing."

They watched a while longer from their corner. Their parents were sitting at a table with some of the Peersons, except that their mother got up about every three minutes the way she always did to make sure that her husband or somebody else had what they needed. And if you looked at all the other tables you could see the exact same thing, people doing what they always did, eating baked beans and ham and apple crisp, talking about the weather, the prices of corn and fuel, loans come due, people with bad luck or no luck, which often came down to simple laziness and lack of effort, the incomprehensible entity that was the government, and hadn't the pastor given a beautiful and affecting homily.

"Yeah," Ryan said, as if they'd been talking all along. "It's like watching a big flock of cranes or something, all of them walking around and honking and flapping their wings and doing exactly what they're supposed to be doing."

"OK," Torrie said. "That's a little strange, but I think I get it."

He stood up. "I was going to go back with Libby and Glen, hang out with them for a while. Unless you want me to drive back with you?"

She shook her head. "Go. Try not to get arrested."

Of course her mother didn't like the idea of her driving home by herself either, as if there really was some mad kidnapper out there, and Torrie pointed out that it had practically stopped raining, and her father said the only way this was going to happen was if Torrie waited until they were ready to leave and then if she drove ahead of them so they could keep track of her. Torrie rolled her eyes and said, "All right, gee," stopping herself just in time to keep from saying *jeez*.

She started her mother's car and got the heater going and ran the wipers to clear off the windshield and then waited for her parents to get it together, saying good-bye, good-bye to everybody and her mother making sure she had her casserole dishes and serving spoons and nobody else's. Her father started the car and Torrie flashed her lights at them and steered her way out of the church parking lot and to the crossroads and from there onto the highway.

It wasn't raining hard enough to keep the wipers running; they scraped and squeegeed over the glass. But every so often she had to flip them on and then off, otherwise the raindrops thickened and obscured her vision and it really was pretty dark out here, even if the road was straight as tape. Her father's headlights reflected off the rearview mirror. She would have liked to explain to him that following too closely was a safety hazard. It was probably her mother fussing at him to keep up, keep up, and after a couple miles of this Torrie waved (they could probably see her hand) and sped up, gunning it on a flat stretch and leaving them behind, at least for a minute or two.

She saw their headlights behind her, gaining ground, and gunned it again, knowing that her mother wouldn't allow her father to exceed a certain speed, and finally the road was all hers, lonely and beautiful and nothing but the white line feeding beneath her wheels. She tried singing, since there was no such thing as a radio station out here, *Hey, Mr. Tambourine Man, play a song for me,* but her voice was all wrong for that one. Singing along, flipping the windshield-wiper switch to on, one instant everything right and the next this shocking noise, impact, the smell of something burnt, the car skidding 180 degrees, the force of it slamming her to one side.

The white lines tore away and she fought the skid, pumping the brakes, but the steering wheel jerked out of her hands and then there was nothing beneath her tires. The car was airborne but already seeking gravity, and in that long, floating, disbelieving second before it began to pitch and fall, Torrie thought that at least she wasn't going to die a virgin.

# *Chicago*

MARCH 1981

The class was supposed to be reviewing the material on research methods, but they could hardly be blamed for wanting to talk about the president, the president getting shot. A momentous thing, even if by now it seemed certain that no permanent harm had been done. By now he was recovering, sitting up in his hospital bed and signing paperwork. By now everyone had heard of his joking with the doctors before the surgery: "I sure hope you're all Republicans!" Say whatever else you wanted about the man, you had to admire his style.

By now the grubby, pathetic shooter had been thoroughly jailed. By now there were public prayers, and people sending cards and teddy bears and flowers. Although a dead president would have been more solemn and dramatic, still they were all conscious that this was history, the taste and texture of it, and they should pay attention.

"Is assassination a political act? Or just a violent act that has political consequences?" Ryan, perched on the edge of the desk, leaning forward to indicate intensity, posed this to the fifteen undergraduates in his discussion section. They bit down hard on the question. You could practically see their brains chewing. They were serious young people, all of them very intelligent, or at least they tested well.

The weather was freakishly warm for March, high eighties, a

record, everybody said. The students had rummaged their closets for shorts and tank tops and it was distracting for Ryan to look out on so much unaccustomed flesh, when they'd all started back in January wearing parkas and wool hats. The room was never the right temperature no matter what the season and now it was thick with heat. They'd forced a couple of windows open but that hadn't helped much, only let in the sound of city traffic, which always sounded like a distant war.

The heat seemed to slow everyone's thought processes. Finally Leo Lautner raised his hand. "It would depend on the intention of the assassin. They might have a political aim, or they might be just disturbed, unstable, like the women who tried to shoot President Ford."

Ryan nodded. He was pretty sure that Leo Lautner was smarter than himself, and it was just an accident of timing that he, Ryan, was the one sitting at the front of the room at the teacher's desk. "Good point. Whereas John Wilkes Booth or Lee Harvey Oswald intended political disruption, acted out of political grievances. Also the, ah, Garfield and McKinley assassins." He was also pretty sure he had that right about Garfield and McKinley. Or that even if he didn't, no one in the class was likely to know it.

None of them were old enough to remember the Kennedy assassination. They might as well have been talking about Lincoln. Ryan had been seven years old, and the undergraduates were just being born. That's what he felt like most of the time, a seven-year-old pulling rank on toddlers.

A girl had her hand up. "What's his name, Hinckley, sounds like a true flake." She was one of the near-naked ones. Her pink bra straps tangled with the thinner straps of her tank top. Some change of decorum or fashion had come about that now made the casual display of bra straps, that previously hidden architecture, acceptable. Still, Ryan felt furtive whenever he found himself looking.

"Hinckley had a thing for Jodie Foster," another boy said, in a tone of wonderment. As if, given a choice of obsessions, he would have made a different selection.

Another student asked if everybody had seen *Taxi Driver*. *Taxi Driver*, in his opinion, was one tight, tight film. Someone else said they felt sorry for the other guy, the press secretary, who had been shot in the head. Could you imagine getting shot in the head? They couldn't. Or rather, they could do so now, but once the damage had been done, the capacity to reflect on it would probably be gone too. They shivered inwardly, thinking of it. They were their heads. Memories, ideas, opinions. What else was there?

The discussion was wobbling offtrack, and Ryan stepped in before he had to hear any more. "All right, people." He was a cool, hip instructor, unconcerned with authoritarian rule-making and discipline, except of course when he had to be. "Say the assassins aren't crazy, or at least, not completely delusional. What might motivate them?"

It wasn't a very good question, and the class pondered it to see if there was some trick to it, if something more than the obvious was called for. Megan O'Brien, who had been encouraged to participate more in class, raised her hand. "They were unsuccessful, or frustrated, in their attempts to participate in the normal political process."

"Yes, and what does that lead to? What kind of feeling," he prompted. Megan was looking stricken, her attempt at participation turning around and biting her in the ass. In spite of her name she was Korean, a shy girl with her black hair cut in pony bangs.

"Alienation?" someone suggested, and Ryan nodded, and Megan O'Brien wilted in a way that he would have to apologize for later, and the rest of the class settled back to blot and fan themselves, the edge taken off their interest, since he was indeed asking for the obvious.

He wasn't a good teacher. It was only a discussion section, he was only supposed to go over the lecture material with them, administer quizzes and approve their paper topics. But often enough he stumbled over the lesson plan, asked wooden questions, as he was now doing, failed to excite or even help them. The students liked him well enough because he joked around, chitchatted with them, took an interest.

They liked him but he was never going to be one of those teachers regarded with awe because they dug deep, stirred something within their students. Instead, he took roll. He reminded them of deadlines, told them what might be on the exams.

And yet today he was trying to work something through in his own mind, take them along with him. What if you hailed from the Great State of Alienation, proud home of the disillusioned, the crazed, the indifferent, the violent? How did it happen that some people lived unquestioning lives, never doubted their place in that enterprise called America, their proprietary involvement, their stake in its successes, while others turned away?

More obvious answers, more hands struggling to rise through the glassy heat. Some people had been excluded due to race, creed, or national origin. Only lip service paid to equality, all men created equal with equal rights to Life, Liberty, Inc. (All *men,* sniffed one of the women students. Right there was a problem.)

Granted, Ryan said. But Squeaky and Sara Jane aside, there had been no legions of women assassins. No black assassins. (No black students in the discussion section either. One could not help but notice.) There had been the Black Panthers, some of whom themselves had been assassinated. Right here in Chicago, the murder of Fred Hampton and Mark Clark by the Chicago police, only a few miles from where they sat. People murdered, ambushed, for their political views, by their own government. Did the students know about this? Well, they should educate themselves.

From time to time, Ryan tried to imagine himself having these conversations back in Iowa.

For once he knew something that his students did not. (That is, everyone except Leo Lautner, who pointed out that it was actually the state attorney's office, assisted by the police and the FBI, who had conducted the raid. Leo, earnest and baby-faced. He had never heard of the concept of piling on.) But most blacks, Ryan went on, demonstrated their view of the body politic not by violent action, but by ignoring elections. They were historically underrepresented. (Leo Lautner one more time, helpfully bringing up the Harold Washington quote. Black voters were "a sleeping giant" that could awaken at any time. Thank you, Leo.)

Alienation, Ryan suggested, as opposed to disenfranchisement, had more to do with those persons who felt entitled (by birth, ethnicity, economics) to their share of the world's goods (money, status, recognition) and had been disappointed.

But surely he had not meant to equate alienation with acts of violence? One leading inevitably to the other? The students shifted in their seats, uncertain and resistant. Because of course they considered themselves alienated. Prided themselves on it. Here he was, making it sound like a tantrum of the overindulged. Alienation was proof of their intelligence, their wised-up perception, their disappointments. They were so young, but already so disappointed. And of course most of them had been born into their share of entitlement, though unlike alienation, this was not regarded as anything cool.

Oh, no, sillies, he reassured them. He meant nothing of the sort. He wasn't calling them assassins. Only inviting them to think about how personal experience, personal grievance, expanded outward into the public sphere. From the individual to the group. From birth, the body of the mother, to the body politic. From the inside of the skull to the outside, a distance of what, an inch? Less? The difference between thought and action. The idea taking root in the brain versus the gun in the hand. The difference between an ordinary day, and history.

The individual and the state, the individual as unwilling participant in the state. The self existed among the great confusion of other selves, each of us, all of us, the cells in the body politic. The political animal. A shuffling, shambling, bearlike creature, sometimes lurching forward, at other times gnawing and swatting at its own troubled innards.

The bell rang. The students gathered their books and papers, anxious to pry their damp skins away from the desks, get themselves gone. He raised his voice above the racket, reminded them to go over chapters seven and eight, they'd catch up next class.

He'd confused them with his fanciful talk. Bears and such. He hadn't found the right words. Maybe Leo could help him.

He checked his mailbox by the department office, nothing. Three o'clock, time for his office hours. He calculated the odds that any students were going to seek him out on such a day and instead took an elevator down and outside, where the sun and heat felt more like a holiday, an occasion for drinking beer at a ball game. Except the season hadn't yet started, and try as he might, he couldn't get that excited about the Chicago teams. This was Hyde Park, you were supposed to root for the Sox, the South Side team. A cultural marker. He'd even gone to a few games, cheered when he was meant to, could hold up his end of a conversation about last year's disappointing season. But he wasn't really a fan. He guessed he suffered from baseball alienation.

The grass on the quadrangle was still winter-brown, the trees bare sticks, the university buildings blank gray stone. Nothing but the temperature spoke of spring. Ryan stopped at a food co-op run by militant vegetarians and purchased bread, cheese, whole-wheat pasta, tomato sauce, mushrooms, salad greens, loading them into his backpack. He made another stop at the Jewel for red wine and hamburger meat and, as an impulse, spumoni ice cream.

It was another four blocks to the apartment he shared with a grad student in mathematics. Burdened as he was, the heat had him dripping and puffing by the time he reached his building and climbed the three flights of stairs. He hadn't minded not having money at first; it was an expected part of graduate school, it even served to validate his dedication to knowledge, his indifference to goods and chattel. But you could get tired of it, especially when you were surrounded by undergrads whose parents had the money to pay big-time tuition, who only dressed as if they were ragged and forlorn. He knew that his own family regarded him with dismay because he didn't seem to be "getting ahead," which to them meant money. And as much as he didn't want to agree with them about this, or any number of other things, it would be nice to have a car again.

He unpacked his groceries. The ice cream had gone soft and he hoped the indolent freezer would be up to the task of reconstituting it. The apartment had a single puny air conditioner and he cranked it to high and set a floor fan running to move the breeze around. He put Miles Davis on the stereo, stripped off his clothes, and padded around until some of the heat left his skin. He took a shower, shaved, put on clean clothes, and by the time his roommate Zev arrived home, he had the salad made and was working on the pasta sauce.

Zev leaned his bicycle against the wall. It was a Le Tour racer, the most expensive thing he owned, and he humped it up and down the three flights every day. He surveyed Ryan's dinner efforts and then Ryan himself. "The girl?" he asked. He had an Israeli accent that sounded like fingers were shoved down his throat.

"Yeah. I'm making enough for you too."

"You are big trouble," Zev informed him.

"You mean 'in big trouble.'"

"No, what I said."

Dinner would be at six thirty. Ryan set the dinky table with bamboo mats and plates, rinsed and polished three wineglasses. A Japanese paper lantern covered the lightbulb over the table and it cast a pink-orange glow. He liked the way it looked and he liked the look of the books and albums on their shelves and the old couch covered with an Indian-print bedspread and the fancy picture frame they'd hung over a square of bare wall as a joke. He liked the music making the room seem so much bigger than it really was. The good smell of the cooking made him happy, it all made him happy because this was the life, the world he had constructed for himself and it was a fine thing.

At six thirty he heard footsteps on the stairs. He opened the door before she had a chance to knock. Megan O'Brien had changed out of the T-shirt and jeans she wore in class. In honor of the weather she had on a sundress, yellow with a print of white flowers, which tied over her shoulders with bows. "Hey, you look nice," Ryan said, guiding her inside with just the faintest, friendliest touch, the palm of his hand on her small, hard shoulder blade. He was thinking that on an older or a more wanton girl the sundress would have teased you with its childishness, like a costume. Megan just looked like she'd been dressed up for Korean Sunday school.

"It's so hot out," she said, with the kind of overemphasis that suggested a long-rehearsed remark.

"Yeah, brutal. Want something to drink? Wine?"

"Oh, I don't know . . ."

"I'll make you a spritzer." He mixed ice, soda, and wine in a tall glass for her. "Here, don't get drunk. I don't want to have to clean up after you."

She giggled. She sipped her drink and stood in front of the bookshelves, taking in the titles. This was the third time she'd been to Ryan's apartment, and on each occasion she seemed to be trying to fathom him, add to her store of worshipful knowledge about him.

"Hey, I'm glad you said something in class today. That's exactly what I was talking about."

"Yeah, well it wasn't like I said anything that great."

"No, it was fine. Really. It gets easier to speak up, I promise." She was a girl who needed a lot of reassurance.

"That Leo guy." She shook her head. Ryan couldn't tell what she meant by this, disdain or admiration.

"Leo sure ate his Wheaties this morning."

Zev came out of his room, making his usual beeline for the refrigerator. "Hello, Meg-Ann." And, to Ryan, "Show me dinner."

"Hi Zev," Megan said. She was especially shy around Zev, although Zev disagreed with this characterization.

"Not shy," he pronounced after first meeting her. "A crying baby." Ryan said Zev should stick to the language of mathematics.

"Spaghetti with mushroom sauce, salad, garlic bread. Get out of there," Ryan told him. "Wait until I put it on the table."

"Can I help?" Megan asked, drifting over. It was the kind of thing girls said when they could see there wasn't anything left to do. Ryan told her to sit down and say *yummy*.

Three weeks ago, when it was still winter, Megan O'Brien had come to see him in his office. She was worried about her grade. The students who came to see him were all worried about their grades. Megan was a music major, piano. She was taking poli sci to fulfill a requirement and she understood politics, or at least, some of it, but it was the *science* part she didn't get, the ideas, the language that was used to talk about the ideas. She knew she hadn't done well on the quizzes or the midterm.

Ryan pretended to consult his gradebook. He already knew where Megan O'Brien stood, somewhere in that great, gauzy territory of B. And not a high B. He told her this. She shook her head and her limp black hair fell against her neck. "I guess I'm a B kind of a person," she said hopelessly. Ryan said he bet she was a pretty good piano player and she said no, she kind of sucked at that too.

By now he was used to students who moped their way into his office to complain about the crushing burdens of being nineteen, by now he knew enough to keep Kleenex on his desk. He told her that she could earn extra points for class participation, and that she could submit a draft of her paper ahead of time so he could give her suggestions.

She didn't cry, just looked wistful. "You must really, really love this stuff, you're lucky, you know what you want to do with your life, pursue your dream, I don't have a dream, I just kept taking piano lessons because my parents wanted me to have, you know, an interest. An accomplishment. I wish there was any one thing I was really good at and people would respect me for it. How does it feel to be respected?"

They went to one of the noisy coffee shops that catered to students, students in lumpy hats hand-knit in the Andes, students in cowboy boots, striped mufflers, navy peacoats acquired at thrift stores, all of them hunched over books and intensely reading. Ryan thought he understood what Megan O'Brien was up against. She wasn't unconventional enough to pass for an artist or a scholar around here. She wore Shetland-wool sweaters over cotton shirts, a parka from L.L. Bean. It was unclear if she had been outfitted by her parents or had no particular taste or aesthetic of her own. She had a small, puzzled, inexpressive face. She told Ryan she had been adopted as a baby, she'd grown up in Philadelphia, and she had no memory at all of Korea. Supposedly she'd been in an orphanage, but there were stories of parents who'd sold their children, particularly the girl babies, due to poverty. For all she knew, her family, her Korean family, was still back there, peasants grubbing around in rice paddies. She'd never eaten Korean food as a kid and didn't like it when she'd tried it. She'd grown up as Megan O'Brien, and when she was old enough to ask questions, her parents explained that she had been specially chosen to be a part of their family, that she was a special, special girl and they loved her very much, etc. For the longest time, she thought that *Korean* and *adopted* meant the same thing.

Ryan said he could see how all that would be confusing. She asked him where he was from and he said Iowa. Darkest Iowa. What he always said, a joke to deflect any further inquiry. He didn't care to discuss his family. They had been bewildered by sadness, by tragedy, and he was no help to them; there was no way to feel good about any of that.

Fortunately, Megan O'Brien wasn't inclined to stray far from the topic of herself. She said again that she wished she was really, really focused, like he was, committed to what he wanted to do with the rest of his life. Ryan was aware that some grade-prospecting might be going on here, some strategic flattering, but that was all right, he had a handle on it. She asked about his thesis, which had yet to take any satisfactory shape, according to his adviser, but in his own mind, and in his recounting of it to Megan O'Brien, it became a magisterial document, a searching examination of identity as experienced by the individual versus political legitimacy as conferred by the state. Wow, said Megan O'Brien. You really are good at this stuff.

At the end of an hour they got up to go and she said that she was going to try a lot harder in class. They walked out of the steamy interior of the coffee shop into a battering cold wind and she said Oh shoot. She was supposed to call her roommate right this minute and tell her how to sign up for a lottery, a lottery that would determine which dorm rooms they would get next year. She had forgotten all about it. Ryan said that his apartment was just down the street, she could phone from there.

That had been her first visit, a brief one. She hadn't even taken off her coat, just stood at the kitchen counter to make her phone call. She flicked her eyes over the apartment, taking everything in. The apartment was a mess as usual, newspapers on the floor, an ashtray with a roach he hoped she didn't notice. A few days' dishes in the sink. Embarrassing. Neither he nor Zev had current girlfriends of the sort that necessitated housecleaning, or who might be persuaded to clean for them. Ryan waited by the door. He felt an unease, a consciousness of trespass on both their parts. It wasn't wise to get too buddy-buddy with your students. It was definitely a bad idea to sleep with them. But she was just a sad little girl in need of some extra attention. Maybe he could finally make a difference, be the kind of teacher who mattered to them.

Ten days ago she'd given him the first draft of her paper. It was so riddled with earnest errors, its thought processes so knotted in loops of language, Ryan gave up trying to write notes on it and invited her over after class. This time he cleaned the apartment, filled three black plastic garbage bags with trash. Stored his drug paraphernalia in a box in his closet. They sat at the kitchen table, chaperoned, more or less, by Zev, who kept coming in and out of his bedroom on one or another errand. Megan took notes, clutched at her forehead, despaired of writing anything passable. Patiently, he took her back to her original argument, refined it, made her write an outline and then some sample paragraphs.

The paper was 30 percent of the grade. Eventually he was going to have to disabuse her of the notion that she could possibly haul herself up to an A. But for now she was so grateful. She was sure he had other, more important things to do than help her, she was so stupid and hopeless et cetera.

Now, tonight, she was bringing a new draft. Ryan had already decided not to read it on the spot, but to wait and hand it back to her with written comments. He intended to be encouraging, while holding back from outright praise. Maybe she could be bumped up to a high B.

The meal was a success, even if Zev complained about the quality of the lettuce in the salad. Out of patriotism or homesickness or both, he felt a duty to complain about all things American. Megan ate in a tidy, ladylike fashion, careful not to get spaghetti sauce on her yellow dress. She laughed at any jokes Zev or Ryan made. It was easy to imagine her reading one of those girls' magazines that advised them to show an interest, be an active listener. When she finished her wine spritzer, Ryan poured her a glass of undiluted wine.

After they finished eating they opened one of the living room windows and climbed out to sit on the roof. They'd furnished a small, flat space there with cushions and upended milk crates. The sun was gone and with it some of the heat and it was pleasant to sit there watching lights come on in the early dusk. The freeway noise muttered behind them, and a mile away in the other direction was the lake, made invisible by the intervening city blocks. Bites taken here and there by urban renewal, the massive project that made it possible for people like himself to live here. The city in a constant slow-motion process of building up and building down, becoming unrecognizable to itself.

Megan claimed she could see the lake, a dark blue corner of it. Ryan said that wasn't likely, and she said how did he know what she saw, huh, and punched him lightly in the arm and rocked backward on the cushion so that the curve of her neck rested against his shoulder.

With a combination of stealth and tact, he waited until there was an occasion to move—Zev needing the wine bottle passed to him— disengaged himself, and when he sat back again he shifted himself slightly away from her.

Then everything was OK again. There was an argument—you could call it an argument because of its emphasis and volume, not any actual ill will—between Ryan and Zev about McCarthyism, of all things, the anticommunist hysteria of the fifties. Zev had made quite a study of it, as he had of anything crummy or crazy, anything that reflected badly on the country. He was living here under protest. Really, the guy had his issues.

Yes yes yes, Ryan said, McCarthy and all that. Shooting the occasional president. But even Zev had to admit that there was something grand, something hopeful, in both the vision and the actuality of the American enterprise, surely Zev could understand that, given his own brand-new and created country? The outlandishness of willing an entire nation into existence. Rough edges and all. Look at the three of them. Genetic material from all over the globe. His domesticated Viking self. Megan, Korean by birth, Irish by accident. Zev, child of Polish refugees, displaced twice over. What an unlikely mix, what possibilities, what tug and pull of human tides allowed them this beautiful evening, this not-quite lake view, their perch on the city's bright edge?

From which, Zev said, so many had been removed. The poor and the black. Inconvenient people. Yes, Ryan said. They had. And the blacks had replaced the earlier Jewish immigrants. Who had in their turn replaced others, going all the way back to the Indians. One should not forget the Indians. The first big losers. Politics always the story of winners and losers. It was written.

Zev said, "The wine is making of you a bad poet." He drained his glass and stepped over the window ledge back inside.

A small silence now that the two of them were alone. The roof, the dark sky above them, were still baking hot, but Ryan imagined he felt some ghost or echo of a lake breeze, a wedge of cooler air. He was tired after the long day and the ungodly heat. He should get some reading done. He was slacking off, he'd spent too much time this semester gabbing when he should have been reading, reading when he should have been writing. It was too easy to fall into the pose of being a graduate student. You were impossibly burdened by scholarly labors, intense and exhausting brain work. And then you sat around on your ass, drinking and complaining about all the work you hadn't done. Megan said, "Zev is so full of it."

"Yeah." Then, paying attention: "What do you mean?"

"What you said? It was great. Passionate." The word, once spoken, seemed to embarrass her. Her shoulders, with their fabric bows, convulsed, as if trying to wriggle out of what she'd said. "I thought that's what school was going to be like. Was supposed to be like. People passionate about their life's work."

"Well, yeah, everybody should be . . . committed to what they do." Which wasn't exactly what she'd said. Passionate. He wasn't sure if he was, or at least, he wasn't sure if he was what she thought.

Maybe he was only passionate about his own preoccupations, maybe everyone was, and your life's work was only yourself writ large, and in capital letters.

"So," he began, preparatory to saying they should call it a night, but Megan hurried to speak over him. "I didn't bring my paper. I need to do some more work on it."

Big relief. He wouldn't have to spend hours going through it. "That's OK, you have another two weeks. Plenty of time. And you know, you can always go to the writing lab." That's where he should have sent her and her murdered sentences to begin with.

Megan waved her wineglass. "More, please."

"You're sure that's a good idea?" He was pretty sure it wasn't.

"It's a great idea."

He refilled her glass and she took a big, punishing drink from it. "If I don't get all A's, my parents are going to send me back to Korea."

"Nobody gets all A's."

She shook her head overvigorously. "They'd look at it as, you know, returning damaged merchandise. But hey, it might work out over there. Roots. The Fatherland. Motherland. One or the other."

A happy thought came to him. He wouldn't even have to read her paper. He could just turn in her grade, her respectable B. School would be over for the summer and he wouldn't have to face her. There was still that part of him that wanted to be liked, that made him commit similar large and small acts of cowardice in the service of being liked. Before he could think about it he said, "Megan, you're not going to get an A in the class. It's just not going to happen."

For a moment he thought she hadn't heard him. She didn't say anything, and it was too dark to see her face. Then she said, "I don't understand. I haven't even written my paper yet."

"Yeah, but it's not mathematically possible. There's a formula, percentages, I don't have anything to do with it. Even if your paper is an A. You still have to write a good paper for a B, and I can help you some more with that. I just don't want you to be too disappointed."

"I don't understand," she said again, and Ryan had the dead certainty that she would never understand, and that for reasons of his own vanity and his own weakness, he had gone about everything wrong.

He said, "It's a course outside your major, you aren't expected to do as well in those. As long as you try your hardest, I'm sure your parents are going to be just fine." She said something under her breath. He didn't hear it and didn't want to. "They might even be impressed."

"I wanted you to be impressed."

Something cold, a current of queasy dread, passed through him. "I am. I'm very impressed by your effort. How important it is to you."

Megan got up from her seat, walked to the edge of the roof, and holding her wineglass around the rim, dropped it over the side. Three stories down, the glass broke with a tiny, musical sound.

"What the hell?"

Her yellow dress turned away from the roof edge as she regarded him. "Sorry."

"You could kill somebody like that. Christ, was anybody down there?"

"How about I buy you a new glass."

"That was just stupid." Ryan wasn't sure if she was just being pissy, a pissy little girl having a tantrum, a booze tantrum, he reminded himself—*Shit, good job of getting her drunk, man*—or if she was nuts in some way that hadn't shown itself until now, and most of all how was he going to backpedal out of it, calm her down, get her feeling all right about things, or at the very least out of his apartment before she smashed up anything else.

"Now look, I know you're upset, but you are way, way overreacting. It's just some dumb paper in some dumb course."

"I guess I'm just some dumb girl."

"Don't say that, come on."

"Sometimes nobody pays attention until you, you know, make some noise."

"I'm paying attention, Megan. Sure."

"Sure you are." She walked over to sit on the sill of the open window. Light from the room behind her polished her thin bare arms and shoulders, picked out the stray hairs growing along her neck in two shadowy triangles. She wasn't a pretty girl. He found himself thinking this and censored the ungenerous thought.

He said, "Look, I don't think you should be comparing yourself to other people all the time. You imagine that everybody's so much smarter and more together than you are and it's just not true. Hey, I'm not that smart or together most of the time, that's the last thing I am. I don't work half as hard as I should, I make stupid mistakes about twenty times a day, I don't know if I want to go on for my doctorate or even if I do, what comes after that. Nobody has it all figured out, Megan, that's my point. And when I was your age? Oh man. I had no clue. It was more like I knew what I didn't want. I've got my share of family issues too. You don't have to be adopted for those."

As if she had only been waiting for him to finish speaking, she swung her legs over the windowsill and stood up. "OK," she said from inside the room. "Thanks. I have to go home now."

Ryan followed her. "I'll walk with you."

"You don't have to."

"Yeah, I do. What if somebody's out there throwing wineglasses?"

A joke she didn't laugh at. "I don't want you to come with me."

"Come on, Megan." At least she didn't seem drunk. But no way was she going to walk home alone through the dark in her child's sundress, even if it was only a few blocks. "I'll walk behind you. You don't have to talk to me or anything."

"If you try to do that, I'll scream."

Zev came out of his room then, sensed something unhappy going on, retrieved his bicycle and headed for the door.

"Hey, Zev? Want to do me a favor, walk Megan back to her dorm? As long as you're going out? That all right with you, Megan?"

Zev said it would be no problem, sure. He gave Ryan a look on the way out. It said, You are big trouble.

He heard their footsteps and the soft bumping of the bike, all the way down.

He wondered if he should try and give her an A after all.

She wasn't in class the next week and that was both a relief and mildly worrisome. He wasn't going to call her, that would have been unwise, an escalation, an admission of complicity or wrongdoing. He'd honestly been trying to help her. Maybe he'd been dumb or naive about it, but aside from providing an underaged person with alcohol (not unheard of on this campus), he'd committed no actual transgressions. It was better to leave her alone to sort herself out. Besides, he had his other students, and his own work to do, and his adviser wanting to see a new chapter, and the new chapter had to be assembled from all the bits and pieces strewn around his carrel in the library.

The weather veered back to damp and cold, and all the campus buildings smelled of wet wool. Ryan spent most of his days and nights at the library, getting back into the rhythm of work, the satisfactions of actual work. It reminded him of running track, of the all-out grinding, gasping effort as he approached the finish line.

He typed up his chapter and put it in his adviser's mailbox. His adviser was also the lecturer for the discussion section Ryan taught. The adviser called the next day and asked to see him. This was unheard-of promptness. It made him nervous. He wondered if he'd made some obvious, jackass mistake in his research or his assumptions, even plagiarized by mistake.

Ryan knocked on his adviser's door and was told to enter. The director of graduate studies was there as well.

He hadn't wanted to believe until now that this had anything to do with Megan.

They told him to sit down. There were two stapled pages on his adviser's desk. Everything else around it had been cleared away. Go ahead, they told him. Read it.

## WHY I WANT TO KILL THE PRESIDENT

Megan O'Brien
Poli Sci 150
Final Paper

In Mr. Erickson's class he talked about how everybody in America is one of two things, either in or out. The people who are out are all the minority people including women. Also poor people. So all the in people are white men. Although Mr. Erickson is a white man himself he thinks this is a problem.

In our system of government, the President is the most in of anyone in our country. Although we have other branches of government they are not as important and so people who are looking to change the government do not kill them as often.

I am of Korean heritage. This in itself is not a big deal. Although my being adopted sometimes is. Mr. Erickson has pointed out that this is not a normal situation and I would be expected to have a lot of problems. This is true but not for the reasons Mr. Erickson says. Korean people have a very strong sense of inferiority complex due to being occupied by the Japanese for fifty years. Although they have many sayings that are symbols of their endurance in the face of obstacles, such as "A living dog is better than a dead dignitary."

Mr. Erickson said that it is only natural for the out people to dislike the in people and want to kill them. This is the basis for political science. We are all a part of political science whether we want to be or not. Everything can be explained by it.

If I killed the President, people would probably think I was crazy, like the latest person who tried to. That person thought he would be good at it but he wasn't. But it would really be because in our system of government we can never change who we are born as. If you kill the President, there will be another President in his place. The rest of us, it's just the one person and nobody will miss them.

Ryan put the pages back on the center of the clean desk. They were waiting for him to say something. His silence buzzed and flattened in his ears. He said, "She was supposed to be writing about checks and balances in the constitutional system."

His adviser asked what he made of this, then.

"I don't know. Maybe she was having some kind of a breakdown."

"Her parents called the Dean of Students office yesterday. They're very concerned."

He thought he should ask why, and if she was all right, but his adviser was speaking again. He seemed to be embarrassed at the necessity of asking such questions, the inevitable air of prosecution. "Why don't you tell us about Ms. O'Brien. How was she doing in the class? I don't suppose you brought your gradebook with you?"

Ryan had not. He noticed that the director of graduate studies was taking notes.

He told them that Ms. O'Brien had been an average student. No serious problems. But she had been very anxious about her grade. He had talked with her about it and tried to give her some guidance.

Just what sort of guidance?

Encouraged her to participate more in class. Helped her with her paper.

That part hadn't worked out so well, had it?

No, sir. He couldn't say that it had.

They had several decisions to make. Ryan should understand that these were serious matters. Killing the president, threatening to kill the president. They had to decide if the police should be involved, if other investigative agencies should be involved. This was not something to be easily dismissed, given the recent events. Even if Ms. O'Brien had only been trying to . . . what did he think she was trying to do, anyway?

Ryan told them he couldn't say. He wondered where Megan was, and if they'd already talked to her. She must have turned in her obscene joke of a paper directly to the professor. That was enough to tell him that the paper was only *meant* to sound as if she were crazy. What she was really trying to do was wreck him.

He thought he could convince them that he had not spoken approvingly of political assassination or urged his students to practice it. It was everything else that stung. *We are all a part of political science whether we want to be or not. Everything can be explained by it.* How easily he had been made to sound like an idiot.

They kept him there for more than an hour. The matter of her visits to his apartment. He didn't deny that they had happened, did he? Extremely poor judgment on his part. As for what he had said in class. Of course they knew he had been misunderstood. (It was beginning to feel to Ryan as if he himself was accused of trying to kill the president.) Of course he had the absolute right and freedom to express his own views. The university supported and protected that right. But there was the possiblity that the student's parents might make difficulties. He should be prepared to answer questions, give some sort of statement if necessary. For the time being, that is, for the rest of the term, it would be best if his teaching duties were assigned to someone else. They were not passing judgment. It was for everyone's protection, including his own.

Ryan said, "If I'd had sex with her, and given her an A in exchange, like she wanted, none of this would be happening."

Further embarrassment on their part. They had been hoping to avoid anything unpleasant. Hoped that he would be mortified enough to go along with everything and allow them to be the chickenshits they had decided to be. He was only a graduate student. His insignificant rights and freedoms more easily dispensed with. Megan's parents must have made some first-rate threats. Sue the university for indoctrinating students in violent anarchy? Sue him for either molesting their daughter or failing to do so? Ryan said, "You know, we were talking about this the other day in class. The difference between stated ideals and actualities. Lip service, it's called."

Their faces hardened. Ryan stood. "Would you excuse me?" And then, because he needed something else to propel him out the door, he said, "Personal experience and personal grievance inevitably expand outward into the public sphere. Boy, do they ever."

He left the professor's office and climbed the two flights of stairs to the office he shared with four other graduate students. No one else was in and he closed the door behind him and sat at the desk.

The self he had created was dissolving along with the life that had sustained it. *In our system of government we can never change who we are born as.* Now he would be neither teacher nor student. He would begin again, in perfect ignorance.

# *Iowa*

APRIL 1983

Before you got married, before you had any idea of who it would be, or how it would all come about, there was curiosity but also a kind of dread, in case you might not be able to pull it off. That happened to people sometimes; they held out too long, or got their hopes set on someone who disappointed them, or maybe they lost their nerve. Anita had known that when it came to marrying, something remarkable was expected of her. It was a small town, and girls like her were burdened with everyone's admiration and spite. And so it was a relief to choose, to be chosen. It calmed something in her, but as time went on, she began to wonder why it had all seemed so important.

Mornings were her mother's favorite time to call, no matter how often, or in how many ways, Anita let her know it was inconvenient. Either Anita had just arrived home after taking Matthew to kindergarten, and the baby had fallen asleep in the car, and it was her one chance to go back to sleep herself. Or else, since Matthew only went to school three mornings a week, she had both of them home and needing one thing or another, a snack or a diaper change, or Matthew attempting to bury his sister in stuffed animals, as he was doing now.

"Stop that," Anita told him, removing a plush frog from the screaming child's face. "What are you trying to do, smother her?"

"We're playing."

"Well she doesn't want to play like that. Go watch *Ninjas.*"

"They're over." Matthew, sulky now. He never had any fun.

"Well go watch something." The phone rang. The baby's face purpled with new, redoubled fury. Anita found the pacifier and tried to get the baby to close her mouth around it. "Go!" she said to Matthew, who was hanging in the doorway to see if he could get into further interesting trouble.

On the third try she got the baby to take the pacifier and dove for the phone just before it went to the answering machine. Her mother didn't like the answering machine and refused to leave messages. She would either keep calling back or, if Anita really wasn't there, she might start calling the neighbors, as she'd done on a couple of occasions.

"Hi Mom."

"Now how did you know it was me? Someday you're going to answer the phone that way, and it's going to be somebody else, somebody important, and you'll be sorry."

"Nobody important ever calls here." The baby was quiet, chomping down on the pacifier. Anita walked into the TV room to check on Matthew. At least she could do things while she talked, try to put the house back together.

"Are you all right, honey? You sound upset."

Her mother always said something solicitous. If Anita ever tried to sound normal, neutral, happy, her mother asked her if she was mad about something. "No, it's nothing. Marcie was pitching a fit, but she stopped."

"Mar-cie!" her mother sang through the phone. "Marcie monkey!"

Anita and the baby looked at each other. Anita thought it was a sad, wised-up look. "She must have heard you, Mom. She's smiling."

Her mother sighed. "You have to bring them up here. It's been so long."

"I will, Mom. Some weekend when we can see Dad too." It was always easier with her father there. He helped keep the lid on things.

"We could—," her mother began, but somewhere in the background a racket started up, a voice without words, high, harsh, changing pitch like a siren, breaking into a sustained sobbing. "I have to go, honey. It's one of her bad days. Love you."

"Love you," Anita said back, but her mother had already hung up.

Anita put Marcie in her crib and wound up the teddy-bear mobile. Tinkly music played as the bears went round and round. She told Matthew that if he got out of his pajamas and put his clothes on, he could have more juice, and that he should take the clothes out of his dresser, not the dirty ones on the closet floor. Then she sat down at the kitchen table with that morning's *Des Moines Register* spread out in front of her. Her mother had not yet read the paper, or else she would surely have called with something to say about it. Anita lived half an hour away from the town where she'd grown up, and usually this was far enough, but not always.

## FT. DODGE MAN KILLS FAMILY, BANKER, SELF

The man in Ft. Dodge had farmed wheat and corn and kept a small herd of pastured cattle. He had taken a pistol and shot his wife, his eight-year-old son, his three-year-old daughter, and the dog. He had used a rifle to kill the cattle. He had driven his truck into town and gone into the bank that was about to foreclose on him, walked up to where the loan officer was sitting at his desk, and shot him through the head. He was on his way to the Farmers Home Administration office when two sheriff's cars caught up with him. He'd stopped the truck in the middle of the street and put the pistol in his own mouth.

It wasn't the first such story, but it was the first time they'd shot the banker too.

Jeff got home late that night. Anita had fed the kids and run the dishwasher. She'd put Jeff's dinner in the oven and watched from the front windows as it got dark. She turned off the oven and tried to call the bank, but of course everyone there was long gone. Matthew asked where Daddy was and she said she didn't know. He started whining and she told him to go to his room. Muffled thuds came from behind his closed door. He was throwing different toys against the walls.

It was almost eight by the time Jeff's car pulled into the garage. Anita hadn't wanted the first words out of her mouth to be *Where have you been?* but of course that was what she ended up saying.

Jeff said he'd had to work late and yes he should have called but he hadn't expected things to go so late and not to start in on him. He had the peevish expression that meant he knew he was at fault. If he ever had an affair, she figured she'd know just from watching him be furious.

She didn't start in. She waited until he'd seen the kids and got his first drink working and was sitting at the kitchen table eating his dinner of dry chicken and lima beans and rice and she said, "I was worried that somebody might have shot you."

He looked at her with his cheeks puffed out, full of food. She said, "Like they shot the banker in Ft. Dodge. A farmer shot him because the bank foreclosed on him."

Jeff chewed and swallowed. "What did you do to this rice? It tastes funny."

"You heard me."

"That was Ft. Dodge. It doesn't have anything to do with me."

"You foreclose on people too."

"I don't, the bank does." Jeff finished off the chicken and left the rest of the food on the plate.

The baby started fussing in her crib and Anita had to get up to tend to her, and then to tell Matthew to brush his teeth. She got everyone settled and went into the TV room, where Jeff was sorting through papers from his briefcase and keeping an eye on the television. They'd got cable, and now he could watch sports of one kind or another anytime he wanted.

Anita sat on the couch, the end closest to the television so it would be easiest for him to look at her. "Could you help me understand something? What's the matter with the farmers, why are they all having so much trouble?"

"Not all of them. Just the ones who can't pay their loans."

"All right, why can't they pay their loans? Come on. I really want to know about this."

He did look at her then, trying to measure her intent. She said, "After all, they're the same farms they've always been. Same crops, right? What happened?"

"They took out more loans because money was cheaper a few years back. And crop prices were higher. Land values were higher. Now that's all changed."

"Money was cheaper?" she ventured.

"Interest rates were lower. That's what banks do, you know that, charge interest."

She did know that. But she'd never really had to know much more. She got up from the couch and started for the kitchen. Jeff reached out and caught her around the hip with one hand. "Sorry I was late tonight."

"All right."

His hand reached down, patted once, twice. "Don't worry about all that. I need you to focus on the kids, worry about them."

"All right."

She wasn't stupid. She hadn't been one of the brainy kids at school, but she hadn't wanted to be. There hadn't been any real reward in it that she could see, and besides, she knew plenty of day-to-day things that were more interesting and useful to her. Sometimes she thought that having children made you dumber, at least while they were small, just because you could get by on mental autopilot, coaxing, threatening, laboring. You were only as smart as you had to be. But she wasn't so stupid that she couldn't follow explanations, if people bothered to make them.

Jeff's bank was in the news a great deal even without anyone's getting shot. His was just a branch bank of the main bank, Citizens Reserve and Trust headquartered in Omaha. Citizens Reserve had made farm loans over four different states, and enough of them had gone bad that if you drove very far in any direction, you were sure to see the bank's green-and-white sign posted on acreage. They owned land everywhere, like a Monopoly game.

Twice a year Jeff traveled to Omaha for business, and on other occasions the Omaha people came into town themselves. Those were evenings when they got a babysitter and Anita had her hair done and put on whatever was best in her closet and accompanied Jeff out to the steak house the Omaha people preferred. Although it was understood that for all its etched-glass partitions and red-jacketed waiters and drinks served in fishbowl-size portions, it was and would always be inferior to the restaurants in Omaha, which served the best steaks in the world, hands down.

Anita and whichever of the wives were there made a show of being happy to see each other, and of paying each other compliments. There was unspoken competition among them and, unlike with the steaks, she wasn't going to concede. She knew she was one of Jeff's assets, the kind of wife people could imagine in Omaha, if such an opportunity were to come his way. She didn't want him to forget her worth. Even after two babies she could still put her figure to good use, squeeze herself into whatever shape was required. It hadn't been so long ago that she'd been the prettiest girl in the room, and that was still the case in many rooms.

On this evening Jeff was picking up the babysitter and then he and Anita would drive together to their dinner. Between the mayhem the kids put everyone through on such occasions, and getting herself ready, there wasn't any chance for the two of them to talk until they were in the car. "Slow down," Anita told him. He was taking the corners fast and she was sliding from one end of the seat to the other. "Jeff, come on! If they get there before us, they'll just go to the bar. It's not like they don't know the way."

He let the car decelerate. He always started out these evenings in an anxious bad mood. He said, "One of these days we're going to have to invite them to the house for dinner."

"And one of these days I'll clean the house and have it stay that way longer than fifteen minutes. My mom called today. She said to make sure to tell you about the Goodells."

"Goodells." He was trying to place them. "What about Goodells?"

"They're cousins of mine. You wouldn't know it on the face of things. But Ruth is Norm and Martha's youngest daughter."

Anita could see the names rolling around in his head, failing to catch hold. "And I need to know this why?"

"Because of their loan. There's some trouble with their loan and Mom said you probably didn't know they're family."

Jeff steered into the restaurant's parking lot. "Trouble, what, they can't get a loan? Nobody's lending anymore. Crap, is that Daniels's car? I knew we were late."

"No, the other kind of trouble."

"Huh."

"It's a Citizens Reserve loan. Mom says to tell you they just need a little more time so they can get a crop in the ground and start making payments after harvest."

"Goodell," Jeff said again. "Hamilton County."

"That's right. They're relatives."

"You're related to half the state." He eased the car into a space and shut the engine off. "Let's get a move on."

"Jeff."

"Yeah, it's been tough up in Hamilton."

"You aren't listening. You can't foreclose on my cousins, that's . . ." She tried to think what it was. "Horrible."

"It's one of those horrible facts of life."

He was impatient to get out of the car but she didn't intend to let him yet. "You seriously cannot do this."

"Not me. The bank."

"Oh, pardon me if it's hard for people to tell the difference."

"Most people," he said tightly, "don't know shit about shit."

"Funny how the guys with the guns seem to shoot the bankers, not the bank." There had been another shooting, this one in Missouri. Another family, another loan officer, all dead. The farmers were always good shots.

"That's not one bit funny."

"Wasn't meant to be."

"When's the last time you even saw these famous cousins, anyway, huh? You spend a lot of time out at the farm lately?"

Anita kept silent. Jeff opened the car door and the dome light went on, making them both blink. He said, "All right, try to understand this. None of these guys are going to be catching up on their payments. Even if they had a crop to sell, it wouldn't be worth enough to cover what they owe for seed and fertilizer and fuel and implements and whatever else they borrowed for. That crop's worth seventy-three cents less a bushel than it cost them to raise it. If your cousins or your second cousins or your third cousins once removed had their loan called, there's nothing I can do about it, they're no different than anybody else. Don't you think everybody's somebody's family? Don't you think I know that? We'll be lucky if the bank doesn't get sucked under from all the bad loans. Oh yes, that can happen. Then let's see who'll feel sorry for the likes of us. The Goodells' paperwork went out through the Omaha office and it's a done deal. They have thirty days for voluntary liquidation. Now can we please get going before Harve Daniels starts drinking his whole dinner."

What else could she do but follow him inside, through the heavy wood doors meant to suggest something or somewhere else—a castle? jolly olde England?—into the restaurant and its clubby bar, where Harve and his wife Linda were being served their second drinks. Harve was white-haired and big-bellied and supposedly a good businessman, not the fool it was so easy to mistake him for. Linda was fifteen years younger than Harve, decorated in an expensive way. She'd frosted her hair blond and got a new, tight perm and the shoulder pads of her dress stuck out like batwings and even as Anita exclaimed over how pretty Linda looked, she was thinking that after all Omaha wasn't exactly Paris, and then she thought what a waste of time it was, the sugary talk and the sizing each other up as if either of them had ever spent five minutes thinking about the other and meanwhile here was Jeff. Shaking hands and laughing and finding whole new ways of saying nothing, all meant to demonstrate that he was at his ease, a man among men, and why should he care about somebody else's grief or ruin, nothing to spoil your evening over, and she hated him. She hated him like poison.

Harve and Linda were on their way to Chicago, where they would stay in a lakefront condo and treat themselves to some world-class shopping and entertainment. Along the way they were visiting some of the branches so Harve could keep an eye on things and write the whole trip off as business.

The four of them settled into a booth and studied the menus, as if they'd changed since last time. "Chicago is amazing," Linda pronounced. "Not just the restaurants and the clubs, but all the cultural things."

Harve made his comical face. "She's always trying to get me into some museum. The only one I ever liked was whatsisname, the mummy."

"King Tut. That's because you're almost as old as a mummy, honey."

They all had to laugh at that. Anita ordered a whiskey sour, with every intention of ordering another. Usually she just sipped a glass of wine with her dinner, since once she got home there was always at least one child who had to be put back in bed, and drinking wasn't good mommy behavior. Jeff could take care of his own children for one night. She said, "Next time you're in town you'll have to come to our house for dinner. See how the other half lives."

This also was received as a witticism. Jeff said, "Seriously, we'd love to have you. Just say the word."

"Finally, we'd get to meet those precious children," Linda said, with the suspect enthusiasm of someone who had no children herself. "It's no fair, you keeping them hid all the time."

"By dinner," Anita said, "we've usually got them chained to a ring in the floor. I guess just the once we could let them out."

The server came to take their orders, and after that the talk moved on.

Anita got the petite filet and the spinach salad, as she always did. She listened to Harve tell Jeff about the prospects for recapitalization and increasing reserve levels, Jeff taking it all in as he forked up bites of steak, nodding at the wisdom and rightness of everything Harve had to say. Linda, stringy from dieting, poked at her soup-and-salad combo. Linda was in the habit of suggesting that she and Anita visit the powder room together. It was supposed to be this normal, chummy thing, two girls peeing next to each other, making an occasion of it. Why was that? She didn't even like the woman, much less want to listen to her on the toilet. What if she said no, she didn't have to go? Or bolted ahead, left Linda in her wake as she ran into the Ladies', did her thing, and met her on the way out?

She giggled, and since it fell into one of those times when everyone else was working their food over, they all looked up at her.

"What's so funny, Sunshine?" Harve asked, smiling his sportiest smile. One of the conventions of these evenings out was that Harve was meant to flirt, gallantly, with her, while Anita was sweetly over-whelmed by his attentions.

"Oh . . . ," she began. Jeff was watching her, stone-faced. The alcohol gave her a floating feeling. Nothing she said really mattered. "Do you ever worry about getting shot?"

Harve said, "Hah," a laugh reflex. You'd have to reach to make it any kind of a joke. "Well, no, should I?"

"Probably not. Omaha's so far away and it's so big, they'd really have to go out of their way. Not like around here, where everybody knows everybody who . . ." Her words were gaining ballast, sinking.

Harve reached across the table and took both her hands in his. She'd painted her nails silver just that afternoon. They caught the light like fish scales. "You're worried about Jeff, aren't you? All those nuts making speeches."

She nodded, her attention fixed on Harve's magnificent nose. So large and red and inflamed, such an intricate geography of pores and capillaries.

"Well don't you be. There's always a few dirty dogs out there, that's the way of the world. But most people understand that business is about risk, and sometimes risks just turn out bad."

"But . . ." She wanted to take her hands back but didn't think she should. "So many people, the farmers I mean, that's all they know. Farming, living on the farm. Where are they supposed to go, and who's going to grow crops if there's nobody left?" She knew she had to stop talking. Right then.

"Ah." Harve released her hands so that he could get to his drink. Anita sat back in her seat and let the hands retreat into her lap. "Here's where it helps to understand a few things about markets. The big picture. See, for everything that's bought and sold, there's a market. A buyer and a seller."

He paused to let this sink in. "Like before there were cars? There was a big market for horses. And horse feed, and horseshoers, and horse-drawn carriages, and so on. You needed to buy a horse, you went to somebody who sold horses. Then cars come along and put all those sellers out of business. But new businesses start up. Car manufacturers and repair shops and gas stations. That's progress. You couldn't stop it if you wanted to. That's easy enough to understand, right?"

"Uh-huh," Anita said. She attempted to look like a serious listener, someone who could take Harve seriously. Next to her, Jeff seemed ready to throw her coat over her head and rush her out the door if he had to. Linda allowed herself to look bored. She must have heard about horses and cars a time or two before.

"So here's your farmer, operating pretty much the same as he ever was, ever since somebody shoved a stick in the dirt, dropped in a seed, and covered it over. Oh, he's got machines, combines, better fertilizer, better crop storage. But he's got the same markets. No need to grow more if there's no place to sell it, right? Then one day that changes. He can ship his corn and wheat all the way to the great Union of Soviet Sorehead Republics, because those boys can build all the missiles in the world, but they can't feed their own people. Now wouldn't you want to buy yourself some more land, and maybe build a bigger barn, and everything else you'd need to take advantage of it?"

She wished Harve would quit asking questions she wasn't really meant to answer. But by this time he didn't seem to be talking to her as much as to some invisible audience of clearheaded visionaries, men who knew a thing or two about a thing or two. "Looking at the big picture. That's the bank's job. Because what goes up must come down. The bank makes its best guess as to how and when that's going to happen and the farmer makes his, and they do business. And some of these guys got a little greedy. Little wishful thinking. There's always winners and losers and in this particular situation, they wound up with the short end of the stick."

"The what end?" Linda asked. "I've heard this story told different."

Jeff said, "That's about the size of it, Harve. Lots of people figured they'd ride that gravy train all the way to Russia and back. They didn't count on the peanut farmer pulling the rug out from under them."

"Or on overproduction."

"Or land values dropping sixty percent."

"But we did," Harve said. "We didn't jump in with both feet, like some of these boys. We had the expertise. The smarts. Survival of the fittest. It's a natural law. Like these bigger outfits coming in now. They got the capital to buy up that acreage and they'll do a more efficient job of working those farms."

Anita cleared her throat. "So farmers are like, what, horses?"

"Don't be silly, honey." Jeff, anxious not to look like he couldn't keep his woman in line. "You're wasting your time, Harve. She's just determined to misunderstand. It's like George Burns and Gracie Allen around our house."

"No, she's right to worry, aren't you, Sunshine? All the poor farmers, they just get put out to pasture? Sent off to the glue factory? Maybe I made it sound like they didn't much matter. But that's not so and I apologize if it came out that way. You can feel sorry for each and every one of 'em and I do. Well, maybe not the real hardheaded ones who argue up and down that black is white and white is black. On an individual basis, feel as sorry as you want. But individuals are not the same thing as economics, or history, or farm policy, or the man in the moon."

Linda said, "I think we're back to the big picture. That train never left the station."

"Now you just possess your soul in patience, Linda Lou," Harve said, trying not to sound as irritated as he was. "The lady has a good heart. She has some serious questions and I'm trying to give her serious answers. Why don't you get them to bring you one of those what is it, Grand Marniers you like so much. Let me finish making my damn point." Harve paused for long enough to get his smile working again. "Any one person, there's only so much they can do when the tide starts to turn against them. Buy themselves a little more time, maybe. But the truth is, a lot of these small operators who just got by, their time is gone. They won't be farmers anymore because we don't need as many farmers. They'll find something else to do here or they'll pack up and leave. The name for it is economic dislocation, and it's a bear to live through, but it all shakes out in the end. Like all those Okies who went west in the Dust Bowl, and now they're sitting pretty out in California, hey?" Harve had managed to get himself all jollied up by now. "We should all have that kind of bad luck."

Linda said, "I guess it's our bad luck that the world always seems to need plenty of bankers."

Anita murmured that she understood a lot better now, thank you. Under the table she formed her right hand into a pistol and shot Harve, POW, in the middle of his roomy stomach. She shot Jeff, POW, straight through the heart. She aimed at Linda but then, liking her better than she had before, reconsidered and shot Jeff again.


Except for the babysitter, it was nothing she planned out ahead of time. You could never be sure if Mrs. Taub was going to be available, but she was. So Mrs. Taub tried to soothe Matthew with vanilla wafers while Matthew cried that he wanted to go too and Anita told him no, it was just for grown-ups and Matthew said *it wasn't fair.*

Then she drove around for a while. She wasn't clear in her mind what to do next. Here was Jeff's bank, and here was his big Lincoln, sitting in its reserved spot. At least she didn't have to wonder where he might be instead. Anita entered the drive-through lane, filled out a withdrawal slip, and sent it through the noisy sucking tube. She chatted with Stephanie, the teller, over the intercom, hinting that some secret or surprise was in the works, in case Stephanie might be inclined to question or comment. It was a joint account, she was entitled to draw from it, but still, it was a lot of money. Anita waved and drove away and stopped at the branch facility next to the Pic N Save. Here she went inside and withdrew an equal amount, waited on by a young and heavyset teller who either did not recognize her or pretended not to, and so she had $5,000 in cash in her purse when she left town and headed north on the highway.

She felt like a bank robber. Technically, it was her own money. But all the money was really Jeff's.

First week of May. A bright, cool day with the wind from the west and the edges of the farm fields greening up. Anita thought, *I can just go there. I don't have to stay. I don't even have to talk to anybody.*

It took her a while to find the Goodells' place. She couldn't remember the last time she'd been there, or even driven past it. But here it was, the old yellow farmhouse set back from the road and, in front of it, the mobile home they'd put up for Bradley and his family. The lane and farmyard were packed with cars and trucks, and a flatbed trailer was pulled up in front of the barn for the auctioneer's use.

The wind was a lot stronger and colder out here in the open. She had to park some distance down the lane and then pick her way along the ruts and the mud from the last rain. Although she'd worn a hooded navy sweatshirt and jeans, outdoor clothes, she hadn't given much thought to shoes, and her flats slipped and twisted on the uneven ground. Once she got closer, she didn't see anyone she recognized, but she had a feeling that plenty of people there knew who she was.

Citizens Reserve must have sent a man out from Omaha to represent them as mortgagee. Anita's fear all along was that Jeff would be there, would have to be there. But someone, maybe Jeff, must have thought better of that. She didn't know this Omaha man but it wasn't hard to spot him. He'd dressed down in a windbreaker and khakis, but he was still the only man there not wearing a hat. He was drinking coffee from a styrofoam cup and talking to a sheriff's deputy.

Two more deputies were lounging around at the auctioneer's stand, and she wondered about them. Nobody in the crowd looked ready to do anything illegal, or even anything very loud. They stood at the edges, as Anita was herself; a few of the men walked among the lots of machinery and tools set out for sale, and in and out of the barn. Anita couldn't remember, if she'd ever known in the first place, if the Goodells kept any livestock. She hoped not. She'd never liked being around farm animals of any sort. They were so helplessly stupid, they made you feel as if eating them was some kind of a charitable act.

The Goodells and Peersons had been off to one side near the farmhouse's front steps, and once Anita positioned herself to get out of the wind, she saw them: Ruth and Jim, who must have been about her parents' age, and the younger kids who still lived at home, and Bradley and his wife and baby, and others of the Peersons.

It was a sad, bad feeling to stand there by herself. She'd always thought that family was family, and that had to count for something. Even as she'd lived her life apart from them, even though at times she had been embarrassed by them.

Her cousin Pat saw her then, and Anita watched her eyes narrow, then she said something to Ruth, who looked Anita's way also, and then Pat began walking toward her. Anita thought she might as well get it over with.

Pat halted a little distance away. She was wearing a plaid wool jacket and denim pants and an old stocking cap. She'd never had one bit of vanity to her. "Hello, Anita."

She didn't sound either friendly or unfriendly, but then, she never did. "Hi, Pat. I guess I . . ." Anita stopped, shrugged. "How are Ruth and Jim?"

"You're free to ask them yourself."

"I wasn't sure if I should."

Pat let this remark settle. She turned away to gaze out over the crowd. The auctioneer was getting set up. He had a microphone hooked up to an amplifier and speakers. The wire that plugged it all in coiled and trailed back to the barn. A loud electrified squeak made everyone look up. Pat said, "They'll be glad to have it over with."

"I tried talking to my husband."

Pat turned back to her. She'd reached that point in aging where the markers of sex begin to fade. Her forehead and jaw could have belonged to an old man. "Always nice, when a married couple talks to each other."

"You know what I mean."

"That it didn't do much good?" It wasn't ever easy to read shades of mood or meaning into Pat, but she sounded tired, and mad on top of tired. "Nobody really thinks this is your fault, Nita. Plenty of them think it's Jeff's. I guess I'm one of them."

"Everybody acts like I can get him to do things and I can't." Anita was struck by the truth of this. He'd never done anything she'd ever wanted, except grudgingly, and out of a vast reluctance.

Pat said, "I guess it's not really about any one person. Anything one person can do when everything's got so wrongheaded."

Anita didn't know whom she meant by this. Jeff? Pat herself? The Goodells? She'd never before thought of herself as helpless, if only because, growing up, she had always been able to get pretty much whatever she wanted. But she had confused that with having any real power in the world.

Pat said, "They were late one payment, and that gave the bank the right to call all their loans. They had four loans with the interest gone up to eighteen percent. Nobody could pay that off unless corn turned into gold."

*It wasn't fair.* Maybe when you were a child, or for a little while longer, you thought that as soon as you pointed unfairness out, a swift and righteous justice would prevail.

The Goodells were grouped on their front stairs as if someone were about to take their picture for a Christmas card. Except that this was spring, not winter, and not a one of their faces showed anything open or pleased. They looked flattened, incurious, as if all this were happening to somebody else. Anita said, "I don't see why they won't let them stay in the houses, at least. A new owner could farm the place even with them here."

"Not the way it works. Everything goes to the debt." Pat nodded at a long table set out at one side of the barn. It held odds and ends of household goods: some Blue Willow china, a lamp with a rose-painted globe, an empty picture frame, a pile of what appeared to be ruffled kitchen curtains. "Pitiful, ain't it. Pull somebody's life up by the roots and set it out for everybody to paw over."

Anita knew then why they were having a conversation in the first place. Pat was furious, and the fury had to come out of her as talk, and Anita was one person who hadn't yet heard it from her. She felt inside her purse and touched the wads of money still in their bank envelopes. Five thousand dollars. Not nearly enough to buy a life back. Pat went on, "Besides, they wouldn't want to stay. They're at our place for now. Bradley and his, they might end up in Sioux City, there's one of Jim's cousins can get him on at ConAgra."

"Why can't they farm Norm and Martha's old place? Wouldn't that do for them?"

Pat gave her a measuring look. "We sold it off more than a year ago. All of us got a share. It wasn't much. Didn't your mother tell you?"

If she had, Anita didn't remember it, or maybe hadn't paid attention.

The speakers squealed again and the auctioneer's amplified voice told them they were just about to start up here, folks, give us a couple more minutes. The crowd stirred, a murmur of talk going through it. Anita asked about the deputies.

"I guess they're worried about the Posse Comitatus people." When Anita shook her head, not understanding, Pat said, "Posse Comitatus. They been kicking up trouble different places, Nebraska, the Dakotas. They say that the government doesn't have any right to tell us what to do, and we're all what they call sovereign citizens, and we don't have to have driver's licenses or pay taxes. Don't have to deal with Farmers Home. Don't have to pay bank loans because the government insures the banks. They got some such answer for everything. Wish they would show up here. Or somebody raise some heck. Back in the Depression they had what they called nickel auctions. Neighbors show up and bid a penny or a nickel on everything. Keep anybody else from bidding higher. Then give it all back to the owner. Used to be farmers, big groups of them, show up at the courthouses with ropes slung over their shoulders. Give the sheriff something to think about. I guess that was then and this is now. Well, I better go back and see about Ruth and Jim."

"I would like to say hello. If you think it would be all right."

"You're here, aren't you? At least that's something."

She followed Pat across the yard, pushing through the crowd of waiting men. The Goodells watched her coming. Ruth had been the prettiest of Norm and Martha's children and she still had a worn-down kind of good looks. Jim Goodell was a big man, heavy in the shoulders. The skin of his face and neck had thickened from windburn and every other weather and you couldn't read expression in it any more than you could a piece of corrugated cardboard. But there wasn't any welcome in it. Other men were grouped around him. Some she recognized—Ruth and Pat's brothers and their sons—most she didn't.

Anita stood in front of them. Nobody spoke until Anita said, "Hi, Ruth. Jim. I just wanted to . . ." She trailed off.

Pat said, "She didn't have to come," and Ruth unbent enough to nod at her. Then it was all right, or at least, all right enough for her to stand there with them. Two of the youngest boys were slinging pebbles at the wall of a shed, making a racket when they hit. On any other occasion, they might have been told to stop. Bradley stood a little distance away with his wife, whom Anita didn't know. She was a pretty girl with red hair, holding a bundled baby, and she looked mutinous, as if she was beginning to figure out she wasn't going to end up with the life she'd thought she was getting. Bradley didn't seem to be paying her any mind. He leaned against one corner of the front porch. A skinny, slouching man, only a few years younger than Anita herself. Already he had the closed-up face he'd wear until the end of his days. His two sisters, teenagers, folded their arms against the wind and seemed to dare people to look at them. It wasn't a family who appeared to be taking any comfort from each other.

Ruth said, "We don't have to stay and watch, do we? I could go on back with Melissa and the baby."

Her husband said, "Just wait," and Ruth went to hold the baby and allow the redheaded girl to rummage in the diaper bag for something she couldn't find, which seemed to put her in an even worse mood.

The auctioneer had a spry, high-pitched voice. He made a few remarks designed to jolly the crowd up, to no visible effect. The machinery was going first. A Massey Ferguson diesel tractor, a six-row cultivator, eight-row planter, hay baler, corn picker, sprayer, grain wagons. One of the men next to Jim Goodell said, loud enough for everybody to hear, "Might as well drive everything over to the bank. Ask 'em where they want it parked." Anita didn't look at him. She thought it had probably been said for her benefit.

The auctioneer slid into his chant. What am I bid, what am I bid, three now four now four bid I got it, how 'bout five, five, five and a half, who's got six, six, here's a six bid, will you give me seven, I need seven. It was all too fast to follow, nor could Anita understand who was bidding on what in the crowd grouped around the microphone, different men holding up bid cards, runners going back and forth among them.

Pat was still standing next to her and Anita nudged her, tried to whisper. "Can anybody bid? What do you have to do to get him to see you?"

"Another time might be better for explanations."

"No, I have some money." It embarrassed her, having to come out and say it. "I brought some money." She opened her purse and watched Pat's eyes lock onto the tidy stacks of bills.

Pat took her by the arm and steered her away from the crowd. "Why is it you want to bid on farm machinery?"

"I don't." Exasperated now, because everyone seemed so willing to misunderstand her and think the worst. "It's for them, I want to give it to them."

Pat shook her head. "Just because you feel bad about—"

"The money doesn't care how anybody feels."

"They won't take it from you."

"Well then you take it for them. Here." She pulled the bank envelopes out and reached for Pat's wrist, shoving the money at her. "I'm not leaving here with it. Either take it or watch me start throwing handfuls up in the air."

Pat let her hand close around it. "Where did this come from?"

"I stopped by the bank."

"Nita."

"You can get some of their things back. Or they can just have it. You decide. I'm going now. I don't need or want to hear about it later."

She turned and started walking away. No one called or came after her.

At the start of the lane she stopped and looked back. She could make out Pat's stocking cap bent over the table where the auctioneer's agents were doing business, and then Pat straightened and joined the bidding crowd. The Goodells had moved in closer to take a look, all except the red-haired girl, still tending to her baby on the steps, maybe wondering just how much a husband was meant to bind you up in a shared loyalty.

She was tired, and chilled from the wind, and too much had happened and she wanted to think about nothing at all. But that was not possible once she reached the place where she'd parked and saw the station wagon listing with one side higher than the other, sunk into a deep rut, all four tires slashed and flattened.

# Reno, Nevada

## JUNE 1985

He was supposed to meet Chip at eight o'clock in the Horseshoe Lounge of the MGM Grand, and since it was now past eight thirty, Ryan wondered how much longer he should wait before he gave it up as a bad job. The lounge was decorated in a style he thought of as faux classy, with club chairs and thick carpeting underfoot and swagged draperies over the walls where there would have been windows, if the Grand had such a thing as windows. The bar itself was horseshoe-shaped. Horseshoes decorated the cocktail napkins, the waitresses' frilly garters, the gold-flecked mirrors mounted above each booth. The room was lit with strips of pinkish orange neon, lurid and overcozy. The cocktail waitresses' long tan legs showed black, their smiles blue. Ryan ordered a second Scotch and soda, one he didn't really want. He guessed he both did and didn't want to see his cousin. Either way would be fine, either way would be something of a disappointment.

Two of his coworkers came into the lounge then, spotted him and headed over. "Erickson," said one. "You can run, but you can't hide." They were both very drunk.

"I'm not doing either."

"We're doing both." Something about this was funny; they sniggered.

"What happened?"

"She wasn't a hooker like genius boy here thought."

"Uh-oh."

"Yes she was. Just stuck up about it."

"You guys are assholes," Ryan said, meaning it but keeping his tone friendly.

"Thank you."

"You know the great thing about this place? You can reset your circadian rhythms. Everything's open 24/7."

"We have to be on the convention floor in twelve hours," Ryan reminded them.

"Yes Mom."

"Everything you need under one roof the size of three football stadiums."

"Is it raining? Somebody said it might be raining."

"We could, you know, actually go outside and see."

"No, let's read about it in the newspaper or watch it on television."

They high-fived. Ryan said, "You should stay inside. Definitely."

"You know what your problem is, Erickson? You lack a lighthearted quality."

"Weight of the fucking world on your shoulders."

"Yeah, man. Always so serious."

"Compared to you guys," Ryan said, "I probably am. But I'm going to try and be more like you from now on."

"Did we order drinks yet? I can't remember."

"You know what I really feel like? Steak and eggs. Maybe a little keno."

After they left, Ryan resettled himself, lifted his drink and put it down again. It was the night before the start of a three-day convention. By day three he imagined his colleagues would have achieved some otherworldly state, some nirvana of debauchery. It was true he didn't drink much these days, or do much of anything else in the way of vices. Sometimes he couldn't believe how boring he was.

The cocktail waitress had made another two passes, asking if he

156                                    JEAN THOMPSON

needed anything else—the drink he hadn't drunk freshened—when he became pretty sure the man sitting at the end of the bar was his cousin Chip.

Ryan stood and made his way toward him. It must have been more than ten years since they'd seen each other. If this really was Chip (hard to see anything clearly in the lurid, unnatural light), some things about him had changed and some things hadn't. Which he guessed was true of himself as well, and a part of him watched himself advance, across the room and through time.

His cousin swung around on his barstool as Ryan approached. "Man," Chip said. "Somebody's been living right."

"I guess you mean the shoes."

"They're some really nice shoes," Chip said, with apparent sincerity.

They shook hands. Ryan took the stool next to Chip and there was a moment of settling in when they didn't have any need to talk and could get used to the idea of each other. He was trying not to scrutinize Chip and instead sorted through his first impressions. Cigarette pack at the ready. Hair cut short and receding into a widow's peak. A permanent-looking slouch, as if he lived somewhere without any such thing as a straight chair. Where did he live, anyway? There had been only a post office box and the briefest of notes back and forth, Ryan saying he'd be in town and suggesting they meet. What he got back was a postcard of a jackalope and Chip's enthusiastically scrawled *Yes*.

Chip said, "This has got to be the weirdest fucking thing in the world, you know? Meeting up here of all places. Two Iowa kids, hanging out in the lap of luxury."

"That what it is?"

"Nah, more like the armpit. And maybe not really luxury." Chip laughed his stuttering laugh. That, at least, had not changed. "Yeah, I never come in the casinos." Chip took a drink from the beer in front of him, looked at it critically. "There's cheaper bars."

"I'd hope so."

"And things like grocery stores and post offices and muffler shops, you know, a real city. The casinos, they aren't just fake. They're like, fake elevated into an art form."

Ryan said he couldn't disagree with that. The open doors of the lounge led directly out to the casino floor, where people crowded around the gaming tables and slots, everyone milling and pushing, like hell's own idea of fun.

Chip tapped a cigarette out of his pack. "Lost much yet?"

"Twenty-five on slots, a hundred and fifty at blackjack," Ryan admitted.

"Ah, that's small change. I bet you're good for a lot more."

He was. "I guess it doesn't have that much appeal for me."

"Small-town boy's not into the bright lights."

That struck Ryan as an annoying thing to say, as if skanky old Chip was calling him some kind of hick. Now that Ryan's eyes were used to the pinkish glow, he saw that Chip looked older than he would have expected. His face had a dry, seamed look that spoke of heat and sun. Ryan said, "So what are you doing out here? Why Reno?"

"No. You first. What's 'information technology'?"

"Short answer? Computers. We're the guys who talk to computers in computer language. We program the machines so they do what somebody wants them to. Keep track of inventory, sales, money. Come up with new things for them to do. It's kind of cool because it's always changing, the systems get better and better, so there's always more to learn," Ryan finished up, aware that he was dumbing down his talk. Most people couldn't follow the details of what he did anyway.

"Weren't you going to school somewhere, so you could be a big smarty-pants?"

"That kind of fell by the wayside." He didn't feel like dredging it up, explaining. How naive he'd been, naive being a nicer way of saying dumb, to think that *ideas* could protect you from the world's catastrophes, or from cruelty or unfairness or your own vanity. "Anyway, the money's better."

It was a lot better. He'd never made this much money, enough to allow him to spend without worrying. He belonged to a downtown health club where members could gather in the attached bar and admire each other's pumped-up and burnished physique. He had mutual funds that were paying off every quarter. He had a two-bedroom condo in Lincoln Park. He bought what he felt like at the grocery, cheeses whose names he couldn't pronounce, fancy prepared dinners from the gourmet counter. He had a company expense account for conventions such as this one. It felt unnatural, even sinful at times, to have so much money—small-town boy lives fast life in big city! Pleasure, the devil's tool!—but everyone else he knew was living the same way, making money at jobs that hadn't existed a few years back, and it would have been foolish to pretend he was any different or better.

He said to Chip, "Your parents were glad to get word of you. Said you'd been out of touch for a pretty good spell."

Chip let that one pass. Ryan guessed he'd had his reasons for staying away and staying hard to find. He didn't exactly look like he'd come up in the world. Chip said, "I was sorry to hear about your sister."

"Thanks." Ryan felt some part of himself tighten, then fall away.

"How's she doing these days?"

"Not great. Not terrible." Not herself. Not recognizably anyone else.

"Is she—"

"Is it OK if we don't talk about her? I mean, not right now."

"Sure, man. Sorry."

Ryan felt Chip watching him as he stared into the gaudy complications behind the bar, the backlit shelves of stacked glassware and liqueur bottles, things nobody ever drank, like Chartreuse and Benedictine. "Hey," Chip said. "You done with that one? How 'bout we take a walk? This place makes me feel like I'm inside somebody's damned rib cage."

The casino floor was brighter and much noisier than the lounge, and Ryan tried to get his eyes and ears up to speed. "Would you look at all this," he said, giving up on any better effort to try and fix it with words. A huge expanse of green felt tables and chandeliers and its multitude of little figures engaged in their separate dramas—fanning cards, throwing dice, acting out pantomimes of winning and losing. Here two old men in cowboy hats and worn-down boots and bolo ties, small-time ranchers on a holiday, Ryan guessed, joined the crowd around a blond woman got up in a pink satin cowgirl outfit, all fringe and sequined stars and white chaps, who was using a microphone to promote some upcoming stage extravaganzas. A pack of Japanese businessmen in dark suits had taken over a blackjack table. There were junketing senior citizens, bikers, women who might have been hookers—he could understand the confusion—women who might have been men, and hard-eyed men who might have been cops, or else convicts.

"You been downstairs yet?" Chip asked. "Come on, you got to see Metro."

"Metro?" Ryan repeated, deafened. His ears were still full of din.

"Yeah, you can't say you were at the Grand until you see Metro. He's the lion."

"I thought you never came here," Ryan said, still trying to make sense of what Chip was saying. Lion?

"Got to make an exception for Metro." Chip led him down an escalator. The moving stairs and the echoing racket gave Ryan a feeling of vertigo, floating between two spaces. He was able to notice more about Chip now without being obvious. He was dressed like a bum, there was no other way to say it, in wash pants of industrial green, a flapping shirt with a faint plaid pattern over a white T-shirt. On his feet, gnarled flat sandals with leather toe rings. He looked down on his luck and used to being that way.

The basement level was a shopping arcade of sorts with a floor of gleaming tile. Signs directed them to the beauty and barber shops, a bowling alley. Store windows displayed clothing whose only real purpose was to look expensive: sporty cashmere blazers trimmed in gold buttons, pearl necklaces, suave leather handbags, golf and tennis outfits in candy colors. It was less crowded than the casino floor upstairs and it was easier to make themselves heard. "Why a lion?"

"Come on, man, MGM? You ever go to the movies? The part at the beginning where the lion roars? They got a whole movie theater down here, show stuff like *Doctor Zhivago*." Chip picked up the pace. "Here you go. Here's the guy."

The lion reclined on a mat of artificial grass like an indoor putting green, like the unnatural irrigated lawns they favored in these parts. A collar around the lion's neck was secured to a cement post with loops of chain. More posts and a waist-high Plexiglas barrier kept him well away from any crowds, but still, it was closer to a lion than Ryan guessed he'd ever been. The lion had a shabby look. His mane reminded Ryan of ancient fur coats stored in mothballs. His muzzle was gray and he blinked without looking at anything around him. Just another day at the lion office, his expression seemed to say.

"They keep him pretty stoned," Chip said. "Plus he's kind of old."

A couple of lion handlers—*lion tamers* didn't seem accurate—in khaki shirts and pants were stationed at either end of the glass, trying to look alert and vigilant. "Old Metro," Chip said. "He was born in a zoo. Never known much of anything different. Now he's a big corporate symbol. And he's bored as fuck. Isn't that perfect?"

"Chip? What's up with you?"

His cousin turned toward him, a leftover smile on his face. "What?"

"Are you OK? You don't look so OK."

"Ray."

"What?"

"I go by Ray now. 'Chip' is a little boy's name."

"That's going to take me a little while to get used to."

"Feel free to start anytime."

"Ray," Ryan said, trying it out.

"See, that's not so hard. You ever get back there much? The old hometown?"

"Holidays, mostly. Thanksgiving, Christmas." His mother usually started in on him around August, trying to extract promises.

"I think I was born there by accident. You know? I can't make any sense of it. Like Superman's spaceship landing in the Kents' cornfield."

Chip laughed. His laugh always sounded fake. "Not that I'm, you know, Superman."

Metro the Lion yawned. He lowered his head and began chewing on one of his front legs. He worked away at it, making wet, repulsive sounds, then tore loose a patch of fuzzy hair that floated loose.

Chip—it wasn't going to be easy to think of him as anyone else—said, "They have this lion ranch a few miles out of town. Sometimes he gets to go hang out there with his lion girlfriends."

Ryan thought maybe the lion was OK with being a corporate stooge. He got regular meals and his own personal assistants. He'd probably lived longer than most lions in the wild, and he'd avoided the humiliation of younger, hipper lions running him off. He showed up for work when he had to and he slept well at night. He had a certain amount of job security.

Chip nodded to the lion attendants. "Hey man. How's that tooth doing?"

"Lots better," one of them said, in the cautious, officially friendly manner of someone who was used to dealing with people who looked like Chip.

"Glad to hear it." To Ryan he said, "He had an abscess. The lion," Chip explained. "They had to bring in a team from U.C. Davis vet school. It was on the news. You imagine being the guy who sticks his hand in that mouth and starts in with the drill?"

Ryan said he couldn't. "When did you change over to Ray?"

"While back. You blame me? Would you want to be fifty, sixty years old and have to answer to Chip?" They were walking again, Chip leading the way. His walk was still loose and careless, just a bit more sore-footed. "You can get jobs at the lion ranch, maintenance, grounds jobs. I'm going to try and get on. Call home and tell my folks I work with lions. Wouldn't that freak them out?"

"Sure. Why lions? What's the big draw?"

"Well I'm a Leo. My astrological sign, ruled by the sun." Chip nodded to emphasize the significance of this. "Always loved the sun. I come here and I find out I'm like, a natural desert rat. All those years freezing my ass off. Even when it's cold here, it's a mountain kind of cold. Totally different."

Ryan guessed he wasn't going to come any closer to solving the grubby mystery that was his cousin. He was wondering if there was a way to give Chip money without its seeming crude or hurtful.

"So, do you have a car?" Chip asked. "A rental?"

Ryan said that he did. "You need a ride somewhere?"

"I was just thinking, if you have any time when you don't have to do convention stuff, you and me could take a drive. Show you around a little. You don't want to spend your whole trip hanging around this place, do you?"

"I don't know, Ray"—he managed the name—"I probably better wait and see how it goes. We have to meet clients, do a bunch of demonstrations, things like that." It was best to get those excuses right out there. "Though it'd be great to see some of the place. Reno, what do they call it, 'the Biggest Little City in the World'?" He'd seen it on the postcards they put in the hotel room. He didn't really get it.

"I always thought you and me should go someplace together."

Ryan kept walking. Cautious. "Yeah?"

"Like, a road trip. Bust loose. See the world."

"Yeah?" Ryan said again. "That would have been something." He was trying to imagine a time, past or present, when such a thing would have occurred to him, would have seemed like any kind of a good idea.

"Because you were like me, you had that same spirit in you, you didn't want to hang around with the home folks watching paint dry. You knew there was more out there."

"I guess so. Sure." They were standing at the foot of another escalator, ready to go up. The noise of the casino sounded like the crowd at a distant football game, or the tiny screaming of people trapped by some catastrophe, fire or shipwreck.

"You ever spend any time in the desert? They got one here."

He never had. *I've been through the desert on a horse with no name.* Nothing he'd seen from the plane, or the drive from the airport, matched up with his idea of *desert.* It was all just highway and bare, baked earth. He hesitated, not wanting to tell Chip either yes or no. Of course he had free time. They set these things up so you could have all manner of expensive, stupid fun. He imagined sitting in bars or game rooms with his coworkers, watching them make idiots of themselves because they thought it was expected of them. Or keeping to himself because he would be too prideful and lonesome to do anything else. He saw Chip's twitchy smile, how he was all too ready to be disappointed, and he was pretty sure that if he said no, he would never see him again.

"How about Wednesday afternoon?" Ryan said. "Around two?"

When he offered to pick Chip up, Chip said no, he'd just be at the hotel, that was easiest, which Ryan took to mean that wherever Chip was living, he didn't want it known.

The convention itself bored him, after the first half day. He'd been to enough of them by now that he recognized the particular energy they generated, the self-created excitement of business and business talk that ran on for a time and then deflated.

He called his girlfriend back in Chicago and assured her he wasn't doing anything lurid or carnal. He guessed it wouldn't be hard to find that kind of thing if you went out to some of the smaller bars and casinos. The Grand seemed to keep everything pretty well policed, a glassed-in pleasure dome designed to make the extraction of money the most natural thing in the world.

He liked having money well enough, liked it better than not having any. He was twenty-nine years old and it was time to give thought to providing for himself, and maybe a family. His girlfriend wanted to get married and he thought he'd probably allow her to have her way. He had to smile, thinking of it. People said that if you could talk yourself out of getting married, then you should. He didn't intend to try. His parents would be relieved that he'd taken this further step into adulthood. He guessed he'd be relieved too. When he was younger he'd never imagined himself married, because marriage was a known and fixed thing and his future was to be both splendid and vague.

You decided that your life would go in a certain direction, and maybe it did. Or maybe you were kidding yourself, and the world was mostly a matter of being in the right or wrong place at the right or wrong time.

Married! It was either the biggest decision or the biggest accident of them all. On Wednesday afternoon he called the valet to get his car and went down to the front entrance to wait for Chip. The glass was tinted and it gave the sky a dark and lowering look. When he stepped outside, fumbling with his sunglasses, the sky lightened to blue, but the heat rushed at him like a wall. The air was oven-dry. His lungs squeezed shut and he had to think about breathing. Down the street, a thermometer in front of a bank registered ninety-five.

As before, Chip materialized without Ryan's being aware of it, standing at the end of the turnaround drive, waving. In the plain light of day he looked even thinner, older, dressed as before in his scarecrow clothes. Ryan waved back and Chip stuck a thumb out, going my way?

Ryan started the car and pulled up to where Chip waited. "Hola," Chip greeted him, sliding into the passenger seat. "Man, look at you, can't you go thirty seconds without air-conditioning?"

"It isn't air-conditioning yet." The car's vents were still sending out hot air. It served him right for trying to save a few dollars on a rental.

"This is a seriously cheap-ass car," Chip announced, It was a little Dodge product, two-door, with a shift that wobbled and threatened to pop out of gear.

Ryan was tempted to ask Chip what he drove these days, that he was such a connoisseur of fine vehicles. The heat was making him surly. "You really like it here? What are you, a lizard?"

Chip laughed his haw-haw laugh. "You are such a pussy. This is high desert, we even get snow here, for crying out loud." Ryan was waiting to pull into traffic, waiting for direction. Chip pointed. "Thataway."

The car's innards clicked and began pumping cooler air, though not at a level that inspired confidence. Ryan steered them into traffic. More casinos, bars, hotels, their outsize signs looking wrong and ugly in daylight. "So where are we going?"

"A little drive," said Chip unhelpfully. "Take this turn."

Ryan followed Chip's instructions, navigating through the business district, then onto a freeway ramp. They were heading north, as far as Ryan could tell, although the sun seemed to be shining in all directions, no escape from the burning heat of the afternoon. Chip pointed out mountains visible in the hazy distance, a subdivision of snazzy houses around an artificial lake. Ryan began to calculate times and distances. A couple of hours jaunting around with Chip was all he thought he could manage before he'd need his frosty hotel room, a cool shower, and maybe a nap. "You never told me. How long you've been in Reno."

Chip was fiddling with the radio dial. "Damned cowboy music," he announced, giving up and shutting it off. "What? What's so funny?"

"You never like anything on the radio."

"That's because all they ever play is crap." Chip reached in his shirt pocket for cigarettes. "OK if I smoke?"

"Crack your window," Ryan told him. It was better to put up with heat than smoke. "Hey, if something's none of my business, just say so. Don't make me keep asking the same stupid questions."

"Oh. Three years. Almost. I kind of moved around a lot. Sorry. Sometimes I have trouble remembering stuff. Focusing." Chip got his cigarette going and sent some portion of the smoke out the window. He was quiet for a time. The road was leading them higher in a gradual grade. The Dodge shimmied whenever Ryan accelerated into the climb. The thing was seriously underpowered. He kept an eye on the temperature gauge in case he had to shut down the air. He wanted to ask Chip what he meant, trouble focusing, but he guessed it was one more answer he wasn't going to get.

After a while Chip finished his cigarette and began the process of starting another. "Twenty percent disabled. That's what they tell me. I guess that means I'm eighty percent normal, right?" He laughed again. "Me and the VA, we have what you'd call a hate-hate relationship."

"You're saying you get benefit checks." Ryan was growing accustomed to Chip-speak, the jumpy rhythm of talk that lit on anything and everything and once in a while circled back to actual information. He guessed the 20 percent part was from the neck up.

Chip pointed back behind them and to the west. "That way's I-80, it takes you into the Sierras and on into California. Over the Donner Pass, you know, the wagon train where everybody ate each other?"

Ryan said he thought he remembered something about that, though he wasn't sure if he did. Scrub pines dotted the hills around them. Away to their left, ridges of pine forest rose on the mountain peaks, fold on fold. Chip said, "Yeah, they got stuck up there in the snow. Ate the horses. Ate the oxen. Ate the harness leather. Ate tree bark. Ate Ma and Pa. It's how the West was won. Take this exit."

Ryan signaled and followed the ramp. The road in front of them stretched, bare and vacant. A line of gravel-colored hills receded into the blue distance. It all had an unfriendly look that worried him. After two, three, six miles by the Dodge's odometer, he said, "They have any gas stations out here? Because you know, rental cars, you can never be sure what might go wrong with them." They hadn't met one car going in either direction since the turnoff. Miles and miles of nothing.

"Relax. Be a tourist."

"What am I supposed to be looking at, exactly?" He was beginning to envision little cartoons, bleached cattle skulls, vultures perched on giant cacti.

"Just a ways farther. Oh, you know what we should have brought? Water. I don't suppose you have a plastic jug, anything like that?" Chip turned around to scan the backseat. "Should have thought of it earlier."

"You're saying we should turn around?"

"Since when did you become such a little old lady?"

"I'm just asking."

"Seriously, dude, you had more spirit before you got those swell shoes."

"Seriously, you need to quit calling me *dude*." He'd had about enough of Chip's abuse, which he had always allowed, perversely, because Chip was such a loser, such a monumental screw-up. But this depended on Chip being aware that he was indeed a screwup. And maybe he was, on some level, but it wasn't exactly on display.

He was annoyed with himself too, for letting Chip make him feel as if he was still a schoolkid who'd never left home. He'd seen a little bit of the world by now, he'd been smacked around enough to have some of the sass knocked out of him. *When you ain't got nothing, you got nothing to lose.* That was Chip, he guessed. The original rolling stone.

Chip lit a new cigarette and said, "Sometimes, grasshopper, the journey is more important than the arrival."

"You suck, you know?"

"Right up there. See that? Can you get off my case now? You sure would have made a piss-poor pioneer."

In the brown distance, a nearly paintless barn. Coming closer, Ryan saw a corral, empty, a house trailer and a cluster of small sheds. Facing the road, a flat-roofed stucco building with an overhanging porch constructed of posts and laths and tented burlap. He slowed the car to take it in. At one time there had been an attempt at decoration, misplaced. The boards of the porch held wagon wheels and pickaxes and a miner's lantern, all meant to suggest antiques but now closer to outright junk. Garlands of crepe-paper flowers, bleached to thin colors, were twined around the posts. It looked like a shabby mirage at the end of the earth. A sign in the window, thickly painted, said ROCKS. GEMSTONES.

Chip directed him to pull up in the front. There was no other vehicle, nor any sign of life. At least it seemed to be the destination Chip had in mind. Ryan was relieved about that. It had occurred to him that Chip's navigation skills were suspect. Chip was already out of the car and looking in at the windows, shading his eyes with his hand. He crossed over to the screen door, propped it open, and spent some time bent over the lock, testing and pulling at it and fishing in his back pocket for something Ryan couldn't see. Finally he tugged at the door and it gave way. "Come on, I want to show you something."

Ryan stepped out of the car to the dirt yard. "Did you just break in?"

"It's OK, I know these guys."

"What guys?" But Chip had already gone inside.

The sun was still just as strong but the heat seemed less, maybe because they'd climbed high enough for the altitude to make a difference. Ryan crossed the creaking boards of the porch, opened the screen door, and stepped across the threshold, blinking to adjust his eyes.

The space was dim and stuffy, with a smell like a long-shut cupboard. Chip's shirt stood out, a spot of blurred brightness. "Hang on, don't move. I gotta go start the generator." The screen door slapped shut behind him.

"Jesus," Ryan said to the darkness. Shapes grew solid as his vision adjusted. A line of counters, shelving, a reflection or luster that might be glass. He heard Chip outside, banging around and mildly swearing. There was the sound of a motor starting, cutting out, and starting again. A bank of fluorescent lights hanging on chains clicked and wavered and grew brighter. An overhead fan began to rotate, stirring the heat.

The glass-fronted shelves above the counter held rocks and minerals of different sorts, some polished smooth, others looking as if they'd been kicked up by an earthmoving machine. One piece, the size of a loaf of bread, had a sparkling green and purple vein through its flattened side. Here was something he guessed to be rose quartz, a central nugget of it surrounded by crystal prisms. Another he was pretty sure was turquoise, though it was rough and cloudy. About others he had no idea. He guessed that even precious stones had to be cut and cleaned and faceted before they looked like anything you'd recognize. Or maybe these were only the kind of geological junk that some people found interesting for reasons of science. On the counter surfaces, different displays of equipment: saw blades, grinders, magnifying lenses, safety goggles.

He turned around and found himself inches away, at eye level, from a rattlesnake curled up and poised to strike, and only after he swallowed his heart down hard did he realize it was stuffed and enclosed in another glass case. He tried to laugh at himself. "Gha gha."

Chip came back inside, looking pleased. "There's a Coke machine. We just have to wait until it runs long enough to get the bottles cold."

"Is this a ghost town, or does somebody live here? Are we trespassing? Just curious."

"It's cool, relax. Did you see this? It's black opal. Very high quality stuff. Friends of mine live here. It's absolutely fine with them if I hang out while they're gone. They went camping. Out at a dig. They do that, go all over the state, rockhounding. It's a way of life."

"They call and tell you to stop by?"

"You see any phone lines out here, slick?"

"All right," Ryan said. "Christ." He was getting thirsty, although he tried telling himself he wasn't. Warm Coke was starting to sound pretty good.

"Come on out back, you can see for about a hundred miles."

It wasn't a hundred miles but it was a good long ways into empty air. Chip led him past the straggling edge of the homestead and its discarded piles of possibly useful junk, and up an incline. Even this mild climb coated Ryan's neck with new sweat. He should have thought to bring some kind of hat. They stood on the loose and pebbled dirt, which was in the process of turning itself into sand, in the next geological era, and looked out at a line of distant, pale green that marked a draw or some temporary watercourse, not yet gone dry for summer. In the farthest distance, very small, another mountain range, like something made of toy blocks.

"You know what you're looking at?" Chip asked, and when Ryan shook his head, he said, "My home planet."

"How do you figure?"

"It just feels right. I dunno. Clears my head, being out here."

Even with sunglasses, Ryan felt the glare bearing down on him. "Kind of a lonesome place."

"Yeah, well, I never had much luck with people anyway."

Ryan kept quiet. There wasn't any point in contradicting Chip just so he could hear himself say something nice. Chip poked at the dirt with his sandal, sending a few small stones skidding down the hill. "It's no-bullshit *real* out here, man. Live or die. Eat or be eaten. The basics. What more does anybody need?"

"How about, Chicago-style pizza and cold beer."

"Always with the funnies. I'm making a serious point here. Modern life, it's turned us soft. We lose . . ." Chip stopped, searched the empty air with his free hand for the rest of his thought.

"Connection?" Ryan suggested.

"Yeah, something like that. All the survival skills get beat out of us. How do you think Indian tribes lived out here? You think we could hunt, or build shelters, or make our own clothes? We wouldn't last two weeks."

"We don't have to do any of that," Ryan said. "I survive just fine, I went out and got a job so I could take care of myself. You might give it a shot."

Chip went on as if Ryan hadn't spoken. "We've lost touch with, ah, actual, physical stuff. What's more real, a computer, or a rock that's been in the ground for five hundred thousand years?"

"Now you're confusing *real* with *natural*."

Chip waved this away. "See, that's what happens when I try to explain. It always turns into an argument."

"I'm not arguing with you, Ray." It was a lost cause.

"Human beings," Chip said, "have evolved too far from their animal origins. I get so tired of trying to figure out words. Maybe I'll just quit on them. Make animal noises. Bird noises."

"I'd miss talking to you." Which was true, in some perverse way.

Chip squinted at him, as if trying to tell if Ryan was making fun of him. "You're OK, you know? You're a pretty righteous dude."

"Thanks." They were back to *dude* again.

"I mean, you could have turned out to be a real dick. Because you always had the smarts and the good looks and the women chasing after you—"

"Oh yeah, sure," Ryan muttered, embarrassed at being the object of Chip's envy. You wanted to be envied, of course, but by somebody cool.

"—but you never acted like that put you in some special category, you know, better than anybody else. You didn't have to look me up out here. I appreciate that."

"You're family, Ray." True enough, although it sounded weak or insulting to fall back on that as a reason: *Even though you're a freakish loser, we feel some obligation toward you.* Which was pretty much the case. "I need to be heading back to the hotel pretty soon here."

"Right. No problem."

"You said something about Cokes?"

Chip turned and skidded down the hillside, his sandals wobbling in the dirt. "Couple a Cokes, coming up."

Ryan walked back to the car and opened the doors to let some of the heat out. He was trying to think what report he could send back home to Chip's anxious parents. *He really loves the weather out there. And officially, he's only twenty percent disabled.*

Chip came around the side of the building, holding four Coke bottles by their necks. "Here, I got us a couple each since they're kind of small."

Ryan took them. They were somewhere between warm and tepid. He opened one and drank down half of it. "The pause that refreshes. Thanks."

"One sec, I gotta . . ." Chip headed back inside the stucco building. Ryan wasn't looking forward to the inside of the Dodge. The steering wheel and the vinyl seats looked hot enough to melt skin. Behind him on the road, the sound of a car engine, still some distance away. He stood and watched it until it became visible. A baby blue pickup truck with a tarp stretched over the bed. It slowed and heaved itself into the dirt lane, pulling up behind him.

It did not occur to him to feel apprehensive.

Two things happened, one right after the other: A man swung out of the pickup truck and crossed the distance between them at a shambling run. Then Chip emerged from the rock shop with a green army knapsack, cradling it in his arms.

"All right, asshole," the man said, pointing first at Ryan, then at Chip, or not pointing, really, since there was a gun in his hand and that was what he was using for emphasis. Ryan looked at it without real comprehension. He was still trying to figure out why someone he'd never met was calling him an asshole.

"Hey there, Otto," Chip greeted him. He'd stopped short, not moving from his place near the door.

*Otto?*

"Put that down. Now, dirtbag." Otto waved the gun around. He had a big black beard and wore a straw cowboy hat. His face was red and sweating and twitchy.

"Jeez, chill," Chip said. He bent down, placed the knapsack on the porch, opened it, and held up a mud-colored rock. "It's just my opals, man. I told you I'd be back for them."

"Soon as you pay me the four hundred you owe me."

"You mean two-fifty."

"Nice try." Otto turned to regard Ryan. "Who's this joker?"

Ryan kept quiet as Otto looked him over. Ryan guessed he was afraid, but it didn't feel like fear. He was just very, very interested in what was happening. Otto kept moving the gun from Ryan to Chip and back again, eenie meenie miney moe.

"Hey," Chip said. "Leave him alone. He's my cousin, he's from Chicago."

"Cousin," Otto repeated. He had small, squinting black eyes and a heavy gut hanging over the waistband of his jeans. "What, a whole family of dirtbags?"

Ryan said, "I think we should just leave now."

No one seemed to hear him. Otto looked him up and down. "The two of you don't favor."

Chip said, "You have to imagine me all cleaned up and with a real classy wardrobe."

The gun had a small black mouth. Otto brought it up to Ryan's nose. "It would be a privilege to shoot any family member of yours."

Ryan said, "Don't." He couldn't come up with any better argument or reason not to get shot. It was going to end up the last dumb thought he ever squeezed out of his brain. Don't.

Chip said, "You're overreacting, Otto. You're a classic overreactor." Chip sounded aggrieved, as if having a gun pointed at him was just one more of life's unfairnesses.

"Shut up or I'll shoot you first."

"You don't want to start shooting people, Otto. Bad things can happen."

"Don't tell me what to do, Tesman. Every time you open your mouth, this whole parade of bullshit comes out."

"I guess we've reached a real crossroads in our friendship."

"Just shut up."

"Say the word, we're gone. Like you never knew me. Like I'm a— what? Figment. Figment of your imagination."

"Shut up, shut up, shut up!" The sound of Chip's voice seemed to infuriate Otto. Chip shrugged and leaned against the screen door, as if to say he'd given it his best effort. Otto hadn't moved the gun from Ryan's face. "Turn around."

Ryan felt the Coke he'd swallowed rising in his throat. He turned so that he faced the car, leaning against it, his legs no longer doing the job of keeping him upright, the sun balanced on the top of his skull like another bullet about to drop, the heat of the car's roof against his bare arms, the gun speaking, CRACK.

Somebody screaming but it wasn't him. "GODDAMNIT FUCK-ING ASSHOLE SHIT SHIT SHIT."

Ryan turned around. Otto rolled on the ground, clutching at his shoulder, his T-shirt filling up with blood. Chip stood over him and kicked the gun away. He held his own gun, smaller, silver-plated, palm-size. Chip said, "Oh, come on, Otto. You've hurt yourself worse having a good time. These tough guys," Chip said to Ryan. "I get so tired of their big bad act."

"FUCKER YOU FUCKIN SHOT ME."

"Well sure I shot you, what do you expect? Was I supposed to think you were just playing some dumb game?" Chip stepped over Otto so that he had one foot on either side of him. "You want a towel, maybe? Ry, look around and see if there's anything like a towel around here."

Ryan went to Otto's truck and looked into the front seat. There was a pile of clothing on the floor; he found a gray sweatshirt and brought it back to Chip. He'd propped Otto up against the wheel of the Dodge.

"CHUNK OF SHIT FUCKHOLE."

"Otto, seriously, you should save your breath. Here, put some pressure on that hole."

Otto groaned. Ryan tried to say something but thought had gone clean out of his head, like the empty balloons over a comic character's head, like the comics Chip used to collect back in Iowa a hundred years ago. Chip said, "You want a ride someplace, Otto? We can give you a ride if you'll agree this was all a big accident. We were messing around target shooting and my shot went wide."

"We need to get him to a doctor," Ryan said, recovering the power of speech.

"Maybe. But first Otto has to get with the plan."

"SCREW YOU DICKFACE."

"Just as well. You don't want him making some big stupid bloody mess in your car. They'd probably charge you extra, you know, for cleanup."

"Say, Chip?"

"Ray."

"Ray. I think Otto is actually very sorry that things got out of control. I bet he's actually trying to apologize, but it's just not coming out right."

Otto groaned again and showed his teeth. Blood was beginning to seep through the wadded gray sweatshirt he was holding to his shoulder.

They started back, Ryan driving, going as fast as he could without hitting any bumps, because the bumps made Otto scream. Chip sat in the front seat, turned around, the silver gun in one hand, cigarette flipping up and down in his mouth. The knapsack with the opals on the floor at his feet. He seemed to be in a good mood.

He said, "Tell me this isn't more exciting than some old convention."

"This is more exciting than a convention."

"You can go back and tell everybody that you had a chance to see the real West."

"If that's what you say it is, Ray."

"Sure it is." Chip took the cigarette out long enough to exhale and reposition it. "Just like in the movies, except Otto wound up all shot."

Ryan drove through the landscape of the real West. Although it didn't look any different from the way it did a couple of hours before, he didn't trust his eyes.

Chip was still pleased with himself, still tickled by his own wit. "I guess old Otto thought he was Charles Bronson or somebody. What do you say, Otto, would you like to be in the movies? You could be a cattle rustler, or a saloonkeeper. You could be the guy who gets hit and falls down and doesn't get up. That have any appeal for you, huh?"

"COCKSUCKER RATFUCKER."

# *Iowa*

## JUNE 1989

She had six grandchildren now. Six! It was bewildering to think how everything changed, fast and slow all at once. She couldn't get her mind around it. If only you could grab hold of time like the end of a string, follow it along, roll it up into a ball until you got where you needed to be. Baby pictures of each grandchild hung in circular frames over the fireplace in the family room. Anita's two and Blake's three and the newest, Ryan's little girl. She stared at them and they stared back. Six wrinkled baby faces looking out at the world in perfect incomprehension. Of course most of them weren't babies now. Matthew was twelve, and Marcie and Kyle were nine, and so on down the line. Or maybe Marcie was ten. She hadn't thought about it in a while and it was possible that some birthday had slipped past her. Who would imagine you could forget a thing like that, your own granddaughter's birthday?

But she did forget. She didn't always pay attention to everything that people assumed you paid attention to. Sometimes she just got tired. So many things piled up in a life, after a while you felt them as a weight. So many babies, hers and everybody else's! They took too much out of you. All the excitement and worry of their arrival and the suddenness of their needs. She must have felt all the right things at the time, happy and fond and anxious. But looking back, she couldn't remember feeling them. Some part of remembering, or feeling, had been blotted out in her.

People said, *I don't know how you manage it,* and you told them that you just did the best you could, day by day, which was what they wanted you to say. They didn't want you to say that sometimes you locked the door to your room and stayed in bed all day and it didn't matter if there was screaming on the other side of the door, screaming and kicking and swearing, you did not get up. *Fuck fuck shit, shittin cunt whore.* Where had her daughter learned such language, and why was it one of the things she remembered?

Some days were sad days and they cried together, as if all the salt tears in the world could change a thing.

Some days were good days when Torrie sat quietly, looking at magazines. She liked *National Geographic*s best because of all the pictures. Jungles with tiny, vivid, poisonous frogs perched on leaves. Bedouin on camels, frozen waterfalls, beaches with frills of turquoise water, with sea turtles and sharks and puffins. At such times Audrey watched her and wondered if her daughter was still in there somewhere, in a far country. Or was she lost inside the pictures?

*How is she doing, is she doing any better now?* And Audrey always said *Yes, thank you, she's a little better,* and people were *So glad to hear it,* because then it meant they didn't have to do anything else.

Better because the emergency surgeries were long past, better because there would be fewer and fewer reconstructive surgeries. Better because the swelling of her face and head had gone down, better because her hair had grown back. Better because Audrey no longer had to change the catheters and urine bags. Better because her shattered pelvis had healed. Better because she was able to use a wheelchair, and after the hip and knee surgeries, a walker, and later, a cane. When she walked now there was a good leg and a bad leg. The good leg went first and the bad leg followed.

The doctors were always encouraged, encouraging. There had been so much progress already, there would continue to be progress. Not as much, or as quickly, as you might want, and not 100 percent, certainly not back to the way she'd been before the accident. That was a doctor for you. They lifted you up with one hand and shoved you down with the other. She hated doctors now.

In the first terrible hours and days and weeks, they had been told not to get their hopes up, no one was sure if Torrie would even live. They kept waiting for someone to give them a real answer, remove the dread. But with doctors, Audrey understood now, there was no such thing as being entirely out of danger. There was only one more day when the patient had not died.

People sent cards and brought casseroles to the house. The church bulletin requested prayers on their behalf. But now it had been almost ten years. There was no longer any crisis, only life and time, which made everything unremarkable.

So that her beautiful, willful daughter had been stolen away and replaced by this changeling creature, a furious and oversize baby who had to be taught all over again how to eat with a knife and fork, toilet herself, tie her shoelaces. Once a week she had physical therapy and speech therapy at the clinic in Des Moines. The therapists were encouraging, like the doctors. They measured out hope on graphs and charts, inches and syllables. *Thatagirl, Torrie! One more time! Great effort!* It was in their self-interest to say that people got better, because otherwise there would be no need for them. So Torrie lifted weights, stacked blocks, blew into tubes, said *A EE I O YOU,* said *see bee tree* and everyone agreed she was making slow but steady progress.

Audrey didn't tell them about the days when Torrie refused to put on clothes, or lit all the stove burners when Audrey was in the bathroom, or cursed at the television so that they hardly ever watched anymore. Commercials in particular seemed to set her off, those inconsequential dramas of people choosing Coke over Pepsi, Ford over Chevy. "What is it, Torrie, what's the matter?" And Torrie made a motion with her hands that looked as if she were trying to wash them and said, in a tone of accusation, "Everybody too happy!"

That was what the commercials wanted you to believe. Buying

things made you happy, and buying the superior brand made you happy. All of it was exaggerated to the point of stupidity and everybody understood that. Maybe Torrie didn't anymore. Maybe she couldn't tell when the world didn't mean what it said, what was real and what were brightly colored lies.

The brain, Audrey had been told, was complex, subtle, fragile. If it was bruised, insulted, torn, it still kept trying to do its job, its neurons firing and looking for connections, short-circuiting and sparking. The brain was the boss of everything. There were the autonomic functions, breathing, the beating heart. Gross and fine motor control. Whatever could be sensed, touched, seen, smelled. Language and speech. Logic, memory, behavior, judgment. It had been explained to her many times that there were some things Torrie could practice so that simple repetition convinced her brain to follow a certain pathway. Other functions might be like a highway that no longer led anywhere.

Insurance only covered part of the enormous bills. They would never pay them off. Randy had planned to retire by now. Instead he went to the office every weekday and sometimes on weekends too. He didn't always have to work, but who would want to be here if they didn't have to be?

If you followed the string back far enough, she was no one's mother. But you could only go forward, and so she would always always always be the one who cleaned up the messes, coaxed and threatened and soothed, loved them no matter what they did except when she didn't. It wasn't one of those things like breathing.

"Eat, Torrie." Torrie sat at the kitchen table, a peanut-butter-and-jelly sandwich cut in quarters on the plate before her. At least there was no more of the strange eating, or not eating, that had gone on before the accident. The things they had found in her room! The food she'd hidden away in drawers and closets, only pretending to have eaten it. It had all gone bad and drawn bugs, so that in the middle of everything else they'd had to clean and scour the room down.

Now Torrie no longer had such secrets. Only the enormous one of who lived inside her damaged head.

"Eat, Torrie." If it was a bad day, she fussed about what was on her plate. Fine then, don't eat, Audrey wanted to say, except that it would be her fault if Torrie got constipated or lived entirely on sugar. "Drink your milk, please?"

Torrie lifted the glass and drank. "Thank you," Audrey said. "Now what do you do?"

Torrie took the napkin from her lap and blotted her mouth with it. "Well then, that's just fine." She was surprised, a little. Maybe it would be one of her good days. "How about some sandwich now?"

Torrie ate half of her sandwich and some graham crackers. Her table manners were so much better now, that is, she could be said to have some.

"Mom."

"What, honey?"

"Show me me."

"Finish your milk first."

Audrey brought the hand mirror to the table. Torrie tilted it back and forth so it caught the light. Her mother watched her watch herself. Her hair had grown back a few shades darker and they kept it short because that was easier. Before the accident the first thing you'd noticed about Torrie was her long yellow hair, a rope down her back. Now it was ordinary, like anybody's hair.

Torrie put her fingers to her face. All the surgeries had left her facial muscles rigid, so that none of her expressions seemed entirely natural. Sometimes if they were out, and if Torrie's hair was combed so that the scars around her scalp didn't show, Audrey saw people staring at Torrie, or trying not to, as they asked themselves just what it was that seemed wrong about her.

Of course she looked older. And her features had thickened. Maybe some of that was the accident, or maybe it would have happened anyway. There was no way of knowing.

"Show me me in the book."

Audrey cleared the lunch plates, went into the den, and brought back the leather-covered album with Torrie's pictures. Each of the kids had one, from babyhood up through high school and beyond, and there was a box of loose pictures somewhere: group shots of Christmases and vacations and different combinations of kids so that sorting them out had been difficult. The things she used to worry about.

Torrie opened the album to its first leaf, the pictures of her at the hospital, a pink bow in her topknot of wispy hair. In one her mouth was open in a yawn or a squawk and her eyes were shut. In others she was sleeping. Audrey held her while her brothers and sister peered at her with cautious expressions. Other pages documented her crawling, standing, walking, then there were gaps and leaps in time to Torrie's older self. She'd been the youngest and picture-taking had fallen off over time. Anita's album was probably twice as large. Audrey used to worry that Torrie had been deprived of her due portion of attention. Well, she was making up for it now.

Audrey moved her chair closer to look at the album with her. "Yes, that's you. Baby Torrie."

"Baby me."

"That's right." *You aren't a baby anymore. Can you grow up again?*

Torrie turned the pages. Some days they didn't get very far. She'd spend a long time looking and either her energy or her interest lagged and Audrey put the book away. But today she made it through to the end, to the empty pages that followed the last pictures of herself with her high school friends, with the volleyball team, and the very last one, where she posed with somebody's new puppy, a dog that would by now be sleeping its way into old age.

Torrie put her hand flat on a blank page. "Where are more?"

"Sweetheart, we don't have any." All that had stopped. There were months and years when it would have been a cruelty to take Torrie's picture.

Torrie shook her head. Sometimes all her old stubbornness surfaced, as if that was the bedrock of her personality. "I want more."

"Well I can't just make pictures out of nothing."

"Make out of me."

"We need a camera, sweetie."

"Then get a camera," Torrie said, sounding for a moment so much like her old self, pert, impatient, mocking, that Audrey gave her a startled look.

There was an old camera of Ryan's in some closet or drawer, she remembered. She rummaged through the back rooms, thinking as she always did what a hopeless mess the house was, crammed with the leftovers of her family's lives. Things no one wanted, but had not yet been able to throw away, so that it was a purgatory for sports equipment, old clothes, and balding stuffed animals. But she found the camera, a Canon with a fancy embroidered neck strap. Her husband cleaned it, peered through its lenses, and pronounced it sound. He brought home film and loaded it.

"What does she want a camera for, anyway?"

"I don't know why she wants anything."

He had nothing to say to that, only went back to reading his newspaper. She knew he grieved for Torrie. She knew his heart hurt just as hers did. But a man didn't show such things, and that only made for more lonesomeness.

"Do you want me to take your picture?" Audrey asked, but Torrie grabbed the camera from her. "Here, at least put the strap around your neck so you don't drop it. Do you want me to show you how it works?"

Torrie knew, or at least she thought she did. She took the camera and went out to the backyard. Audrey watched her from the kitchen window. There was nothing out there that any of them hadn't always seen. Why take pictures of the old picnic table? Why lie on the ground taking pictures of dirt?

Torrie used up one roll and demanded another. Audrey tried to load it for her and Torrie took the camera and set to work on her own. Her hands were slow, like the rest of her. Audrey wasn't supposed to help her do things but sometimes she did. It was just easier. But from that moment on, Torrie never let anyone else near the camera.

That was how it began. Her parents, and everyone else in Grenada, grew used to Torrie walking the streets with her camera, poking the lens into anything and everything.

At first Audrey tried to keep her in her own yard, or at least, their own street, but Torrie was too determined to escape her, and Audrey was too reluctant to follow, and you had to hope that Torrie, who had grown rather heavy over the last few years, heavy as well as tall, would be able to fend off any trouble by herself, at least on such familiar ground.

Everyone told Audrey how good it was that Torrie had an interest now, something that got her out of the house. That was what they said to her face. She could only imagine the kind of jokes they made among themselves, or their annoyance when Torrie jammed her camera into the windows of their parked cars, or appeared in their front yards, clicking away. She was out in all weathers, bad leg and all, patrolling the streets of town, or what was left of it.

Times were supposed to be good again, but not here, where too much damage had been done during the farm troubles, and too many people in the county had lost their livelihoods and moved away. The high school had to be consolidated with the one fifteen miles away. Two restaurants and one of the drugstores closed, and the Fashionaire, and the pie shop, and one of the banks, and the library went to reduced hours. The little country towns were in worse shape, some of them without even so much as a post office anymore.

Sometimes Audrey found herself thinking that she'd been born into one world, hopeful and normal, and now she lived in another, full of sadness and failure.

The pictures Torrie took were an odd lot. Some of them were just patterns of light or shade, or ordinary things like gravel, or telephone wires against a clear sky. With people, she favored close-up portraits. There was a range of faces and expressions, from those who were clearly annoyed, clearly trying to avoid the camera, to those who seemed to pose, no matter how uneasily, offering up their tentative smiles. Audrey recognized neighbors, shopkeepers, even some of Torrie's old friends and schoolmates, grown up now, peering down through the camera at something they didn't want to see.

Because that was how the pictures made the most sense: It wasn't so much Torrie looking out at the world as the world looking back at her. So that clouds or railroad tracks or buildings had a peaceful aspect, nothing there to judge or react, and every shot Torrie took of Audrey showed her exhaustion and wariness.

The only picture Torrie put at the end of her old baby album was a portrait of herself that she'd managed to take, with a timer? With someone else pushing the shutter? There was no telling; it was another occasion when she'd gone off on her own. She stood inside someone's old garage, her face just visible through a window of cracked and shattered glass.

One day Torrie came into the kitchen where Audrey was scrubbing out the cupboards. She held the camera out with both hands. "Cook it."

"You don't cook a camera, Torrie." Audrey still found herself explaining such things.

"Cook pictures," said Torrie patiently, with a smile lurking in one corner of her mouth as she waited for her mother to get it.

It made sense to set up a darkroom for her in the boys' old bathroom, and to get someone from the camera shop in Ames to come and show her the basics of developing. They had been spending quite a bit of money getting film processed at the Walgreens. Torrie caught on quickly enough—it seemed easier for her to learn new things than to remember old ones—and hung strips of negatives along a clothesline in the old bathtub, printing different versions of the same shot, lining them up on the kitchen table and scrutinizing each for a long time. That unnatural slow patience seemed to serve her well. "I like that one," Audrey might say, pointing to one of what seemed to her ten identical pictures, and Torrie would shake her head no, seeing something different.

The pictures grew larger, eight by ten, twelve by fourteen. Audrey and Randy framed a few of them and hung them on the walls, but frankly, they were often too odd or disturbing or puzzling to want on display. Here was a dog's open mouth, its eager tongue, and its teeth like a miniature mountain range. Here was an elderly man photographed with such high contrast that the lines around the mouth and eyes became crevasses. Here was the abandoned high school, Torrie's old school, the windows boarded up, a school for ghosts. The photos bewildered Audrey. She liked pictures of gardens or playful animals, things polished up or made fanciful. Maybe Torrie's pictures were more real, but that didn't mean you wanted to spend all day looking at depressing things. You could see that anywhere!

Now it seemed they hardly saw Torrie. She was either out taking pictures or shut in the darkroom, developing them. She sat at the table with them for meals, but she was always impatient to get back to her work. "Why do you like taking pictures so much?" Audrey asked her, but Torrie only said, "Photographs. Not pictures." Her speech was getting better too. She no longer sounded like a deaf person speaking, guessing at the words.

As much as Audrey had chafed at taking care of Torrie, now it felt as if she had been left behind. It was lonesome in the house without her, which was probably why each new picture Torrie took of her mother looked a little sadder than the one before.

# *Iowa*

He was twelve and in a hurry to get to thirteen and then sixteen because you could drive and then twenty-one, when no one could tell you what to do.

Sunday morning. If he stayed quiet in bed long enough, there was a chance the rest of them would sleep in and they wouldn't have to go to church. Sunday school was at nine thirty and often hit-or-miss, but church wasn't until eleven, so it was harder to avoid. He'd gotten up very early, while the house was still dim and shadowy, fixed a bowl of cereal in the kitchen, and brought it back to his room to eat. Then he got into bed again and waited, doing nothing, which was boring but not nearly as boring as church.

Just before ten he heard his sister get up and turn on the television in the den. He got up and padded down the hall after her. "Hey, turn that down," he said in a whisper that he tried to make loud.

She waved the remote at him, smiling her triumphant smile.

"Gimme that."

"No."

"Bitch."

"I'm telling you said that."

He started to say it again but his attention was caught by the television screen. "What's that?"

"Hurricane stuff."

The hurricane had been going on for a while in places like tropical islands and now it had come to the United States, which made it more interesting. There was a picture from the weather satellite, a huge white flat saucer of cloud slicing into the map. Then the television showed pictures of wrecked buildings, cars upside down, huge trees leveled.

"Cool," Matt said.

"Do we have hurricanes here?"

"Nah, just tornadoes."

"I don't like hurricanes," his sister said. She was small for her age, a thin-wristed girl with hair that was nearly white at its ends, darker near her scalp.

"That's because you're a dork."

"Shut up."

"Make me. A hurricane would be"—he tried to find the best word—"majorly cool."

"Yeah, because you'd die in it."

"No, you would," said her brother, but he was no longer paying attention to her. The television was showing pictures of the storm coming ashore. Waves smashed into the beach and the little houses in its way staggered and fell. Palm trees bent double. Their leaves streamed behind them like hair. It wasn't fair that he had missed it all.

From upstairs, footsteps, a toilet flushing. Matt and Marcie looked at each other. "Shit," Matt said, but under his breath so his sister wouldn't hear it and add it to her list of things to report.

Their mother came in, wearing her bathrobe and slippers. "Morning, guys."

They said good morning, sort of, their eyes on the television. She went into the kitchen and they heard her making coffee. When she came back in she said, "What's this you're watching?"

"The hurricane."

"Those poor people," she said, watching, then, "Why aren't you getting ready?"

"Are we going to church?" Matt asked. As if there was any room for argument.

"You have twenty minutes to get dressed."

"Is Dad coming?"

"I don't know, he's still asleep."

Behind their mother's back, Matt made his fist into a beer can, popped the top of his thumb, and raised it to his mouth to drink. Marcie giggled.

"Move it," their mother said, going into the kitchen again.

Half an hour later the three of them were in the car. Marcie sat up front and Matt had the backseat to himself. He slouched down and watched roofs and treetops slide past the windows. Church was boring. God was boring. God was like everybody's parent. He figured he was probably going to hell, not because he'd done anything too bad, but because of his private, ugly thoughts.

"Mom?"

"What?"

"How come all the Norwegians are Lutherans?"

She sighed, as she did whenever he asked a question, as if all his questions were designed to test and aggravate her. "I don't know, they just are. Like all the Irish are Catholic."

"Not all of them. Some of them are Protestants, they fight about it."

"You shouldn't ask things you already know the answer to," she said, her attention given to something in the roadway.

"I don't. Dad's not Norwegian. So we're only half."

"You're Norwegian enough to go to church," his mother pronounced, and Matt settled back into his slump. He wished he was all one thing or the other.

They parked and joined the stream of other people moving toward the front doors. Matt dawdled behind his mother and sister. At least his dad wasn't here. Then they would have been the complete dork family. Church wouldn't be half as bad if you didn't have to dress up for it. He hated the strangling tie he wore, and the shoes that required polishing, and his mother telling him to comb his hair, what was he *thinking*? His mother was all done up in a way that turned her into a separate creature who smelled powerfully of perfume, whose made-up face was all eyebrows, and who stalked along on high heels. Even Marcie looked weird. Her church clothes were from a store their mom liked that specialized in bright pinks and turquoises and purples, like cheap stuffed animals.

Scanning the parking lot, he caught sight of a friend. "Mom? Can I sit with Josh and his family?"

"No."

"Why not?"

"Because I say so," came back the unsatisfactory answer.

The organ was playing as they took their seats, too far up front for Matt's liking. It was better when the church was crowded and they had to sit in the balcony, where you could at least look down on people and imagine yourself parachuting on top of them. Today there would be no way not to look at the minister right in front of them, and no way to fold the program into a fan or airplane without people noticing, nothing you could do to keep from being eaten up and digested by boredom.

The organ changed its note and everybody stood as the choir marched in, singing in their stagy, loud voices. He didn't know why they weren't all embarrassed. Everything about church was profoundly embarrassing to him, as if religion was something that only took place in the most unnatural circumstances.

The organ played its final chord and the congregation's reedy singing trailed off. At a sign from the pastor, they sat down again. Matthew studied the program to see how many more times they got to stand up. During the long stretches of sitting he went through a complicated, furtive calesthenics designed to keep one leg or another from falling asleep.

He shut out the minister's voice as best he could. The minister was a dramatic speaker, given to pauses, whispers, and thundering crescendos of emotion that you knew he wrote out ahead of time and practiced, probably in the shower. It was all a big fake act. Nobody got as excited about anything as the preacher did, every week, on cue.

A hurricane at least was something real, and although he had not been there, he was able to imagine it as if he had, as if he were on a ship in the ocean with the storm building, and sheets of rain washing over the decks, as if he was one of the rescuers on the beach, making one last desperate effort to reach the injured and the stranded.

But the minister was talking about the hurricane also. That was weird; Matt looked around him, as if he'd been talking out loud and people were laughing at him. The minister asked the congregation to pray for those who had suffered losses in that terrible storm. The usual minister talk. Matt relaxed again.

The minister figured he'd latched onto a good thing and so they got a whole sermon full of hurricane. Life was full of powerful storms. They could blow us off course. Faith was our compass, Jesus was our anchor, heaven our safe harbor. The minister could make even a hurricane boring.

Because, see, our souls were a boat and life was the sea. This was our home port, right here, our church, our community, our family. He made it sound like a board game, the kind they brought out after dinner at one of Matt's relatives' houses, relatives who never let you watch anything good on television.

It didn't sound like much of a life, going straight from here to heaven.

Finally the service was over and he stood up, waiting his turn to file out of the pew and inch along in the herd of dressed-up people until he got himself out of the sanctuary and the reach of the creepy organ music and out the front doors into the open air. Josh was at the bottom of the steps kicking at a loose brick in the walkway. They were laid out in a crisscross pattern that was supposed to be fancy, but over time the ground's freezing and thawing had heaved them up. The church was trying to raise money to have them replaced.

"I'm getting a Game Boy," Josh informed him.

"No way."

"Way."

Matt took a turn at trying to dislodge the loose brick. His mother and Marcie were still inside somewhere. His mother liked to gab with people after church. Josh said, "Uh-oh, here comes Tolliver. What a skank."

"A skank ho," Matt agreed.

They watched the blond girl with the ends of her hair crimped by a curling iron. She came down the steps with her parents and made a point of ignoring them.

Matt's mother came out then, searching for him. "What are you doing?"

"Nothing."

"It doesn't look like nothing to me. What if somebody trips over that and hurts themselves, then how are you going to feel?"

Matt shrugged. You weren't meant to answer. Josh sidled off to find his own parents.

Back home his mother fixed Sunday dinner, which was supposed to be some kind of a special treat but usually turned out to be one of her bad ideas, like today's ham-and-potato casserole. It had some kind of white glop all over it that was so thick, your fork could practically stand up in it. Marcie said it was making her sick to her stomach. Their mother said to finish what was on her plate and drink her milk and Marcie said she had to go to the bathroom and could she be excused please? On her way out of the room she made a secret, triumphant face at her brother, who wished he'd thought of the bathroom idea himself.

His father was scraping the white sauce off a piece of ham. His mother watched this, then said maybe from now on she should just pick up something from Kentucky Fried Chicken after church and see if that would suit them. She made it sound like something they would want to talk her out of.

His mother said, "My classes start tomorrow, so you're going to have to order a pizza for dinner." She was taking community college classes in English and history. It was weird to think of his mother doing homework.

His father said, "I don't get it, why you want to go back to school, what's the point? You going to get a job or something?" He winked at Matt.

"I might want to do just that," his mother said. "Or I might want to get out of the house once in a while and have an intelligent conversation with other adults."

"I don't remember you being this big-time scholar. You didn't ever crack a book if you could help it. You used to say those people were too smart for their own good."

"I guess I used to think you were a lot smarter too."

"Can I be excused?" Matt asked.

After dinner he took his basketball out to the driveway and practiced his layups. Dribble right-handed, plant left foot. Head up, eyes on the backboard. Drive through any defenders, shoot right-handed, elevate right knee. He scores and he's fouled! A chance for the three-point play!

He was hoping that maybe Josh would come by on his bike, or somebody else he knew. Instead his dad came out of the house. "Hey tough guy, how about some one-on-one?"

Matt muttered that he was just messing around.

His dad took a stance between Matt and the basket. "Let's see what you got."

"Dad."

"Whatsamatter, afraid to try? Huh?" His dad put his arms out and shifted his weight from side to side. He looked more like a wrestler than a ballplayer. Whenever Matt went up against his dad, his dad just reached out and clobbered him, smothered him with his weight. It wasn't any kind of a game.

Matt backed up to midcourt to draw his dad out. His dad would be expecting him to fake left and go right. Instead he went straight for the basket, pulled up, took the shot, missed, followed it, grabbed his own rebound on the baseline and came back out again.

"Hah!" his dad said. He was winded and his face was sweaty. He wasn't used to much running. He'd probably had a couple of drinks after dinner too. "Sneaky guy. Let's see you hit something."

"I don't feel like playing."

"Bawk bawk bawk." Chicken noises. His dad was always wanting to arm wrestle with him, or race him, or beat him at some stupid game. Sometimes it was fun and sometimes it was creepy.

"Half-court," said his dad. "Play to twenty-one."

It started off pretty even. His dad was a lot taller than he was, but Matt was quicker. He got off a couple of shots and made one, then his dad got the ball and sank one of his famous belly-floppers, where he just about ran to the basket and heaved the ball in. Matt called traveling but it never did any good.

"I don't want to play if you're not going to follow the rules."

"Aw, whatasa matter wid da widdle baby? Did somebody steal his ball?"

That pissed Matt off and he started to play in earnest. He scored on a reverse layup, leaving his dad flat-footed at the head of the drive. Then they fought for a rebound and his dad got it but couldn't hang on to it and Matt scrambled and came up with it and tipped it in.

"Up by two," Matt called out, but now his dad was really red in the face and really mad, though he was trying not to show it. His dad got the ball and cleared out with his elbows. Matt planted himself right under the basket. His dad was so slow, everything he did took about five minutes. When his dad went up for his shot, Matt did too, but his dad leaned in and came down right on top of him and Matt caught an elbow under the chin and went down hard.

"You OK?" his dad asked.

His mouth was bleeding where his teeth had jammed into his upper lip. His tailbone hurt. His dad put a hand out to help him up. "Come on, let's have a look."

Matt rolled onto his knees and got up from there. "Leave me alone."

His dad bounced the ball against the drive. "What, you quitting? You quitting because you got hurt?"

"Fuck you."

"WHAT DID YOU SAY TO ME?"

Matt turned his back on him and headed into the garage. His father's hand fell on his shoulder. "GET BACK OUT HERE, MISTER."

He swatted the hand away. His heart was going so hard he felt light-headed. There was no way to unsay it. All he could do was to keep disobeying. He went around his mother's car so as to keep it between him and his dad. His dad cursed too, but in a lower voice, something Matt couldn't make out. Matt ran into the house, into the kitchen.

His mother was running water in the sink. "Matt? What happened?"

His dad shoved the back door open and it cracked against the wall behind it. "DON'T YOU WALK AWAY FROM ME WHEN I'M TALKING TO YOU. YOU WANT TO TELL YOUR MOTHER WHAT YOU SAID?"

"Will you stop shouting? What did you do to him?"

"Yeah, that's right, run and hide behind your mommy," his dad said, and now he was mad about not being allowed to be as mad as he wanted to be. His face was all twisted up and purple.

"He's bleeding! Matt, let me see that."

Matt put his hand to his mouth and shook his head. He didn't want her near him either.

His mother wheeled around to face his dad. "Why can't you just leave him alone?"

"Go ahead, treat him like a baby." His dad looked for something to hit or kick. He upended two of the kitchen chairs and sent them skidding across the floor.

"Now who's acting like a baby."

"Get out of my way!"

"Matt," his mother said, "go to the phone in the den and call the police."

"Go ahead, call them. Tell 'em you lost a ball game."

His mother said, "Matt, I want to apologize to you for not finding you a better father."

His dad sat down in one of the chairs he hadn't thrown and put his

head on the table with his arms around it. He made a horrible squealing sound that was crying.

Matt and his mother looked at each other. His mother said, "How
about if the two of you apologize to each other for whatever it was?"

Matt didn't want to. But he said, "I'm sorry, Dad. I was just upset."

"All I ever wanted was a little respect." His dad was still crying. It
was awful.

"I do respect you, Dad."

His mother said, "One of these days he's going to be bigger and
stronger than you are, and he's going to be the one knocking you
around. Matt, let me get you some ice for that."

"I don't need any."

"Come on," she said in her coaxing tone, and he shook his head
because it was true, she wanted to make a baby out of him.

His dad raised his head. His eyes were red and weepy, but he'd recovered his voice. "Do what your mother says."

His mother put some ice in a plastic bag and wrapped the bag in a
dish towel and told him to keep it on the cut. She asked if he wanted
anything else and he said a Coke, and she poured one out in a glass for
him. He wasn't the one who'd been crying, but his face was hot and his
stomach hurt as if he had.

"Now," his mother said. "Let's all just calm down and try and be
considerate of each other."

His father took a paper napkin from the holder on the table and
blew his nose. "I'm taking down that goddamn basketball hoop."

"Good riddance," his mother said.

Matt took the ice and the glass of Coke back to his room. His
dad wouldn't take down the basketball hoop. He never did any of the
things he said he was going to. Just like his mother never really called
the police.

He had posters of Michael Jordan and Karl Malone, big ones, on
his closet doors, which was the only place his mother let him tape
posters. He had a *Star Wars* poster on heavy cardboard propped against
one wall. It was from the first *Star Wars* movie, the best one, before

they got into gross stuff like Leia was his sister and Darth Vader was his dad, and you had to look at Darth Vader's leaky old bald head under his helmet.

It was better when you had parents who weren't your real parents because then somebody could kill them off and nobody felt too bad about it. Luke didn't get to do anything while his aunt and uncle were still around.

In case God was listening, he thought he'd better take back the part about wanting his parents dead, so that if they should happen to die, it wouldn't be his fault.

His mouth had stopped bleeding but it was going to hurt a while longer. If you were the hero of a movie, like Luke, you could save the whole galaxy. If there was ever a movie of his own life, most of it would be the waiting-around part, before anything you did mattered to anyone.

# *Chicago*

He couldn't sleep. He hadn't slept well for weeks, months. It began with one bad night here and there. Then two or three or four in a row, then the dread of them piled up and, as his intelligent, reasonable wife pointed out, his mind became the enemy of his body.

In the beginning Ryan hadn't been too concerned. When he'd got his first jobs in computer programming he'd often worked odd, late-night, all-night hours, because that was the way the work got done, how everyone did it, and if you slept on a cot next to your desk and lived on snack food and Mountain Dew, so much the better. It proved you were an ace, a pirate king.

But he'd been younger then, and if he needed to, he could sleep twenty straight hours over a weekend to catch up. This was different. He stayed awake for no reason, then wore himself down with fretting over it. He went through his days draggy, wired, gravel-eyed. Nothing helped. Drugs didn't work; they shoved him into a black tunnel and drew him only partway out again.

His wife and daughter slept. He prowled the apartment, barefoot on the cold floor. Most nights he went to bed when his wife did, then woke up two or three or four hours later, unable to get back to sleep. The windows were cold to the touch, rimed with white frost. Outside, the same frozen street, same dirty-pink mercury-vapor streetlight, the same stick tree throwing its bare shadow. Although they lived on a Wrigleyville street regarded as quiet, if you watched for even a couple of minutes, some car or truck always rolled along, even during the dead and frigid hours. It was easy for him to imagine, at such times, that he was lost in a nightmare loop of time, when it would always be a black night in stark and staring winter and he would always be awake to see it.

His wife, who had not yet entirely lost patience with him, suggested he enroll in some kind of sleep study. She'd heard of such things. Surely they had them at the big university hospitals. He told her he'd call around and see, although he never actually did. He didn't like the thought of filling out nosy questionnaires, or trying to sleep with wires attached to his head in some blue-lit observation room. If you could fall sleep in a place like that, why would you need any help? His wife (still trying to be constructive, she didn't mean it unkindly) remarked that maybe he *wanted* to be sleepless, for some reason that he himself did not comprehend, it filled some need.

Ryan didn't like the idea that he was bumbling around with secret, destructive motives he was too stupid to figure out. "What, I need to be miserable?"

"Maybe you just need some time alone."

He'd had to think about that one. At work he was often isolated, but never alone. His daughter, a boisterous and piping two-year-old, made any normal adult privacy hard to come by, and solitude impossible.

His wife said, "God knows, if I could keep myself awake long enough, I might try a little insomnia now and then." She stayed at home with their daughter and had her own complaints.

Every effect had a cause, you had to assume that, and maybe the cause for his sleeplessness was a simple matter of fizzing brain chemistry. Not some big hurt that needed worrying about. Only the usual modern complaints: dullness, impatience, staleness. Maybe he should take up some expensive, challenging hobby, such as skiing. A lot of guys he knew were into skiing.

He was thirty-five, which didn't feel either old or young. He didn't know how to measure. It wasn't an age anyone looked forward to, as in "someday, when I'm thirty-five." By now many things had been decided, or decided for him. He missed the sense that everything he did was important and urgent. A kid's feeling. That didn't make it any less true.

But what portion of his life would he change if it meant that his daughter would never have come to be?

His wife said, "Maybe you should get back into running. It used to tire you out."

He'd run along the lakefront in good weather. Lots of people did, at times the whole city seemed to be made up of rangy, purposeful runners pounding out the miles. There was always the lake to watch, its boats and circling birds, its moods in sunshine or its metallic look beneath clouds. There were the beaches, the volleyball games in summer, the strolling pairs, the roller skaters and bicyclists, everybody out to enjoy the city's great front lawn. He guessed it had been the closest he ever came to alone time, taking his place in the communal scenery. It was his city now, and he belonged to it as well. He didn't volunteer to people that he was from Iowa. They always thought that meant he'd grown up on a farm.

But he kept injuring himself, which depressed him because it meant age creeping up on you a little more every year no matter how you tried to stiff-arm it, and by the time he'd healed, the weather had turned cold, and though there were still runners out there, wearing propylene and goggles and earmuffs, he just wasn't that hard-core. He missed it, sure, but he didn't think it was making his body have some kind of nonsleep tantrum about it.

Then there were a few days of thaw, the false warmth you knew not to trust, and a little after midnight, marooned in sleeplessness once more, on impulse he dug out his running shoes and a down vest and a wool hat and wrote his wife a note in case she woke up and missed him. He let himself out and jogged a few blocks over to the Inner Drive and set himself a course of four easy miles, two up and two back. The temperature was in the forties and the sidewalks were wet but not slick. There wasn't anyone else out on foot, but that in itself didn't make him feel unsafe. He had enough confidence in his speed to think he could outrun most problems, he had enough confidence in his judgment to believe he could spot them ahead of time.

Nevertheless, he carried an ID with him, so that in case of accident, his family wouldn't be left to worry and wonder what had become of him. He did such things now, it was second nature to him. It hadn't been that long ago since he was responsible to no one but himself.

North was the direction he chose, with the lake and the streaming traffic on his right. He'd stretched out at home, but the cold made it difficult for his muscles to loosen. All his old injuries (hamstring, knee, hip pointer) made themselves known, though mildly. He thought he could work through them if he didn't push himself too hard. The air was cold, although not so cold that it hurt his lungs. After three-quarters of a mile he struck a good pace. His breathing eased and he took pleasure in his own motion. He'd always liked running at night, though it was another thing his wife had objected to, objections Ryan had dismissed as unrealistic and overcautious. She'd come into a mother's worrying nature.

He couldn't have said what he was thinking—if he was thinking anything at all, or if his mind had been quieted into perfect blank calm—it was not the same as carelessness. In any case he hadn't seen it coming, the false step, the toe catching on an uneven surface. It up-ended him hard, his left knee taking the full impact, the whole of his left side on the cement and his head skidding.

It felt like sleep, like waking up from a restful sleep. There were feet around him, very close to his face, and voices a mile away. Man's voice, woman's voice. Back and forth. His knee hurt like hell. The pain brought him around, otherwise he would have been content to lie there listening to the mere sound of the voices without their taking on meaning. "Shit," he said, or tried to say, tried to bend his knee up to where he could massage it.

A man knelt next to him. "Hey buddy, how you doing?"

"That's a stupid," Ryan said, meaning, *stupid question*. Something was wrong with his mouth as well.

The woman said, "I think he needs an ambulance." He saw her feet, her dressed-up shoes.

"No." He shook his head. It felt loose on his neck. He was determined that there be no ambulance, although he could not have said why.

The man said, "He's got a head injury, he ought to get it checked out." The man sounded like a bossy type. Ryan decided he didn't like him.

He would have to proceed with cunning. He forced himself to sit up briskly, as if his head didn't feel like it was full of sparkling confetti. "S'my knee that hurts." He rolled his leg from side to side, demonstrating.

The woman said coaxingly, "Let's get a doctor to look at that knee, how about it?"

Ryan thought about standing up. If he could stand, he could get out of their clutches. "Lil help here," he said, attempting a jaunty tone.

Instead they took a step away from him and conferred in low voices. Then they surrounded him again. He thought maybe there were more than two of them. The man, or a different man, said, "You live around here? Someplace around here?"

"Yeah." They were waiting for him to tell them where. He felt in his vest pocket and came up with the flat wallet that held his ID and house keys. This was taken from him and passed around.

"Buddy?" It was the bossy man again. "The lady's willing to give you a ride home. If you got somebody there to look after you."

"Ah, yeah." He was expected to say more. "Wife."

Then he was hoisted to his feet. He found himself draped over the bossy man's shoulder, unpleasantly close to his jowls and large unclean ear. A car—the woman's—was pulled up to the curb, and after some discussion it was agreed that he should be placed in the backseat so he wouldn't have to bend his leg. He felt something wet leaking from the vicinity of his knee, either blood or melted snow. The woman got

behind the wheel and waited while the others arranged him length-
wise on the seat. "Thanks," he said, waving. Then the door closed on
him and the car started up. It was a Mercedes, luxurious, new smell-
ing, with a leather interior the color of vanilla pudding. He hoped he
wouldn't bleed on it.

"How you doing back there?" she asked. "Still with me?"

She pulled away from the curb. He wanted to say something clever
about where else would he be, then he realized it was a question about
his mental state, much as you might ask someone if they knew the day
of the week or the name of the current president. "Huh," he said.

"I was driving right behind you when you fell. Scary. You practically
cartwheeled."

"I feel like an idiot," Ryan said. His first complete, coherent sentence.

"It could happen to anyone." She turned around and smiled, then
turned back again to attend to her driving.

He hadn't seen her face until then. He stared at the rearview mirror
where now only her eyes were visible, passing in and out of strips of
light and shadow.

She said, "I'm just going to go up two blocks, then turn around and
go down Archer."

"Fine."

"I could still take you to an ER, if you want."

"That's OK."

Silence as she braked at intersections, turned back south again. He
was afraid his damaged head would make him say something wrong or
crazy, he was afraid he was mistaken about everything. He was afraid of
not being mistaken. "Here," he said, once they approached his block.
"The one with the courtyard."

She eased the car up to the entrance. "Do you want me to help you
out? Can you put any weight on that leg?"

"Ah, I think I'll be . . . if you could just . . ." He was having a hard
time maneuvering himself to the edge of the seat. He didn't think he
could get the door open.

She set the parking brake, got out, and walked around to the curb side. She opened the car door and peered inside. "Stuck?"

Ryan planted his good leg and pivoted out to the street, holding on to the Mercedes's roof. There was no way not to look at her. A lady doing a favor for a stranger, her smile pleasant and impersonal. Something about the way she was dressed—heels, good coat, perfume—suggested that she might be on her way home from a party. "Thanks again," he said.

"Let's see if you can walk."

He took a hop, lurched, crumpled halfway over, straightened himself. Led with his good leg, then let his bad leg catch up. "Like a champ."

"I'm hoping you don't have to climb any stairs," she said. Which stopped short of an invitation to help him.

"Elevator. Lucky."

"You should probably stay awake for a while, in case you have a concussion."

"No problem."

"I'll watch and make sure you get inside," she said, and walked back around to get behind the wheel of her car.

It was now a point of pride for him to get himself to the front door, and he did so, panting, cursing, but keeping up his pace so that she wouldn't feel obliged to come after him and embarrass him further. At the door he turned around and waved. She tapped the horn and pulled away.

Maybe she hadn't recognized him. But she'd had his ID. Or maybe she'd forgotten him, but he didn't believe that. Or had she hoped that he would not remember or recognize her?

Once inside the apartment he managed to peel off his pants, clean up the bruised and shredded skin of his knee, apply ice, take a Vicodin left over from his last injury, get back in bed beside his sleeping wife, and in spite of all the wisdom about concussions, and in spite of all his history of bad sleep, he was asleep almost at once.

His knee swelled up and made walking near impossible. He spent the rest of the week at home, trying to work at the kitchen table, or navigating around the apartment using a mop as a crutch. His wife didn't come out and say that it served him right for sneaking out and roaming the streets so imprudently, but it was clear this was what she thought. The weather turned cold again and the three of them stayed inside, an extended period of togetherness. His daughter was delighted to have him home and heaped him with toys and books and baby dolls, all the loot of the recent Christmas, gone slightly stale until they were revived by the wonder of his presence.

"Daddy look! Daddy read!"

He was sought after, importuned, courted. His complete and constant attention was necessary to her happiness. She had silky hair the color of honey that might in time turn into his blond, or his wife's darker shade. Her eyes were blue, their lashes damp and spiky, her skin a perfect layer of bloom. He had never imagined loving anything as entirely, as violently, as he loved her. And she loved him and her mother because she had no choice except to do so.

But she would grow beyond them and into the wider world, and at some point he would become more and more the background of her life.

Ryan had to sleep with his leg elevated, and if he tried to roll or shift positions, it sometimes woke him up. But although neither his mind nor his body was at ease, he got through his nights without those numb hours of wakefulness. It was as if they had served their purpose. They gave form and shape to a restlessness he hadn't known was in him.

He'd already tried finding Janine in the phone book, and as expected, there was no listing for her. He was certain, intuitively, that she lived here, she hadn't been just visiting or passing through. She'd been cautious with him because she knew she could be found.

Once he returned to work, he had the opportunity to better proceed. There was no question that he was going to try to find her, if only because she didn't want to be found. Beyond that, he didn't permit himself to go, because he knew very well that he was being willful and perverse, poking a stick at something that might rise up and do him harm.

There was a Pasqua in Lake Forest—her father, Ryan was pretty sure. But he didn't think he would get anywhere by calling and nosing around, claiming some vague old acquaintanceship. Her father wouldn't have given someone like him the time of day. He wasn't glib enough, or inventive enough, to come up with some better cover story. He believed she must live in the city, and perhaps not all that far from him, given her presence on that particular street at a late hour. He kept his eyes open as he went about his rounds of commuting and errands. No sign of her.

Her car had looked new. She'd always driven new cars; it seemed that prosperity had not left her. He searched out Mercedes dealers in the northern suburbs, found three of them. It was another two weeks before he was able to make his way there (his wife and daughter dropped off with a friend, another mommy, for a play date and shared lamentations). He sauntered around the lot, admiring the high polish of the new, immaculate metal, until a salesman joined him. They shook hands, and Ryan asked about this model and that one, heard about their features, their value, their many virtues.

And didn't Dr. Pasqua's daughter have one of these?

At the first dealership he drew a blank, but at the second he was told that yes, Mrs. Burnham had this year's model, she was pleased with it. Burnham. Now he had a name.

Then he went no further. He carried his new knowledge as he might a gun in his pocket. He and his wife had a discussion, verging on argument, about money, and another one about sex. If they could get around to in-laws, they'd achieve the full trifecta of married conflicts. It might have reassured him or consoled him that their problems were the same as other people's, and other people got by or muddled through them. But it made him impatient and melancholy.

As part of an effort to create more time for each other, which they both agreed they needed, one night they got a babysitter and went out for dinner at an elegant Gold Coast Italian restaurant, the kind that served nothing in tomato sauce. It was still winter. They had to park a couple of blocks away and quick-walk through the trampled slush at the curbs. Their eyes watered from the wind. At the restaurant his wife unwrapped herself, took off her heavy coat and wool hat and muffler and gloves, revealing her pretty dress. They were shown to their table. They settled themselves and shook their heads and took a steadying breath. These days it seemed to take so much effort to do anything.

They ordered drinks; the waiter brought bread and olive oil. His wife looked around the room. The restaurant was new to them. "What do you think?"

"Nice." He thought it looked like any other restaurant, with its recessed lights and expensive surfaces and gliding waiters. Nor did it smell of food. "You look great tonight."

"Thank you." Her fingers touched her hair, her throat. Since their daughter's birth, she'd worried about her weight. She went on grim campaigns of dieting and exercise, doing battle with her extra ten pounds, although Ryan told her truthfully, no one noticed or cared about them but her, she was a beautiful, sexy adult woman whom he still had the hots for. The fight about sex had made it necessary for him to say this from time to time.

"You look good in red." The dress had a low neckline. His eyes rested on the place between her breasts where there would be just enough space for his exploring fingers.

She shrugged. "Trying to make up for the days when I never change out of sweatpants."

The waiter brought their drinks. They opened the menus and studied them. The different courses were presented in florid calligraphy, and there were words with which they were not familiar. *"Carpaccio?"* Ryan ventured.

"We can ask the waiter."

"It's not important." He hated asking about things he thought he should already know.

"You are so funny sometimes. That's what the waiter's here for, to answer questions. And why are you whispering? You always whisper in restaurants. Yes you do."

He guessed he did. A stupid, hick habit he hadn't broken. A good restaurant still felt a little like church, or a library, a place requiring solemn good behavior.

He didn't much like having it pointed out to him. As if she was some born sophisticate! She'd grown up in Grand Rapids, Michigan, for Christ's sake!

Because he didn't want to spoil the evening with ill humor, he said, "I will ask the waiter about the carpaccio. I will bellow at him."

They ordered and their food came, and it was all very good. Things such as veal, and gnocchi, and thin-shelled pastas filled with wild mushrooms. They agreed that this must be cuisine from some fortunate part of Italy where life was so good, no one ever emigrated. Unlike the poor Sicilians with their meatballs and pizza. "I'd like to go there sometime," his wife said. "Italy."

"Really?" This was a mild surprise. "Why Italy?"

"Because it's so different from everywhere else. Everything I grew up with."

Ryan knew what she'd grown up with: the Dutch Reformed Church, as pious and grim as anything the Lutherans could offer, the expectation that she would settle down within twenty-five miles of her birthplace and raise up a family of equally pious, grim, judgmental, fault-finding progeny. Really, it was extraordinary that their two Old World ancestries had dispersed to the New and united themselves in marriage. They had laughed about it and resolved to leave behind them all the conventions and strictures of their upbringings.

His wife said, "Not that I knew any Italians. Just what you'd see on television. Or like, *The Godfather*. They had big messy families, they sang opera, they had passionate fights, they drank a lot of wine . . ."

"They stomped grapes with their feet. They danced the tarantella."

"Something like that." His wife gazed around the well-mannered dining room, where no one was doing anything boisterous, shouting *Salute,* or planning hits.

Ryan said, "Clearly, we have to get you to Italy. Let you bust loose."

She shook her head. "When is that supposed to happen?"

"When Anna's a little older. When it's a little easier to travel with her, when she can appreciate it."

"What about Spud?" Spud was the name they had given to their planned, yet-to-be-conceived second offspring.

"Spud can come too."

"That means, maybe we'll get there in about fifteen years."

"Not if we make it a priority."

"A priority," his wife said in the patient, instructive tone he had come to dislike, "is saving for college educations, or for a house, or an orthodontist, or something we really need."

"Maybe what we really need is a little bit of pleasure once in a while."

"*Pleasure* meaning 'self-indulgence.'"

"You say that like it's a bad thing," Ryan said, trying to deflect her mood. Once she began in this dreary, my-life-is-a-series-of-burdens vein, they often ended up in an argument. He thought she didn't really regret her life up until now; she just wanted to complain about it.

"If you have a child, the child comes first. The child gets her orange juice when she needs it, and her vaccinations when she needs them, and her vitamins—"

"It's not like we leave her out in the car while we go have a few beers. Jesus, Ellen."

"If you have a child," she went on doggedly, "then you've made certain choices. You've said, 'This is important enough for me to be unselfish. Because someone depends on me entirely for her very existence.'" His wife slumped back against her chair, looking both tragic and irritated.

"I get that," Ryan said. "Why would you think I didn't?"

The waiter appeared then, asking if they would like to look at the dessert menu. "By all means," Ryan told him. "Is there anything particularly self-indulgent tonight?"

She flicked her eyes over the menu and closed it. Ryan said, "A little gelato wouldn't kill you."

"I'm already going to have to swim extra laps to work off this meal." Swimming was his wife's exercise two days a week. The Y had a kids' program and his daughter was a Water Baby, working her way up to Tadpole.

"Tiramisu," Ryan told the waiter. "And an espresso, please."

"Good luck sleeping," his wife said, and she was right about that, but by now he didn't care.

When his dessert came, he offered her a bite of it, and she said no thank you. She watched him eat. She said, "Men can do that. Pretend that life doesn't change entirely once you have a child. They're not on the front lines. In the trenches."

"Right." He saw no point in arguing with her when she got like this. It wasn't even an argument.

"I don't forget about her for a minute. I can't. It's almost like I'm still pregnant, when everything I did or ate or even thought affected her. Fed straight into her."

Ryan reached across the table and took one of her hands in his. "I'm a little worried about you."

She shrugged. "Well, maybe you should be." Her hand stayed inert, neither drawing back nor squeezing his.

He paid the check and they retrieved their coats and he said he would go get the car and come back to pick her up so she wouldn't have to go so far in the cold. In truth, he wanted to get away from her for even the ten minutes it might take him to walk to the car. Alone time.

For the first time, he found himself wondering if his wife had some kind of mommy depression, the kind you read about. More and more often there had been scenes like this one, when she seemed determined to take no delight in their child, no delight in their present or in their future.

And that wasn't like her. She was as levelheaded and focused as any woman he knew. She'd wanted to be married (to someone, presumably to him), she'd wanted a child, children, she would stay at home for three years and then reattack the job market. Now it seemed that none of that was worthwhile.

He would talk to her about seeing her doctor, getting a prescription. Lots of people took things nowadays. Half his office was probably on Prozac.

It wasn't true, as she'd accused him, that he was lighthearted about having a child, or that he separated easily from his responsibilities. The terrible weight of loving his daughter was with him always.

The car was up another block and down a side street. This block of north Clark was home to any number of restaurants, their windows allowing views of warm light and of people taking pleasure in each other, in the food and sparkling glassware before them, so that on this block, at least, you could believe the whole world was a place of elegance, abundance, and good cheer. He was passing by one of these, its windows outlined in small white electric lights, its tables blooming with arrangements of white flowers, when he saw Janine Pasqua Burnham sitting at a table next to the glass.

He kept walking, then once he was out of her view he looked back to see who sat across the table from her. A man, Ryan couldn't make out his face, only a general impression of his dark shirt, casual, undressy. He took two steps past the restaurant's door, then turned around and went inside.

A host stood at the entry, checking off names; the restaurant was busy and even this late at night people were waiting in the bar to be seated. Ryan walked past them, not wanting to explain himself, turned a corner and went up to Janine's table. Her back was to him; the man saw him coming and narrowed his eyes, a question, an alarm. "Hi," Ryan said to him, then turned to her. "Hello, Janine."

It jolted her, he saw it in her face; the jig was up. Then something careful and amused took its place. "Hello, glad to see you're back on your feet."

To the man Ryan said, "Beg your pardon. Just saying hello. Ryan Erickson." He held out his hand.

"John Delgado." Not her husband, then. Or at least, not Burnham.

They shook. To Janine, Ryan said, "I just wanted to thank you again." She wore a black turtleneck, a necklace of big silver chunks and matching earrings. Her old style, translated into a more expensive key. They must just have arrived; they had drinks in front of them but no food. To Delgado he said, "I was running and I wiped out on the street. The lady was kind enough to help me up and clean me off."

Janine said, "I'm good about things like that."

Delgado looked at her, then at Ryan, trying to get a read on them. "Care to join us?" he said, not meaning it. Either he wasn't in a good mood tonight, or he was never in a good mood. He was one of those men so determinedly bald, it was hard to imagine them ever having hair.

"Thanks, no. Pleasure to see you again. Nice meeting you, John."

"Watch your step out there," Janine said, her game face still on.

He nodded and went back out through the crowded bar and outside. He reached his car and drove around an extra block so he could pass the restaurant again. They sat as before, and he thought he saw Janine turn her face toward the dark street, scanning it.

He pulled up to the curb at the Italian restaurant. His wife emerged and made her careful, teetering way across the sidewalk. When he stepped out to open the car door for her, she waved him away. "I got it."

That night he had trouble sleeping, which his wife said was what you could expect if you drank espresso at that hour.

A week later, he found a J. Burnham in the phone book. He looked up the address, one of those far-north enclaves, where town-house and condo developments had been constructed around leafy squares. When he called the number he got an answering machine—her voice—and hung up without leaving a message. Then, fed up with himself, he called back. "Hi Janine, Ryan Erickson. I guess we could wait and run into each other a third time, but I hope you'll give me a call so we can have an actual conversation before then. This is my office number."

His phone rang. "What did you do, get in touch with the Alumni Association?"

She meant, finding out her name and phone number. Ryan said, "I thought you were never going to get married."

"At the time," she said, "it seemed like a good idea."

"Who's Delgado?"

"None of your business."

"You look good these days, Janine. I wanted to tell you that, even if I don't get to say anything else."

She didn't speak for a moment. Then she said, "Look, I like my life exactly the way it is."

"Glad to hear it."

"You're like, a hallucination or something."

"Thank you."

"I mean, overnight, you changed from a hippie punk into a—how old are you now anyway? Thirty-six?"

"Thirty-five."

"So, who did you get to marry you?"

"Her name is Ellen. We have a little girl, two years old."

"Ellen," Janine said, as if the name was something you could shake out and examine, like a piece of fabric. "That's nice that you have a little girl."

"How about you, any kids?"

"Not at present."

He waited, but she didn't elaborate. "Why didn't you say something. The night I fell."

"I don't know. It was like *The Twilight Zone.* Too, too weird. You know you practically did a cartwheel. As if that wasn't strange enough."

"So why did you drive off and leave me, I'm talking back in Iowa, I'm talking however many years ago, that was a genuinely crappy thing to do, you know?"

While he waited for her to answer, he looked out the slice of window that had been allotted him. His office was in the north Loop, off Dearborn. His view, facing north, was hemmed in by a commercial building, occupants unknown, with a coffee shop and shoe repair and a couple of other retail outlets at street level. He was five stories up, near enough to sort out people as they passed along the sidewalks and waited at traffic lights, bundled against the cold, burdened with parcels, filing through a roofed construction tunnel built out into the street, intent on getting from one place to another. By six o'clock, the streets would be empty and unsafe. No one lived here.

She said, "Were you following me the other night? At the restaurant?"

"You're kidding." She wasn't. "No, Ellen and I had dinner at Delphine, and I was getting the car."

"I don't remember giving you my phone number."

"I don't remember you answering my question."

"I don't know if I want to do this," Janine said. "I have to hang up now."

The phone clicked in his ear. "Do what?" he said to the empty air.

Ryan went home at the end of the day and his wife was standing at the kitchen sink, running water. She had been at the kitchen sink when he'd left that morning. His daughter demanded that he listen to a story about her baby doll, the baby was on the roof and she fell and her baby's friend fell too. "Oh no," Ryan said. "Did they get hurt? Did they have to go to the doctor?"

"No. They ate some candy."

Both of them, wife and daughter, required his attention. From the moment he walked through the door, he was divided into slices and parceled out. There was a sound of metal slamming in the kitchen, and he looked up. His daughter sensed his focus wavering. Her voice rose, a treble spiral. Her two hands pulled at his fingers. Her story grew more and more desperate, packed with marvels. She—Anna—and the baby saw a dog and the dog stole the candy. It was a red dog. The dog's name was . . . She was running out of details.

"Was the dog named Tickle Me?"

"No!"

"Are you sure? Because I saw a big red dog and you know what his name was? Huh? You know?"

She collapsed in giggles, wanting and not wanting to say it. "Tickle . . ."

"Huh? What was that?"

"Tickle Me!"

She shrieked as his fingers found her ribs. Red-faced, helpless, writhing from side to side. Her little Winnie-the-Pooh shirt riding up over her tummy. "Woof," Ryan said. "Woof woof."

His wife called from the kitchen. "Please don't get her all stirred up. I have to feed her."

He left off tickling. "OK, Anna Banana. Mom says we gotta calm down."

His daughter said the dog was Tickle Me, Tickle Me, and Ryan said the dog was all gone now. He redirected her attenton to the television and one of her Big Bird videos.

In the kitchen his wife was shaking a strainer of potatoes. Steam made her face look like something boiled, and her hands were enveloped in oven mitts. At times he wondered if she purposely made herself into a drudge. "Hey," he said, kissing her bare neck just below her pinned-up hair.

His wife said, "I'm going to feed her and get her in her pajamas and then we can eat. If you aren't too hungry to wait."

When they did sit down to dinner, his wife said that it was time to look for a day care, she had decided to go back to work, or at least look for a job. Ryan knew better than to react right away. These days he treated her as if she were a piece of glass with a crack in it. He forked up a piece of chicken, chewed and swallowed. He asked what had brought all this on, wasn't it a little ahead of schedule? His wife said, "I feel like I'm locked in a box, just the two of us, there isn't anybody in the building who has kids her age, there's nobody to talk to, if I want to go outside with her we have to mount an expedition. And you know there's all these other boxes with other moms and kids all over the city. It doesn't seem like people ought to live that way. Maybe if we were near family, yours or mine, it'd be easier. I don't know."

"If you think it would make you happy to get a job, then that's the way you ought to proceed."

She looked at him with a measuring look. "Happy, you mean, to not be such a drag all the time."

"I don't think you're a drag, Ellen. Maybe bored. A little over-whelmed."

She only shrugged. They went back to eating. Their daughter was playing the *Sesame Street* video again. She never got tired of it. Ryan said, "You don't really want to move, do you? I mean, the family part."

"Oh, I know we can't. Even if we wanted to. Where would we work? But sometimes I think, we blew it, we were both so anxious to get away and not be one bit like our parents and we had to, it was so smothering. But back home, I can look up and down just about any street and there's people I'm either related to or I've known them all my life and my parents have known them and my grandparents knew their grandparents and there's a comfort in that. I miss it. That's all I'm saying. Here, it's like we're not from anywhere."

"You wouldn't really want Anna to grow up in a place where they think you're going to hell, and they mean that literally, if you don't vote Republican."

"They know they're a part of something," his wife said. "We're just a part of each other." She got up from the table and went to check on their daughter.

The Great State of Alienation. It stretched from sea to shining sea. *Everybody in America is one of two things, either in or out.* His wife was right, they'd worked so hard and were so proud to be on the outside of everything they'd grown up with. But they were inside of nothing but themselves.

City of brutal and wayward temperatures, of horizontal snow and lashing rains, city of instant potholes and blackened slush. By the end of February, winter had rolled back far enough to make you believe in spring. The gutters ran with snowmelt, the sidewalks gleamed. His wife found a part-time paralegal job, work she'd done before the baby, with the promise of full-time work to come. Their daughter went to a private day care a mile or two away, at the home of a lady who had come highly recommended. There was some squalling at first, some crying when she was left at Mrs. Carter's, but that was short-lived, and it appeared that they had made a good decision. His wife seemed happier, more energized, and she dealt efficiently with all the chores and items necessary to get both herself and Anna out the door in the morning and ready for their days. Ryan dropped Anna off at Mrs. Carter's and Ellen picked her up when she got off work in the early afternoons.

It seemed that they had navigated one of those bump-in-the-road times, one of those comes-with-the-territory crises that you ought to see coming but you never did.

He thought about Janine from time to time, but he made an effort to regard their encounters as something freakish and isolated, like seeing a celebrity on the street. Then she called him again at his office. He picked up his phone to hear her announce, "I wanted to clear a few things up."

"All right. Good." He was treading water, wondering how to deflect, or answer, what might be coming.

"I don't write poetry anymore."

"OK."

"Not in any organized, disciplined way. It would be fair to say, occasionally."

"Well that's . . ." He was about to say "better than nothing," but stopped himself before that particular train wrecked. "Do you miss it?"

"I miss a lot of things."

Another of their silences. Janine said, "It would be all right if we saw each other. Just to talk. There need to be some ground rules here."

"What the hell, Janine. You decide whatever it is you want and then do it. You always did anyway."

"And you always got pissy about it, you big Nordic palooka, because you never had an impulse you didn't stifle or second-guess. Sorry. That's a little harsh. Besides, I believe *palooka* refers to boxing, a second-rate boxer. I still have a poet's precision with words."

In a nearly businesslike tone, they agreed to meet the next week on an afternoon Ryan believed it would be possible for him to leave work early.

*Just to talk.* He guessed he believed that was all it was.

Janine's neighborhood was much as he'd expected it. Pretty, upscale, home to bookstore cafés and a rotating series of ethnic restaurants: Thai, Korean, Basque, Aztec. People walked past with copies of the *Reader* beneath their arms, or with trotting dogs on leashes, or both. Grown-up hip, with money. Janine's building was a redbrick compound trimmed with white doors and woodwork and a carpeted lobby with a chandelier. It reminded him of those suburban banks meant to resemble gracious homes. He spoke through the intercom and was admitted.

Her apartment was on the third floor. Janine was standing at the entrance when he got off the elevator. "Over here." Since they couldn't decide whether to shake hands or embrace, they did neither. Janine stood aside to let him enter.

"Nice place," he said. "As a Nordic palooka, I think I'd probably be more comfortable out in the barn."

"I said I was sorry about that." She shut the front door and stood next to him. He kept forgetting how short she was. "Give me your coat."

She took it away and Ryan was left to assess the raised, beamed ceiling, the fireplace made of slate and distressed wood, white walls, the flood of light from the high windows. There were a couple of large paintings, slashes of color. His Iowa/hick self couldn't have said if they were good, bad, indifferent, art or non-art, but they were at least real, paint-on-canvas paintings.

Janine had disappeared down a hallway—he had no clear sense of how large the place was—he felt a kind of vertigo, the strong sun coming in at this unexpected angle—wondering what blazing stupidity or delusion had brought him here in the first place—then Janine's footsteps walking back to him.

She was carrying a tray with two tall glasses. Ice cubes chinked. "Pomegranate juice," she said. "It's my new kick. Go on, try it."

She sat. Ryan sat too, but on the couch opposite her. The pomegranate juice was deep pink, like a stain. It tasted pink too. She was watching him. "Interesting," he said, and set it back down.

"I could get you a beer."

Ryan said no thanks. Janine leaned back in her chair and crossed her ankles in a tidy way. She was wearing sandals and her toenails were painted coral. Narrow black pants and a shirt that was some echo of her old gauzy florals, jade green and peacock. Hard to get a sense of her body beneath it, what might have changed. He tried not to think about any of that.

Hair a little shorter, but still dark and wild. Her skin looked very white against it, even in the room's strong light. Gold earrings and a gold cuff bracelet. No rings. The shape of her face, that perfect roundness, was now smudged or blurred. It was as if the face he remembered, her younger face, lay just beneath it, and every time he looked at her he had to try and bring his vision into focus.

"So . . . ," he began, spreading his hands to indicate the room around him. "All this . . ."

He waited, but she only looked at him, politely expectant. "I thought you'd be living in a commune or something." The wild girl he used to know, now looking every bit at ease in such a place.

"We all grew up and got better furniture."

"Come on. What do you do for money?"

"My dad got the car for me. I saw you eyeballing it."

"OK, but . . ."

"My husband died."

"What, he . . ."

"Died."

"I'm sorry." He wasn't sure if this was meant to be an answer to his question about money.

"Three years ago of liver cancer. He never knew he had it, never had so much as a bad cold. He collapsed on the street, went into the hospital, and was gone six weeks later. His name was Walt, by the way. Walt Burnham. He was only forty-five."

"I'm sorry," he said again. Her face flickered with something—impatience?—from having to tell the story too many times, from having to accept sympathy. "I'm sure you . . . somebody you loved . . ."

"That's usually why you marry a person."

There was another leaden silence. Marriage was love gone public. He had married Ellen because he loved her. He loved her because he had married her.

Janine said, "He ran a brokerage house. A smart, smart guy. He had a nutty side too, that's why we got along so well. He liked talking, cooking, company, goofing around, going places. We were married five years. I miss him."

Again Ryan murmured that he was sorry. Her hair fell into her eyes and she brushed it away. It was a gesture so familiar to him—and yet the woman herself had become so strange—it took him another moment to get his bearings.

He said, "Do you remember my little sister, Torrie?"

"Sure I do."

"She was in a bad car accident when she was seventeen. She's better now but it left her with brain damage. Impairments. She still lives with my parents."

"Crap. *Crap.*" Janine glared at him. "That's horrible. I'm sorry. Oh crap."

"I'm not there as much as I should be. I can't be OK around her. Or be any way. It's too sad. And she sees it in me, she can tell."

The sun lowered and Janine turned on the lamps. They talked about her family—they were as nuts as ever—and his job—he managed an IT division for an educational publisher. She asked him whatever happened to political science, and he said political science wasn't the growth industry people made it out to be. They talked about Bush, whom Ryan said at least wasn't as scary as Reagan. Janine said that nobody who ran the CIA should ever be president. Ryan's eyes slid to his watch. He'd be expected back home soon.

She saw him preparing to leave. "Would you like to see the rest of the place?"

He said he would. They stood up and she walked him back through the hallway to a den—the white walls gave way to brick—dining room, a kitchen done in some high style, with the cupboards painted glazed orange. "Walt liked to cook," Janine said. So this was the place where she'd lived with a husband. Too many things to comprehend, coming at him too fast. He felt as if he was in a movie running backward and forward in fits and starts.

Another hallway—a hesitation, then she led the way—bedrooms, a pearly bathroom—Ryan ducked his head inside each, not really seeing anything, issuing fatuous compliments—"Nice! Great!"—until he could back himself out to the safety of the living room.

Janine brought his coat. Smiled up at him. "Well," he said. An experiment in speech. They leaned toward each other, attempted a hug. He felt the warm weight of her. He stepped closer and ran his hands along her blouse. Tried to get to her breasts through her shirt. Although he had spent years without thinking of it, he'd never forgotten the way the two of them fit together.

Janine said, very softly, "Oh," nothing more, and then they were kissing, and that felt amazing, better than you would have imagined just kissing to be, and then the dumb commotion of his dumb dick overwhelmed him, a slow fuse just now going off in his skin, and he was trying to reach every part of her, lifting her on one of his knees so she straddled it.

Finally they backed away from each other. Janine raised his hand to her mouth, ran her tongue along one of his fingers, then back again. Her head bent over it, moving side to side.

"I have to go," Ryan said. His voice gone hoarse.

"You were always like catnip to me, you know?"

"I have to go now."

"You can come back." Her face, a stranger's face, suddenly close to his.

"I don't know." And he didn't. He didn't know anything. He got himself downstairs and into the street. He didn't look up in case she was watching him from her windows.

His wife and daughter both wanted to tell him about their days, and he listened like a good daddy, presiding over dinnertime and story-time and bathtime and nobody noticed anything different about him and maybe there wasn't. Then the weekend came and there were chores to do, and an excursion his wife wished the three of them to make to a children's fair. He and his wife were good-humored with each other, one of their easy times.

What did it mean that he could wall himself off in this way, keep one current of his life separate from another? Which part of him was false? He did and did not know himself, just as he did and did not know Janine. He felt that old bleak lonesomeness, that sense of standing outside the lit circle, looking in. That at least had not changed.

On Monday afternoon he called Janine from the office. She said, "I wasn't going to call. If you didn't."

"Well, here I am."

They were used to silences by now and they let this one take its time. Then Ryan said, "Everything seems like such a long time ago. Not just you, but everything when I was a kid."

Janine said, "I'm sorry we didn't go on that trip together. You know, for spring break."

"Yeah, I know the one." He could better picture her, now that he'd seen where she lived. He imagined her in the sunny front room, or lying back in bed with her white legs bare.

"I was really, really mad at you. Because you were acting like this furtive, chickenshit horny teenager. Then when we got back to school, you wouldn't talk to me."

"Yeah, things kind of fell apart after that. No surprise." His hand prying her legs open. Her eyes closed, her mouth making shapes.

The line stayed silent. Ryan wanted to ask, *Are you still the same person you used to be? Am I? That same kid, in there somewhere?* Instead he said, "Could I ask you why you don't write poems anymore?"

"I guess once Walt died, it became . . . it was all I wanted to write about, and it seemed . . . disgusting. To use something like that as fodder. The man *died,* for Christ's sake. And all I could do was write a poem?" There was a rustle of sound that Ryan was able to identify as her shaking her head, the sound of her earrings against her hair. The way she used to crouch above him, her hair falling over his face.

"Maybe," he said, "you'll feel differently about that in time."

"Maybe."

After a moment Janine said, "Look, I do want to see you again. I want you to come see me. You decide. You decide what it means."

They said Friday afternoon, same as before, and got off the phone as quickly as possible.

He had never made a pact with himself that, once married, he could go outside of his marriage from time to time. But now he had to admit that he'd held something back, left one page of the contract unsigned. So that was one part of himself.

The night before he was to see Janine, his wife said, "What's the matter with you?"

"What?"

"You heard me." They were in bed. The door to their room was left open and the light in the hall was on in case Anna needed to come find them in the night. Lately she'd been having her own fit of sleeplessness and woke them with requests for play or conversation. His wife raised herself up on one elbow, listening. "I thought she was up. Guess not. You've been ten miles away all night. What gives?"

He could deny it, or come up with some lame excuse, something at work. "I don't know. Just tired, I guess." Lame-o. He attempted a small yawn.

"You're sure?" His wife had a habit of persistence. "Because you can tell me. Even if it's something not so great."

"If there was anything to tell, I would tell you."

"I don't want there to be these empty spaces between us. I want us to work through things. Like before I got the job, that wasn't a good time for me but we managed. We came out on the other side of it."

"I'm glad you're happier now." He found her shoulder, patted it.

"I don't want us to be just coparents. You see couples like that, all they have in common are their kids."

Ryan said Of course, and Of course not. One or the other of those had to be the right answer. His wife rolled over in bed until the length of her body pressed against his. Her hands ventured over him. He froze. He felt a kind of desperate shame. Guys back in school who used to brag about it, *I fucked two different girls in one day.* He guessed he'd been envious. He guessed he'd had his own fantasies. But now . . .

The mechanics of arousal, already under way. Maybe it was something you could get used to. He hadn't thought it through yet. He didn't want to. He didn't want to make love to his wife all the while pretending she was Janine.

He covered his wife's hands with his own, stilling them. He kissed her forehead and turned his face deeper into his pillow. After a time she withdrew her hands. Ryan pretended to fall asleep, and sometime after that, he did.

The next morning he called Janine from the office. "Hi. Just checking in. I'll be there by two. Earlier, if I can manage it."

"All right."

He didn't trust the sound of her voice: remote, even a little sad. He didn't want to start asking, What's wrong? as his wife had the night before and hear her say, Nothing. It was only natural that one or the other of them would have a case of shaky nerves, or cold feet. All you could do was blunder through. He said, "I'm looking forward to seeing you. Really."

"Me too."

"OK then. Got to go."

He had his afternoon covered. He was always free to take more leeway with his work hours if he wanted; except for meetings and some of the corporate training sessions, all that mattered was getting tasks done and keeping systems up and running. It was just better if he was there, presiding over the cubicles. He had to wonder how it would look if he started ducking out regularly on Friday afternoons.

His wife's call came a little before twelve. "You have to go pick up Anna at Mrs. Carter's. She has some kind of dental emergency. I mean

Mrs. Carter. I can't do it, I have to leave here for a deposition, it's going to last all afternoon."

It took Ryan a minute to sort this out. "Pick her up, what am I supposed to do with her?"

His wife said she had spent the last hour trying to get that covered. She'd talked to Delia, the college girl who occasionally babysat for them. He could take her to Delia's apartment in Wicker Park, Delia could keep her until five, then one of them would have to get back there. Ellen would give him the address and phone number. "Or you could leave early and just go home with her."

"I can't do that." There would be new complications. Phone calls.

"I'm sorry but this is what happens sometimes with day care. Do you have a pen?"

He copied the numbers, already making calculations. North to Mrs. Carter's, south again to Wicker Park, far north to Janine's, then back in rush-hour traffic to pick up his daughter if he had to. He could still be at Janine's by two. They'd still have a couple of hours. He tried to lay the groundwork for his not being able to pick Anna up at five. There was a meeting, it might run late . . . Every lie he told came out sounding punier. She had to hear it. But his wife was in a hurry to get off the phone and only told him to call her later.

Dental emergency? He left the office, using his brand-new and genuine excuse, and retraced his morning's path to the day care. Lake Shore Drive to Belmont. He drove as fast as he could, cruising just ahead of the traffic zooming around the lake. It was grotesque to think that everything was at the mercy of one old woman's toothache. He got to Mrs. Carter's—she had a mouthful of ice cubes and a washcloth pressed to her jaw, her apologies coming out in god-awful mumbles— collected Anna, plus Anna's backpack, snack containers, boots, mittens, hooded winter coat, and buckled her into the car seat in back. "Where's Mommy?" she asked.

"Mommy's at her office. Now you get to go see Delia at Delia's house."

"I don't want to!"

"Well, you have to. Mommy's at work. Daddy has to go back to work." Stinking lying Daddy.

"No!" Her face bunched into a knot.

"Sounds like somebody needs a nap," he said cheerily.

His daughter got her hands on one of her toys, a doll whose hair she had pulled so often, it stood straight up like a fright wig, and began beating its plastic head against the window. "Anna, quit that." She didn't. "Do you want me to stop the car and give you a spanking?"

It wasn't a threat he could have acted on. He was preoccupied with trying to find his route south, wondering if he'd gone past Ashland already. When he found it and headed south, the traffic moved like a clog through a pipe. All manner of people he didn't know and never would, taking up space with their grubby cars and grubby, depressing errands. There were times he hated the city and everyone in it. The doll's head whacked against the window glass. "Anna? Did you hear me?"

She lost her grip on the doll and it slid to the floor. "I want Baby!"

"Well you weren't being very nice to Baby. She can stay on the floor."

In the rearview mirror he saw her lower lip trembling. A squall ready to break out. Ryan coaxed her into the song about the little green frog sitting in the water, the little green frog, doin' what he oughter. There were three or four verses, which carried them as far as North Avenue. He didn't know the streets here and he didn't much like the look of the place, with its air of incomplete urban renewal, its fortified corner groceries and druggie coffee shops. He didn't think that his wife had been to Delia's either, and now it seemed like an entirely wrongheaded plan to bring their daughter here. He had a moment of pointless anger toward his wife, then he made up his mind to offer Delia extra pay if she'd come back with him, watch Anna at their place, as she always had. It was already after one o'clock, but things could still work out.

Delia wasn't home. Her roommate, another sooty-eyed college girl, came to the door and said that Delia was in class, she'd be back a little later. "Are you sure?" Ryan said. "I mean, my wife talked to her . . ."

The roommate gave him a what-do-you-want-me-to-do look. The apartment behind her gave off a whiff of cat. The hallway looked like a crime-scene photograph. The roommate bent down to speak with Anna. "What's your name, sweetie?"

"When is it you expect Delia?"

The roommate said she couldn't say, Delia must have got hung up somewhere. She got his daughter to answer her, finally, and the roommate said that Anna was a pretty name for a pretty girl.

He couldn't and wouldn't leave Anna here with the roommate. It was a relief to recognize his limits.

Back in the car, Anna announced that she had to go potty. "We'll be home real soon," Ryan told her, although they would not. It was after two when they reached their own door, then there was the rush to the bathroom, Anna's coat to get off, her demands for juice, animal crackers, the *Sesame Street* tape he couldn't find. "You can watch this instead," he said. It was a soap opera that he counted on her being too young to understand. "I'll find your show in a minute, OK?"

In the bedroom, behind the closed door, he called Janine. "I am so sorry," he told her. "This whole day's been a landslide." He began explaining: the phone call, the toothache, and so on.

Janine listened until he reached the end. "Next week," he said. "Either Friday, or, if Friday's not good—"

"Ryan?"

He ran out of breath right then and there. "Yeah."

"Maybe I'm not as OK with this as I thought."

When he didn't answer, she said, "Look at everything you had to do today, tie yourself in knots, get your little girl all upset . . ."

"If I was there right now," Ryan said, "you wouldn't be having all these unselfish thoughts."

"Well maybe they wouldn't be uppermost in my mind. That doesn't mean I wouldn't have them."

"This is shit, Janine."

"You're angry. I can understand that." Her tone was calm, reasonable. She sounded almost like his wife.

"So I guess you're bailing on me one more time. Wow. History repeating itself."

"I can't be your, whatever it is you want. Long-lost fantasy girl. I can't live the way I used to, all crazy and dangerous and wild. It takes a toll on you after a while. I've had to realize I need to protect myself. I need to protect myself from myself, if that makes—"

Quietly, Ryan hung up the phone.

When he was younger he had wished to see the world, and then he had wished to change it, and then he had been afraid it was passing him by. And his mistake had been to confuse a particular woman with the world.

In the living room his daughter sat on the couch, deep in the folds of it so that her legs didn't reach the edge of the cushions. On the television screen a handsome couple were having a serious conversation that appeared to have gone on for some time. His daughter was transfixed by them. Ryan sat down next to her, hoping to become engrossed in any story not his own.

# *Iowa*

Anita sat at the kitchen table, writing out her day's list of things
to do. She had pretty handwriting, a small, rounded cursive. People
often gave her compliments on it. Sometimes she thought she was
mostly a collection of minor talents.

The phone rang. The cordless receiver sat next to her on the table
so she didn't have to get up. "Hello?"

"Girl, how are you?"

It was Rhonda. "Fine, I guess," Anita said. With her free hand, she
took her pen and crossed *Rhonda* off her list.

"How's Jeff?"

"I found a bottle in the garage last night. In a storage bin."

"They like garages."

"He said it had been there a long time, he forgot it was there."

"Good one," Rhonda said. Rhonda was her Al-Anon friend. Rhonda
had already divorced her own drunk husband. "You check the garbage?
See if there's any empties?"

"You think I should?"

"Oh honey, I'm not saying try to beat him at his own game. You
have no idea how talented these jokers can be. They are pure cunning.
Bill P. used to bury his Wild Turkey out in the potato patch." Bill P.

was Rhonda's ex-husband, so called to distinguish him from Bill H., her new boyfriend. It was an AA joke. Bill H. was an alcoholic also, but he was in recovery and went to meetings. "Always out there digging his potatoes. Took me a long age to figure it out. I would of laughed, if I wasn't so scalded mad."

Rhonda did laugh then, her big hawing laugh. One of the interesting things about Al-Anon was that you met people with whom you would not otherwise have anything in common.

Anita said, "I know you aren't supposed to be the alcohol police. I know they can always get more. But I poured his damned bottle down the sink. It felt good."

"How are the kids?"

"They won't talk to me. You'd think I was the one who drove the car through the garage wall and peed on the kitchen floor."

"Give them time. They aren't sure he's going to stay sober."

"Neither am I," Anita said. A month ago Jeff had got his second DUI and was sent to court-ordered alcohol counseling. The counselor said Anita should go to Al-Anon, so she did. Sometimes she thought it was helping, and sometimes she thought it was only one more way that everything had to be about Jeff.

"Just work your steps. Let go and let God."

Anita said she would. She told Rhonda she would see her at the meeting and hung up. She was still learning all the AA lingo. It was kind of funny that she'd lived with a drunk all this time and was just now figuring out how to talk about it.

That night at the meeting, there was a guest speaker, a man with one arm. He told them he had lost the arm driving drunk on a motorcycle. But he'd never really made the connection between drinking and losing his arm. It was just one of those things. He shook his head, marveling. Then, a few years later, he left work, stopped at a bar, got back in his car, and T-boned somebody at an intersection. Killed a man. A man who never made it home to his family that night. He'd woken up in the hospital without remembering any of it. Total blackout. He'd gone to jail. Finally, he'd made the connection. Every day he thought about that man. Every day, that was what kept him from taking another drink.

The man with one arm was thin, with bushy sideburns. Having one arm didn't keep him from lighting and smoking cigarettes, one after another. He was ordinary looking, in jeans and a cotton shirt. He looked like somebody who worked in a gas station or a factory or whatever job you could do with one arm. You didn't like to catch yourself thinking this way, but Anita had to wonder if there were other, different AA meetings for drunk bankers, drunk doctors or drunk lawyers, drunk . . . well, people more like her.

But Jeff could have killed somebody too, driving around drunk. Could have gone to jail, lost his job. Killed his stupid self while he was at it. It could still happen. She and the kids could be left on their own. Every time she thought of it she felt scared and furious. Alcoholics were sick, it was a disease. But he wouldn't be sick in the first place if he wasn't an asshole.

The meeting was over. They stood and said the Lord's Prayer. Anita only did a halfhearted job of it. The God who was in charge of alcholics didn't seem the same as the church God. After the prayer they all held hands in a circle and said, "Keep coming back, it works if you work it." You had to do all sorts of embarrassing things at meetings. She felt bad about her attitude, she wished she was more openhearted, more sincere. But there were also plenty of times when she resented all the things required of her when she wasn't the one who got DUIs and phoned in sick to work with hangovers and made everybody miserable.

Anita stood next to Rhonda at the back of the room while Rhonda said good-night to people. Rhonda knew everybody. She'd been coming to meetings for a long time. Rhonda was the first one she'd met at her first meeting. Rhonda had opened the door for her. Anita couldn't even imagine what her own face had looked like. "You're in the right place," Rhonda had said, drawing her in. You had to love her for that.

Anita worried that she'd dressed up too much. She was always doing that, even though she knew better by now; meetings weren't a real showy place. She had worn a blue blazer and a red silk blouse, black crepe pants and her red pumps. She didn't believe in leaving the house without making an effort.

Rhonda wore jeans and a sweatshirt. She was thin and wore her hair long, like a country-western star, and she smoked a lot of cigarettes. Most people in AA smoked, though Anita hadn't yet figured out what that meant. Rhonda worked as a cashier in a restaurant. She'd had a lot of different jobs and not one of them, she said, ever paid you enough for the misery of it all. Anita and Rhonda were what was called codependents, meaning people who put up with the goddamn drunks. Bill P. had broken Rhonda's nose. He'd taken the Breyer horse figures she'd collected all her life and melted them down in the burn barrel.

When Rhonda had finished saying the rest of her good-nights, she and Anita walked out to the parking lot. "It could storm if it wanted to," Rhonda said. It was already dark, but to the west they could make out the darker shapes of bulging clouds. The day had been warm. It smelled of rain and a breeze was kicking up. The meetings were held at the Grange building on the west edge of town. There was a truck stop a little distance down the highway, and a few farm lights. It was the same lonesome emptiness all the way to the Missouri and the Nebraska border, and beyond that, to the Rockies. Bad weather always came through on the west-to-east track, nothing between here and the mountains to slow it down, like a big black mouth opening right on top of you.

"I should get on home," Anita said, although now she was reluctant to leave. The lights were still on in the building behind them. They had a welcoming look. "Rhonda? I'm mad all the time. I don't know how to not be mad. Don't tell me 'fake it till you make it.' I'm tired of slogans."

A flare of lightning lit up an edge of cloud. The lightning was reflected, still some great distance away and too far for the thunder to reach them. Rhonda pulled her jean jacket tighter. "Oh that sky has a wicked look, don't it? You can tell Jeff you're mad. Just don't be mad the very minute you say it."

"I feel like I've been married for a hundred years."

"Yeah, the first hundred years are the hardest." Rhonda leaned over and kissed Anita on the cheek. "Call me, OK?"

Anita said she would. She got into her minivan and Rhonda into her old Pontiac with the loud exhaust. They drove back along the access road, Rhonda in front and Anita following. Rhonda's back window displayed two baseball caps, one for the Hawkeyes and one for the St. Louis Cardinals. Bill H. was a big Cardinals fan. Bill P. had been a Cubs fan, so the caps had to change. When they got to the stoplight, Rhonda honked and turned off to the right.

Anita reached her own driveway, pressed the garage-door opener, and eased the minivan into its space next to Jeff's sporty Mazda. Of course he couldn't drive now. Anita dropped him off at work in the morning and picked him up in the afternoon. For now Jeff told everybody that the Mazda wasn't running right, they were having repairs done. Anita didn't think they were fooling anybody. People always found out. It meant that Matt couldn't drive the Mazda even if Jeff would have let him. One more lousy secret. They talked about that in Al-Anon, how unhealthy it was to protect the alcoholic from the consequences of his behavior.

But what if Jeff lost his job? Not that those guys at the bank didn't all poison themselves with booze. They just thought it was a sign of weakness to screw up and get caught.

She came in through the kitchen and put her purse and keys on the counter. The TV was on in the den. Her son was stretched out on the couch, a glass of Coke and ice on the floor within his reach. "Hi honey."

He made one of his noises in greeting. He wore a gray T-shirt and basketball shorts. These were the clothes he slept in and sometimes spent whole days in. Some things she had given up trying to make him do. "Did you get any dinner?"

"Grilled cheese."

"What are you watching?" It was a documentary, something with old brown-and-white pictures and a serious narrator.

"The orphan train."

"What?"

"It's for school," Matt said, as if that explained anything.

"Where's your dad and Marcie?"

"Upstairs."

His silences and his telegraphic speech had different tones and qualities and she knew them all. Most often he was just being a teenager who communicated with his parents as if he was a soldier captured behind enemy lines: name, rank, and serial number, nothing else. But more and more he seemed furious at having to live under the same roof with her.

The first long, low roll of thunder broke.

Anita stood, pretending to watch the television while she watched her son. He looked more like Jeff than like her side of the family, but he didn't have his father's matter-of-factness or incurious nature. He kept a zone of secrecy around him that she was not allowed to enter. The only way she ever knew if he had a girlfriend was when his sister told everyone else about it. He'd taught himself to play the acoustic guitar and spent a lot of time in his room practicing old Bob Dylan songs. He went in for solitary sports, like swimming and distance running. She worried that he might turn out like one of her family's oddballs, the ones with peculiar talents and discontents. Her crazy cousin Chip, or her too-smart-for-his-own-good brother, or Torrie and her freakish pictures. None of that kind ever settled for being happy in any normal way.

She wondered if she should go away, as Matt so obviously wanted her to, or inflict herself on him further. She sat down in the armchair across from him. Damned if she was going to raise one more man who felt free to ignore women.

The program must have just started. A man in a book-lined office, some professor-type expert, Anita guessed, was talking. There were more old-time sepia photographs, crowded city streets, horse-drawn carriages, men in derby hats. Pictures of grimy children, dressed in clothing so peculiar, it was difficult to identify any of it as particular items, shirts, say, or pants. But it was always the faces that stayed with you: young, shy, dead.

After a couple of minutes, she understood enough of the story. Poor, orphaned, and distressed children were rounded up from the miserable New York City streets, packed onto trains, and shipped west to the farm states, where new families could be found for them. There was a general belief in the virtues of rural life and useful labor. Sometimes there were happy endings, families who had lost their own beloved children and welcomed these new ones into their hearts and homes. Other times less good: people looking for field hands or household drudges, children standing on train platforms while their teeth and muscles were appraised. If children weren't chosen, they got back on the train and went on to the next stop, carrying with them only their cardboard suitcases and a change of clothes.

Anita said, "Do you think any of those trains came through Iowa? I bet they did. I bet some of those orphans wound up right around here. There's this noncredit course in local history this summer. I was thinking about signing up for it. That would be a way to find out."

Matt didn't answer. She couldn't stop talking. "That is just the saddest thing. Can you imagine, being packed up and shipped off like that and not having any idea where you'd end up?"

Matt reached for his glass of Coke. "Some of them were probably just as happy they got to leave."

She stared at him but he didn't say anything else. She said, "What do you have to do for school? Shouldn't you be taking notes?"

"I just have to watch it."

"Don't knock that glass over," Anita told him, falling back into Mom-speak, good old nagging. It was all she was really allowed to say to him.

She made the rounds of the house downstairs, checking doors and windows. It had become her habit to do so. Those nights when she went to bed before Jeff did, she got up later to make sure he hadn't left the front door wide open, or the stove burners on. He was capable of doing those things. Rain was beginning to spatter. Lightning flashed its SOS.

Upstairs, television sounds came from the bedroom where Jeff was watching—baseball? Something with an announcer. Her daughter's door was closed and she knocked on it. "Marcie?"

"I'm on the phone."

"I need to talk to you."

She waited while Marcie wrapped up her end of the conversation. Giggles. Whispers. Probably a boy. "OK," Marcie called, and Anita entered. Marcie had made her room into something resembling a giant bowl of peach sherbet. Peach curtains and bedspread and lampshades and throw pillows. Peach sherbet garnished with strewn clothing, magazines, papers, plastic bags disgorging recent drugstore purchases.

Anita lifted a peach-colored towel draped on the back of a desk chair. "This is still damp. Hang it up in the bathroom."

Marcie rolled off the bed, took the towel and pitched it toward the adjoining bathroom. When it landed on the floor, she sighed and got up to retrieve it. Sometimes Anita thought they'd all be just as happy if she let them live like pigs in a sty, wolves in a den. Nobody else cared about how the house looked. Maybe she didn't really care either.

Anita said, "I have class tomorrow night so Matt's going to drop me off and pick me up and in between he can take you to Susan's, and Susan's father can give you a ride back, OK?"

"I don't understand why you have to keep taking those dumb classes."

"Because I wasn't smart enough to take advantage of all my opportunities when I was younger. I was too busy goofing around and having fun. Like somebody I know."

Marcie rolled her eyes. She was the prettiest girl in her class and always had been. Queen bee of the hive. There was no mystery whom she took after.

"Mom?"

"What."

"Are you and Dad getting a divorce?"

Her daughter dropped back down to sit on the edge of her bed. She wouldn't look up at Anita. It was as if she'd embarrassed herself.

Anita reached behind her and pushed the door shut. "Why would you say that?"

"I don't know."

"That's not the idea. The idea is we all try really hard and work things out. It just takes a while."

"It's OK if you do. But would you tell me about it ahead of time? Because I'd want to know."

Everything in the room was sad. The ribbon board with its photographs of laughing girls, documented friendships. The troll figure dressed up in school colors, the beaded bracelets and fashion magazines, scattered CDs and the rest of the music paraphernalia, inside-out sweaters that should have been folded and put away. Her daughter's accumulated life, both careless and careful. All of it at the mercy of her loutish and squabbling parents.

"Honey, nobody's planning on any divorce." *Nobody can afford one.* "We just have to hang in there while things get better. They will. You just need a little patience."

She watched her daughter not believe a word of it. Well, why should she?

"Mom? Could I stay at Susan's tomorrow night?"

Anita said she'd think about it. She might as well load both her children onto the next orphan train.

All she'd ever wanted was a family of her own. It hadn't seemed like a greedy or an outrageous thing to want.

She crossed the hallway to her own bedroom. Jeff was propped up in bed, watching his ball game. One pillow lay across his stomach, his arms resting on it. He looked up at her, his usual furtive expression. Ever since the DUI, he alternated between guilt and belligerence. "Is it raining yet?"

"Just started." Another boom of thunder. The lights flickered.

"Crap. It's only the fifth inning."

Anita went into the bathroom to change clothes. Back when they were first married, she'd tried to be interested in who was playing whom, or why it was important. She didn't care. She'd never cared.

The window frame ticked as the house made its minute adjustments to the rising wind. It was a well-insulated house and could stand up to any weather short of a tornado. Anita took off her jewelry, placed it in the china saucer she kept by the sink, washed her face, brushed her teeth, and changed into the sweatpants and T-shirt she kept hanging on the back of the door. It had been a long time since she'd worn anything to bed that might suggest sex. Jeff only wanted it when he was drinking, which was exactly when she wanted nothing to do with him. She didn't expect any of that to change just because he'd managed to go a couple of weeks without getting liquored up.

She came out with her armload of clothes and went to her closet to sort them out and hang them up. The closet had a mirrored door and she saw Jeff looking at her. He could look all he wanted, as long as he didn't get any big ideas.

Anita got into her side of bed, switched on her light, and picked up one of the magazines she kept on her nightstand. She'd got tired of the women's magazines, their worrying tone, like there was always something you were supposed to be doing: starting an exercise routine or a craft project or trying Mexican seasoning in your next meat loaf or learning about some new dread disease. She'd come to like *Better Homes and Gardens* and *Architectural Digest* because you knew you'd never live anywhere like that and could just relax about it.

The baseball game droned. The thunder boomed, right overhead now, then the loudest part of the storm passed over and the rain came on harder. Anita reached up and turned her light off. She rolled herself up in the covers with her back to Jeff. He turned his light off also and lowered the volume on the television to a buzz. It was a routine neither of them had to think about.

Anita wasn't yet asleep. The rain sound was carrying her away. Jeff's leg moved against hers. Then the nudging pressure of his hip and shoulder. The television was off and the room was dark. Had he done it on purpose?

He knew she was awake. They knew each other's breathing, their dream speech, their restless turnings. Anita kept still. His hand cupped her shoulder. He said, "I don't know if I can do anything. Without the drinking."

Anita rolled over enough to cover his hand with hers. She left it there a moment, then withdrew it, and after a time Jeff also turned away back to his side of the bed.

The telephone went off like a bomb. Anita's first, swimming-to-the-surface thought: the kids. But both of them were home. Or her parents. Or Jeff's. The phone shrilled again. She reached it on its third ring. "Hello?"

"Anita?" A woman.

Next to her, Jeff fought with his pillow. "*Whas?*"

"Go back to sleep." She lifted the phone from its cradle, took it into the bathroom and shut the door. "Rhonda? What's the matter?"

Rhonda laughed. It came out skittery. "Son-of-a-bitch bastard."

"Tell me what happened. Are you all right?"

"Could I get a ride?"

"Where are you?"

"Out in the rain like a damn wet cat."

"Tell me where you are and I'll come get you."

Rhonda gave her directions to a 7-Eleven on the far side of downtown. The store was closed but she was using the pay phone. Anita said, "Are you all right there? Should I call the police?"

"I flushed his car keys down the toilet. He's not coming after me."

Anita said she'd get there as soon as she could. She got off the phone and went back into the bedroom. The clock on the bureau said it was one thirty. She slid her hands through the bureau drawers, found her jeans and shoes in the closet. When she'd finished dressing, she shook Jeff by the shoulder hard enough to wake him.

"I have to go out. I'll be back in a little."

He groaned, staring up at her in the dark. She said, "I have to go help somebody, it's an emergency. It's OK, go back to sleep."

Downstairs she found her coat and purse, then went to the linen closet and took a couple of towels. She left a light on in the kitchen and went out to the garage to start the van.

The rain had settled into a steady drizzle. She couldn't remember the last time she'd been out this late. She was wide-awake, all nerves. The strangeness of it all fueled her. Her neighborhood was laid out in curved boulevards, each house lit by an electric carriage lantern in the front yard. It wasn't hard to believe she was the only person awake for a mile in any direction.

The streets shone with rain. A traffic light reflected blurred red on the pavement. She headed south through the silent downtown, then east, away from campus. She had some idea of where Rhonda lived, a neighborhood of little cottages set close together, dog pens in the backyards, cars parked with their tires up on the curbs, a district of Dollar Stores, muffler shops, a place that sold day-old baked goods, a VFW. The rain made everything look broken, dissolving.

She couldn't find the 7-Eleven at first. The sign was off and only the security lighting was on inside. Anita slowed, unsure, and that's when Rhonda ran from around the corner of the building and pulled at the passenger door.

Anita pushed the unlock button and Rhonda climbed inside. "Take off, hurry up." She was wheezing. Her hair dripped water. "What are you waiting for, an engraved invitation?"

Anita hit the gas and the van bucked forward. "What happened, talk to me."

"Goddamn his stupid drunk ass."

"Bill P.? I thought he left town."

"No, no, Bill H.! The one who hadn't had a drink in eighteen months, or so he said." Water pooled in the seat around her. Anita handed her a towel. "Stood up in meetings and testified up and down, how he was blood-bought and sold out to his Lord and Savior Jesus Christ who kept him on the sober path. I'm thinking Jesus got a raw deal."

Anita was driving around and round the block in widening circles. She didn't know where Rhonda wanted to go. "What happened?" she said again. She figured she might have to keep saying it for a while. The rain had picked up again. Veils of it blew across the road.

Rhonda scrubbed her face with the towel. Her long hair had gone limp and draggled and she tried to set it right with her hands. She opened her handbag, looking for a comb. "I came home from the meeting. He was out in the garage. What did I say about them liking the garage? First I set eyes on him I knew, but I didn't want to know it. That little alarm buzzes in you. The way he says hello, all loose and breezy. I went back into the kitchen, I started in on the dishes. He comes up behind me while I'm standing at the sink and starts fooling with me. You know how they grab all over you when they're drunk?"

Anita knew. Rhonda said, "I pushed him off me and said, 'You've been drinking,' and he acted like that was funny. A funny drunk."

"I'm sorry. Why did he start? After all this time?"

"Because it's Tuesday. Because he couldn't find his blue socks. It's alcohol, it don't need a reason." Rhonda hugged herself and Anita passed her the second towel. Rhonda wrapped it around herself. "We had us an argument then. It got kind of lively. I threw some stuff from the refrigerator at him."

"Stuff?"

"Frozen corn. Frozen peas. Frozen spaghetti sauce. That was in some Tupperware."

Without looking at each other they started giggling. Indelicate snorting laughter. It bent them double. They laughed until their ribs ached.

"Oh Lord."

"Too much."

Anita pulled up to an intersection with a stop sign and idled there. Moisture was condensing on the inside of the windshield; she rubbed it away. Main Street stretched in front of them: the coin shop, gift and china shop, H&R Block, a photography studio. Jeff's bank, a brick-and-glass cube whose architecture, he had told her, was meant to express both financial solidity and customer service. Fog was moving in, blurring the streetlights into hazy moons. "So," Anita said, as a way of asking, Now what.

"Either he finds a new place or I do. What do they call it when you see stuff you already saw."

"Déjà vu."

"He'll wake up sorry and make his promises and then the whole shitslide starts all over again."

"You can come to my house."

Rhonda didn't say yes and she didn't say no. "Huh. How would that go over with the old man."

"If he doesn't like it he can build himself an actual doghouse out in the yard."

"Maybe just for tonight. Or what's left of it." Rhonda used the towel again on her eyes. Her makeup had been rubbed off, and without it she looked like she'd just woken up. "By the way, thanks."

"Sure." Anita flipped her turn signal, then flipped it off again. They hadn't yet seen another car anywhere downtown. "Force of habit," she explained.

"You crack me up."

Anita glanced over at her. "No, really," Rhonda said. "Here you are, Miss Lady, running the streets with the down-and-out."

"It can get pretty down-and-out at my house too, Rhonda."

Rhonda stayed quiet on the drive back to Anita's neighborhood. While she'd been talking she was the same as she always was, quick with an answer for everything. Silent, the worry looked to be piling up in her. Anita could imagine most of it. The disruption of moving, or of having to get Bill H. to move. Money. The guy you shared a bed with and all that fed-up love.

"Here we are," Anita said, pulling into her driveway and letting the door roll open to the brightly lit garage with its tool bench and bicycle rack and tidy shelving. Their garage, her son used to say when he'd been in the habit of talking, was so big, a few third-world families could live there. He had a sense of humor that Anita just couldn't follow.

She and Rhonda got out and Anita led the way into the kitchen. She listened, but the house was quiet. "Are you hungry?" she asked Rhonda. "Or, you want coffee?"

Rhonda still had the towel wrapped around her. She took a few steps then stopped in the center of the kitchen, as if she'd run out of forward momentum. "Not now, I guess."

Anita pulled out a chair. "Here. I'm going to make up the guest bed."

"You have one of those?" Rhonda asked, with a little of her old spirit. "Where am I, the Holiday Inn?"

"Sit," Anita told her, and went out into the hall. The guest room—it was a little grand to call it that, with its piles of junk and broken computer—was next to Matt's room. His door was open and she closed it, then located the sheets she needed in the linen closet.

When she was finished, she went upstairs. It took her a while in the dark, but she found an extra bathrobe, wondered what Rhonda would like to sleep in, pajamas or a T-shirt, scooped up both. Took an extra toothbrush and a new bar of soap from the bathroom. Jeff stirred and she waited to see if he'd wake up, but he turned over again and was still.

Back downstairs she heard voices from the kitchen. Her first thought was that Bill H. had followed them, broken in somehow.

Her son sat across the kitchen table from Rhonda. A bag of pretzels was open between them and they were both drinking from cans of Coke. "Hi Mom," Matt said.

"Oh, honey. I'm sorry, I didn't mean to wake you up."

"It's OK." He looked rather unsurprised about encountering a strange woman in soaking clothes in his family's kitchen.

"This is my friend Rhonda."

"We already met," Rhonda chimed in. "You never told me your boy was a musician."

Matt shrugged. "She asked."

"That's nice," Anita said, wondering just what Rhonda had asked. She sat down between them. "Rhonda's spending the night."

"Yeah. She told me."

They sure seemed to have broken the ice in a hurry. "Rhonda, you don't want to sit in those wet clothes. I brought you a robe and some things."

"You didn't have to do that."

"If you get changed, I can run your clothes through the laundry. The bathroom's down the hall."

Rhonda finished her Coke, stood up, and gave Anita a damp, one-armed hug. To Matt she said, "Your mom's a total sweetie, you know that?"

Left to themselves, Anita and Matt were quiet. They heard the shower start up in the bathroom. Anita said, "You should go back to bed."

"Yeah, in a little." He was still wearing the T-shirt and shorts he'd had on earlier. His legs and arms looked unaccountably large and man-like. She was used to her children's sudden shifts and lurches in growth, but she marveled at each one.

"Rhonda's had kind of a bad night," Anita began.

Matt reached into the bag for more pretzels and sorted them according to some principle Anita couldn't fathom. "She said her boy-friend got drunk and they started slugging each other."

"Did she." It was true that Rhonda had a lot of AA practice talking about such things. "Well, she doesn't need us asking her a lot of questions and making it worse."

"I don't see how we'd be the ones making it worse."

Anita held up her hand for quiet. There was the sound of feet on the stairs. Marcie came in, blinking in the light. "What's going on?" She wore an oversize nightshirt and her hair was in a frowsy ponytail. Her slippers had long-eared bunny faces on the toes, and a white pom-pom at the heels, meant to represent bunny tails.

"One of Mom's drunk-meeting friends got thrown out of her house."

"Matthew."

"She's not the drunk, her boyfriend is."

"God, Mom."

"Both of you, just put a lid on it." The sound of the shower had stopped. "You can go back to bed, it's none of your business."

"Why was she taking a shower? Is she dirty?"

"Quiet," Anita hissed. The bathroom door opened. Rhonda padded into the kitchen, holding her wet clothes in a bundle. She wore
a pair of Anita's blue-flowered pajamas, too big for her, and a white
terry-cloth robe. Her hair was wrapped up in a blue towel. Next
to the children in their peculiar nighttime costumes, she looked
like a model for sleepwear. "Where do you want these? Oh, hi. I'm
Rhonda."

"This is my daughter, Marcie."

Rhonda said Pleased to meet you. Marcie said something that
might have been "Yeah." Anita took the clothes from Rhonda
and stepped into the utility room to start them in the washer. She
couldn't believe both the kids were awake. Usually they could sleep
through a bomb going off. She wanted some privacy, a chance to talk
to Rhonda.

But when Anita went back into the kitchen, Matt and Marcie were
still there, sitting at the table. She guessed they didn't want to miss any
of the dramatic goings-on. Rhonda was rubbing her hair dry with the
towel. Her hair was an ashy blond, and wet like this you could see the
gray next to her scalp.

"Rhonda, I've got your bed made up, you can go lie down anytime." It was almost 3:00 a.m.

"Thanks. Still a little wound up for sleep." She looked tired, but
maybe she didn't want to start sorting through everything that had
happened yet.

Marcie said, "You know what would be great? Some hot chocolate."

Her brother said, "Yeah, too bad you broke your leg and can't get
up and fix some."

Any other time, Marcie would have started in on him. But probably
due to Rhonda's presence, she just gave him a dirty look and got up to
put the kettle on.

Everybody but Anita said they wanted hot chocolate. She was on
one of her diets again. Sometimes she thought she'd been dieting her
whole life.

The four of them sat around the table. There was that middle-of-the-night feeling, when whatever was said had a heaviness to it. Rhonda said, "You could fit the whole of my house into this kitchen. My ex-house. I'm moving. I decided."

"You can do better than him," Anita said. There didn't seem any point in trying to keep the conversation private.

"Of course I can. Anybody could. I felt sorry for him. See where that gets you."

Anita had seen Bill H. at meetings. He wouldn't have been anybody she'd feel sorry for. A big man with a beat-up face and hands like shovels. Rhonda said, "At least I didn't marry him. So there won't be that mess to undo."

Matt and Marcie were trying not to look fascinated at all the real-life grown-up stuff available for viewing. Matt cleared his throat. He said, "You could make him leave. You wouldn't have to move. Especially if he's the one who started the fight."

"Well that's sweet. But he wouldn't see it that way. It's not how a drunk thinks. Nothing's ever their fault."

They hadn't heard him, but they looked up from the table to see Jeff in the kitchen doorway, his face sleepy and confused. "Rhonda?"

Rhonda opened her mouth, shut it. When she opened it again, she said, "Well I'll be damned, Jeff."

Anita gaped. Rhonda said, "Coffee."

"What?"

"He comes in for coffee every morning. At the Hot Spot. That's where I work," she explained to Matt and Marcie, who were staring, stricken. "We do breakfasts and lunches." To Jeff she said, "I had some trouble at home tonight."

"So, what do—"

Anita said, "We go to Al-Anon together."

"Jesus H. Christ." Jeff sat down in the extra chair at the end of the table.

"Small world," Rhonda offered.

Marcie spoke up. "So you guys go to your meeting and talk about Dad?"

Anita said, "It's supposed to be anonymous. It's supposed to be confidential."

"It still is," Rhonda said. "We're just having a little bit of a moment here."

Jeff said, "Don't anybody take this the wrong way, but I could use a drink."

"Not funny, Dad." This from Matt. He was fidgeting with the pretzel bag, crumpling it with one hand.

"It was meant as a joke, OK?"

Nobody said anything to that. Jeff tried again. "So, a guy goes into a bar—"

"Don't," Anita told him.

"I'm not a bad person," Jeff said. He started crying, right there at the table. His face bunched up and turned red.

"Oh, right," Matt said. "Go ahead and feel sorry for yourself."

Marcie was crying too. "Why is everybody being so horrible?"

Anita and Rhonda looked at each other. Rhonda said, "Maybe me calling you wasn't the best idea I ever had."

"You know none of this is your fault." Anita couldn't remember the last time they'd all been in the same room together. At least that was something.

Jeff blew his nose on a paper napkin. "I've been sober a month now."

Rhonda said, "All due respect, Jeff, but you're not sober yet. You just don't stink so bad."

The idea came to Anita fully formed. As long as Rhonda didn't wake up with a changed mind about moving out. But then, none of them looked like they were going to get to bed before sunup anyway.

Somebody to help smack sense into Jeff. Listen to Matt's music and draw him out. Maybe even shame Marcie into being a little less spoiled. If Rhonda got her car back from Bill H., she could give Jeff a ride in to work mornings. The spare room would have to be set to rights.

Her idea branched out, set forth shoots and leaves, details, questions, strategies, all the things she was more than capable of managing. She felt a surge of energy, even optimism. She would be the engine, the driving wheel. So clear was her vision of this future that it seemed as if it had already come to pass.

There would be persuasion needed, with assurances made all around, how Rhonda would be the one doing them the favor. Which was perfectly true. There were times when a family needed an orphan.

# Veracruz, Mexico

## OCTOBER 10, 1996

*Hey man,*

*I got your new address from my folks, they said you'd moved. I guess if you have the kids, they have to have a place to ride bikes and dig in the dirt and all that kid stuff. Well that's great. Tell them Uncle Chip says hi. Yeah, I gave up that fight. To the home folks, I'm always going to be Chip.*

*Notice the funny stamp? I got my sorry ass down to Mehico. It's a long story. It always is. There were some business opportunities. It's nothing I'd put in a letter. But it all worked out pretty sweet. There's times I've had money and there's times I've had no money and I'm here to tell you, one is better than the other.*

*Veracruz suits me fine. I been a couple of other places this side of the border and this is the best one I found. It has all the old-timey stuff like the cathedral and the Zocalo, that's like a plaza with places for dances and domino games and hanging out all night drinking cervezas. You imagine doing that back home? Acting like every day was a party? But it's also a big dirty city, sort of like Detroit with palm trees, so that keeps the tourists down.*

*Veracruz is where Cortes landed in 1519 and everybody's luck*

*started to run out. More and more I like reading about history
and historical events. I don't know why. Maybe because it's
all written down so I don't have to worry about forgetting it.
(Ha ha.)*

*So if I'm 45, I guess that makes you 40. Whoa Nelly, like the
old folks used to say. Except now we're the old folks. Blows my
mind.*

*Boy I don't know if I'm old yet, but parts of me sure are. There's
things I worry about.*

*You should come visit. Just say the word. I've got a nice place,
actually it's my girlfriend's but she is very big on family. She would
knock herself out cooking and cleaning for all of you and think it
was a big treat. She's different that way. Her name is Mayahuel.*

*There's a phone number, I'll put it at the end. If Mayahuel or
one of her kids answers, they don't speak a lot of English. Just say,
Llame Senor Ray. That's me. What a trip.*

*Sincerely yours,*
*The Old Gringo*

# *Iowa*

It was Torrie's moving day and the last thing you could expect was for it to go smoothly. Everybody would see to that. Blake only wanted to get it over with.

There had been a little rain overnight, just enough to make puddles and clear the air. This morning he was looking at a blue sky, a good twelve hours of daylight, and a whole string of jobs backing up on him. Calls to return, somebody wanting an estimate on a room addition, somebody else needing a rental property repaired and needing it now. Supposedly, he was his own boss.

He threw the last of his cigarette out the truck window. The whole world wanted him to quit smoking. The world was going to have to wait.

It was only a ten-minute drive to his parents' house, tops, but he took his time, the last piece of the day he could call his. His coffee mug in the cupholder, the radio tuned to the PBS station nobody ever believed he listened to. The roads he'd just about worn a track in by now, into town past the abandoned high school somebody was going to have to either fix up or tear down someday, past the used-to-be-a-gas-station-bakery-insurance-agency-barbecue-joint.

Once he reached town, he went out of his way to go down Main

Street. He wanted to look at the brickwork one more time. The old bank building, his contribution to civic pride, and Torrie's new home. The mall had just about killed off the last of downtown. The bank project got everybody all excited about the revival of the business district, which always seemed just about to happen but never really took off.

He slowed and went around the block. He'd worried about the brick, but he'd ridden the mason's ass until they got it right. The down-stairs spaces, which were meant for commercial use, were just roughed in, waiting for somebody to sign a lease and decide what they wanted. Torrie's place, upstairs, was the only real finished part.

There wasn't an inch of the place that hadn't fought him. The old gas piping had to be dug up and sealed to suit the inspector. The celings had to be dropped an extra six inches to fit the ductwork and that had thrown everything off. Next time somebody asked him to rehab a pile of ancient batshit and asbestos, he'd say no thanks.

Except next time, he'd know how to do it better. There ought to be some way of learning things that didn't take the hide off you piece by piece. And he'd done good work. Anybody with eyes could see that, if they thought about it in the first place.

The night before, his mom had kept Trish on the phone for most of an hour, going on and on. His mom was all bent out of shape and Trish was the only one who'd put up with it. Blake would walk into the kitchen for a beer and Trish would still be sitting at the table with the phone up to her ear. He'd raise his eyebrows, a question, and Trish would shake her head. "Of course not," she said. "Sure." A laundry basket was in front of her and while she talked, or rather, listened, she was folding towels.

He went back into the den. Friday night. His daughters were out running the streets, his son was planted in front of the television. Blake stood and watched the show, trying to figure it out. It was one of the *Star Trek*s, but he didn't recognize any of the characters.

"What is this?"

"*Deep Space Nine,*" his son answered. Which explained exactly nothing. There seemed to be an effort under way to show more black people in outer space. Good luck with that one.

He had paperwork to do but he waited until Trish hung up the phone. Then he went out to the truck for his ledger and receipts. In the kitchen Trish was loading the dishwasher. She said, "They want you over there by ten."

"Yeah, OK." He sat down at the table and opened the ledger. His business checks were laid out in notebook style and he didn't always fill out the stubs. Another bad habit, like smoking. Once he had the ledger straightened out, Trish would enter it all in the computer. He still wasn't much of a computer guy. "How was Mom?"

"She's convinced that something horrible's going to happen to Tor."

"Something horrible already did happen to her."

"And you're all aiding and abetting."

"She'll get over it." His mother and Torrie drove each other crazy. The move was the best thing for everybody. It was just going to take some prying loose on his mother's part and she wasn't very good at that.

Trish moved around the kitchen, setting things to rights, then she went into the laundry room to start the next load. She worked twenty-five hours a week at Farm and Fleet. It felt like neither of them ever quit working. They could barely keep three kids on two salaries when his parents had raised four on his dad's job alone. The math of the world had got screwed up somehow.

The phone rang. Trish picked it up and tried to find a place between the squalling noise of the dishwasher and the laundry, gave up, and handed it to Blake. "It's your brother."

"Hey Ry. Hold on a minute." The noise drove him out of the kitchen and into the bedroom. He closed the door, lay down on the bed with his beer balanced on top of a newspaper on the nightstand. "OK."

"How are you, man?"

Everybody said he and his brother sounded exactly the same, you couldn't tell the difference between them on the phone. Maybe if he made about ten times as much money, this was what he'd sound like. "I'm good," Blake said. "Friday night and the beer's cold."

"You talk to Mom yet?"

"No, but Trish did."

"She still on the warpath?"

"Yeah, you're evil." Ryan had bought the old bank building, an investment, he called it. Another big idea from the idea man. Then Torrie had jumped all over it. "How's everybody at your house?"

"Great. Crazy, but great. Sam's a pistol. His new thing is arm wrestling. One of these days he's gonna take me."

Blake said you could count on that. Silence. He wanted a cigarette but he'd have to go out in the garage for that, and he figured he might as well wait for whatever his brother really wanted to talk about.

Ryan said, "You think I should have told her she couldn't."

He hadn't asked it as a question. "No, I think it's a good thing. Or will be, once the dust settles."

"Thirty-five years old, for Christ's sake. I figured, this is the only way it would work for her. Something with a lot of support systems."

"True."

"Mom and Dad aren't going to last forever."

"You don't have to pile up a lot of reasons to convince me."

Another silence. Then Ryan said, "I should call Mom."

"Probably."

"Call me if there's anything funky. And thanks."

"No problem. This time tomorrow, it'll be a done deal."

He hung up the phone and went out for his cigarette. It hadn't occurred to his brother to be here himself.

Torrie was going to live there rent-free, part of what would make it all work, and that was generous of his brother, a good thing, and buying the old bank in the first place was another good thing, one that got him into the newspaper. It was a more complicated kind of good thing for Ry to ask him to do the rehab. It was a paycheck for him and the two or three guys he could take on. Winter work, you were always glad to have that.

But his brother didn't understand that if it was anybody else but family, he could have set his bid a lot higher, really made it pay off for him. And Ryan wasn't going to have their mother in one ear and Anita in the other, giving him grief. And Trish, the one they'd decided they were going to look down on for all time, would still be fielding their phone calls, because they'd decided she was good enough for that. Ryan didn't understand any of this because he didn't live here and hadn't for a long time now.

Torrie was already outside waiting for him. A dozen plastic storage bins were lined up on the driveway. When she saw the truck pull in, she began dragging one of them toward it.

"Whoa, Tor. Let me do that."

She straightened up, puffing a little. She was strong, but she wasted a lot of energy flailing around. "So, you excited about moving?"

"Yeah, excited." She grinned and punched him in the arm.

"Well, I'll go see what the old folks are up to."

"Ha," Torrie said. Wise-guy style.

Ha it was. Blake walked into an empty kitchen. *Crap.* He went farther back into the house. "Mom? Dad?"

His dad was in Torrie's room, taking apart the bed frame with a wrench and a screwdriver. The mattresses were leaning against the wall. His dad didn't swear, but he looked as if he would have liked to. "Ah, these bolts," he said.

"Let me give it a shot." Blake took the wrench from him and worked the bolt until it loosened. "Where's Mom?"

"Resting."

That meant she was pitching one or another kind of fit, but if they were lucky, she'd stay put until they got the truck loaded.

Today they were moving the little bit of furniture Torrie was taking with her, plus her clothes and whatever his mom and Anita had put together for a kitchen. Not that either of them believed Torrie was capable of cooking a meal or keeping herself fed. Blake had already picked up most of Torrie's photography equipment, mostly to keep his dad from doing it himself. His dad didn't like to think he was slowing down, but he was almost seventy and didn't need to bust himself up for no reason.

Somehow, Torrie's moving a dozen blocks away was some kind of epic event that brought out everybody's peculiar side.

Torrie even earned a little money these days. She'd started making different things out of her photographs: cards, calendars, even T-shirts. She sold them at the gift shop at the mall, and a guy in Seattle had them for sale out there too. She'd found him on the Internet. Every so often Torrie took a box of her stuff down to the post office to send to him. It was hard to understand why anybody normal would want to look at one of Torrie's pictures on a daily basis. A whole calendar of them? That would make for a real strange year.

He and his dad got the bed frame outside and slid it into the truck, then propped the mattresses next to them, then braced everything with the clothes dresser and some of the storage tubs. Torrie kept coming out with different odds and ends: pillows in a plastic garbage bag, a milk crate filled with her old schoolbooks. A lamp with its base in the shape of a cartoon owl.

His dad straightened up from where he was working in the truck bed. "You know, Tor, you can leave some of your stuff here if you want."

Torrie just laughed and stumped back inside for more.

Blake said, "She's really cleaning the place out."

"Yeah, it's going to feel a little empty."

They made room for the rest of the plastic tubs, trying to get the load square. It would be too much to hope for that he'd get it all in one trip.

"You and Mom ever think about moving? Get some place smaller?"

"Ah, your Mom wouldn't want to. You know how she is."

Blake said he knew. He was pretty sure that if he asked his mom, she'd say it was his dad who was set on staying put.

He didn't like thinking about his folks getting old. Older. As long as Torrie still lived under their roof, everything had stayed the same. In a sad sort of way, because in other, normal circumstances, his sister would have moved out years ago. They'd had to be parents for way too long. Blake was fond of saying that when his kids turned eighteen, they were each going to get a handshake and a new suitcase.

They just about had a full load roped in when Anita honked at them and pulled up along the curb. She'd driven the Mazda, which meant she wasn't intending to haul any furniture, but she'd brought his nephew. At least now he'd have somebody besides his dad to get the heavy stuff upstairs.

Torrie, who had been standing in the driveway, turned and made a beeline for the house.

Anita picked her way along the street in her sporty shoes. The Shoe Queen, Trish called her. Among other things. "Hi guys. Dad, I told you Matt was coming, you didn't have to do anything."

"We've got it under control," his dad said.

Matt looked like he didn't much want to be here, and who could blame him. It was his spring break and probably all his friends were off on a beach somewhere, having drunken college-boy fun.

"I brought some curtains," Anita said. "The ones we used to have in the den. If Torrie doesn't want them, I'll take them back. Does she have enough towels? I have an extra set, blue and white stripes. Matt, tell your grandfather not to climb up there, you'll do it. Where's Mom?"

Anita went in through the kitchen door. She seemed to leave a little space of stunned air where she'd been. Matt put his hands in the pockets of his jacket, then took them out again. "Hey Uncle Blake. Hey Grandpa."

"Hi Matt. How's college treating you?"

"It's OK. You need me to do anything?"

"Not this exact minute."

Blake figured it was a good time for a cigarette, as long as they had to wait for the women to tell them what to do. Smokem if you gotem. He leaned back against the truck, exhaling into the blue sky. "You smoke, Matt?"

Matt said he didn't. "Do yourself a favor and don't start," Blake told him. He figured the kid did all the usual college druggie stuff. He went to school out in Arizona. Studying history, which to Blake's way of thinking was a waste of time, since everything about it had already happened.

"How's your father these days?" This from Blake's dad.

"He's good," Matt told him. This was how people asked after Jeff. *Good* meant, Not Drinking. There had been some bad times. A stint in the Drunk Hospital. He'd had to change jobs.

But Anita had him towing the line now. You had to give her credit, she hadn't given up on the sorry son of a bitch. She was all about AA now. She went all over the place for conferences. Organized meetings, wrote newsletters. She was back on top of her game, like it was high school all over again. There was usually some down-and-out character living at their house. No wonder his nephew had run off to Arizona.

Jeff sure seemed to know he was licked. Anytime you saw him, he had that hangdog look. It almost made you want to sneak him a drink.

Blake's dad said, "I'm wondering what the holdup is. You think we should just head downtown?"

If you had to ask the question in the first place, the answer was no. His dad seemed to realize this and sat down on the open tailgate. He said, "I saw on television where a rocket was going to take some dead people up in outer space. Their ashes. Shoot 'em out the window."

"Yeah?" Blake hadn't heard about that.

Matt stirred. "One of them's Gene Roddenberry. The guy who created *Star Trek*."

"You're kidding."

"No, really, he wanted to be buried in outer space. You know. The Final Frontier. He wanted to be part of it. It's not so weird. Outer space is where people always thought heaven was. Or maybe they still do. You know another guy they're taking up in the rocket? Timothy Leary. He invented LSD."

"You're kidding," Blake said again.

"LSD," his dad said. "I thought that was illegal."

Matt, who had just said more than Blake had heard from him in about the last three years, seemed to be done talking. He sat down in one of the old dining-room chairs Torrie was taking with her and zipped his jacket closer around his neck.

Blake's dad said, "You can't count on anything to stay the same anymore, can you? Every time I read the paper or watch the news, I have to learn some brand-new thing."

Blake didn't know if that was all bad, but he kept this opinion to himself. His dad was in one of his moods and you pretty much had to give him the floor, so to speak.

"Even the wars nowadays. I don't know where half those places are. They don't even sound like real countries."

"You got a point there, Dad."

"Not that I recognize much about this country anymore. It's been picked clean by thieves. Everybody out for their own selves. Look at what they did to the farmers. Let them try to eat money when they get hungry."

"That was a while back, Dad." Blake wished he'd stop with this line of talk. It probably wasn't anything Matt needed to hear. There was no reason to stir all that up again. Sometimes he thought his dad forgot about things like that.

"Well we're still dealing with the ruin of it. Look at downtown. Look at everybody's downtown."

"Give it a little time."

"Then what's left of America rots from the inside because people only think about their low-down pleasures. Hard work, sacrifice, discipline, who cares about any of that."

"You make it sound like we're all having way too much fun," Blake said, trying to joke him out of it.

His dad shook his head. "You think a country can't die off just like a flesh-and-blood creature? Talk to anybody from the Roman Empire lately?"

Blake had to say he was glad when Anita came out of the house just then. "Mom wants to know if you want lunch now or later."

"Later," Blake said, fast enough that nobody else had time to speak. If they sat down for lunch, it would add another hour.

Anita surveyed them with her hands on her hips. She was thin these days. She took yoga classes whenever she wasn't busy telling everybody not to drink. "Mom wants somebody to talk to Torrie and tell her she can't move until her phone gets put in."

"Little late for that," Blake remarked.

His mom came out then. "Oh, Matt! Why haven't you come in to see me yet?"

"Hi Grandma." Matt stood up and let her hug him. "I didn't want to get in your way." He was the oldest grandchild and he'd had more practice at it than anybody else.

"It's not safe over there with no phone. If something happens, she couldn't call." His mom wasn't about to let herself get distracted from the main event.

Blake said, "If something happens, she can stick her head out the window and holler at the police. They're right down the block."

"She can't call us!"

"Why don't you go out to the mall and get her a cell phone? If that would make you feel any better."

His mom shook her head. "You know the kind of bills people run up on those things?"

"Audrey," Blake's dad said, "it'll take her about ten minutes to walk back here. What are you so worried about anyway?"

His mom sat down in the same chair Matt had used. She was wearing her big brown winter coat even though the day had warmed up. "I don't know why I bother. She won't call us even when she has a phone."

Nobody said anything to that. It was probably true.

Blake's dad stood up from his seat on the tailgate. "What's Torrie doing now?"

Anita said, "She locked herself in the bathroom and she won't answer when we try to talk to her. And that's exactly the kind of behavior we ought to be worrying about."

Blake was still standing in the bed of the truck. Something at the side of the house caught his eye. A window nudging open. Then a leg wearing blue jeans poked its way out, followed by his sister's complete hindquarters. She balanced for a moment on her stomach, toes straining for the ground, then the rest of her slid out and landed with a wobble. She steadied herself, then crouched low and made a beeline for the back of the garage.

He hoped she'd unlocked the bathroom door before she left.

He said, "How about Matt and I run this load downtown, get some of the heavy stuff taken care of. Now come on, Mom, we're not taking it all back into the house."

"Come in and have some barbecue beef first," his mom said. She didn't give up easily. Her worrying was one of the great unharnessed forces in the universe.

"We'll get something downtown." Blake reached for his keys. Matt went around to the passenger side and got in. He was probably just as happy to get out as Torrie.

His mom and Anita were still yakking at them even once he started the engine and couldn't hear them. Whatever it was, he waved and nodded, then pulled out of the drive and away.

They caught up with Torrie on the next block. She was stumping along with her usual energy. She wore a white sweatshirt she'd silk-screened with one of her photos. The photo was of a brick wall with what looked like bite marks taken out of it. She'd done it on a computer. While Blake hadn't been paying attention, computers had taken over photography too.

Blake pulled up next to her and leaned out the window. "Hey, need a ride?"

Torrie grinned and shook her head. "Feels good to walk." Her speech was so much better now.

"You sure? OK, we'll meet you there." He waved and drove off. To

Matt he said, "You hungry? We could go to Sonic. Didn't mean to drag you away from lunch."

"Maybe later. I thought Aunt Torrie was back at the house."

"Jailbreak."

Matt looked like he wasn't sure if he was supposed to laugh at that or not. Poor kid. Blake had always liked the guy, felt sorry for him. Growing up with Anita and Jeff for parents probably killed off your sense of humor. His own boy didn't know how good he had it.

Matt reached into his jacket pocket and brought out a flat plastic case. "You want to listen to my band?"

"Your what? Band?"

"Yeah, we just made a CD."

"You see anything that looks like a CD player in this truck?"

"Yeah, sorry. Forgot who I was talking to."

"Smart guy." Blake made the turn onto Main Street. The post office was closed on Saturday now but a few cars were parked down by the doughnut shop. The rain had washed them clean and their window glass sparkled. "A band, huh?" He guessed Anita and Jeff might not be crazy about the idea. "I didn't know you were still playing music. I bet Torrie has a CD player. We can have us some tunes. This band have some weird-ass name?"

"Canned Rats."

"Yup, that's weird." Blake found his cigarettes. Time for one more before they got started.

"It's supposed to be something you remember."

"How about, something you wish you could forget. Kidding." Blake thought his nephew had the right kind of serious, miserable good looks for a musician. He bet a band was a great way to get girls.

"We got a spot on a tour. With some other bands."

Blake pulled up in front of the bank building but kept the engine running. He wanted to finish his cigarette. If his nephew had more to say, here was his big chance. When Matt didn't speak, Blake said, "So when is this tour?"

"It starts in August. We have some festival dates in Texas and Arizona. We think we can get one in LA too. I'm not going back to school after this year. I already decided. My folks don't know yet."

"Well, they won't hear it from me." He couldn't imagine Anita and Jeff were going to be very happy about the news. They were the kind of people who talked about college as an investment. Matt was going to be money down the drain.

"There's other things I want to do besides school."

"Yeah, and don't let anybody talk you out of them."

Blake threw his cigarette butt out the window. Then he thought twice about it and decided he should pick it up. No reason to have trash out in front of the place. "What's Arizona like?"

"Not bad. Hot, like you'd expect. But I kind of like that."

"You're lucky you can get out and see some of the world," Blake said. It surprised him to realize he meant it. He'd never been much of anywhere. Minneapolis and back a few times. Trish had family there. One summer he and a couple of buddies had worked a firefighting crew in Montana. He'd do it again in a heartbeat if he ever thought he could get away from work. Time was money and he never had enough of either one. Plus he'd have to close his ears to all the female screaming that would greet his announcement of any such plan.

But wasn't it also true (carrying the thought with him as he got out of the truck, bent to pick up his cigarette butt) that he'd settled into the life he'd wanted. He guessed he was just one of those old dogs who was happiest at home.

Sometimes, though, he wished he was a different breed of dog.

"Come on," he said to Matt. "I'll show you around the place."

He unlocked the street door at one corner of the building. It led into an entry hall where a flight of stairs took you to Torrie's place and another door gave access to the ground floor. Blake unlocked this also and they walked through the echoing space. Everything had been drywalled and a wood-laminate floor laid down. HVAC up and running, 220 service, a roughed-out space for restrooms with the piping already in place behind the walls. You could even put food-service equipment in the very back if you wanted to. "Your Uncle Ryan's thinking somebody might want to open a restaurant, coffee shop, something like that." You could subdivide the space too, fit two or three smaller shops into it. The realtor had a big For Rent–Commercial sign in the window. Now everybody was waiting for the ball to get rolling.

"This turned out great." Matt stood in the center of a pool of sunlight, taking it in. "It must have been a ton of work."

"You got no idea."

They climbed the stairs to Torrie's apartment. Two big rooms. The one in front had the original windows, arched on top, practically floor to ceiling. Matt said, "I don't expect our old curtains are going to end up in here."

"Yeah, the light's the best part, isn't it."

There was a bathroom in the hallway, and a galley kitchen in one corner of the front room. The back room was Torrie's work space and studio, and she'd already organized it, put up worktables with her computer, her enlarger and silk-screen press, file drawers holding different kinds of paper, portfolios for her finished prints. A closet was fitted out as a darkroom. She really was a photographer. She always had been. She'd just needed a place where people could see it for themselves.

Some of her framed prints were already on the walls. He and Matt walked from one to the other, taking them in. Here was a fish, a trout, with all its beautiful dappled colors. Torrie must have found some way to take pictures underwater. The trout was swimming on a dinner plate. Bizarre.

"What do you make of this one?" he asked Matt.

"A fish out of water."

"Huh." He guessed that made sense.

There were faces that looked as if they'd been painted on glass, then the glass broken into shards and reassembled. Trees whose roots were visible underground. Landscapes Blake thought he recognized— farmhouses, woods—but with the curve of the earth so exaggerated, they seemed to be about to slide off. Black-and-white, most of them, but shot through with the colors Torrie had given them: orange, twilight blue, green, violet.

Matt said, "Hey, here's one of you."

Blake came and stood next to him. "Yeah, I've seen it. Not sure if it captures my natural beauty."

Torrie had taken his picture while he worked on this very building. He had a board laid out on the sawhorses and was bending over it with the circle saw. Somehow she'd drawn in the grain of the wood, not just on the board, but extending onto his hands and bare arms, up his throat and covering his face with its lines and whorls.

Matt said, "This is pretty cool. It's saying something about working. About your work becoming you."

"If you say so, Professor. How about we start unloading the truck?" Blake wasn't one of those people who looked at a thing and made something else entirely out of it.

The staircase had a turn that was tricky to negotiate, but once they got the bed frame and matresses up, that was the worst of it. Torrie arrived and carried some of the chairs and lamps herself and told them where she wanted the furniture. She unpacked the sheets and made up the bed and covered it with a sky blue quilt. There was a love seat upholstered in rose velvet that she must have rescued from somebody's attic. It looked like something Blake could almost recollect from another room, another house. There was an oilcloth for the kitchen table with an old-fashioned pattern of flowers in baskets.

Blake wasn't used to thinking of his sister as somebody who cared about the way she lived, somebody who decided things, even something as small as the color of a bedcovering. But here was the evidence all around him. The things she'd wanted, planned out, brought into being.

"So what do you think, Tor? You like the way it's shaping up?"

"It's great!" She grinned. They'd done a good job on her face, everybody said so, which meant you could get used to it. The way it separated above the one eye, and the eye itself, turned ever so slightly up and out, seeing its different pictures.

Matt said, "I think it's great too, Aunt Torrie. Plus there's a fire escape you could use for a porch if you wanted some fresh air."

"Family escape," Torrie said, a joke.

The gas stove still had to be hooked up, and Blake had Matt help him with that. "Where did Torrie go?" Blake asked after a time. He'd lost track of her, and even though he wasn't his mom, he felt a tug of worry, which was stupid. She was going to live here alone and come and go as she pleased. That was the whole point.

He went to the front windows, with their view of what used to be a five-and-dime and then a discount grocery, and down the block, the old Rialto, its marquee still in place, an *R* and a *T* dripping off the edge of it. A lawyer's office hung on, and the ad agency that put out the free flyers. A realtor specializing in agricultural properties. A furniture consignment store. The American Heart Association, the Knights of Pythias on the second floor. A place for orthopedic shoes. The laundromat. His brother was either a real estate genius, about to catch the crest of the next big wave, or else he'd spent a lot of money on a really big For Rent sign.

Torrie came into view, the top of her head bobbing along the sidewalk beneath him.

They heard her on the stairs, then she came in, blowing a bit with effort, a brown paper bag under her arm. "What you got there, Tor?"

"I got lunch." She set it down on the oilcloth table cover and lifted out a number of foil packets with their edges crimped together, and different styrofoam containers, and a quantity of paper napkins. It smelled of something hot and cooked.

Matt said, "Hey, Mexican." He unwrapped rolled burritos and containers of rice and refried beans and salsa, and a waxed-paper sleeve of tortilla chips.

"Where'd you get this, Tor?" There were some Mexicans in town now; Blake guessed this was what they ate.

"La Tienda." She scooped her hand to indicate a little distance. "It's on the next block."

"Well that's something new." He picked up a burrito, pried the foil open, sniffed it. Sometimes Trish made taco salad, with hamburger and sour cream and guacamole. He guessed he wasn't a real adventurous eater. Unknown Mexican people cooking in a back room somewhere, that made him think food poisoning. But he'd have to chance it, for politeness' sake.

Torrie brought out plates for them, an old melamine set of his mother's. They opened the door to the fire escape and moved the table so it caught the breeze. He asked Torrie if he could smoke, remembering that it was her place now. Just before they sat down, Matt brought out his band's CD. Torrie didn't have a stereo, but Matt said they could play it on her computer.

"Really?" Blake said. "You can do that?" Matt and Torrie laughed at him and said, Sure. He shouldn't be surprised. Computers did everything but wipe your ass for you these days.

Matt's band was like the Mexican food, in that it could have been a lot worse. The music was a little on the screechy side, but in parts of it you could make out an actual tune, some harmony you could latch onto. "Is that you singing?" Blake asked. Like most people, Matt's speaking voice was one thing and his singing voice was another. The singer was all bothered about something, a no-good low-down woman. "You sound pretty good."

"Thanks, Uncle Blake." Matt was pretending to be embarrassed at the praise, but you could tell he was all kinds of pleased with himself.

"Aside from your, like, brokenheartedness."

Torrie punched Blake lightly in the arm. "That's just the song," she informed him.

"Oh, beg your pardon. Here I was feeling sorry for him."

"Ha ha," Torrie said. When she was teasing him or making fun of him, that's when he could see her as she used to be.

You couldn't let the thought all the way in or it would kill you with sadness. The life she might have had. She would have got married, had kids. There wouldn't be any of that for her now. She was a fish out of water.

Pretty soon they'd have to go back to the house and let his parents and Anita pick on them for a while. His mom and Anita would probably want to come over here with every cleaning product in the world and turn the place upside down. But not just yet. The sun slid over his face, warming it. It was a nice moment, and he felt a kind of useless melancholy at the idea that the three of them would never again sit here in just such a moment and that no moment of life was like any other and as soon as you became aware of them, they were as good as gone. He must have been tired.

Matt stood up. "I brought you something for your new place."

He showed them. It was a small flat metal shape, a rabbit hunkered down on its front paws. Its eyes and whiskers and toenails were indicated by raised lines. "It's a cookie cutter," Matt said. "It was Great-Aunt Martha's."

Blake took another look at it. "I'll be damned. You remember that, Tor? Aunt Martha used to bake a ton of cookies and bring them over in potato chip canisters." He hadn't thought about that in years.

Then he thought about the night of Martha's funeral and he went cold.

"How'd you get this?" he asked Matt, wanting to move the conversation along.

"I don't remember. Mom says Martha gave it to me. Here you go."

Torrie held the rabbit in her open hand. It wasn't Matt's fault. He'd been too young.

If Torrie was upset, Blake couldn't tell from her face, which wasn't able to do much in the way of expressions anymore. Torrie closed her hand around the rabbit. It seemed like everything was going to be OK, and he felt a careful relief.

You couldn't pretend that people didn't exist, or that things hadn't happened.

Torrie said, "Don't you want it?"

"I kind of think it should stay around here."

Because Matt wasn't going to. That much seemed clear. He was going wherever it was that a guy with a guitar went these days. So many kids left here now. They felt they were missing out on things, they wanted a chance to earn the kind of money that everybody except him was pulling down these days. He worried about his own kids.

You didn't raise them just so they'd grow up and you'd never get to see them.

He guessed he should be happy for Matt because he was doing what he wanted. Maybe some people just weren't born to stick around. They already had a ticket on that rocket to the Final Frontier.

Torrie put the rabbit up in a windowsill where you could see the shape of it against the light. It looked more like a cat perched up in a tree than anything else.

Blake was just getting ready to say they should head back. Torrie crossed the room and came back with a T-shirt she spread out on the table. The picture printed on the front was the one Torrie had taken of him, the one where he was turning into a board or a tree.

"What's this? I'm a shirt now?"

"I owe you money."

"Money, what for?"

"Guy in Seattle sold a bunch of you."

"Wow," Matt said. "You're a hit in Seattle."

"He says, to Japanese tourists."

"You're shittin' me." He couldn't get his mind around it. People on both sides of the Pacific Ocean walking around wearing him on their chests.

"Hey Uncle Blake, if I ever get to Japan, I'll look you up."

"You do that, slick." He saw it behind his eyes: the ocean waves slapping against each other, the cities and trains and temples, the slash-stroke writing, the women dressed up like fancy, teetering dolls. The Land of the Rising Sun.

He told Torrie she didn't owe him money. They listened to the rest of Matt's music for another moment and a moment and a moment more.

# *Italy*

This was the trip his wife had always wanted to take, although like most things she wanted, Ryan had needed to talk her into it. And it had been a wonderful vacation. They reminded themselves of this whenever they had to get past some unavoidable and predictable space of boredom or irritation. The great time they'd been having was on one side of the chasm. They had only to ride things out, reach the other side, where a new and unexplored great time awaited them. Although they tried not to think of it in such terms, the grand amount of money they were spending made happiness feel like a matter of some urgency.

The kids had done really well, better than expected. They had probably been more awestruck by the plane ride than anything else. Sam had never flown before, and Anna had been too young to remember it. So that the airport crowds, the loudspeaker announcements, the smiling stewardesses in their trim uniforms, the cunning little packages of peanuts were all new to them. As was the terrifying skyward lurch. There were a few bad moments then, but soon they were coaxed by the impossible views of clouds, close up, all around them, underneath! Anna was ten, Sam was six. Anna was her mother's. Sam was his. Everybody said so. They were a little genetic laboratory, a real-life demonstration of selected traits. Anna had Ellen's sturdy seriousness and gray eyes. Sam could have been any one of Ryan's Norwegian farm relatives from the last century. "Mom," Sam said, looking down at this new country of sunlit fleece, "how do clouds stay up?"

While Anna just stared. Ryan put an arm around her shoulders. "Look," he told her. "There's another plane over there, do you see it? I wonder if it's crossing the ocean too." Sometimes he thought he understood his daughter better than his son, if only because she'd been around longer. Sam was still a cheerful savage, immune to most terrors. Anna needed to be reassured that hurtling through space in a pressurized tin can was absolutely normal, natural, and delightful. One of the lies parents told children for their own good.

When they first arrived in Rome (the children cranky, jet-lagged, complaining of tummyaches, earaches), it was hard for them to be impressed by anything. The Colosseum, which was too hot for anyone's comfort and had the look of something that ought to be either built back up or torn down. After one museum gallery, the pictures all looked alike to them and talking about the Renaissance only made them fretful. This although Ryan and Ellen had primed them for weeks beforehand with *Let's Go to Italy!* coloring books and storybooks and fun examples of Italian vocabulary. *(Buon giorno! Grazie!)* Children only saw what was here and now, not any of the past glories. Here and now, in Rome at least, had been the staggering, murderous traffic, clouds of unfurling exhaust, trampling herds of tourists, food the kids didn't want to eat. Thank God for gelato.

"Hey Anna," Ryan said. "It's lemon. You like lemon, don't you?" And her little round chin stopped its trembling. What wouldn't he do to comfort her, coax her, shield her from hurt? How much longer would ice cream be enough?

Florence, Orvieto, and Venice had gone better for all of them. The kids had settled into the routine of travel and regained their noisy energy. There were the family-friendly activities that had been promised: the hands-on pasta-making workshop, the mask-making workshop. The actor dressed up in pantaloons and doublet and plumed hat who scared Sam at first with his extravagant delivery, his barker's spiel designed to convey historical narrative in an entertaining manner. So it reminded them of Disneyland. Kids liked Disneyland.

Ryan and Ellen were also privately relieved by the presence of other peoples' loudly misbehaving kids, those who screamed and squalled and provoked their parents into shows of public discipline. Although they were always mindful not to invest or project too much of themselves into other people's opinions of their children, since it might be their turn next to deal with tantrums or brattiness. Still, how well Anna and Sam looked by comparison to this or that raging child, how comely, how sweet, how serious. They were good and vigilant parents. It was nice when some of that showed.

And if parenting had come to replace other parts of marriage, if every other sentence seemed to begin with "The kids," if unspoken things took up more and more space between them, well, none of their problems were anything new, in the history of the world. Especially this ancient world they had come to view, its palaces and fountains and statuary, its courts and grottoes echoing with old secrets. So much that was bloody and splendid and barbaric and grand had happened here. They were content to be eclipsed for a time. That was part of a vacation too.

It was the height of tourist season, you could hear English spoken on every street, which struck Ryan as somehow rude. And disappointing, as if they'd waited too long to come, and now everything had been tamed and colonized for them. There were charter tours that catered to Americans, with cheerful Italian guides and well-plumbed hotels. Even though Ryan and Ellen decided against these, it was hard to avoid incongruous reminders of home. An Italian TV lady with a Jennifer Aniston hairdo introduced a feature on Jennifer Aniston. The Stars and Stripes lurched into view, a whole field of them, worn on the T-shirts of some girls' high school athletic team. Basketball? Lacrosse? Ryan couldn't tell. They clomped off in their shorts and braided hair, the flags jigging over their breasts.

"Maybe if we were Italian," Ellen said, frowning. "I mean if it was our heritage, there would be things we'd recognize, things that would resonate for us. Not that it isn't all amazing . . ."

Where was the real Italy? How would they know? So much strangeness in the midst of so much strangeness. The elegant carabinieri, certainly the tallest men in Italy. The little golden towns, the walls of ancient, lichened stone, the excellent wine, both red and white, that they drank and drank without, it seemed, ever getting drunk. All the things they had been warned against: pickpockets, beggars, overpriced taxis, scams. In Florence, two young men on a motor scooter slowed beside them in a concerning way. "Where you from?" one called, and when Ryan said, "Chicago," they laughed and brandished imaginary machine guns, *rattaratta tat tat,* waved and rode off. What a goofy, happy moment, a relief, a release. In Venice the gondoliers were bored, oh painfully bored, with having to haul the tourists around. They waited sourly on the landings in their silly striped shirts and ribboned hats. Ryan and Ellen opted for the vaporetti instead. There was no reason to pay money for such guaranteed contempt. And this made them happy too, as if they had escaped some circle of tourist hell.

At Peggy Guggenheim's museum they were certain they saw a figure from a long-ago American scandal, a man whom in other circumstances they might have approached and wished well. But he was so clearly on vacation and off duty that they decided to leave him be. A small and thrilling miracle from the god of coincidence.

They discovered that Spaghetti Caruso, a particular dish, was prepared with chicken livers and so was rightly and passionately rejected by Sam. When he was older they'd remind him of this. It would attach itself to him, the story would become part of him.

For their last five days in Italy they rented a hillside villa in Umbria with a view of olive and cypress and lemon trees, its own swimming pool, maid service, and satellite TV. There were a number of other such vacation villas occupied by tourists, although they were all designed and sited so that they each felt entirely private. There was a fully equipped kitchen and a modern supermarket to serve the villas. And, in the pretty town at the top of the next mild hill, some excellent restaurants. It was a chance to relax, their reward for having been so many places and dutifully seen so many sights.

Ellen was worn-out and complained of headaches and spent a lot of time napping under the ceiling fan in their bedroom with the curtains drawn. The kids liked the pool, but it seemed that once the momentum of the trip slowed, much of the fun was over for them. "When are we going home?" Anna demanded on their first day.

"On Sunday," Ryan told her, glad to have an answer for her, even if it wasn't the answer she wanted. He was close to being vacationed-out himself. He was ready to sleep in his own bed, turn the trip into pictures and souvenirs, put a bow on it. But first there would be this interlude.

The villa had a shelf of books and magazines left behind by other, mostly English-speaking guests. While Ellen slept, he supervised the kids in the pool and leafed through the old copies of *Time* and *Der Spiegel,* a couple of glossy and forbidding literary journals, the detective novels and thrillers that were considered ideal for vacationing. None of them engaged him. He was always saying he wished he had more time to read, but either that was untrue, or else none of these materials were what he thought of as reading.

He and the children piled into the tiny rented Fiat and made a trip to the supermarket, where Ryan allowed them to select American breakfast cereal, processed cheese, and hot dogs. He made fried chicken for their dinner, and for himself and Ellen, pasta with lemon and artichokes and shrimp. She was still pale and puffy-faced, but felt well enough to come to the table for dinner, eating a little and smiling fragilely at the children. Later she sat with Ryan on the terrace.

The kids were inside in front of the television. Of course. "What are they watching?" Ellen asked. The colored smear of the television screen was behind them in the living room.

Ryan went inside to check. *"Baywatch,"* he reported back. "David Hasselhoff, dubbed in Italian."

"I guess that's OK. I worry about the commercials. They always seem to be showing bare breasts or some such thing."

"Well then, Italian kids must see that stuff too." He wasn't sure what sort of point he was making.

"I guess so," Ellen said, seeming to lose interest. Ryan stood behind her and rubbed her shoulders. "Mm," she said. It wasn't really that hard to be nice to her.

"How's the headache?"

"Better. Kind of a dull roar. Background noise."

"You can just take it easy tomorrow. There's nothing we really have to do." They had considered taking some excursions into the countryside, tours of wineries, tours of olive-oil factories, but nothing they'd planned out.

"It's boring for you here," she said in a regretful tone.

"I can go into town if I get antsy." He hadn't been aware of feeling bored until she'd spoken. Now he felt it weighing him down as if he were underwater.

At some point in their life together he had assumed the burden of making her happy. Her most familiar mood, what he thought of as her default position, was one of exasperated suffering. Which he must attend, coax, tease, and try to reason away. He would never be entirely successful; at best she would only be not unhappy. But he would always be obliged to try.

Was that the worst thing he could say about her? If he was looking for excuses, was that the best he could do? He shamed himself with these thoughts, but not enough to keep him from dishonesty.

He'd had two affairs, one of them brief, one of them lengthy. He believed that Ellen had suspicions, but no actual proof or knowledge. It had sobered him, how easy it was to get away with such things, also how little effort it would take to deal a marriage, his or any other, a fatal and rupturing blow. And that he had not been willing to do.

Both had been women he knew at work or through work. One, the first, had been younger than he was by fifteen years, a reckless, adventuring girl who alarmed him with her highs and lows, her crying jags, her cocaine, her theatrics, which, although deliberate and calculated, she thought of as impetuous charm. She was exactly the kind of girl you worried might show up to a rendezvous naked underneath a coat. It had only lasted a few weeks, then she'd moved to Toronto to be with an old boyfriend. Even now, if his phone rang at odd or unexpected hours, Ryan's first sweating thought was that she was calling.

The next woman had been his age, divorced, and lonely enough to accept what he had to offer without wanting more, or at least, so it had been in the beginning. But over the year and a half of their time together, she'd made more and more space in her life for him, become more and more wifelike, fussing over his health, his clothes, stocking her kitchen with the brand of coffee he liked, even aquiring a bathrobe for his use. He began to back away. He'd hoped to let things die a natural death and avoid a scene but there had been one.

They'd been in her car, she was driving him to Union Station for what would be the last time. Ryan said, "I thought we were just going to enjoy it until it was over." It was at that point in the argument: anything more generous and less craven had already been offered and dismissed.

"Fuck you," she said. "I don't remember signing that piece of paper. I don't exist solely for your convenience."

"We could still keep in touch," Ryan said. Another remark he would be ashamed of later.

"You mean, Dial-A-Geisha. You mean, you call me whenever it fits into your fucking *schedule,* and I will soothe and entertain you and listen with great interest to all the tiny events of your tiny life. No thanks."

He didn't answer. She was driving too fast then hitting the brakes heavy, and he concentrated on just being able to get out of the car alive.

"You know what the hell of it is? You probably love me, in some chickenshit way. It's just not important enough for you to do anything about it."

"Would you Jesus Christ watch where you're going," Ryan said. Brake lights were flaring red in front of them, and she was looking straight at him.

The hell of it was she was probably right. Chickenshitedness. An important component of screwing around. He wished she would become a good memory, not someone who came to mind, as she did now, only when he felt irritable and guilty.

Well, if he felt guilty, it's because he was guilty. He'd tried to reclaim some notion of himself as he had been: not just younger, but certain that his journey through the world would be a blazed trail, not one stupid foot in front of the other.

From the terrace at night you could see the lights of other villas through the weaving, waving trees. A scent of eucalyptus mixed with the residue of the day's baking heat. At a little distance was the walled town that dated back to before the Etruscans.

Ellen said, "I just wish we'd met more Italians. Besides hotelkeepers and tour guides, I mean. I wish the kids had. Everybody we ran into was from Dallas, or Los Angeles."

Ryan said that was the way it was set up, these trips. Parts of the country were just big holding pens for tourists. Walking with Anna and Sam on a sidewalk in Florence, they'd seen two little Chinese boys, dressed in shorts and kneesocks and jackets, walking alongside each other, one's arm thrown over the other's shoulder as they looked at a book. Miniature Italians, in almost every respect. "Who are they?" Anna had asked, and Ryan said he didn't know, just some boys. There would be a story there, but he wouldn't be able to guess it. All over the world, people ended up in the damnedest places.

He said, "I think I will run into town for a bit."

"What, right now?"

"Just to get a drink. Blow the stink off." He spoke lightly so as to disguise his sudden and irresistible urge to be alone and free in a strange country, if only for an hour. "It's not even eight o'clock. If you think you can manage with the kids . . ."

"I always have," she said levelly. She was appraising him in a way that seemed unfriendly.

"I don't have to go out. If you still aren't feeling—"

"No, go." She waved her fingers at him. "Scoot."

He was careful driving in the dark in the tiny, unfamiliar Fiat, but the road was well marked, and other pairs of headlights were winding their way down from the hills, like marbles on a slope, other tourists on the way to their own gratifying evenings. Couples, people with their kids. For a moment Ryan considered turning around and going back. The idea of being alone, so welcome to him earlier, now seemed like a miserable punishment. But cars hemmed him in ahead and behind and anyway, if he didn't want to be alone, it was one of those times when he wanted even less to be with anyone he knew.

As it was impossible to drive very far into the town itself, there was a car park just outside the old gated entryway. Ryan joined the others passing in under the arches, the dressed-up women picking their way carefully along the uneven cobblestones, the men in the sports jackets they'd been made to pack for just such occasions. Strings of colored lights decorated the streetlamps and crossed overhead. Small shops were open, selling postcards, papier-mâché puppets, key chains, ashtrays, guidebooks. He slowed to look into the shop windows to demonstrate the normality and harmlessness of his presence. Without his family he felt conspicuous, even a little sinister.

Ryan followed the stream of people uphill, where most of the bars and trattorias and restaurants were. He passed columned entrances, windows with elaborate plasterwork cornices, looking as if figures from a different century might appear there at any moment. Yellow roses grew from urns made of soft pink clay. Small, starlike red and white flowers cascaded out of window boxes. The stream of tourists was emptying into a larger current of townspeople out for their own entertainment, sleek young men in polo shirts and jeans, ornamental young women, older people on stately promenades. Here were cafés with tables set outside beneath their awnings, placards advertising their different specials. A large window, its shutters open and lined with tiny white lights, gave him a view of linen-covered tables, ranks of candles, people attending to their dinners with apparant delight. And this he stood and watched also, until someone inside noticed him, and he hurried away, brushing aside the ghost of a memory he couldn't quite place.

A little farther up the same street he found a small bar that looked to be something other than a nightclub, that is, he didn't hear any of the hectic, brassy music that might indicate dancing. He entered, peering around him—the light was dim, yellow as candlelight, although it was in fact electric. He took a place at the bar and ordered an Americano. Vermouth, Campari, soda, and an orange slice. The barmaid, who had a broad, businesslike face, repeated it, "Americano," and set to work. Ryan reached into his pocket for some of the pretty, confusing Italian bills and held them up. The barmaid extracted a bill and brought his change, which he left on the bar.

The drink was sweeter than he remembered, disappointing, almost perfumey. Maybe it was supposed to be this way. He decided to drink it rather than complain.

"German," someone next to him said, and it took Ryan a moment to realize the word was being applied to him.

"American," he said to the man. The bar had no seats and they were both standing. The man was shorter than Ryan, as were most people, but heavy in the chest and shoulders. Italian, certainly. Graying hair worn pushed away from his forehead in a pompadour. Jowls that gave him the look of a prosperous bulldog. He wore a white shirt open at the throat and a summer jacket of some light material, only a shade darker. In the dim light he glowed like a photographic negative.

"Apology," he said.

"Not a problem," Ryan told him.

"So many are Germanys." The man nodded and said something to the barmaid, who took Ryan's nearly empty glass and refilled it with another of the treacherous sweet drinks.

"Thanks very much. *Salute.*"

"*Salute.* First time here?" His English was strongly accented and Ryan had to pick his way through it over the noise of the bar.

"Yes, my family and I."

"*Benvenuto in Italia.*" The man finished his own drink and motioned for another. Ryan wondered if it was his turn to buy, but he was too slow. "Everybody in the world is here," the man announced.

"The American, the German, the Englishman. We are the big world playground." He smiled. The notion seemed to make him happy.

"Yes, it's a very beautiful place," Ryan said politely. From what he could see of the rest of the room, he was the only foreigner. There were some small metal tables, unoccupied except for an old couple occupied with not talking to each other. At the back of the room was another door, and waiters were passing in and out with plates and silverware. He hadn't noticed this when he'd come in and he wondered if he'd mistaken the nature of the place. More people were crowding in at the front entrance, apparently for some occasion. He began to think about leaving the watery end of his drink on the bar and slipping away.

Before he could do so, another man, this one older, slighter, with a ring of grizzled hair, came up to the bar and put one arm around Ryan, one around the pompadour man. Greetings were exchanged in quick, incomprehensible Italian, then this new man said to Ryan, "German?"

"No, American," Ryan said, allowing himself to feel annoyed. He guessed it had to do with being blond.

There was another pantomime of apology. Ryan hoped it wouldn't lead to another drink. The smaller man edged in between the two of them and spoke to the barmaid. Then to the pompadour man, who relayed it to Ryan. "He says, American is better than German. More new."

"What's new, you mean, it's newer that Americans come here?" The bar was getting noisier by the minute. People were lining up at either side of the front door, as if in expectation.

"New country," the man shouted at him.

"Is that good?"

"New and shiny." The man smiled with apparant approval.

Yes, Ryan guessed it was. At least compared to a few thousand years of emperors, plagues, invading Huns, Medicis, and Mussolini. It would give you a different worldview, all those centuries of triumph and wreckage.

But new and shiny? The shine was pretty much knocked off by now. Or maybe that was just him feeling old and tired and cynical. He was past forty. He guessed it was hard to live through forty years of any kind of history without cynicism.

Ryan straightened and looked around him. Family groups were coming in now, moms and pops, little girls in flower dresses, leggy teenagers, everybody excited and chattering. The waiters in the back were now hurrying into the unseen rear room with platters and trays of food, wineglasses, bouquets in crystal fishbowls.

Clearly he had come in on some private party or celebration. Maybe there had been a sign he couldn't read. "Good night," he said to his new friends, waving foolishly. "Ciao. Nice meeting you."

But he was too late, because at that moment the doorway filled with applause, and a bride and groom entered, carried along by some momentum, as if they had been hurled into the room like projectiles.

The couple was young, handsome, and attended by a squadron of other splendid-looking young people. The bride appeared to have been inserted into a structure of white satin shells and swags. The groom resembled a man in the last period of a strenuous athletic contest, attempting to get to the final horn. A general cheer went up. Someone went behind the bar and tried to start the recorded music. After some amplified skips and scratches, a love song, he guessed it was, began, with a singer who made Ryan think of the term *crooner*. Were weddings the same everywhere? Every one he'd seen, his own, certainly, all of them more alike than different. The strain of so much public happiness. The promises everyone expected to keep. A procession of couples all the way back to some dim start of time, the past gaping like an open pit at his feet.

He had to wonder at himself, such strange and windy notions. He was tired, he didn't belong here. But there was no clear path to the door, and the best he could do was to sidle around the edge of the room. Sooner or later he supposed the wedding party would go into the back room for their supper. Or maybe someone would shoo him away: no Germans allowed. Trays of wineglasses were making the rounds. His new friends from the bar were raising their glasses to him, and so he took one also and toasted them. It was fizzy, some kind of sweet champagne that coated the inside of his head with another layer of dullness.

A group of young girls, teenagers, was between him and the door, and just as he became aware that they were staring and goggling at him, one of them walked up to him. "Hello. I am winning a bet."

"A bet?" She had a thin, vivid face with eyebrows that moved as rapidly as antennae, a cloud of dark curls. She was wearing a black silk dress that looked too old for her, and a pair of stiltlike high heels.

"My friends, ah, say I am scared." She pivoted toward them and then back to him, with a humorous expression.

"They dared you to talk to me."

She laughed and showed her pretty teeth. "What is your name?"

"Ryan." She was very young. He was nervous about talking to her. Not that it wasn't flattering to be singled out. He'd reached the age when he'd begun to tell himself that he looked pretty good, considering.

"I am Gianna." She did another pirouette back to her friends, who were twittering like a flock of sparrows. "You want to dance with me?"

"Sorry. I'm not much of a dancer."

"Are you from California?" she asked, sounding hopeful. "You look California."

Better than Germany, at least. "No, Chicago." He guessed that she wouldn't have heard of Iowa.

"I like California. And New York. And Tokyo. Here I am going very soon."

He tried not to smile. She reminded him of . . . it was difficult to say. Of every pretty, bold, knowing young girl in the whole world. The bride and groom were in the center of the room now, being admired and congratulated. "Who got married? I didn't even know there was a wedding going on here."

Her mobile face registered an exaggerated boredom. "Ah, my *cugino*. Cousin. And some silly girl. Who are perfect with each other. I will never get married."

"And why is that?" Her certainty amused him.

"I will be a fashion model." She struck a pose, hands on her jutting hips. "And a singer."

"Opera singer?" He couldn't help teasing her.

Gianna hit him lightly on the arm. The freight of gold bracelets on her wrist rang. "Funny man!" She sang along with the recording for a few bars in a trilling voice. "Good? You think?"

"Very nice. And I think you speak very good English."

"Thank you. I practice. What are your business?"

"I own a computer-software company." She inclined her head toward him, puzzled. "Computers," he said, moving his fingers across an imaginary keyboard.

"Ah," she said, comprehending. "Do you have a lot of money?"

"Gianna, I have to tell you, in America that would be considered a rude question."

"So you do have," she said happily.

Ryan shook his head, attempting to deflect her. But in fact the leap he'd taken six years ago, putting the skills he had to work for himself instead of for everybody else, had paid off extravagantly. He'd never expected to have so much money. He worried about his kids growing up thinking it was the way everybody lived. "What's the Italian for 'none of your business.'"

She tapped his arm again in punishment and swayed toward him. Her perfume was a warm wind. He really did have to leave. "Well, Gianna, it was awfully nice to meet you. I hope you have a very successful career."

She was distracted by something behind her, some kind of ecstatic signaling from her friends. "They want to talk you too."

"Sorry, but I have to go home now. Ladies." He made a mock bow in their direction, which set them off into paroxysms of laughter. "Enjoy your evening."

"Good-bye." Disappointed in him, she made another face. "Funny funny."

He gained the doorway and walked two dozen paces downhill before he realized he didn't have the keys to the rental car.

He stopped where he was, in the middle of the promenading crowds, then moved to one side of the street and conducted the sort of calm, methodical search he made his children go through at such times. Were they sure, were they absolutely sure they didn't have whatever it was? Yup. No keys.

He tried to remember if he'd had them in the bar, perhaps taken them out of his pocket. He didn't think so, and he wasn't inclined to plunge back in to look. It was more likely that he'd dropped them on the street or stupidly left them in the car. He set off again downhill, at a quicker pace now.

The car was gone. Ryan stood at the edge of the lot, marking the empty space. He really had been that stupid. How was he going to get back to the villa? It had a phone but he didn't know the number. He'd left his cell phone behind because it didn't work here. He turned and went back in through the arched entrance, heaping abuse on himself, even if it was only a rental, even if this was what insurance was for, because it was all going to be a giant pain in the ass.

No doubt there was a police station somewhere, that would be a good place to start. Except he couldn't find it. He hiked a little farther up the hill, straying into what turned into sleeping residential districts, other streets that dwindled to alleys. By the time he made his way back to the main thoroughfare, and the square he'd seen in daylight a couple of days ago—the statue of somebody or other on a horse, the fourteenth-century church—there were fewer people about, and most of them seemed to be hurrying home. The square had a creepy look, veiled with shadows, the cobblestones ringing with echoes. Ellen would be worrying about him by now.

Finally, at one of the streets leading into the square, a *polizia*, engaged in what seemed like casual conversation with a couple of loitering young men. Ryan approached. *"Scusa . . ."*

The officer turned toward him, looked him over. Did he even know the word for *car*? For *stolen*? If he ever had, he didn't now. And he wasn't drunk, exactly, more like thickheaded, out of his element. *Macchina!* His brain presented him with a gift. *"Scuza, signore, mi macchina . . .*" He ran out of vocabulary here. "Stolen." He made a pantomime, shading his eyes with his hand, looking from side to side, giving up and shrugging his shoulders. "Stolen," he said again, reduced to idiot repetition. He made a show of sticking his thumb out, hitching a ride.

This was the funniest thing they'd ever seen. They laughed and smacked each other on the back. Ryan laughed along with them, politely. It occurred to him that he didn't know the license-plate number of the car or have any of the useful documents that detailed the rental agreement. They were in the car, of course. He'd have to wait until tomorrow, then call the English-speaking office of the rental company. Oh ha ha ha.

The three men recovered from their laughing fit. Each of them stuck his thumb out in imitation of Ryan. Then they waved, bye-bye, turned their backs on him, and walked off into the shadows.

Maybe he'd said something unintentional, maybe sticking your thumb out in Italy meant something it didn't in other places, something along the lines of "I like to pick my nose." He left the now vacant square, hoping he'd found the right street. They were all narrow and they jogged first one way then another, so you couldn't tell where they led. His eyes were tired and the streetlights were developing veils and halos. Maybe if he got back down to the car park, he could catch a ride with some other tourists on their way back to the villas.

From some distance, another street beyond him, voices floated toward him. Ciao, ciao, good night.

Then silence. The street was so narrow, the ancient houses built out so far over it, there was very little sky overhead. Strips and lozenges of stars. Here and there, a light behind a curtain. A voice he didn't realize was coming from a television until it was shut off in midword. How quickly the streets had emptied out, everyone gone home. He wondered if the wedding party was still going on, and if he could find his way back there. Let his new friends buy him more drinks. Marry him off to Gianna.

He'd thought that all he'd need to do was keep heading downhill to

reach the gates, but the street ended suddenly at a wall, solid except for
a drainage pipe along its lower edge. Well all right. Ryan retraced his
path, uphill this time. The effort made him break a sweat but the cool
air turned his skin clammy. He was trying to get back to the church
square and take one of the other streets down to the gate, but he was
out of his reckoning and the square refused to materialize. He began
talking to himself, silently, once more using his calming, father's voice:
Let's just try to figure it out, it won't help, getting upset. And really, it
wouldn't.

Think of yourself (he continued, as if speaking to Anna or to Sam,
as if there was an answer for everything and one had only to ask the
right intelligent question) as a more persevering sort of tourist. Someone who's gone off the map. Pushed a little farther into unknown
territory.

Another, broader avenue presented itself, this one with a mercantile
character, a row of shops beneath a columned archway. Ryan passed
along a wall of glass windows, looking sideways at his own reflection.
He looked old, even a little soiled. He couldn't imagine why Gianna
and her friends had bothered flirting with him, except out of perver-
sity. Pretty girl, made brave by her own newness. His own daughter,
he foresaw, was going to give him merry hell in a few short years, with
all the reckless behavior he could imagine, as well as those things she
would actually do.

Uphill? Downhill? His legs were tired. He hobbled a little way in
one direction, then the other. For a town that made its living off tourists, they could have put up a few international street signs. Someday
his daughter would be not just a teenager but a young woman, a
mother, old. Beyond that he could not go. It was easier to imagine his
own death. Oh too easy. He was all his history at once, a big boo-hoo
story. It was the Bronze Age and he was overrun by tribes of prehistoric
Greeks. He was a papal state. He was liberated by Garibaldi.

He laughed to show himself how foolish he was being, foolish and
fanciful, but it was the cold truth that although he mourned many of
the things he had done, the broken chain of his own good intentions,

he might not have done much of anything differently even if he could, including the difficult territory of his marriage, for fear of making some worse mistake.

Chickenshit.

As if he'd reached the end of thought and need go no further, he arrived without warning at the main gate, draped with its national and city flags, lights still blazing even though no one but himself was there to see them.

A little mist was seeping in through the ancient gate. The car park too was illuminated with a grid of overhead lights, a doleful concrete island in the ground fog. It was nearly empty except for a couple of older wrecks that looked as if they lived there and, in its own marked square, his rented Fiat.

Ryan approached it, tried the driver's door, which was open. The keys were on the floor mat. He got in and engaged the ignition. It started right up.

Had he been mistaken before, had the car been there all along? Or had someone taken it for a joyride and then returned it? He put the car in gear and started off, with exemplary caution, on the road back to the villa. He guessed he'd never know. He guessed it didn't matter, and he was the beneficiary of a small piece of dumb luck, accent on dumb.


They took more pictures, they bought the last of their souvenirs, they packed and tidied and made arrangements for their travel and it had been a great trip, a success in all the ways they had imagined. They were glad to have attempted it and now they would be glad to have it behind them. It was a beautiful country in so many respects, but they'd had enough of being foreigners.

The car was packed and Ryan made a last circuit of the rooms to make certain that important items had not been forgotten. The wet towels from the children's last swim spread out to dry on the terrace, the money for the maids set out on the kitchen table. The beds stripped, the linens gathered into bundles. Satisfied, he crossed the tiled floor to the front door, passed through and locked it from the outside.

The sound of the car's engine faded. Little by little, silence regained the rooms. The sun rose higher and the morning light grew and trembled, almost liquid, like a drop of honey on the lip of a jar.

By design, Ryan and Ellen had left behind them for future tenants some paperback books and a few magazines, added to the pile in the main room. Neither of them had found much entertainment in the available selections. Although if Ryan had paid real attention to one of the high-end magazines, he would have been struck by a particular name in the table of contents. Understandably, he'd only glanced at it. It wasn't the sort of thing he read, those serious, artsy productions with their daunting pages, and besides, the god of coincidences couldn't be expected to attend to everything.

## SPRING, 1975

*Long ago, on a far road*
*A hundred blackbirds perched.*
*They were young, they loved the day with song.*
*We were young too, uncertain of our real*

*natures. Were we free to fly,*
*like blackbirds? Was that pretense? Would our road*
*take us back and back again, to our real and*
*far from airborne selves? We loved*

*to think we were the road itself,*
*and blackbirds sang their far and farther*
*songs to lead us into love. Was any of it*
*real, or were we simply young?*

*In that far spring our road*
*found its real end. We did not know enough*

*to say how much was pride, careless,*
*like the blackbird, love just one more song*

*when so many might be sung. My road*
*was the blackbird's wing, yours was the bird's real*
*nature. I never got better at love.*
*You went too far and vanished into air.*

*Were you? Was I? Too late to know. We were so*
*young. Ah, love, the blackbirds at least were real.*

# *Iowa*

DECEMBER 2000

Friday morning. Squalls of light snow blew up and down the length of Main Street, twisting like a curtain come loose. Chip Tesman looked out from the first floor of the old bank building, watching the snow ride the wind. He guessed it was going to keep up the rest of the day like this, pissy little stuff. He still didn't have any use for snow.

The great state of Iowa, celebrated for its agriculture, commerce, and industry. Land of the good neighbor and the firm handshake. Cold enough for you? Hot enough for you? Weather was one thing you were allowed to complain about. Sturdy, cheerful, hardworking folks. Soul of generosity. Salt of the earth. They looked at him cross-eyed. What had he expected, the key to the city? He'd never wanted to be back here.

Chip left the shop by the side door, not bothering to lock up, and climbed the stairs to Torrie's place. She was playing some of her old Dylan music and he had to knock pretty loud.

"Holy Bob," Chip said, once she let him in. "I'm gonna get you some new tunes."

"I like this one." Torrie tilted her chin to smile at him.

"Yeah, I figured that out. You coming with me?" Torrie shook her head. "Come on, a little expedition. Don't you get tired of the four walls?"

She shook her head again and Chip knew it was time to stop asking. He turned to the huge windows and watched this new view of the snow, as if it was a drive-in movie, a movie about snow. The movie would go on all day and night sometimes. Where else was there snow? Lots of places he'd been. Bits and pieces of them. They spooled out behind his eyes. Then he was noplace.

"Chip?"

He turned away from the window, crisp, smiling. "Right."

"Careful driving."

"Yes, extracareful, I promise. If I don't get back tonight? It doesn't mean anything bad happened. Just that I didn't make it back."

He probably shouldn't have said that about not coming back. Now she was giving him this stricken look.

"You have to quit worrying about stuff all the time."

"I'm don't."

"Seriously, cut it out. Why won't you come with me? What if Dylan never toured again after his motoryele accident?" She wanted to laugh at that but she wouldn't let herself. "I got it. You should take some skydiving lessons, jump out of a few planes. Face your fears."

"Dumbass," she said affectionately.

"Hey, I like your hair these days." She'd grown it out just past her shoulders and it looked like she might be putting some blond stuff on it to hide the gray.

She touched the hair above her ear. "It's just hair."

"Now who's a dumbass."

The plain honest truth was, he'd never thought Torrie's face or anything else about her was so bad. Maybe if you didn't see somebody for, what, twenty-odd years, all their growing-up time, you didn't have some big expectation of how they should look anyway. When he first got back, he saw how everybody fluttered around, making a big deal out of not making a big deal, waiting for him to have some kind of horrified reaction. And he just couldn't come up with one. Torrie looked sort of cracked, but he'd seen worse. It wasn't like he was any beauty queen himself.

Sure they felt sorry for her. Were so proud of themselves for being nice to her. Were so pleased to have her around to feel sorry for. Torrie must have learned to ignore them a long time ago.

She said, "There's lots of places . . ."

"What, baby? What about them?"

"Nothing going places." She shook her head, frustrated. She still did that sometimes, got her words backward and on top of each other. But he thought he knew what she was saying. Lots of places she'd like to go. If only.

You didn't give up wanting things because your life had put them out of reach. Even if everybody else tried to make you into some kind of crippled saint.

"What's this?" He picked up a print from her worktable. "It looks new." It was a blue-green swirl, like those pictures of Earth taken from outer space. But blurred and threatening to unravel. It had a floating, almost 3-D quality. "How'd you do this?"

"I don't know. Just a trying."

"Ms. Artist."

"Yeah yeah yeah."

"All right, you change your mind, I'll be downstairs for a while. Hey, can I take that print with me?"

When Chip got back to the shop he found, not unexpectedly, one of his regulars, Ferd, making himself at home in an armchair with a vintage copy of *Silver Surfer*. "Dude," Chip said, slapping hands with him.

"What up, Chip." Ferd was fifteen, a spotty, furtive, ignored kid. The kind who moped his way through school, spoke in monosyllables, beat off in the shower. The kind of kid Chip knew pretty well, from having been one himself.

"I've got to close up today, I got some business to tend to." Ferd looked stricken. "But you can hang out here, if you don't let anybody else in."

"Yeah?"

"You can do inventory if you feel like it. You remember how to do inventory?"

"Yeah, sure I do." The kid looked as close as he ever got to happy. You'd think he'd been asked to sweep up piles of gold coins.

"And don't mess with my shit. There's some Cokes in the fridge. Here." Chip took a $5 bill from the register. "Get yourself a sandwich or something from Lena's."

"Thanks, man." Ferd had to struggle to maintain a properly indifferent face. Chip knew he'd just given the kid the gift of a perfect day. He could hunker down by himself, singled out, made special. He wouldn't have to go back home, hide in his bedroom, listen to his mother ask him for the ten-thousandth time what on earth he did in there.

He hadn't been meaning to start a business. He'd just been looking for something to do with his old comic book collection. Then he'd added to it at swap meets, along with Magic cards, Dungeons & Dragons, posters of wizards, space aliens, warriors. He had to admit, he got a kick out of all that stuff. What everybody really wanted was video games, so he sold those too: *GoldenEye, Counter-Strike, Warcraft.* And he'd ended up with this dandy clubhouse for the town's lost boys.

"Ferd? How much snow are we supposed to get?"

Ferd looked up from his comic book. He had thatchy hair long enough to get in his eyes, giving him the look of a small, furtive animal. "Ah, I dunno. Some."

"Right." He guessed Ferd wasn't a guy who paid much attention to anything real, like weather. Chip went into the back room for his coat and keys. He pretty much lived back here, had a bed and a little bit of a kitchen, even a shower set up in what was meant to be a mop station. Illegal as hell, so if anybody asked, he lived at his dad's.

Not that they were likely to do anything to piss off Ryan, who might be persuaded to dump more money into downtown one of these days. Even if Chip's establishment wasn't exactly what the Chamber of Commerce had in mind for the space. Still not too many people taking advantage of all the swell retail opportunities. And the ones who'd always dreamed of opening their own flower shop or knitting boutique had smacked their heads into a pretty solid economic wall.

Everybody thought he was a drug dealer. Him and the boys, sitting around smoking or snorting or cooking. Every so often somebody he didn't know came by, acting all curious and interested. You had to figure that was Officer Friendly keeping track.

Sorry to disappoint them. It wasn't like the old days. He'd learned to be very, very careful.

He locked the door to the back room, also the shop's front door. "So, go out by the side. Pull it shut behind you, switch off the overhead lights. Leave it open if you're coming back."

By the time Chip got out to the sidewalk and looked in through the shop window, Ferd had curled himself around the armchair like a snail, like an advertisement for bad posture, moving his lips slightly as he read.

The snow had stopped for the moment, leaving the thinnest, sifting layer on the pavement. Chip waved at Lena as he passed her window. She was cooking up a grill order, her wild hair held back with a red bandanna. He was rooting for her to stay in business and she just might make it. She served lumpy whole-grain bread and alfalfa-sprout salads, but also the kind of food people didn't cook for themselves anymore: pot roast, scalloped potatoes, lemon meringue pie. Good solid Iowa chow, and it didn't seem to matter that Lena was a Jewish girl from New Jersey who'd followed a husband out west and then lost him to the usual kinds of bad luck. She cooked like she'd grown up winning blue ribbons at the state fair.

The old Chevy coughed and rumbled and took its time warming up. He felt the cold in all the usual places: ears, back of the neck, rib cage, thighs. He was too skinny to live in this damned climate. Not enough fat on him. The Chevy was a tank, a bumper-dragging wreck with 175,000 miles on it. It didn't get crap for mileage but in bad weather it was the safest thing on the road short of a garbage truck.

The snow picked up again just outside town, heavier now, enough to coat the ground. It was blowing in from the south so it was going to be in his face all the way to Des Moines. Kaleidoscope snow. The kind that burst into patterns on the windshield. Tricky shit. Hypnotizing in a way he didn't like. He pounded the car's radio on and off, singing when he wouldn't find a station. *Row, row, row your boat, gently down the stream, merrily merrily merrily merrily,* any dumb thing he could think of, anything to keep himself in the right here and the right now.

He'd done something to his head, or something had been done to it so that he had these moments of free-floating confusion, a blackout, he guessed, except it had a grainy look, like an old movie. Once he'd been talking to—somebody? in the shop?—he was pretty sure of that much, and the next he was out on the sidewalk, squinting up into the sky with his mouth open. Like chickens who drowned when it rained because they were too stupid to swallow.

He understood how people went out in public naked, or had long arguments with themselves, or any other genuinely crazy thing. The movie in their head skipped a few frames. So he was crazy too, but just a little bit around the edges, just enough to need careful tending. The last thing he wanted to do was tell some doctor who would load him up on big chalky unfun pills or alert the pain-in-the-ass concerned authorities.

After all, your head only had so much room in it. No surprise if it overflowed once in a while with little bits of sparkle and electrical fizz. He'd finally quit smoking—had to, the lungs were shot—and sometimes he wondered if that was part of the problem, his brain having to adjust to a nicotine-free state, no soothing pillow of smoke to cushion it.

He'd got a map of Des Moines and spent time studying it, so once he reached town he had it knocked. Without so much wind the snow was back to acting like normal snow, the kind you could reasonably trust to fall from up to down without any weird stuff, so he could keep his head balanced right where it was supposed to be and didn't have to worry about its sliding off one or another shoulder. Ha ha.

And here was the college, showing up just where it ought to. It took him some driving around to find the building he needed, but he'd left himself all kinds of time, a couple of hours. Fine with him. He could look the place over, figure out if this was any kind of a good idea.

He parked and entered through the big double doors. Cool, echoing tile floors, white walls, one of them glass. The snow outside mounding up, another layer of white. Students coming and going, the artsy sort, with big portfolio cases and scuffed boots and funky knit hats, and they looked at him kind of strangely because after all he didn't belong here and it showed and it was funny that these kids who were all about looking peculiar and different seemed to draw the line when it came to his peculiar self.

He could have ended up as one of them. It wasn't so hard to imagine. He'd always had a knack for drawing. Just not much of a knack for school, for sitting still and paying attention and giving a shit.

Here was the gallery, a hallway branching off into a couple of different rooms. Nobody was standing guard or charging admission, so he walked on in and found himself face-to-face with a poster, a black-and-white photograph of a long, dark hillside, a slice of sky above it, and a single tree silhouetted against the sky. Only when you looked closely at the tree did you see it was really part of a painted backdrop, a billboard maybe.

On the poster:

### NATIVE LAND:
### PHOTOGRAPHS BY ELTON POTTER

December 2–January 31      Allen B. Drinkwater Gallery

Chip made a circuit of the room, stopping in front of each picture. All black and whites. Some of them were landscapes, out west by the look of them, canyons, highways edged with scrub, mountains reflected upside down in a long trough of rainwater. All of it with a sense of being borderless, stretching out to empty space. Other pictures were cityscapes: windows, wires, traffic, signs, a solitary man crossing a street. A shot of a kid who reminded Chip of a young Elton, waiting at a bus stop, his round face sullen with loneliness.

On a table near the gallery entrance was a stack of flyers, and he picked one up. They went along with the show. There was a list of different exhibitions and talks and other art stuff that Elton had been up to. It looked like he'd kept busy. There was a picture of him and Chip studied it for a time.

Then there was something called Artist Statement:

When people learn that I'm a Native American, they often have certain expectations of me and of my work and life. I find it necessary to explain to them that I don't know how to track a wolf or catch a salmon with my bare hands. I don't have a totem animal or a medicine pouch. I grew up with bits and pieces of my own history coming at me sideways, filtered through television and movies and cartoons, Chapter One in American Studies, a story that was supposed to be over by now. I never felt like a "real" Indian, even though I could trace my lineage back through three Northwest tribes who had lived on the same land a thousand years before Columbus.

Tribes. It all came back to that, one way or another. He read on.

I think I started taking pictures because I didn't (and still don't) have the right words to express the unease of a life lived outside of categories, boundaries, and ready-made narratives. My photographs are informed by a sense of loss, myself made strange to myself, and a country that too often has seemed to belong to everybody except me.

Jesus. Whine much, guy?

He still had time to kill, so he walked outside again, pushing up the hood of his coat against the snow. In the building next door he found a snack bar, and a lounge where students were absorbed in tapping at computers. Or they were plugged into headphones, eyes closed. Everybody communing with their private machine. Chip bought a cup of coffee and a hot dog and some nachos and ate slowly, thinking about nothing in particular.

When he got back to the gallery, waiters in white shirts and black pants were setting up tables of wineglasses. He picked a spot in the lobby to wait. Trying not to look like a guy who was there just for the free drinks.

People began to gather in ones and twos and threes. Enough to call it a crowd. Even though he'd been watching, he didn't see Elton come in. But there he was, it couldn't have been anybody else, having a conversation with a man and a woman, two of the grown-ups.

Chip got up and joined the group in the gallery. He walked past Elton and his fans and pretended to examine a photograph nearby. Elton was still on the chunky side, but he'd grown tall enough to balance it out. Still that round, baby face, now spreading out around the chin. He wore his hair pulled back in a ponytail. Jeans, a black, open-neck shirt, and he'd picked up a pretty nice leather jacket somewhere along the way. Chip guessed the jacket was the artist part.

He dawdled over the picture, trying to catch what the three of them were saying behind him. The woman must have been a teacher, she was talking about a class. The class had so enjoyed blah blah. "I'm really glad I got to meet some of them," Elton said, and damned if he didn't sound exactly the same, like this was back in Seattle, in his mom's old kitchen. The woman said they were looking forward to hearing more from him about blah blah. "Of course, that would be great," Elton said, and even though Chip had his back to him and hadn't talked to Elton since 1976, he was just about positive that the guy wasn't looking forward to it one bit.

Chip moved on to the next picture. He hadn't yet figured out what he was going to say to Elton, but it would be pretty chickenshit not to say it.

He kept Elton in the corner of his eye. As the guest of honor, he was in demand. Everybody kept wanting him to talk about the fine points of this or that picture, including a couple of the juicier girls. Elton, my man! The girls couldn't have been more than twenty-two. And Elton had to be, what, over forty now. Only seven or eight years younger than Chip was. That was part of what had made Seattle such a funky little time.

Elton and his satellites were moving in one direction around the room, Chip in the other. When they intersected, Chip managed to get close enough to come into Elton's field of vision. Chip nodded. "Good to see you again," he said, and kept moving.

He was aware of Elton staring after him. Some fuzzy expression on his face. It was another five minutes before Elton detached himself from his groupies and walked over to him. "You're shittin me," he said. "Ray?"

"The one and only."

"I don't believe it."

"Yup. Same old me, just smarter and better looking." He had to say, he was tickled at being recognized. It meant he didn't look as bad as he thought.

"Take a flying fuck at a rolling doughnut," Elton told him, and then they managed a little bit of back pounding and handshaking. "Goddamn, what are you doing here?"

"I live here. Around here. I read about you in the paper and I thought, 'These people have no idea what a lame-ass character you are, I better go straighten them out.'"

"Total mind fuck," said Elton, shaking his head. Close up, Chip could see that his eyes were pouchy, older than the rest of him. "Shouldn't you be dead or something by now?"

"Were you always such a smartass? I'm trying to remember."

"So catch me up, you been living here all this time?"

"Nah, not that long. You know what they say. Home's the place where, when you show up, they have to take you in." That was pretty much the size of it. "So when did you turn into a big shot?"

Elton ducked his head, a movement that recalled Elton the Kid. "Oh yeah, that's me. Here in the land of the big shots."

"No, really, those are pretty righteous pictures. You still in Seattle?"

Elton said thanks, and yeah, he was, mostly, but he worked here and there. Different gigs. Chip thought this was probably already more conversation than they'd ever had way back when. How long had he lived out west, anyway? A couple of years? He should have made a habit of writing things down, so he could remember exactly. And then, since they had to get past this part, he asked, "How's your mom?"

"She's good. She got married. He's a pretty nice guy. They bought a house out in Port Angeles."

"Yeah? That's great." Chip tried to feel one way or the other about Deb's being married, but he couldn't, aside from a mild curiosity about whether her husband was a white guy or another Indian. Deb. She must be most of the way to old by now. It gave him another of those floating, cut-loose feelings.

"I was married for a while," Elton volunteered. "Actually, twice. But the first one didn't count."

"There are those kind."

"The second one lasted longer. But she was mean as a snake. I give her credit for launching my career. I was always wanting to get out of the house, so I started driving around taking pictures."

Chip was getting a kick out of this new Elton, the talky one. Who would have guessed, way back when, that the guy had any such thing as a sense of humor?

"I have two kids. Boy and girl. Teenagers. They're good kids. Smarter than I ever was. They live with their mom, but I see them as often as I can. Counteract some of the snake venom."

"You, a dad," Chip said. "Now there's a mind fuck." He guessed it was his turn to talk, but he didn't have anything in the way of wives or kids to offer up. From across the room, a little delegation was headed toward them. The lady art teacher and a couple of dressed-up older guys. "Here comes your fan club," Chip said.

Elton saw them too. "Look, I have to go do the art thing."

"Understood."

Elton hesitated, then went for it. "There's a party later. At some students' place. Very, very casual. I think I can promise that. Why don't you come with?"

Chip was all ready to say no. Trying to imagine himself at any kind of a party, especially one with a bunch of college kids being all cool and talking art and then throwing up in the sink. "Sure," he said. "Thanks."

"Great. I'll come get you, give you the high sign."

Elton went off to glad-hand the fan club and Chip strolled over to get himself a glass of wine and some of the mingy cheese and crackers. He shouldn't have said he'd go to the party. But he'd be fifty on his next birthday and he didn't have much to show for it except a bunch of stories he couldn't always remember because they slid back and forth too fast and maybe Elton could at least make one of them hold still for a little while. Besides, Elton actually seemed happy to see him.

By his third glass of wine, whatever was happening at the gallery was winding down, people heading for the doors. Elton came up to him, accompanied by one of the juicy girls. "Hey Ray, you still good to go?"

"Absolutely." The girl was tall, every bit as tall as Elton, with short dark hair streaked a fluorescent red. She didn't look like the smiley type. She wore shiny black knee-high boots, a flippy little skirt, and a jacket made of some patchwork stuff. It was as if everything she had on meant something, but he couldn't have said what.

"This is Alisa, she can give us a ride. Or if you want, we could go in your car . . ."

"I'll take a ride." The inside of the Chevy wasn't exactly house-broken.

The three of them went out into the snow, a few inches deep by now. Nothing more was coming down but the wind had picked up and turned frigid, which was pretty much the miserable cycle of weather here. The girl, Alisa, led the way to her car, a new-looking Japanese model. She and Elton were having a little conversation, while Chip trudged on behind. He wondered if being an artist meant you got next to a lot of girls, if Elton was such a great photographer that they fell over backward for him. Because if you were going to be honest about it, he wasn't the world's best-looking man.

The Japanese car at least had four doors, so when Chip said he'd sit in the back, he didn't have to fold himself entirely in half. Elton sat up front, his arm all casually across the seat, just resting on the back of Alisa's neck. Chip said, "So, you do this kind of thing a lot? Show up places where they have your pictures?"

Elton turned around. "It's called visiting artist, yeah, I do them from time to time. Come out to a school, visit classes, maybe do a gallery talk. Then they buy me drinks."

Alisa said, "We had Gabrielle Wyse earlier this fall. She was incredible."

"That's great," Chip said. "I mean, I guess they pay you and all. Great." He should probably stop talking now. The car's tires made a soft noise in the unplowed snow. He sat back and watched the streets and houses slide past, little square houses with frosted roofs that could have been anywhere, *Des Moines.*

Elton said, "I'm liking the hair. Very intense. Like red feathers, like you're a tropical bird. So Ray, man, tell me what you're doing these days. Tell me what you've been doing the last twenty-five years."

"Ah, all kinds a shit." He rummaged around for a story. "I went to diamond-cutting school. Carson City, Nevada."

"Yeah? You turn into some international diamond smuggler or something?"

"Oh yeah, ha ha ha. It's great work, if you can get it." OK, next story. "I lived in Mexico for a while. Florida. Austin, Texas. Man, times I woke up and had to look at a matchbook to remember where I was. Now I'm back in the old hometown."

Alisa said, "Gabrielle Wyse was a revelation. The way she approached pigment. It made you reexamine every formalist assumption you had."

"I'm going to have to take a look at her work. You're going to have to tell me more about her. So what are you doing with yourself, back in the old hometown?"

"I run a little business. Comic books, video games. You could even call it a pop-culture art gallery." This in the way of a joke, but the laughs weren't coming. "Just something to keep me out of trouble."

"We're here," Alisa said, pulling the car over to the curb. Other cars were already lining the street, and people were walking toward a house with the porch lights blazing. The three of them got out. Chip caught up with Elton and held him back for a moment of private conversation.

"Hey I don't know if this is such a great idea, you know, it's supposed to be your party."

"What are you saying, you want your own party?"

"No, fool." Alisa was already stalking away toward the house. Elton's gaze tracked her. "Nice girl," Chip said. "Very high style."

"She makes videos. Sensitive art videos." Elton took hold of Chip's arm and steered him along. "Now don't get all stupid on me. You take off now, I'll wake up in the morning and think you were just a bad dream."

"I'll stay for a little while." Chip thought he could walk back to his car if he had to. Or find a quiet corner, fall asleep under somebody's bed.

The first thing that hit him walking in was the smoke, sweet sweet cigarette smoke. He let it ignite in his head. Whammo. There was probably some pot mixed in there too. The rooms were decked out in Christmas lights, big slashed-looking paintings, 1950s kitchen chairs, a sofa upholstered in orange vinyl and one in turquoise vinyl. Lamps made from industrial-looking metal cans. Horseshit music on the stereo. He bummed a cigarette from a kid in a little squashed-looking hat. In the kitchen he helped himself to beer from a cooler. Maybe it wouldn't be such a bad party after all.

The place was crowded with kids leaning up against walls or draped over the vinyl sofas. Chip made a circuit of the rooms, wound up back in the kitchen by the cooler. The kids all had the same look of calculated goofiness, the art crowd. It didn't look so hard to achieve. He could imagine Ferd, with a few years and a little wardrobe updating, fitting right in.

Elton came into the kitchen. "You having fun yet?" he asked. On each side of his face, a piece of hair had come loose from the ponytail. He'd taken off the leather jacket. Sweat stains were drooping beneath the armpits of his black shirt, like bats hanging upside down in a cave.

"Yeah, I'm great." Chip watched Elton open the refrigerator, rummage around and come up with a can of Coke. "Coke?" he ventured.

"Oh yeah, man. Otherwise I turn into a drunk Indian. Not a good thing."

"Where's your girl?"

"Alisa? She operates on a higher intellectual plane than most people."

"I'll be right here if you need me for anything," Chip said. If he started walking around, he might step on something he shouldn't, like Godzilla squashing skyscrapers. The drinks and the smoke were making him balloon-headed.

After Elton left, he edged in on a group smoking by the back door and asked one of them for another cigarette. A blond girl wearing pink-framed glasses shook one out of her pack and he bummed a light too. They had the back door open and cold air was coming in like a fist, but that felt OK in the overheated room. Chip stood with the rest of them, smoke and frosty breath mingling.

He wasn't paying attention to their talk at first. His hearing had a blotted quality, but the cigarettes were making his brain percolate. They were talking about the president. Nobody had won the election yet. They were still counting ballots and suing people. "We're going to get fucking Bush," one of the boys was saying, "and everything's gonna go off the edge of the cliff."

"They sent goon squads down to Florida to intimidate the county clerks."

"Unreal."

"Gore should grow a pair."

"Yeah, don't hold your breath."

Chip felt his lungs beginning to squeeze and grind, and a cough rising to the surface, no way to stop it. An ugly wet hacking erupted from him. It lasted a long time, and though he bent over in an attempt to make it more manageable, or at least keep it out of people's faces, when he stopped and straightened up, they were all staring at him.

"Sorry," he said, and then, because they were still staring, he said, "Which one's Bush?"

A space of silence, then a boy said, "You're kidding, right?"

When they were pretty sure he wasn't, the girl with the pink glasses said, "He's the Republican. Did you vote for him?"

"Vote . . . no, pretty sure I didn't." He was actually very sure. He'd never voted in his life.

"You know," the same boy said, "if you don't get involved in the political process, you don't have any right to complain." He had red hair and blotchy brown freckles. The kind of kid who makes a cute six-year-old, and it's all downhill after that.

"I'm not complaining," Chip said. He drew in more of the cigarette smoke to keep the cough where it belonged. "So, are all of you artists?"

"Yeah," said Red. "Who are you?"

"Friend of Elton's. Big Chief Thunderthud." He turned to the girl in the glasses and tried out a smile. "What kind of an artist are you?"

"A photographer."

"Great." She wasn't very pretty, and he'd hoped that would make her friendlier, but he guessed not. "What kinda pictures you take?"

"I'm cold," she announced, and stomped off into the house.

"Yeah, I guess she is."

At least that got a smirk out of Red and the other two sock monkeys and he would have liked another cigarette but crap he should have quit while he was ahead and anyway he didn't want to be a total cigarette whore. He tilted the beer bottle to get at the last of it. "I like artists. Art."

"Why's that?"

He could hear the snot in the kid's voice, not that he gave a shit what any of them thought. He'd only been running his mouth. Art art art. Woof woof woof. Still, he was glad when Elton wandered into the kitchen. "Elton, hey. Come tell us the story of your life. The artistic part."

Elton shook his head. He looked glum, like maybe he'd just found out Alisa only liked girls. "Not much of a story. Fat kid starts taking pictures. I wanted this one little space I could control, this little square of the world. It gave me power when I didn't have any. Made me feel less disenfranchised."

"Disenwhat?"

"Not able to vote," Red said, smirking again.

"You're a clever guy," Chip told him. "I can tell that just by looking at you."

Elton said, "What's the deal, Ray? Chill. You wanted to hear a story, right? I kept taking pictures. I spent more and more time and money on it. I started to think I might be good at it. That was this huge thought for me. I never thought I was very good at anything. Ask Ray here. He knew me when." Elton gave him a solid nudge in the ribs.

"You were a pretty sorry fuck, yeah." Chip nudged him back, had to grab a wall to keep his balance. Smooth.

Red and the sock monkeys finished their cigarettes and flicked the butts into the snow. "Fuckin freezing out there," one of them said. They wandered away, following the noise of the party.

Chip pulled the door shut. "I don't think I like them."

"Yeah, the bigheaded boys. I see a lot of that kind."

"What's their problem?" Chip rubbed his arms, trying to warm them. He thought maybe he should eat something.

"Ah, I never went to college, so they either think I'm stupid, or maybe they're stupid for wasting their time going to school when they could be living an actual life. Or both."

"You make an excellent point." There was a cupboard behind Chip; he opened it, extracted a box of Cheerios, and began eating them by the fistful.

"Plus they think I got everything handed to me because I'm an Indian. You know, affirmative action. What do you think, man, you remember any big privileges I got back in the day? You think guys named Jason and Brent are tragically, tragically getting the undeserved shitty end of the stick?"

"No," Chip said, which he hoped was the right answer. He'd lost some of the thread of what Elton was saying, probably because he was being pissed off and sarcastic. It was a new side of the new Elton.

"Yeah, not so much. But you know something? Those guys are never going to do squat, because they have all the creativity of one of the four basic food groups. They might as well be dark green leafy vegetables or dairy products."

"Wow."

"The only people who have enough of a soul to *make* something with a soul are the ones on the outside looking in. You can't be at home in the world and see what you need to see about it. Crap." Elton pushed the hair away from his face. "Sorry. I get myself too worked up."

"No, that's OK." He was looking in the refrigerator now. He found a pack of some kind of lunch meat in plastic wrap and set about trying to get at it. "I'm understanding you." And he was, he did. Because this was his real tribe and always had been: the funky, the dispossessed, the out of it, the freaks and cripples. But he wasn't any artist.

Elton said, "Look, I have to do a lap here. Circulate. Make nice. Then we can go, if you want. I'm done here, they already gave me the check."

"Yeah?" He was mildly interested. "How much they pay you to come by and be a pet Indian?"

"I'm not telling."

"That little, huh?"

Elton shook his head and walked off into the living room. From behind he looked a lot like the kid he'd been: round-shouldered, lumbering, intent on getting out of the line of fire.

Chip grabbed another beer to wash away the slightly sick-making taste of the lunch meat. It must have been hanging out in the fridge for a pretty long time. Then he followed Elton into the living room. The party was all revved up by now. It was a loud son of a bitch. The music was jacked all the way and the little art punks were all screeching away at each other with their lungs practically hanging out at their elbows. He didn't see Alisa. She must have taken off with somebody else who also liked her hair color.

The same shitty electronic music had been playing all along. It was making his brain itch. He walked over to the stereo and punched the OFF button.

"Hey!"

"What's your deal, man?"

"Put something else on. This crap blows dead bears."

"Hey, you don't like it, you can leave."

Elton intervened then. "Ah, can you cut my friend a little slack? He has this nervous disorder. On account of serving in Vietnam."

That made them gawk at him. Chip put on his best cross-eyed psycho face, like he might snap and go into a jungle warfare flashback. Funny that with all his other brain farts, that never happened.

One of the girls held up a CD. "How about Indigo Girls? Very mellow."

"Sure," Chip said, because whatever it was would have to be an improvement. It turned out to be girls playing guitars. Fine.

"How do you guys know each other anyway?" This from Red, who you had to figure didn't know when to leave well enough alone. How about a nice big cup of shut the fuck up, buddy?

"He used to sleep with my mom."

Maybe it was just another sign of the party getting a little crazy.

"Dad," Elton said, putting an arm around Chip's shoulders. "It's one of those Indian-ritual things. He adopted me."

"Son," Chip said, since he didn't have much choice except to go along.

Nobody knew if they were supposed to be laughing. Chip said to Elton, "Where's your damn camera. Somebody should take a picture of the family reunion." His ears were doing that blotting thing again. He had to shout to hear himself.

"Assholes," he thought he heard Red say, but it was also possible he'd said something like "Hamster cages."

The guitar girls stopped singing, and the next minute the repulsive, throbbing music was back at full volume: CRUD CRUD CRUD CRUD CRUD.

He was across the room in three strides. The stereo was on some kind of bookcase and he upended the whole fucking thing in a waterfall of smashing and collapse. Then he got his hands on the stereo console, half lifting, half dragging it, trailing its tangle of wires. He got the front door open and then kicked it shut behind him. One of the speakers had made the trip too, like a tin can tied to a car's bumper. He stood on the top step of the porch, balanced the load, then let it fly. It hit a couple of steps on the way down and landed, thud, on one end in the snow of the front yard.

The door behind him opened and he braced himself to throw a punch, but it was only Elton, his leather coat over one arm. The room behind him was full of commotion, then the door closed like a mouth. "Come on, man, we got to get out of here."

"Waitaminnit." Chip left the porch and gave the stereo a final kick as he passed it. In the fresh snow of the front yard, he picked a spot and began scuffing a path with both feet.

"What are you doing?"

"Making art."

Elton watched him for a moment, then busted out laughing. "Give me an *F.* Give me a *U.*"

"Here, you want to help?"

Elton got his coat on and started in on the other side of the yard. Pretty soon there was a complete message spelled out in four-foot-high snow letters: FUCK YOU.

Chip said, "It needs something else."

"What are you talking about?"

"It's kind of plain. I want it to blink on and off in neon. Or, how about we piss on it?"

"Can we get the hell out of here before the cops come?"

"I don't regard it as my best work. I just want to get that on the record."

They ran to the corner and ducked behind a hedge to travel down a side street. The wind was vicious and the body heat they'd worked up was gone in an instant. Chip wanted to make some joke about them being outsiders, but he was too cold. Elton said, "I don't believe you tore that shit up."

"Music has always affected me powerfully."

"You should probably be on some kind of medication, you know?"

They walked a few more blocks without anybody coming after them. Snow started up again, small, sleety stuff, like salt. Shit. It was going to mess up the letters. "I'm hoping this is the way back to my car," Chip announced. The cold was clearing his head even as it bit into his skin.

"Yeah, I'm pretty sure. Listen, sorry if I dumped some funky remarks on you back there."

"It's OK. Probably had to get said." His feet, he noticed, were wet. His toes felt like they'd already got frostbite and been amputated. "What are you like when you drink, huh?"

"You were always decent to me. You were just, no bullshit."

"Well, sure. Thanks."

"Of course, if anybody asks me about that stereo, I never saw you before."

"Of course."

"They aren't all bad kids," Elton said, sounding gloomy. "But that's what they are. Kids. I got to get a different life."

The snow was revving up. The sky looked like it could bust loose with some serious shit. He hoped they were almost to the car. He hoped Elton knew where they were, because he had no clue. He was glad he'd been nice to Elton way back when, or at least, nice enough. He guessed he had this talent for taking in strays.

Here was the art building and the gallery, empty-looking and glassy, and for a bad couple of minutes he couldn't find his car, but there it was, all alone and marooned in a snowy parking lot. They got in and Elton cussed a little at all the junk on the seat. "What's this?"

"A caulking gun. Where you want to go?"

"They got me a motel room. You want to crash? There's an extra bed. What's this?" Elton picked up Torrie's print from the dashboard and studied it under the streetlight. "Hey. Interesting."

"Ah." His toes were thawing. The idea started there and rose all the way through him and first he thought it was his head going loose again, but it was just the excitement of trying to get the idea out of his mouth. "You in some big hurry to get back to Seattle?"

"No particular reason to. How come?"

"There's somebody I want you to meet."

# *Iowa*

"The well checked out. The septic checked out."

"Then the whole crud heap is yours."

"Not until the closing. But yeah, almost."

"You're nuts, you know."

"Always have been."

Ryan and Blake stood on the front porch of the farmhouse that had belonged to Norm and Martha Peerson, and to a couple of Peerson generations before that. The blacktop road in front of the house was hogbacked and bordered by deep, weedy ditches. Across the road was a field of knee-high corn, the leaves like green straps. Here and there along the farmhouse's circular drive you could see the remnants of the old border of whitewashed rocks. The windbreak evergreens still stood on either side of the yard, but the plowed fields now crowded right up to their edges. The sky was hot and blue and dotted with the white puffs of summer clouds.

Ryan turned to his brother. "Shall we?"

The decorative squares of red and blue and yellow glass set into the front door transom had a few cracks and missing corners. The frame had settled and Ryan had to put his shoulder to it to get it open. Different people had lived here on and off over the years, though none recently. The air inside was almost a solid thing: dry, acrid, sour.

"Oh yeah," Blake said. "I'm liking it."

"Tell me about the floors."

Blake stamped his foot at different places on the entry hall's floorboards. "Dougie Osgood looked at the foundation?"

"Yeah, foundation's good."

"I need to get down in the cellar."

"Let's do the kitchen first." Ryan led the way. He already pretty much knew what his brother was going to say.

The kitchen had been updated at some point, but on the cheap, and any of the new feel had long since been battered down. There was an electric range with two sprung burners, and a copper-colored refrigerator. The floor was a piece of textured vinyl. Blake walked to the sink and let the water run. "Pressure could be better. You might need a new pump. Especially if you want a dishwasher in here." He opened a cabinet. "Looks like you bought you some mice."

"Sure. I expect there's raccoons in the attic. Bees in the walls. Anyway, it needs new cabinets."

"Let me do some measuring."

Ryan watched as Blake flicked his tape measure into the corners of the room, then made notes. They weren't in the habit of talking about things. But Ryan would have liked to know if his brother still enjoyed his work, if his manner of going about it as a series of exasperating chores was only a kind of cover for taking pleasure in it. His face was a permanent windburned red, like a farmer's. He'd mentioned some back problems. It was work that used your body up like one more tool.

The house was stuffy, but the temperature inside was cool and not unpleasant. Ryan walked out to the mudroom porch and opened the back door. The old cow barn still stood, though bare of paint. In this direction some of the original parcel had been included in the sale. A far-off tree line marked the boundary. A few gnarled orchard trees stood in the deep grass.

When Ryan went back into the kitchen, Blake said, "Makes you wonder how they managed, back in the day. You wanted Kentucky Fried Chicken, you had to kill and pluck your own."

"Canning. Baking. Churning the damn butter and hoping the milk didn't spoil."

"Eating involved some serious work, yeah."

"You wonder if they were happy, or if that's just a bunch of nostalgic crap."

"They didn't think in terms of happy," Blake said. "Let's see the rest of the place."

They inspected the downstairs ceilings for water damage, and the ancient cellar. The whole house was going to have to be rewired, and the bathrooms were pretty sad. Blake said he'd seen better down at the Marathon station.

"Funny how this house always seemed so big, when we were kids," Ryan said. They were standing in the upstairs hall, looking into the three narrow bedrooms. Sunlight slanted across the bare floors. A white dresser stood in what had been the girls' room, supporting a mirror in a frame of painted roses. He crossed the floor and bent down to look into it. Mistake. The mirror was dim and wavy and God knew he was looking old these days, but he was 47, not 147.

Blake was rocking the radiator back and forth where it joined the wall. "You might want to get some ductwork done. I'm just saying."

"Yeah." At some point the Peersons had added a little room off the kitchen, a sleeping space for a grandparent, maybe. There was nobody now alive that he could have asked.

Back down the steep-pitched stairs. "I need a smoke," Blake announced, heading out to the porch. Ryan followed. "So how much money you want to spend here? Because you could just keep going."

The legend of his money wasn't going to die anytime soon, even though a lot of the money had. His family didn't understand how divorce vaporized money, since none of them had ever got divorced. They didn't much understand what he did for a living, just something with computers, so there wasn't any point in explaining that what they'd begun to call the tech bubble hadn't felt like a bubble until it burst. He still had two kids to support. He'd moved into an apartment in the city, he'd cut way back, he'd had to work like hell to keep his company from going under, and there was no guarantee it would ever come back to anything like what it had once been.

There had been seven fat years, and now there were seven lean ones, all this with the country gone into an ugly, shaky tailspin with braying headlines about the enemies among us and the need for mighty and muscular vengeance.

But he'd wanted the farmhouse. And it had come cheaper than almost anything with four walls and a roof, though Blake was surely right, it was going to suck up money on a major, full-time basis.

His sister Anita had told him it was on the market. Anita was now the local real estate queen. Her picture—smiling, impeccably got up, hair sleek and gilded—presided over billboards, full-color supplements in the Sunday paper, even the flaps of grocery carts, which were now used for advertising. "Come On Home," her ads urged, with commercial solicitude. She'd made agent of the year twice now.

Good old Anita. She was hardwired to end up on the top of whatever heap she chose to climb. He had to give her credit for getting out there and learning the trade, getting certified, putting in the hours. And for finding a job that allowed her to exercise her particular combination of charm and bossiness.

"Norm and Martha's old house is for sale," she'd told him over the phone. "Just listed."

"I would have thought they'd already knocked it down for the acreage."

"They never got around to it."

They hadn't phoned much over the years, aside from holidays and birthdays, but ever since their mother died and he and Ellen had parted ways, Anita seemed to think he needed some sort of female monitoring.

"Huh." He didn't have any immediate reaction. He couldn't remember the last time he'd even thought about the place.

Anita wanted to know about Anna and Sam, how were they, what was new with them, and he told her the things he'd saved up for just such an occasion. Anna was still on the volleyball team. Absolutely vicious competitor. He guessed he didn't find it strange to have an athletic kid—they were doing so much to encourage girls' sports these days—a little snort from Anita suggested she had some opinion about this, though he couldn't guess what it was—but Anna's intensity? She must have come up with that on her own.

And Sam, age eleven, took karate lessons, played computer games—didn't kids used to collect bugs or rocks?—and wanted to be either a computer-game designer or a race-car driver when he grew up.

Anita said it was great that he worked so hard at being a dad. She'd seen so many divorced guys just give up on their kids. Ah, well, Ryan muttered, as if to suggest modest agreement.

The truth was, his kids had mostly given up on him. They lived with Ellen, and his participation in their lives was always a disruption of some sort. They were polite, for the most part, and uncommunicative, in large part, with him, and even though some of that was just kids being kids, he had upended their lives and by now they were used to it, and to his absence.

Anita said, "You should bring them out here for a visit. I haven't seen them in the longest time."

"It can be a little tricky, with everybody's schedule. You know, softball, summer enrichment courses . . ." Ryan was imagining the battle to the death that would result if he announced his intention of taking them off to Boredom City, Iowa. "But I'll work on it. How's everybody there? How's Dad?"

"Pretty good. He's planning a trip to the Grand Canyon. He says he's never seen it. I know. We're trying to talk him out of it."

Ryan knew better than to say, Good for him. He asked about Anita's family.

Anita said that Matt was still in Los Angeles, being a music bum. When he wasn't in Amsterdam, or Prague, or some other place you'd never heard of, and she worried about his flying when there were terrorists everywhere and she guessed he made enough money to live on, but honestly, there were some things you just didn't want to *know*.

Marcie was still working in the office part-time and taking courses. She was all about the boyfriend and buying clothes and going out and Anita figured they'd be paying her car insurance and medical a while longer, until she got serious about either the boyfriend or earning her own keep. Kids. She didn't remember, did they used to sit up nights thinking of new ways to drive Mom and Dad crazy?

Jeff was fine; he said hello.

They'd got off the phone and a couple of weeks later Ryan called her back and asked, just out of curiosity, how much they wanted for the old farmhouse.

Anita was supposed to come by soon and give him the mortgage documents so he could look them over before the closing. And because he'd rather have his business with Blake finished up before she arrived, Ryan said, "How about you just give me your best guesstimate on the kitchen. Some kind of laminate for the floor. Medium-grade appliances. We can fine-tune it later. I'll worry about the bathrooms when that's done."

"All right. But I'd jump on that rewiring first thing. I can tell you who to call. And I'll shave down that door so you can get in and out."

"You're sure you've got the time? Because if you have other jobs you need to get to—"

"If you've got the money, I've got the time."

"OK then," Ryan said. But his brother was still working on his cigarette in a way that suggested some kind of powerful bad mood, and of course you weren't allowed to ask him what was the matter. So they stood on the porch for long enough to watch a truck hauling an anhydrous tank on a trailer pass on the road. "I guess they'd have to spray pretty close to the house. I hadn't thought about that."

Blake threw his cigarette butt into the yard. "Jimmy wants to enlist."

"Holy crap." Too late, he wondered if he was meant to offer congratulations. Double crap.

"He says he wants to do his part. Help the country."

"What do you think about that?"

"He's eighteen, we can't stop him."

"That's not what I asked you." He was trying to imagine his nephew got up as a soldier, plunked down in the middle of the heat and dust and loony violence. It wasn't hard. He was just what the army wanted. One more small-town kid for the war to smack around and chew up.

Blake said, "I'm proud of him for stepping up. Somebody has to."

"Sure. What does Trish think?"

"You're going to keep on asking until you get me to say it's a bad idea, aren't you? She's not happy. But she's his mother You wouldn't expect her to be."

"It's the wrong war to get all patriotic about."

"I don't need to hear that, you know?"

Ryan had forgotten the part about keeping his mouth shut. They let some silence settle in between them. Locusts started up, a rising and falling *zeee* sound. Blake said, "This looks like Anita."

Their sister's silver SUV was visible in the distance as a burnished reflection, a moving point of glare. It slowed to get into the driveway and parked behind Blake's truck. Anita got out holding a manila envelope. She was wearing a summer suit, white jacket and pants, and red sandals. She stopped at the bottom of the porch steps and said, "This yard needs mowing."

"I'll get right on it," Ryan promised.

"No, I meant Carolyn, the realtor. It's not the way you want your properties to look."

"Well, it's my problem now."

Anita came clipping up the steps and stood between them. Still a girly girl, with her perfume and her little gold earrings and her painted toenails. You just had to smile, looking at her. He and Blake were just two big lugs. She offered up her cheek and Ryan kissed it. "You smell good."

"Thanks. When did you get in?"

"Couple hours ago. That for me?"

Anita handed him the envelope. "Ten a.m. tomorrow. Be there."

"Yes ma'am."

"Then dinner tomorrow night at our house." Anita was hosting the family get-together. To everyone's relief, she was having it catered. She turned to Blake. "You guys are coming, aren't you?"

"Sure."

"Jimmy be there?" Ryan asked, and his brother said yes, and that was how they left it.

The locusts shrilled. It was the first real heat of summer. Anita made a swatting motion with her hand. "You'd think there'd be a breeze out here," she said in an accusing tone. "So, you think you can find tenants, all the way out here?"

He'd put off telling anybody until now. "Actually, Chip's going to stay out here."

"No way."

"Well, yeah." They didn't like the sound of it, he could tell.

"Oh no. I didn't invite him to the dinner."

"That's OK. He probably wouldn't come anyway."

Blake said, "This his idea? Or yours?"

"It all just kind of came together." No one was convinced. "He can help keep the place up."

Anita said, "Well, he doesn't keep himself up particularly well, does he?"

"He's just an old soldier who needs a home," Ryan said.

That stopped them, or at least gave them something else to think about. Chip's comic book emporium had run its course, and a metaphysical-book store had taken its place. Hippie businesses seemed to be the only thing that would grow downtown, like weeds in sidewalk cracks.

After a moment Anita asked just what was wrong with Chip, exactly.

"Hard to tell. Maybe Agent Orange, though the VA doesn't like admitting it. Maybe whatever else." *Whatever else* covered a lot of ground. He knew that people were inclined to blame Chip himself, just because they always had. "Anyway, we'll see how the house works out for him."

Blake looked at his watch. "I have to go. You need a ride back to town?"

Ryan told him no. He and Anita watched him drive off, the sound of the truck's engine dropping away. Anita said, "What's the matter with him? He's even more surly than usual."

"Was he?" He figured he'd let Blake, or Jimmy, tell their own news, so it wouldn't end up on one of Anita's billboards.

His sister gave him a familiar look of disapproval. "God forbid either of you should talk about anything important. Don't you get tired of that?"

"Yes."

She raised her eyebrows, but she wasn't used to instant capitulation and didn't answer back. Instead she turned and regarded the house. "Sad to see it so beat-up, isn't it."

"Come on. Help me decide what to do with the kitchen."

They went inside and Anita said the kitchen ought to be towed out to sea and burned. She had opinions about the cabinet finishes and the type of sink and the light fixtures, and he let her run on because after all he'd asked her, and she probably had a better sense than he did of why all these things were important. Maybe it was the old house itself that made him feel more fond of her than usual, Anita being Anita, all her exclamations and professions of disgust or enthusiasm, as if time had already passed them by and he was standing outside himself and watching a memory.

"By the way." She interrupted herself midsentence. "Dad wants to take you out to dinner tonight."

"Oh yeah? I was going to take him out."

"We think he has a girlfriend."

"Huh." Ryan couldn't quite fathom it. "Girlfriend."

"Try and get him to tell you. He's been acting real pleased with himself lately. I want to see the upstairs."

"A girlfriend," Ryan said again. "That could take some getting used to." Their mother had died of a heart attack almost three years ago. He guessed he should be happy for his father, who must have been lonely. Or not happy. He guessed it depended on the girlfriend.

They stood in the upstairs hallway. The western windows were full of sun blaze. "This wallpaper has to go," Ryan said. It was dark green, darker where it had been worn slick, with a pattern of mustard-colored bouquets.

Anita was crying, or trying not to. Her eyes and nose were red. Her face a crumpled photograph, suddenly old. "Hey," he said.

"I miss Martha."

"Well sure." He was uncertain how to comfort her and settled for a too hearty pat on the back.

"Right in there, that's where she died."

If there were ghosts here, they were uncomplaining ones, sifting through the sunbeams like the dust, like time itself. After a moment Anita said, "I miss Mom too. And Torrie."

"Torrie isn't dead, come on."

"Well she sure isn't here anymore."

Torrie had moved out to Seattle with Elton, and the two of them seemed perfectly happy living together and taking their photographs and not caring what anybody else thought.

Ryan said, "I think that once Chip's moved in, they'll come back and spend some time with him."

"Really?"

"We've talked about it."

"You're just full of surprises, aren't you?" Anita opened her handbag and took out her compact and began to dab different things on her face.

Ryan shrugged. "Didn't want to get ahead of things."

"Mom wouldn't have been happy about her being out there."

"Why? Because they aren't married? Because Elton's an Indian?"

"That's what she would have said." Anita gave her face another glaze of powder and snapped her compact shut. She looked like her Realtor of the Year self again. "But really, the two of them never got along. One of them was always disappointing the other. I think Mom had to be gone for Torrie to have her own life. Listen to me. You'd think I knew what I was talking about."

They went back downstairs and outside, and when Anita started down the porch stairs to her car, Ryan said, "Chip's supposed to come out here a little later. I'm going to wait for him."

"Oh, good idea. What if he doesn't show up?"

"I'll be OK."

Anita shaded her eyes with her hand. "I don't think cell phones work out here."

"Well, if I'm not at the closing, you'll know where to come after me."

"There are no adults in this family," Anita said, getting into her car and closing the door after her. When she turned onto the road she honked the horn and waved.

Ryan sat down on the top porch step. The locust song shrilled and droned as the sun dropped lower. A breeze kicked up and the leaves of the corn stirred.

It was possible that he'd bought the farmhouse just so he could sit here this one time and let the thought drain out of him.

Chip's old Chevy came down the road, leaning to one side as if it had two flat tires or a sprung frame. Chip got out and pushed against the door to try and get it shut.

"Nice car," Ryan called out to him.

"Yeah, want to buy it off me?"

Ryan came down the steps to meet him. They shook hands. "Just look at you all dressed up," Ryan said, because Chip was wearing a shirt of some once-white fabric, a red plaid tie, and a newish pair of jeans. "You getting married or something?"

"Just a little sense of occasion." Chip had lost some more weight he hadn't needed to lose. "On account of you're a farmer now." He laughed, his old cackle, now a cough.

"Not exactly."

"What is this shit, field corn? Whose fields are these anyway? We should go introduce ourselves. Be neighborly."

"Sure, let's go do that."

"Seriously. I want to talk to him. I might want to borrow a tractor. So I can start a garden. It's not too late to plant sweet corn, is it? And tomatoes and cucumbers and melons. I want to start eating real healthy."

"You can dig in the dirt tomorrow, if you want." It probably was a good idea to get ahold of whoever farmed here, pay them to shovel the drive in winter. Haul Chip's car out of the ditch when needed. "I don't know when Blake can begin on the kitchen. It's going to be kind of a mess."

Chip waved that away. "No problem. This is gonna be perfect. You should move in too. It'd be famous times."

"I think I'd need better Internet access."

Chip went back to his car and took a cardboard box out of the trunk. "I brought a few things over. You want a beer?"

"I have to get back and have dinner with my dad. All right. Break my arm."

They sat down on either side of the porch steps. A car passed and Chip waved at it.

"Who's that?"

"Damned if I know." Chip grinned. His teeth hadn't held up well. He pointed. "What kind of tree is that?"

"Some kind of maple." It was shady and beautifully shaped, each leaf like a green star. He'd been staring into it before Chip arrived without really seeing it. The beer was loosening him up but making him more alert, or would at least until he started yawning. He was still tired from his long drive.

Chip said, "You didn't have to buy this place, but I'm sure glad you did. Thanks, man."

"Sure. Thanks for the beer. We're even." He filled his mouth with it, swallowed. "Jimmy wants to enlist. Blake's boy."

"Ah shit."

"Pretty much what I said."

"You know you've been handed a fucked-up life when you've seen two useless obscene wars."

"Patriotism," Ryan said, "is running high these days." He understood why kids signed up. He still remembered when a war seemed like an adventure he was being cheated out of.

"I spilled beer on my tie," Chip announced.

"It's the kind of tie that looks better with a little beer on it."

"Maybe it's not such a terrible thing for Jimmy to go into the army. Seriously. The only jobs around here are putting tires on for Farm and Fleet. And meth is a really evil drug."

Ryan's full attention returned. "What are you saying?"

"So much of it around," Chip said vaguely, which was either more of his spooky knowledge about the bottom layer of life or else total bullshit, and Ryan decided not to ask any more for fear of learning more. His nephew was a good enough kid but he was just a kid, he didn't understand all the different ways the world was out to kill you.

He said, "I hardly ever see Anna and Sam."

Chip got up from the porch and took two more beer cans from the carton and handed one to Ryan.

"I thought I could make it work with them. You know, plan the great weekends, help them with their homework online. Give them the benefit of all my terrific advice. I'm just the ATM. The guy who writes the checks." He cracked open the new beer. He didn't know how it had happened, that the only person in the world he could really talk to was his derelict cousin. "A few years, they'll be gone, living their own lives. Don't get me wrong, it was a good move to get the hell out of that marriage, it's such a relief that not everything's my fault on a day-to-day basis. But I didn't think I was divorcing my kids too."

"Bring 'em out here. End of the summer, once we get the place cleaned up. Once Tor and Elton are in town."

"They won't want to come."

"I thought you said you wrote the checks."

He could make them do it. He'd have to pay, not just with money, but with sullenness and whining and lots of eye-rolling. What did he have to lose? They already thought he existed mostly to annoy them. "Learn a little bit of their own history," he said.

"Now you're talking."

"Even if they hate every minute of it." They no doubt would. He felt his confidence ebb, the decision waver.

"Sort of like camp. The kind where they send juvenile offenders."

"I feel old, Chipper."

His cousin scrutinized him. "You don't look half-bad, man. You still have that Nordic-prince thing going on."

"Don't make me laugh. I'll get beer up my nose."

"Me, I'm not that old. But my lungs and my liver are." Chip brought the cardboard box up to the porch and rummaged around in it. "Help me with this."

"With what," Ryan said. He'd meant, *old* as in he didn't know what came next. What you were allowed to look forward to. "What the hell, Chip." His cousin was unfolding an American flag the size of the front door.

"Just hold this end up." Chip produced a hammer, and he positioned the flag so it hung down from the front edge of the porch, the blue field on top. He reached up and tapped a nail into a corner, then took Ryan's end and did the same. Then he went down the stairs into the yard to admire his work. Ryan followed him.

"I don't think that's, you know, Boy Scout–authorized display."

"You see any Boy Scouts around here?"

The sunset breeze caught the loose fabric and made it bell out. Ryan waited. Chip said, "Why not, man. It's my goddamned country too."

"Sure it is."

"It's like family. No matter how fucked up it is, it's the only one you got. Let's go look at the barn."

And here was the barn, with its good smell of ancient must, its dirt floor baked into something as dense and layered as peat, its shallow central pit where generations of cows had trampled. The old milking stalls, the feed bucket still hanging from its nail, the hayloft, the corners filled with rusted and spiderwebbed junk. Chip kicked at a bale of gray stuff that might have once been hay, came up with a horseshoe, worn thin at its top lip, the nail holes still visible. Hey look, he said. Good luck!

He said the barn would be a great place for whatever you felt like doing, practice space for some band, maybe. Make all the noise you wanted, nobody'd care. Tor and Elton could store equipment here; it looked dry enough. Do their photography stuff. You'd have to put in a floor. You could do that. These beams are solid, man. They built this sucker to last, those old-timers.

Built to last, Ryan agreed. It filled him with holy dread to stand in this place that testified to their grinding, incessant labor. How hard they had worked, and how stubbornly, every day of their lives, for their little bit of ease, little bit of pride. They had done so much. They had meant to do so much more. Imagine them slipping off to death regretting the task unfinished, the field unplowed, the child unloved. It could break your heart. He felt an urgency in him, a clamoring. Compared to them, he wasn't old at all. Chip stooped and picked another horseshoe out of the soft dirt and handed it to Ryan and Look, he said. You're lucky too.